MYTH

******

Jessica Lietz

For Poppa,
because he's the best.

ISBN – 978-1-7388456-0-6

Table of Contents

Prologue

The Legend of Myth

As told by the philosopher Glazgo,
(A fine man, but somewhat excitable and given
to strange ideas)

There are many constellations in the sky above this land, our land, the wonderful land of Allaria. They are all beautiful, but the most beautiful of all is the constellation of Myth. A great golden star, surrounded by six lesser stars in a halo of light and brilliance, it shines above our land like a beacon of hope.

There are many legends about how it came to be, it's significance, and why, some years ago, the golden star in the center disappeared. Already, some are saying that there never was a center star at all, that the legends concerning it are false. How quickly we forget.

The legends of Myth are as numerous as the people who tell them. However, I, Glazgo son of Glopzite, at the age of ninety seven, in the fourth year of the reign of King Anthus Rudbeck the Mighty, declare that, after extensive study and research, I have uncovered the truth.

This is the tale of the great dragon Myth, who brought much to this earth, both grievous and beneficial, and became the constellation so named. It is a true tale. I have much evidence in the matter, which I will reveal to any who are so ill-bred and uncouth as to question my word, specifically one self-proclaimed High Philosopher in Chief by the name of Stephanio, a most pompous and disgusting old man, who has the mind of a weasel, the tongue of a snake, the laugh of a hyena, and eats all the honey cakes at dinner parties. I hope he chokes on one and dies. But I digress. This is the legend of Myth, as told to me by several very reliable sources, one of whom lived in a cave and ate only snails.

✳ ✳ ✳ ✳ ✳

Long ago, when the world was young and wild, there was no magic at all. It was buried deep in the fire of the earth and hung dormant high in the heavens. The forests and wild places were empty and quiet. No dangers haunted the high hills. The only thinking beings were humans, and even they did not think too much. All men were safe, but life was dull and tedious.
Until, one day,
the heavens bent down,
the fires of the earth sprang up,
and for a moment,
they touched.
One ordinary falcon was caught in the middle.
And changed.
This was how Myth was born. She was a great golden dragon, born of pure Magic, beautiful and vicious. The world of Man trembled where she went, wreaking havoc on towns and cities. The ground trembled when she roared. Crops flattened from the wind of her passing, and forests withered from the fire of her breath. However, Magic does not only destroy, it also creates. As Myth traveled about the world, the magic that clung to her rubbed off on the things around her. When she breathed her fire upon people, many died, but some changed. They became the first Faerie, also called Elves, able to use magic and live for centuries. They were cast out of human society, forced to live in the woods, where they built their own society,

beautiful and powerful and hidden from human eyes. During this time, Myth gave birth to five creatures. The Siren, the Phoenix, the Ice Creeper, the Sea Serpent, and the Griffin. These creatures spread throughout the world and inhabited all the wild places. Many people scoff at the idea that this could happen, since Myth was the only dragon, but bear in mind that the term "birth" can have many meanings. In this case, it is most likely that Myth did not create these creatures so much as she changed creatures that were already living, giving a part of herself and her magic to give them strange forms, abilities, and some greater intelligence or presence of mind than is normal to find in dumb beasts.

The Siren, for example, has many properties of water, such as the enchanting liquid voice, and also many properties of a fish, such as gills, scales, and fins. The Sea Serpent is quite like a snake, the Ice Creeper like a leopard, and so on. To learn more of these creatures, their habits, abilities, and characteristics, refer to *Glazgo's Book of Fascinating Magical Creatures that Defy the Laws of Nature* for further study.

In that time, there were still true Heroes living. One by one, however, they came forth to fight Myth, and one by one she killed them. The last Hero of all was Gilead. He knew that he could not best Myth while she was at her full strength. So he concealed himself and waited until she was about to give birth to her sixth creature. Then he leapt out from his hiding place and stabbed Myth deeply with his enchanted sword. (refer to *Glazgo's Book of Historical Magical Items* for further study.) It did not kill her, but it wounded her most grievously, so that the Darkwing was born only half alive, a creature of shadow and fear. It could not eat, drink, or sleep, but neither could it die, unless it was exposed to the full light of the noonday sun. It fled screaming into the darkness. Gilead tried to kill Myth, but she escaped him and flew high into the night. She flew so high that she became nothing but a burning golden star, forever looking down on earth from afar. Her constellation is still there today, surrounded by the stars of her children. (refer to *Glazgo's Book of the Significance of All the Stars that We Know Of, An Exhaustive Study*, for further study.) As for Gilead? No one knows. Some say he died after a short and violent life, others say he was killed by Myth. And some, myself among them, think that in his fight with Myth he survived her fire and was given long life like the Faerie. Perhaps he is even still living today.

Chapter One

A Baby in a Sack

* * *

"The Black Market trade of Magical children may be wrong, but Great Firth, who cares? It makes money."— Thetius Smoke, First Treasurer of his Majesty King Rudbeck the Mighty.

* * *

The moon was barely a sliver. The thin half circle shed no light on the beach, a swath of black sand overshadowed by dark, tangled trees. All was quiet except for the soft swish of waves, the stirring of leaves in the breeze, and the muffled splash of oars.

The eight men in the boat were quiet. The small sack in the boat was quiet too. However, when the boat bumped on the beach, it hiccuped and wailed. "Shut it!" hissed a man, and kicked it. It was quiet.

"You sure this is the place?"

"Yeah. It for sure landed near here."

"Unless it fell in the bay. You ever think of that?"

"I would've seen the steam."

"Oh yeah. I guess so. Let's get started then. Look for burnt patches."

There was a brief scratching sound, then a match flared and was passed around. Once everyone had lit their torches, they spread out along the beach, peering into the dark forest. Suddenly, one of the torches began to swing in a circle. All the other men made their way over. Their combined light illuminated a patch of burnt and broken branches near the top of a tree.

"It just grazed the tops here, see? Which means it should be… maybe thirty feet in? Depends on the angle."

"Let's go then. Who's got the machete?"

Like all deserted woods, the trees writhed with unnerving darkness and whispers. The men were relieved when, twenty minutes later, they arrived on the edge of a crater. The trees on either side had been blasted away. In the center of the crater was a bubbling pool of what looked like molten gold. Little streaks of red and silver danced across its surface. Every time a bubble burst, golden sparks were thrown up into the night. The man in the front whistled softly.

"Amazing. Never seen the like. Gold ones don't fall 'cept maybe once in a hundred years. We better hurry before someone else gets here."

Two of the men stepped up to the edge, one with a long pole and the other with the small sack, which was crying again. They attached the sack to a hook on the pole, and swung it out over the pool. With a swish and a plop, the sack fell in. The men jumped back as a wall of gold fire shot up into the night. Then it was gone, and the forest was plunged once again into darkness.

The pool was gone. The sack was gone. The only thing in the crater was the baby. One of the men cautiously edged his way down into the crater and picked it up. It's eyes were open, and they were a bright, glowing gold.

"Hey Tom, How much does a gold Starfall child sell for?"

"I dunno. Probably a couple thousand pieces."

The men grinned at each other.

"We're gonna be rich!"

"With a thousand pieces, we could buy a palace!"

"We could buy the king's palace!"

"Won't the mother notice, though? The house we took her from was a rich one. It won't do to have an angry baroness on our heels."

"She won't catch us. She wouldn't recognize this baby now, anyways. She'll probably just think that the Faerie stole her baby. Besides, when a person buys a Starfall, they never ask where we got it. Buying stolen goods is illegal. People who are rich enough to buy a Starfall are always stuck-up nobles who would hate to admit that they've committed a crime."

"Okay. Let's go then. Market opens in three hours."

They put the baby into another sack, climbed into the boat, and paddled away. Under the trees, dark eyes glowed, watching them row away. Moonlight glinted off of a pale hand, lifted as if in farewell. A soft chant, in a language no human had ever spoken, hissed after the boat, making the sleeping child stir in her sleep and whimper softly. A faint light glowed through the sack, near where the child's head was. The boat rocked.

✳ ✳ ✳ ✳ ✳

A soft breeze was blowing through a silver wood. The stars were the same as those hanging over the boat, but here the moon had already sunk to the edge of the horizon.

The inhabitants of the wood were elsewhere that night, watching a boat row away into the darkness. Their great city stood empty and silent. But one heart still beat *in the empty wood.*

In a place where the trees grew dead and twisted, one man stirred in a fitful sleep. With a strangled cry, he woke and stared about him with haunted eyes. His arms were covered in old, knotted battle scars, and lines of despair ravaged what should have been a handsome face. The man would have seemed young, not a day past his prime, except for the deep, ancient darkness in his eyes. It was the darkness that only comes from hoarding hate in the heart for a long, long time.

He stood up slowly, his eyes instinctively searching the sky for the source of all his grief and hatred.

It wasn't there.

He froze in utter disbelief. At first, he seemed confused, but then the truth dawned on him, and his face drained of color.

"Not again." He whispered. Fear flickered across his face. It was only there a moment before he mastered his emotions, and the fear was replaced with determination.

He went looking for his sword.

Chapter Two

In Which a Voluntary Kidnapping Occurs

"Why are you asking me for a quote? I don't have a quote. Go away."— An old hermit named Ham who lives in the Hills.

***

"This is the girl?"

"Obviously. Do you see any others?"

"She's a Starfall, you say?"

"Yep. Sure is."

Ellia stood perfectly still and pretended she couldn't hear them. She hated it when people stared at and talked about her as if she weren't there. The Squire and her master, Baron Opulus, both turned and looked at her. The Squire studied her with greedy eyes. She felt sick with fear. If this man bought her, her life would be terrible. She had seen how he treated his servants. How much worse would he treat a slave? *Please don't buy me!* She thought desperately. She met his eyes and glared at him. *You don't want me, You don't want me, You don't want me.*

A queer tingling feeling raced down her skin. It felt silky and slimy at the same time.

"You don't want me." She whispered. Her voice seemed to echo and hiss as it slipped into the Squire's head. He squinted, blinked, and frowned.

"Why aren't her eyes a funny color? Aren't they supposed to be gold or something?"

"What do you mean? Of course they're gold!" Opulus turned and looked at her. His expression changed to confusion, and then anger.

"See here girl, what's the matter with your eyes?" He slapped her, as if that would help. The Squire snorted. "Nothing the matter with her eyes. She's got perfectly normal *blue* eyes." He glared at Opulus. "I should've known. A *real* gold Starfall would never be sold for so cheap. This girl's completely normal! You've cost me a full day's journey for nothing!" He turned and stormed out of the hall, ignoring the baron's protests. *That was weird.* Ellia thought. She felt weak with relief. However, her relief was short-lived. Opulus was livid.

"Useless!" He roared. "No magic, No skills, and a horrible attitude! Not to mention all the trouble you bring down on us from those awful Kurdians! They don't know you're useless, do they? They all think a gold Starfall must have marvelous powers! Powers worth sending raiding parties all the way down here to get you! Do you have any idea how much I have to pay for soldiers to protect you? DO YOU? And yet the King would have my head if I let the Kurdian king get his hands on a Starfall, and every time I try to sell you something goes wrong! Maybe I should just leave you out for the wolves!" He turned towards the door.

"MASON!"

"Sir?" A large, beefy guard with a speckled gray moustache stumped into the room. Ellia's heart sank. John Mason was the most brutal of all the hired guards living in the manor. Sharon, the cook's daughter, had received a terrible beating from him after she spilled soup on his jacket.

"Please, I didn't do anything!" she pleaded, but Opulus merely sneered at her before turning back to Mason.

"Take this miserable creature to the whipping post and beat her until she shows some magical ability."

"Yes sir." He grabbed her by her arm and dragged her out of the hall.

As she was being dragged across the courtyard, Ellia kicked, scratched, and bit. After all, she was going to get a whipping anyway, so why behave? She was so busy kicking him that it was several minutes before she realised that something was wrong. "Hey, you big idiot, the whipping post is that way."
Mason just ignored her. He continued to drag her in the wrong direction, towards the gates. He kept glancing back across the empty courtyard as though afraid that someone might be watching him from the manor's windows. Ellia began to suspect what was happening. It was not the first time that someone had attempted to kidnap her. She felt relieved, since he couldn't possibly escape all the other guards, and it looked like she wouldn't get a whipping after all. However, when they reached the outer gate and still had not been challenged by anyone, she began to be nervous.

"You're going to get caught." she said uncertainly. "The other guards won't let you take me."

Mason just laughed. "The other guards were the ones with the idea."
Oh no. Ellia thought. This was bad. With no guards, this kidnapping might work. She didn't like Baron Opulus, but according to Sharon, her best friend, the Kurdian king killed people regularly and wore a crown of human wrist bones. "If he found out you were useless, he'd chop you into little pieces and cook you in a stew!" Sharon had cackled.

Not a nice thought.

Ellia considered screaming and fighting, but then they rounded a corner and she immediately discarded that idea. Five guards were standing outside the manor walls, holding six horses, already saddled and ready to go. One of them frowned at Mason.

"You didn't tie her up?"

"No. Why would I? The Baron's never been nice to her. Why would she want to stay here?"

"I dunno. But we're kidnapping her, and she's a Starfall. She might be dangerous."

Mason snorted. "You're such a wuss, Tuck. She's about as dangerous as a kitten. Nothing I can't handle."

Ellia began to be annoyed. For the second time today, people were treating her as if she wasn't there.

"Hey! What's going on? I thought you guys served the King! What happened to your loyalty?"

The guards seemed amused.

"We're not selling you to the Kurdu, if that's what you think." The guard named Tuck told her. "The king of the Kurdians isn't the only one interested in acquiring your kind. Our good king Rudbeck the Mighty recently bought three Starfalls as his personal attendants, and the queen is feeling jealous. She's offering a hefty reward for anyone who can bring her a pretty girl Starfall for her handmaiden. She's always trying to beat her husband at everything, so she'll be mighty happy with you." He grinned at her.

Ellia was confused. "But I don't have any powers."

Tuck shrugged. "I wouldn't be so sure about that. They might show up later than most, but the queen won't care about that. All she cares about is looks, and you've got the only gold eyes in a hundred years."

Ellia was about to protest further, but another guard cut her off. "We don't have much time. Are you

coming willingly, or do we have to tie you?"
Ellia considered this. The Queen might turn out to be
nasty, but Baron Opulus was awful. Besides, she didn't
really have a choice in the matter.
"I'll come."

After several days on the road, Ellia decided that
she liked being kidnapped. The guards were a jolly lot,
and she was treated far better than she had been at the
manor. Every day she got to ride with Tuck, since he
was the thinnest, and he was very nice, telling her
everything he knew about the castle and the royal court.
At night the guards would make stew and tell jokes
around the fire. Ellia had never before eaten such good
stew. Baron Opulus had begrudged her every scrap she
ate. She was only ever allowed to eat the food that no
one else wanted. One of the guards, named
Wopscallion Malacus Gumphria, but called Wop, was a
very good cook, and could turn almost anything into a
good meal. Ellia wished that they would never get to the
palace, but instead just keep traveling like this forever.

Chapter Three

In Which Our Heroine Spits Some Ice

***

"The fear of Wild Places is a disgrace to the honour of Man. Has anyone actually ever *seen* a Darkwing? Of course not! They're just bits of shadow. So, if you can't see them, the logical conclusion is that they aren't there."— The Philosopher Sithia.

***

After four days of travelling, they came under the shadow of the darkest, thickest, trees Ellia had ever seen. They towered over the path, and creeped with a slithering, almost tangible darkness. Where the path turned into the wood, they seemed to reach out over it with roots and branches, as if trying to block out travellers. The sight sent a chill down her spine, and the men spoke in hushed tones. Even the horses were nervous.

"Keep real quite." Tuck whispered in her ear. "Yonder's the Shadow Wood. It's full of wild animals, Faerie folk, and all manner of queer creatures. We best make no noise when we pass through, otherwise they might *do things* to us. Word is there's even been an Ice Creeper sighted in there."

Ellia shivered. She didn't know much about

Creepers, except that they were a legendary creature like a large cat made from snow, fog, and ice. Their breath could freeze a grown man, and their teeth and claws were icicles.

"Where does the darkness come from?" she whispered. Now that they were closer, she could see that it was unnatural, moving through the trees in smoky ribbons, twisting and curling although there was no wind. Tuck glanced swiftly around, then leaned closer and whispered.

"Darkwings. It's shadowed enough under the trees that they can live there even in the daytime… If you call what they do living."

As they entered the trees, the darkness writhed, and a heavy blanket of silence seemed to fall over them. Suddenly, Ellia knew that she was being watched. Through the shadows a few paces away, she half-glimpsed beautiful, terrible figures. They seemed very young and yet immeasurably old at the same time. *Where did they come from?* She wondered. Out of the corner of her eye she saw burning cold eyes watching her. The owner of them raised a pale arm towards her. In the back of her mind, a vivid memory suddenly surfaced.

The moonlight glinting off a pale arm, raised as if in farewell… a soft chanting… the child stirs in her sleep… the boat rocks... Suddenly, a dark voice shattered the scene. *WE ARE WATCHING YOU.*

Ellia jolted awake. Had she been asleep? She looked into the trees, but there were no faces in the darkness. There was also no unnatural silence. *What was that?* She wondered.

"Did you say something?" She asked Tuck. He frowned at her and shook his head, confused. Ellia wondered what she could have been remembering. She had never even been in a boat. *Weird.* She must have been imagining things.

They continued to travel in darkness for what seemed an eternity. Trees loomed on all sides, tall and dark and strong, like the pillars of some ancient, underground hall. They were beautiful in their way, and Ellia could imagine living here, in constant night and stillness. There were no leaves on the ground, although there were long silver ones in the trees. It seemed as if time stopped here, that the leaves had never fallen, would never fall, unless they were torn from the trees by force. It was cold. There was no wind. The only thing that moved was the darkness, and the only thing that changed was the path; winding this way and that, climbing up and down through the silent wood. No one spoke. The horses clomped steadily onwards. Ellia was tired, hungry and saddle-sore, but she dared not dismount and walk alongside as she usually did. They passed small, moonlit clearings where strange flowers glowed and the darkness was less deep. They saw large things and small things slip through the shadows, but nothing challenged them, or seemed to care that they were passing through.

As the hours passed, however, the darkness began to seem more and more sentient. Wings flapped, leaves rustled, and soft hisses sounded from behind them. Once Ellia even felt something like hot breath on her face. The men were no longer relaxed. During the Faerie's silence, Ellia had longed to hear noises, but these noises were worse than the silence had been. She could feel the Darkwings, and other things too, drawing closer, growing angrier. Ellia felt that they were moments away from attacking. She braced herself, hunched over, waiting for something to happen. A wing brushed her arm, and she yelped in surprise.

The sound seemed to infuriate the creatures. The hissing rose to a blood chilling screech. Dark shapes darted forward, slashing and biting at the travelers. Ellia felt Tuck hunch over her, shielding her, as the horse broke into a gallop. Through the gap between the horse's head and Tuck's shoulder, Ellia could see the others getting farther and farther away. The creatures were closing in on either side. The other riders disappeared around a bend. Suddenly, something leaped from a branch and into the path in front of them. It let out a horrible scream, and the horse stopped frozen in mid stride. It's chest and front legs were coated with ice. In front of them crouched a great cat made of icicles and frost. It snarled, and even the Darkwings behind them retreated in fear. The cat looked at them, and Ellia held her breath. The horse struggled, bringing her to her senses just before the cat screamed again. They dove from the horse just in time, as a barrage of icicles hurtled over their heads. In a panic, Ellia realized that she was separated from Tuck, on the wrong side of the horse. The Ice Creeper stalked towards her. She couldn't run, she couldn't hide. So she picked up a stick and yelled "Go away!"

It didn't work.

The Creeper pounced. It's weight landed on her chest like a boulder, knocking her to the ground. It's claws stabbed into her shoulders, sending icy pain shooting through her body. It's breath was freezing on her skin. She could feel ice forming on her face. She couldn't breath.

Deep inside, she felt a cold pressure building up, as her breath ran out and her vision grew dim. *This is it.* She thought. *I'm going to die.* Then she screamed.

The ice over her face shattered, and the cold rushed out of her lungs, forming icicles that flew from her mouth straight into the snarling face of the Ice Creeper. It leapt back with a startled yowl, icy fur standing on end. It dashed into the trees and vanished.

Shaky, cold and bleeding, Ellia realized that she was crouched on all fours, and stood up. The Darkwings had retreated into the trees, but she could still hear them, waiting for the right time to attack. She screamed at them. No icicles formed this time. The cold feeling in her lungs was already fading, but a cold wind shook the trees, and the Darkwings drew back.

Tuck appeared around the horse, which had almost succeeded in freeing its front legs. His eyes were round and scared.

"What happened?" he demanded, "Are you alright? Was that *another* Ice creeper that I heard screaming?"

"I don't know." Ellia shrugged, then regretted it as pain flared in her shoulders.

"The Ice Creeper attacked me but then another one screamed from the bushes and it ran away." Tuck shook his head in rueful astonishment.

"Just our luck. Most people live their entire lives near this forest and never ever *glimpse* an Ice Creeper. We get attacked by *two* of them!"

"Yeah." Ellia agreed, pretending to be unhappy, but inside she was brimming with excitement.
I have an ability! I can… shoot icicles?
She wanted very badly to share this revelation with someone, but experience had taught her never to share information. Especially not with kidnappers, even if she liked them.

The last of the cold feeling faded from her lungs, and with it her adrenaline. She suddenly felt all the pain and exhaustion come flooding back, and she collapsed.

It was the morning of the next day when they finally limped out of the trees and rejoined the others. As they tended to the wounded and made breakfast, a guard named Silas came over to bandage her shoulders.

"Tuck said you got attacked by an Ice Creeper, and then another one came and scared the first one off?" He gave her a searching gaze. "That what really happened?"

Ellia felt a stab of guilt. "Yes. That's what happened."

The guard smirked. "Funny. I've been in and out of these woods for years, and I've heard all the stories there are about those cats. They all agree on one thing. Creepers always hunt alone. Matter of fact, they never even let another Creeper enter the same woods as them." He tied off the bandage and looked up. "What really happened?"

Ellia didn't meet his eyes. "I already told you."

Silas snorted and stood up. "You're a bad liar, girl, and bad luck to boot. Whatever really happened in there, I'll be glad when we're rid of you." He started to walk away, but then changed his mind and turned back, with a slightly softer expression. "A word of advice, I'd work on your conviction when you lie. Those palace jackals will sniff out any weakness, so if you don't act confident, they'll treat you like dirt. You got to meet their eyes and never be the first to look away." He hesitated, and then reluctantly added, "It's not your fault you're bad luck. Starfalls always have it bad."

Chapter Four

In Which Ellia Chases a Cat and Gets Lost

"I once went to Thalis. Horrible place. The smells upset my stomach, the streets had me lost in an instant, and someone stole my wallet."—Duchess Angelona Clemency, a rather depressing woman.

It was an early spring morning when they finally reached Thalis, the King's City. The gate alone was bigger than anything Ellia had ever seen. The guards on top looked like tiny bugs. Ellia couldn't admire it as she wanted to, though, because she had to keep her head down to prevent people from noticing her eyes. Tuck pointed out that, although people seldom asked questions, it was still better not to be too obvious when engaging in illegal activities. Word might get back to Opulus. Once through the gate, they followed the crowd of people in the general direction of the palace. The city spread out haphazardly, in complete chaos. The main road led straight from the gate to the palace, but Ellia knew that if she strayed off of it she would never be able to find her way back. Tuck said that there were actually six main roads, and six gates, but Ellia couldn't imagine why. The road they were on seemed wide enough to encompass the entire population of Allaria, human and otherwise. Why would you need five more? The idea seemed ridiculous.

Only thirty meters from the gate, the crowd became so thick that they were forced to dismount and lead the horses. The crowd pressed in close to her on all sides, and Ellia was surprised to discover that most people rushed by with their heads ducked and eyes on the ground. No one looked up or met her eyes. Taking courage from this, she dared to raise her own head, to better see where they were going. She began to think that no one ever interacted with each other in this city. That is, until she met her first vendor.

She was struggling past a wagon, when suddenly a man grabbed her by the arm and started yelling at her.

Oh no. I've been caught. She thought in a panic, until she realised what he was yelling.

"Salamander sticks, fresh off the grill! Warm your insides on a cold day! Only five pieces! What a bargain! Feeling cold? Feeling hungry? Buy a Salamander stick! You know you want one!"

Ellia ducked her head, but not before he had seen her eyes. He cursed under his breath and dropped her arm, backing away like she was an infectious disease. Tuck's hand tightened protectively on Ellia's other arm, and he tugged her away.

"Ignore him." He advised her. "The merchants in this city are all a bunch of superstitious, money-grubbing fools."

Suddenly, the air was shattered by a piercing shriek.

"Help! Help! I've been robbed! Somebody stop that thief!" A woman across the street was yelling in a hysterical, nasally whine. People turned to listen, and were bowled over by an old beggar. He was leaping with surprising agility through the crowd, fleeing from the furious woman. She tried to pursue him, but was cut off

by a small hoard of street urchins. They leapt into her
path, blocking her and clamoring for attention.

"Spare a penny, Ma'am?"

"A hand with your baggage, Miss?" She fell back,
perplexed. Several men in the crowd were attempting to
stop the escaping thief, but were hindered at every turn
by clamoring street urchins. It seemed that half the
street was in league with the old man.   Things were
fast becoming an outright brawl, as a squad of city
guardsmen waded into the mess. Tuck let go of Ellia's
arm and touched his sword hilt. Suddenly, the old
beggar leapt out of the crowd, shoving between Tuck
and Ellia. Both of them were thrown to the ground in
opposite directions. Surrounded by trampling feet and
noise, Ellia gasped, trying to reorient herself. It was
impossible. Clouds of dust stung her eyes and clogged
her throat. Someone kicked her in the ribs. Her hair
caught in someone's sandal strap. She curled into a
ball, trying to protect herself. The chaos continued. In
the distance, she could hear Tuck's outraged yell.

"Hey! Now my wallet's gone too!" Then his voice
faded.

Ellia felt a hand slip into her back pocket. Without
thinking, she twisted around and punched the pick-
pocket in the nose. He skittered away, dripping blood.
Good thing I have nothing to steal. She thought dryly.

Gradually, the tumult died down, and she was
able to get up. The crowd was returning to it's regular,
chaotic business. Ellia turned to hurry after Tuck, but
found that he had disappeared in the crowd. She rushed
forward blindly, the clamoring noise and shoves only
adding to her panic and confusion. She was turning in a
circle, trying to see over the heads of the crowd, when
she heard a voice behind her.

"Lost, little girl?"

A tall, greasy man with a sharp foxy face leered

at her.

"I can help you, sweetie. Just come with me."

Ellia turned towards him, and the blood drained from his face.

"Holy mother of Firth, It's a Faery devil. Don't curse me!" He threw his hands over his head, dropping to his knees. People all around him began to stop and stare. Ellia quickly pulled her hood down over her eyes and ran away through the crowd.

Faces flashed past her, looking up with surprise at her hurried steps. She immediately slowed down and tried to blend in.

All the buildings and storefronts were unfamiliar, and Tuck was nowhere to be seen. *Oh drat I'm lost.* She thought. She kept walking, at a more leisurely pace, and considered her options. She finally decided that it was probably best to return to the place where she had lost sight of Tuck and wait to see if he would come back for her. She walked back along the main street until she heard the loud voice of the Salamander stick man. He was further down the street now, still yelling. She carefully went around him, ducking her head, then settled herself on a stack of crates behind a vegetable stall and waited, carefully scanning the crowd.

Nothing happened. The sun was hot and the road was dusty. The mixed smells of vegetables and sweaty people filled the air, and Ellia began to grow bored and hungry. She went for a short walk up and down the street, pocketing various edibles from the food vendors, and then settled back on her crate to eat them.

The day dragged on. The sun gradually sank, and a cool evening breeze began to chase away it's heat. Many vendors began to pack up their wares for the night. Most of the people had gone home for dinner.

It was only when the street was almost empty that Ellia noticed the cat. It was sitting in the opening to an alleyway across the road from where she sat. It was a dark color that blended in very well with the shadows, and she wouldn't have noticed it at all if it hadn't been staring straight at her. It's eyes gleamed in the darkness, looking far too intelligent for an animal. They looked very young and yet immeasurably old at the same time. Ellia's heart thumped. *That's not a real cat.* When the cat saw her watching, it quickly looked away, lay down, and closed its eyes. Ellia knew it wasn't sleeping, though, because she still had the prickly feeling of being watched. She casually got up and headed down the street. The cat got up and headed deeper into the alleyway. Ellia pretended not to notice, and kept walking. However, at the next alleyway she came to, she stopped just short of it, pressed flat against the side of the building, and waited. A few minutes later, the cat's head poked out of the alleyway and looked up the street to see where she had gone. Ellia dove to grab it, but it hissed and dashed back down the alley. Frustrated, Ellia chased after it, determined to catch and interrogate it. Whatever it was, it had to know a lot more than she did, and knowledge was power.

The cat streaked away, turning several corners, heading deeper into the maze that was Thalis. Finally, it streaked around a corner and disappeared. Ellia rounded the corner and ran smack into something hard and warm. That something said,

"Oof."

Ellia landed hard on her back, and looked up into the face of a man. Well, a boy, really. A scrawny, dirty, ragged street urchin who hadn't even begun to grow facial hair yet. Nevertheless, he was still considerably bigger and stronger than her, so she felt quite nervous.

"Are you all right?" He asked, and offered her a hand. Ellia took it warily, and stood up.

"Yeah. Sorry for running into you. Have you seen

a black cat run through here?" *Act confident.* She told herself, as the boy raised his eyebrows.

"A *cat?* Have I seen a cat? Of course I've seen a cat. This place is full of them. Might I ask why you were chasing a cat through Thalis at night?"

Ellia shrugged. "You can ask, but I don't see how it's any of your business. I was looking for my cat, and if you haven't seen him then I'll be on my way." She pushed past him with her chin in the air and kept walking down the alley. Several twists and turns later, she still had seen no sign of the cat. She turned another corner, and found herself facing the same boy again, leaning against the same wall. His eyes glinted with amusement.

"Lost your cat? Or lost yourself."

Ellia stopped short.

"I'm not lost." She stared him down, daring him to contradict her. *Never be the first one to look away.* He smiled.

"I can't help you find your cat, but for three pieces I can lead you back to the street, or wherever it is you want to go."

"No, thank you." Ellia replied stiffly, and started to push past him again, but he stopped her.

"Thalis isn't safe at night, especially for a girl like you. Are you sure you won't reconsider my offer? Not many people are as nice and helpful as I am."

Ellia hesitated. "Fine. But only two pieces, and when we get there, not before." She decided not to mention that she didn't have any money at all, but figured she would deal with that problem once she got to it. The boy nodded, and then took off without another word, walking so fast that she had to run to keep up.

The street was completely empty when they came to it. All the vendors had gone home, and the only living things were the rats, the cats, and one lone horse, tethered to a post. Or, at least Ellia thought it was empty. A lump on the ground next to the horse stirred and Ellia realised that it was Tuck, crouched against the wall with his head in his hands. At the sound of her footsteps, he looked up slowly, every line of his face showing exhaustion. When he saw her, he jumped up with a yell and hugged her, grinning with relief.

"Thank Firth you're safe! The others gave up looking hours ago. We'd better hurry, or the Inn will close for Curfew before we get there." He walked to the post and began untying the horse.

"Tuck, wait. I need two pieces to pay my guide. He helped me find my way back here..." She turned around, but the boy was gone. "Oh... Never mind. He's gone." Tuck chuckled darkly as he swung onto the horse. "And a good thing too. The only thing he would've had from me is a knock to the head. Anyone who's willing to guide you for a mere two pieces is up to no good. It's a good thing I was here, or you might've come to a bad end." Ellia blushed, ashamed for having trusted a complete stranger. From now on, she decided, she would be more careful.

She ignored the hand Tuck offered her and leaped up behind him. They started off down the street.

The cat watched them go, then followed quietly behind.

Chapter Five

In Which Ellia Kicks a Nasty Boy

"Being a guard is the most tedious job I've ever taken. Standing, just standing, all day. My only pleasure is in denying people entrance so that they can see what it's like to just stand there, too."—Jonquil, a palace Guard at the Southern Gate.

"If you want to see His Majesty, you'll have to wait like everybody else. Spring Petitions are over." The palace guard sneered. His armor was so decadent you could barely see his face beneath the ornate helmet. His plume would make peacocks seem modest, but his face was deadly serious, and it was all Ellia could do not to snicker. Silas sighed impatiently.

"We're actually here to see *Her* Majesty. The Queen. As we've told you several times already. Do I have to speak slower for your little mind to grasp that concept?" This time Ellia really did snicker, which caused the guard's face to redden with rage.

"You dare mock me?"

He glared at Silas, his hand on his sword hilt. "You can stay out here forever now. I don't let in cheeky peasants." With a sniff of disdain, he reverted to his original rigid pose and stared loftily over their heads. Ellia finally lost her patience. She marched up the steps to the guard, threw back her hood and glared up at him. "Let us in this instant, you idiot." She snarled. The guard turned white as paper. With shaking hands, he unlocked the side door behind him and pulled it open. "Her majesty's waiting room is two corridors down and to the left." He muttered as he shrank back and practically hid behind the door. Tuck gave her a proud look, and Ellia smiled wickedly back. It seemed people in the city were much more superstitious than at Baron Opulus's mansion. Good. She could use that.

They filed past the guard and down the corridor. It was empty, but when they got to the Queen's waiting room they found that it was actually quite busy. The queen was not present, but several harassed attendants were trying to calm several noisy merchants and nobles who looked ready to break into a fight. There were also several girls in the room, each bearing the signature metal cuff of a Starfall in bondage. Some were made of gold or silver, and bore the crest of whatever noble house they belonged to, and some were more simple iron, but all were the same distinctive shape, two bands twisted together and pounded flat. Ellia herself had one, but Opulus's crest had been scratched out for fear someone would realise that she didn't belong to Tuck and his friends. The girl's eyes were a range of metallic colors. Other than their eyes they looked quite human, and they were all very pretty. Ellia suddenly felt self conscious about her slightly pointed ears and unnatural looks. She had never met another Starfall, and so had assumed that they must look like she did, with sharp features and an elvish appearance. Her heart sank at the sight of these girls. *I won't even blend in with the other Starfalls here. Will I be an outcast everywhere?* She was distracted from her mournful thoughts by a sudden commotion at the far side of the room as the queen finally entered.

She was extremely tall, with a gigantic pile of intricate braids on top of her head, dyed red and dusted with golden glitter. A tiny crown was stuck precariously onto the top of this monstrosity, hardly noticeable amid the fantastic braids. Her clothes were equally fancy, with so many layers that they swept out for at least five feet in every direction. Her face was powdered and painted into a frighteningly perfect mask. All in all, she was the most terrifying and imposing person Ellia had ever seen.

Everyone in the room immediately knelt, fist to forehead in the royal salute. The queen waved them up imperiously. "Show me the girls." she ordered, giving the room a bored sweep of her eyes. "Maybe today there will finally be something worth looking at." The nobles and merchants flushed with embarrassment, and pushed their Starfalls forward. One by one the other Starfalls shuffled to the front of the room and formed a line. Ellia was still frozen in amazement and panic, staring at the queen. A gentle nudge between her shoulder blades forced her forward a step, and she whirled to face Tuck, suddenly realising that this was the last time she would ever see him, or the other guards. He would leave and she would be stranded in this strange city, with thousands of people who were either terrified of her or wanted to exploit her.

"Don't leave me!" she pleaded in a desperate whisper. He gave her a sympathetic smile, but his eyes were impassive. Ellia's heart sank, as she realised that this was the whole and entire reason for their brief friendship. The only reason he had cared about her was because of the money her sale would give him. She felt like crying. *No friendships are real. How could anyone really care about a Starfall?* Tuck gave her an irritated look.

"Go on." He hissed. The other guards were also looking at her with impatience. *Keep your head up. Don't let them see that you care.* Taking a deep breath, Ellia stood up straight, flung her hood back and marched to the front of the room. She felt like she was leaving her heart behind. A hollow feeling filled her, but she was determined not to show it.

The room had fallen silent, as she had come to expect by now. Even the queen was looking at her, greed and interest sparking in her eyes. "Finally," She purred. "*This* one is *much* more interesting than anything my husband has. I'll take her. Who do I pay?" Tuck and Silas stepped forward, and the queen waved for them to follow her into another room to begin negotiations. The other Starfalls and their owners were glaring daggers at her. Ellia couldn't imagine why any of them would want to be bought by this woman, who treated them like they were merely expensive ornaments. The attendants began to usher the others out of the room, and one by one they turned to leave. The merchants cursed under their breath, while the nobles simply glared at Ellia, then swept disdainfully out of the room, Starfall in tow. One Starfall with rust-red eyes actually spat at Ellia's feet, leaving a sizzling hole in the carpet, a biting reminder of Ellia's own lack of powers.

Finally they were all gone, and she was left with the attendants. None of them smiled. A short blond one looked her over skeptically, then shrugged. "You will have to be washed, and we'll have to find you something more acceptable to wear. I'll show you to your room, and then tomorrow we'll deal with all that and also get you fitted for a new cuff. Come on then." She strutted out of the room, Ellia following in a daze.

For some strange reason, it seemed that the room prepared for Ellia was at the opposite end of the palace from the Queen's chambers. They walked and walked, passing through grander and grander rooms, but seemed to have no destination.

"Um, if I'm to be Her Majesty's handmaiden, shouldn't I be nearer to her rooms?" Ellia finally inquired, but the attendant just snorted. "Her Majesty has no need for another handmaiden. You belong to her in name only. The real ones you will be looking after are in the King's side of the palace. He keeps them there because he wants them to love him more than their mother." She shook her head. "As if those monsters could love anyone other than themselves." Ellia was very confused. "The king and queen live in opposite sides of the palace? And who are the monsters I'm going to be taking care of?"

At first she thought the attendant was just going to ignore her, but then she glanced carefully around, leaned in close, and started speaking in a quiet, hurried voice. "It is unwise to speak about the king and queen's division. They are very jealous of each other, competing constantly for everything, even the affection of their children. However, it is not spoken of. Their majesties like to pretend that all is well between them, so this news does not leave the palace, understand?" Ellia nodded. She had heard some of this from Tuck, but had had no idea that the rivalry of the two royals went so far as to build two separate wings of the palace.

"So the monsters you spoke of are the Prince and Princess?" She asked. The attendant gave her a stiff nod, but it seemed that she had decided she had said enough, because she pursed her lips tightly shut and stared straight ahead.

Ellia was quite thoroughly lost by the time they reached the King's wing of the palace. The doors were huge and gilded, with many guards lounging around outside of them. These ones were perhaps less superstitious than the guard at the gate, or they were accustomed to strange sights, because they merely raised a few eyebrows at the sight of Ellia, before pulling the gates open.

Beyond the gate the rooms were even more extravagant, but in a much different style. There was much more gold everywhere, along with vaulted stone ceilings and statues lining the walls, whereas the queen's side had been mostly smaller rooms with carved wooden walls and tapestries everywhere. They entered into a large hall stretching away from the gates towards a huge open door through which Ellia could see firelight and hear many voices talking. However, the attendant pulled her into a much smaller side passageway with torches lining the walls.

"Servants and staff do not enter the Throne Room unless invited." She stated stiffly, practically dragging Ellia away from the firelight. They hustled down the passageway, where the rooms Ellia caught glimpses of were very different from the rest of the palace, simple wooden doors leading into plain stone sleeping chambers. The attendant shoved her sideways into a small empty room, with only a bed and a table, nothing else.

"This is your room. Do not go anywhere until noon, when you will eat with the king's attendants and their Highnesses' nursemaid. The dining room is seven doors down and to the left." She rapped out.

"Dinner is served when the sun goes down. You will be shown your duties tomorrow. Until then, stay out of sight, don't cause any trouble, and, above all, do NOT wander. Everyone is much happier when the Freaks stay out of the way and keep their Demon Eyes where we don't have to look at them." She said this with a completely business - like attitude, so Ellia was uncertain as to whether she meant this last statement as an insult, or whether Freak and Demon Eyes were common terms used to refer to Starfalls here. The attendant spun on her heel and left, slamming the door behind her. For the first time that day, Ellia was alone, with nothing to do. She sat down on the bed and tried, for the hundredth time, to summon that cold feeling she had experienced in the woods. Nothing happened, as usual, so after a while she decided to give up. It was almost noon, so she decided that she might as well try to find the Dining hall, or at least another person to talk to. Both things, it turned out, were very easy to find. She had only walked past three empty rooms before she passed an open door and someone stumbled backwards out of it and into her. His elbow banged into her shoulder, still very sore from the Ice Creeper's claws. She yelped in pain and kicked him in the shins. Laughter echoed out of the open doorway, but the man who turned to face her was not laughing. Burning copper eyes glared down at her. Suddenly, the flames leapt off of the torches on the walls, formed into balls of fire, and flew at her.

Uh oh. Wrong person to kick. Ellia thought. She dropped to the floor just in time, as the flames flew over her head, and somersaulted into his knees. He crashed to the floor. All the balls of fire ceased to defy gravity and did likewise. The other young men in the room came to the door, still laughing. There were two of them, and they weren't facing Ellia but she could see from their matching gold cuffs that they were Starfall.

"Hey Burke, what happened, did you trip over the door frame?" A tall, skinny Starfall asked, stepping out of the door. Burke jumped up. The fireballs rose up off of the floor and hovered around him like a bunch of very large, angry wasps as he looked around for the person who had kicked him. Luckily, the tall skinny man was standing in front of Ellia, or he would probably have thrown the torches at her again. He sputtered in outrage.

"I didn't trip over *anything!* I stepped out into the hall and then that vicious little imp kicked me!" He pointed at Ellia, but he was glaring at the other Starfall. The tall one turned around, and his silver eyes widened at the sight of Ellia.

"Be careful who you sling insults at, Burke." He hissed. Burke turned to protest, but then he saw Ellia, and really *looked* at her for the first time. His mouth dropped open.

"Great Firth, what *is* it?" He exclaimed in astonishment. The Silver Starfall shot him a glare.

"*She* is a Gold Starfall, you idiot."

"But she looks like a - " Burke began, but was stopped short by a kick in the shins from the other Starfall. The Silver one turned to Ellia, swept his brown curls out of his eyes and gave her a flirtatious smile.

"What he was *going* to say," He began in a flattering tone, "Is that you look like a stunningly beautiful young lady, and that he is terribly sorry for running into you." He offered her a hand. "Lovely to make your acquaintance. I'm Jasper. Would you care to join me for lunch?"

Ellia was not a very trusting person. She could tell right away from the looks of Jasper that he was bad news. However, when he looked into her eyes, something like a headache clouded her vision. She found herself suddenly thinking that she had never seen such a nice and honest gentleman before in her entire life. Logically she knew she shouldn't trust him, and yet she found herself smiling, taking his hand, and following him down the hall to the Dining room.

During lunch and the rest of the day, Jasper introduced her to many more staff, but she found it hard to remember their faces. Burke and the other Starfall, who also had copper eyes, and who's name was Roy, tried to engage her in conversation, but she couldn't pay attention to what they were saying to her. She would start to answer, but then Jasper would look at her, with his silver eyes practically glowing, and she would trail off, thinking, *Wow, He's so nice. I like him so much.* Usually, if a boy was too forward, she would kick him. However, whenever Jasper put his arm around her or called her pet names, she didn't mind at all. She just kept dreamily thinking about how much she liked him. She wondered why he spent time with Roy and Burke, since they were so obviously unsavory people. Burke was a bully, violent, crude, and not very intelligent, while Roy was just creepy. He had shifty eyes, and seemed to have the ability of animating statues, because every statue he walked past would move, either making an inappropriate gesture or a weird face at passers by.

When the day finally ended, they walked back to their rooms. Jasper's room was the biggest, and so the other young men liked to spend most of their time there. When they reached it, Jasper said good night very politely and went in. Ellia was just about to leave for her own room when out of the corner of her eye she saw Jasper stagger and then collapse onto the bed with his hand over his eyes. She immediately turned back, anxious to help him, but Burke blocked the doorway.

"Jasper's fine." He growled. "He just gets tired from using his ability too much."

Ellia was very confused. "What's his ability?" Burke didn't answer, just glowered at her until she finally gave up and went to her room.

As she closed the door, the head-achy feeling that had been plaguing her all day began to fade. She remembered everything that had happened that day, all the sneers and veiled insults she had received without even realizing it. She wondered how she could have been so unwise as to travel about with the King's own Starfall attendants. Weren't they the whole reason the queen had wanted Ellia? They were supposed to be rivals, so there was no way they had good intentions towards her. She would have to be careful of them, she decided, before she fell asleep.

Chapter Six

In Which Ellia Has a Dream and a Bad Day

***

"The wise man walks on the straightest path. That's to avoid bandits, you see. Also, he should make sure to ask for directions, and avoid paths that are muddy, unless he wants wet shoes."—Demitrius Scallop, a highwayman with absurdly clean boots.

***

The forest was dark. The moon was low and dim. The wind was cool as it rushed over her face. It felt good on her hot scales. She flapped her wings, and the trees below tossed. They rushed past underneath her, silver leaves glinting in the glow of her scales. She reveled in the freedom of the night, the open sky, the power in her muscles. This is what it meant to be alive. She swept over a lake, admiring her reflection, a burning golden fire on the dark surface.

At the edge of the lake there was a town. It was dark and silent, but on the hill above it watch-fires glowed. They were ready for her. For a moment she considered changing direction, but then discarded the idea. Men could not stop her. She could go where she pleased, do what she wanted. She was free, and no one could ever take that from her. She let out a roar, and a jet of flame exploded over the hillside, illuminating frightened, upturned faces around the watch fires. The men of the town had armed themselves with pitchforks, arrows, and clubs, determined to defend their homes and livestock. She snorted at such a pitiful display of bravery. They could never stand against her. With a sweep of her wings, the campfires went out, raining smoke and sparks into the men's faces. During the chaos that followed, she attacked. Arrows and pitchforks bounced harmlessly off of her scales. The men cried out in dismay as her fire destroyed their comrades. She opened her mouth to roar in triumph and exaltation at her own strength and might. However, she suddenly stopped short as a sharp pain flared in the back of her throat. She coughed and snorted, desperate to get rid of this horrible new sensation. An arrow flew out of her throat and fell to the ground, the tip flecked with blood. Her blood. She stared at it in utter astonishment. Then in anger. The men who were still alive had gathered together, watching her in fear. Standing among them, his shaking hands holding an empty bow, was a boy. This boy had shot her. This puny, insignificant human boy had caused her to feel pain. She roared in such anger that the forests echoed with it. The rage inside her grew to a blinding fury, and she flew at the men, biting, crushing, clawing, burning. Even after there was no one left to resist her, she continued to rampage all over the hilltop. She destroyed the livestock enclosures, stomping on the animals. Then she turned on the town, and lit it on fire with her breath. At last, her rage spent, she threw herself into the air and sped away into the night.

Ellia stood alone on the hilltop, in complete shock and horror at the pointless carnage she had just witnessed. Had she really witnessed it? Or had she actually done it? The idea was too horrible to contemplate. She looked around the smoking hilltop, watching as a few dazed survivors slowly made their way to the top, staring at themselves and each other in astonishment and fear as they began to change, growing more beautiful and elegant, but also completely inhuman. What had even happened here? And, most importantly, why was she here?

She stood there in confusion before becoming aware of someone standing next to her. He was tall, and shrouded in a long dark cloak. She had no idea who he was, until he spoke.

"It cannot be. This is not where you were Gifted. I would have known if you were really this old. You must have been born into the Gift, but then how do you remember this?" He turned towards her, and she suddenly knew who he was. The boy from the alley. She was certain of it, although she couldn't have said why. This person was nothing at all like that boy. He was taller, far more elegant, and although she couldn't see his face clearly through the shadow of his hood, she could tell that he didn't have the same features.

"I don't know what you're talking about. This is just a weird dream, not a memory. I've never even seen this place before. Also, why are you here?" She tried to see his eyes, but he stepped back and turned away. "This isn't just a dream, Starfall. This is deeper, and I think you know it. You have some role to play that I can't figure out yet. You have something that many people have been waiting a long time for, I'm just not sure what. I will have the truth from you, eventually. Until then, know this.

We are watching you."

Ellia woke up in a panic. What was going on? Had that really been a dream, or something more? She had a feeling that she was in over her head, deeply involved in something that she didn't know about. She needed to find out what was happening.

The boy from the alley. Ellia thought, but then dismissed the idea. Why did she keep thinking about him? She had barely met him, and he hadn't been very special, just an ordinary street urchin. So why had he seemed like something more in her dream? She was about to put it out of her mind as a silly fantasy, perhaps her subconscious had found him attractive or something? But then she remembered something. She had looked him in the eye, denying that she was lost, and he hadn't even blinked. *He hadn't even blinked.* As if he wasn't surprised at all to see an elvish face with golden eyes staring at him. As if he was expecting her to come around that corner and run into him. But how could he have known? *The Cat.* The answer suddenly came to her, so obvious she couldn't believe she hadn't seen the connection before. The cat had disappeared at the same time as the boy had appeared. The cat had had Faerie eyes, and in her dream the boy had seemed elfin as well. Also, he had used the same phrase that the Faeries in the woods had used. *We are watching you.*

I have to find that boy. She thought, leaping out of bed. Only then did she remember that today was the day when she would begin her duties as a servant in the palace. She sat down again with a groan. The many days spent traveling and then the one day of leisure in the palace had caused her to get used to freedom. She had almost forgotten that she was still a slave. *How am I going to find the boy if I'm stuck in the palace?* She wondered. She would have to just wait for the opportunity to arrive. Sighing, she got up and went to the door, only to have it bang open in her face. On the other side was the same attendant from the day before, along with several other maids and a manservant, all weighed down with piles of cloth and sewing materials.

"Good, you're up. We're here to get you ready for your new post." She bustled into the room, and immediately began firing orders left and right. The manservant measured Ellia's wrist for her new cuff, raising his eyebrows at the scratched out coat of arms, but making no comment. He recorded the measurements and then left, greatly to Ellia's relief, as the maids had started to strip off her old clothes in order for her to try on new dresses. They bickered and argued about shades and styles for several hours, until Ellia was thoroughly fed up with trying on dresses. No sooner would she put one on, then they would all be clamoring for her to try on a different one. The maids and attendant were also getting irritated, as none of the dresses had been made to fit Ellia's slender, elfin build. Finally they decided that her dresses would have to be made from scratch, and so they spent another hour arguing over which type of fabric to use. When that was finally decided, Ellia assumed it was over. However, she was mistaken. The attendant sent a maid out for a hairdresser who, when she arrived, took one look at the state of Ellia's hair and groaned.

She was immediately rushed off to a different room, filled with steam, perfume, and large basins of water. Ellia was scrubbed and doused in several tubs of water before the hairdresser finally pronounced her clean enough. Then they sat her in a chair and proceeded to "do" her hair, which involved a lot of yanking and cutting and rubbing with strange oils. Ellia usually washed and dressed herself, and so she found this whole process very mortifying. Also, it annoyed her that the hairdresser was constantly moaning about the state of her hair, how it was the most boring shade of brown she had ever seen, and how it was more tangled than a sheep in a thorn bush. Finally, they were done. It was a complete waste of time in Ellia's opinion, since her hair still looked about the same, an ordinary brown, only a little bit shinier and with less tangles.

Several maids came in with a new dress made to fit her, much to her astonishment, as it had only been a few hours. She put it on, and was hustled along through the servant's quarters until they emerged in the Armory, where a huge hairy man cut off her old cuff, and wrapped the new one around her wrist, sealing the ends together. When Ellia saw it, she nearly fell over in shock. The Queen clearly wanted to outshine her husband in this aspect, and the smiths had outdone themselves to please her. The bracelet was made of gold, with the signature design of two bands woven together. However, there were really two cuffs. Both were identical, but one was slightly larger and fit higher up on her arm. The two were connected with an intricate lattice of interwoven vines, birds, and flowers, made of different shades of gold and studded with tiny gems. There was no crest, as the queen didn't have one, but on the larger band there was a clear and perfect diamond, cut into the shape of a six - pointed star. Ellia wasn't sure whether to laugh or to cry. With this on her arm, there was no chance of slipping out into the City unnoticed to find the boy from the alley, nor was there any hope of ever escaping the palace. On the other hand, it was a clear sign of her status as the Queen's servant, and people would be less likely to bother her. The other maids and attendant seemed similarly stunned. The attendant finally groaned, and said, "We'll have to change your dresses to match, I suppose. Well, come on then. It looks like you won't be able to start your duties until tomorrow."

It was decided that the palace maids would work through the night, embroidering tiny gold vines into the hems and collars of Ellia's dresses, and she was finally released as the sun went down. She suddenly realized that she was very hungry - she hadn't eaten anything all day - and so she rushed to the dining hall and joined the throng of servants all headed in the same direction.

Jasper was waiting for her. She had completely forgotten about him, but as soon as she saw him leaning against the wall in the Dining hall the memory rushed back. *I had better be careful of that guy.* She thought, but then he caught her eye, and the thought fled her mind. The head-achy feeling rushed back, and she was overwhelmed by the desire to be near him. All thoughts of the day, her new duties, and her plans to find the boy from the alley rushed out of her head as he smiled at her and told her she looked beautiful. She didn't even notice the flash of dark jealousy in his eyes as he saw her new cuff. All she could think of was that she had never met a more charming person.

Chapter Seven

In Which Two Children are Horrible But Not Really

***

"The solution to badly behaved children is simply to not have any children in the first place."— High Philosopher in Chief, Stephanio.

***

Ellia didn't even have to meet the Royal twins to know that she was in for a rough day. The face of the nursemaid who opened the door said it all. Her eyes were red, from lack of sleep, crying, or both, and her hands were shaking. She couldn't have been more than thirty, but her face was so wrinkled and creased from exhaustion and worry that she looked much older. Her eyes kept darting back and forth, so much that she barely seemed to notice Ellia standing there in front of her. Ellia shifted uncomfortably.

"Um… Excuse me? I'm supposed to take over for you?" The woman's eyes finally settled on her in a distracted kind of way.

"Take over? For me… I can go? But who will take care of the children? They need their lunch at noon, and someone has to take them to see their father, His Majesty, I mean, keep them from screaming … causing a scene, last time the chaos… Oh dear."

Ellia swallowed. "Maybe you could stay, just for today, to show me how to do all those things?" She suggested, but the woman's eyes widened in panic.

"Oh no, I'm sure you'll do fine. Don't worry. As long as you're here to take care of them they'll be fine, you don't need me. Just remember to feed them occasionally, and keep them clean and tidy for when Their Majesties want to see them. Oh, and be careful of chairs. I'll be off then, goodbye." She pushed past Ellia and practically ran away down the hall. Ellia sighed, wishing she had someone to help her. The Prince and Princess were kept in a very fancy but out of the way corner of the palace, not far from her own room. She considered running back and asking Jasper to help, but he had his own duties serving the King. She was on her own. *Oh, well.* She took a deep breath and walked through the door.

Nothing happened. The room beyond was empty. She walked carefully inside, stepping over several trip wires. She glanced curiously at the chairs in the room, which, sure enough, were covered in something that looked like honey. *Be careful of chairs, indeed.* She thought with a smile. She envied the children the fact that they could get away with these kinds of things. The children themselves were nowhere to be found. She was thoroughly confused, until she walked into one of the bedrooms and noticed the open window. There was a note on the table, scrawled in untidy writing.

WE DoNT WaNt ANotTer SToOPID NuRSse

Ellia considered calling the guards, but thought better of it. There was no way she was going to let anyone know that she had lost her charges before she had even met them. She sighed in irritation, then jumped out the window.

The window was two floors up, overlooking an overgrown garden. The twins had probably climbed down using the brickwork, but Ellia didn't have time. She had discovered long ago that she was physically capable of more than most people. Even so, the fall still jarred her legs quite a bit. She stood still underneath the window, listening hard. She couldn't hear anything. There were three doors in the wall around the garden. Two of them led into other gardens, and the other led out into a neater, richer part of the city, with mostly straight alleys and tall brick houses. *If I were a runaway child, where would I go?* The answer was obvious. She ran through the garden and out into the city.

The Prince and Princess may have been good at setting traps, but they weren't any good at running away. Ellia spotted them down the first turnoff she passed. They were dressed in bright, clean, and incredibly fancy play-clothes, and they stood out against the drab houses like two spots of sunshine in a dungeon. They were running away as fast as they could, but Ellia was faster. She caught up with them a few houses down, caught them by the backs of their shirts, and planted her feet.

The girl squealed and started to throw a tantrum, but then caught a glimpse of Ellia's face and stopped with her mouth hanging open. The boy's eyes grew wide with fear, and he struggled frantically to escape, biting and kicking. The little girl took her cue from her brother and began to do the same, letting out a horrible high pitched shriek at the same time. Ellia held on grimly. Early that day, she had worried that she wouldn't know what to do, since she'd never taken care of children, let alone royalty, before. However, these weren't children. These were little animals, and she knew how to deal with spoiled animals.

"Stop it." She spat, giving them both a shake. "I

don't care if you're royalty, if you don't behave you're going to regret it." This got their attention. They had obviously never been spoken to this way before. They gaped at her in astonishment. Finally the prince spoke up. "Are you a Faerie? Are you going to curse us?" He asked uncertainly.

Ellia grinned. "No. I'm your new governess. I'm going to take care of you, but I can't if you won't let me. So, you have a choice. You can cooperate with me, and we can have lots of fun, or you can be a nasty brat and I promise I will make your life miserable." For a second they just stared at her, as if under a spell, but then the boy seemed to wake up, closed his gaping mouth, and screwed his small face up into a sneer. "You can't do anything to us. If you hurt us our daddy will kill you."

"Yeah!" His sister echoed. "He'll chop your head off." She added with relish. Ellia felt slightly sick. She knew she was playing a very dangerous game. She often rushed rashly into things without first thinking through the consequences. *I don't care.* She thought recklessly. *I'm going to teach these kids to obey me, no matter what.* She smiled wickedly. "There's a lot of ways to make you miserable without hurting you." She said. The prince crossed his arms. "Yeah? Like what?"

"Well, for a start, I could feed you only oatmeal for breakfast, give you baths every day, lock you inside and give you lessons on grammar, etiquette, and mathematics. Also, you would have to wear formal clothing all of the time. For every prank you played, you would spend an hour alone in your room..." Ellia easily continued to rattle off all of the things that she herself had been forced to endure as a child, when Baron Opulus had hired several strict tutors in an attempt to conquer her rebellious spirit. She watched the children's smug sneers quickly fade into looks of horror and dismay. The girl's face finally crumpled and she burst into tears. "I hate you!" She wailed. "You're a horrible witch!"

Ellia tried to remain stern, but her heart went out to these poor children, whose parents didn't love them, and who reminded her so strongly of herself.

"Listen." She said softly. "It doesn't have to be like that. If you just listen to me, and stop playing pranks and running away, we can have a great time together. We can go exploring in the palace. We can build blanket forts, climb trees, go for walks in the gardens, wear whatever we like, eat whatever we like, and maybe, if your father allows it, I can even take you out into the city. Deal?" The children thought about it. Finally, the prince reluctantly muttered "Deal." And his sister followed suit. Ellia grinned with relief, spat on her hand, and held it out. The children stared at it in utter confusion.

"What are you doing?" The prince finally asked warily. Ellia was astonished.

"You spit and shake. That's how you seal a deal in the place that I came from. Haven't you ever done that before?" Both children shook their heads. The prince's eyes lit up. A delighted grin slowly spread across his face. It had evidently never occurred to him that any older person would ever willingly let him do such a nasty thing. He spat on his palm and shook her hand with relish. The sister also did so, but with less enjoyment.

"So..." Ellia began, taking their hands and steering them back out of the alley, "I'm Ellia. I'm a Starfall so I don't have a second name. What are your names?"

"I'm Myrgen." The prince replied shortly, dropping her hand and striding a few paces ahead in a show of independence. The Princess stared at their joined hands with something like wonder. She drew closer to Ellia and held on tightly to her hand with a tentative, sweet smile.

"My name is Myria Rose. My favorite food is mushrooms and cheese. Sorry for calling you a witch."

They walked back to the palace slowly, talking the whole way. Ellia quickly realised that the main reason that these children had acted so terribly was because no one ever paid any attention to them. Clearly no one had ever actually *listened* to them before.

Not wanting to alert the guards to their escapade, they climbed back up the brickwork and entered the royal apartments through the window. The first thing Ellia did was call a maid to bring lunch, and also to clean the honey off of the chairs. After the kids had eaten their fill, they began to grow bored, and began to behave badly. When they started to throw food at the walls, Ellia recognized that if she didn't put their restless energy to good use, she would have a very big problem on her hands.

"Alright," She said cheerfully. "Lunch is done. What do you normally do after?"

"Scare the nurse maid so that she runs away screaming." Myria stated matter-of-factly. Ellia sighed.

"Other than that." They thought about it for a moment. Then Myrgen's face lit up.

"Sometimes when she's gone we run around in the palace and outside so that it takes her hours to find us." As he said this, Ellia was struck by a brilliant idea. This might just be an answer to her problem of finding the boy from the alley.

"Where are you allowed to go?" She asked carefully. Myrgen laughed.

"Anywhere, except out into the city. Nobody can tell us what to do." Ellia smiled. This was wonderful news. If they could go anywhere, then she, as their governess, could also go anywhere with them. Also, many of the gardens had entrances into the city. They were almost always guarded. It had been a lucky coincidence that the one they had left out of was unguarded at the time. She would need to learn about the guard's rotation schedules first. She needed information, and the best way to get it was by going all over the place and listening to the gossip. If the children often disappeared for hours at a time, she might be able to sneak into the city and spend a few hours looking for the boy.

"Great." She said. "I'm new here, so today we're going to go exploring in the castle, and you can tell me everything you know about it."

The palace was far bigger than Ellia had at first thought. However, as they walked she began to see a sort of pattern to the many hallways and rooms. The palace was made up of a large, circular, middle section, which was mainly large conference rooms, banquet halls and ballrooms. The roofs were two stories tall, with secret passageways and catwalks hidden in the vaulted ceilings, behind statues and across the tops of pillars. These were not known to most people. The children had discovered them quite early in their wanderings, and described in detail how one could climb across the arches and dump water down onto the heads of banquet guests. They climbed up, and Ellia was amazed by the way that the walkways were designed so that you could look down without being seen. She decided that they were probably created for spies, or possibly archers if the king were afraid of assassination. The middle section of the palace was surrounded by many gardens, fountains, ponds and woods, except where the six roads of the city cut through them to reach the two main gates on either side of the palace. The two wings of the palace were attached on opposite sides of the main section. They were made up of smaller rooms, mostly stacked two floors high, except for the towers that flanked the four corners of the palace. Although the wings were symmetrical from the outside, they were vastly different on the inside, as the rooms were all different sizes, and the hallways were more tangled than a Siren's hair. The upper rooms were mostly those of the royalty, and various noble men and women in the court. The lower floors were the servants quarters, the baths and other facilities for servicing the upper classes. Each sovereign, she learned, had their own set of servants, baths, and the rest in their separate wings. They didn't share anything at all, except the court nobles, who spent time in both wings in order to curry the favor of both. There was only one smithy, and it was underground, almost as if the king and queen didn't want to be reminded of something that they had to share with the other.

The palace was so expansive that even though the children had lived there their entire lives, they still had not been everywhere in it. They explored the palace all day. Ellia was delighted by the fact that the children could get away with anything, and, because she was with them, so could she. Despite this, they still took quieter back passageways. Ellia hated all the stares and whispers that both her and her bracelet received from the palace residents. The servants spat and muttered curses at the sight of her, but the noblemen were the worst. They would at first stare in astonishment, and then their eyes would take on a calculating, greedy look, and they would immediately come up to her with simpering, oily flattery. She saw the hunger in their eyes, though. She knew their sort. Baron Opulus was one of that type. The only thing they saw in her was power. All Nobles were drawn to power like starving wolves to fresh meat. She avoided them whenever possible. However, the higher classes were not always avoidable. Ellia ran into many of the nobles, and even the Queen, once. She caught sight of Ellia, took in her new outfit, and gave her a satisfied smirk. Then she saw her children. Her face took on a look of distaste, and she swept past without stopping. Ellia also saw the King that day, but he was leaving a large room just as they entered from the other side, and he didn't notice them.

The most interesting encounter, by far, happened as they came out of a side passageway into the main hall leading from the gates to the Throne Room. The main gates were swinging open, but not from the guard's hands. Rather, the guards were standing pressed against the wall in terror. The gates were blasted open by a gust of warm wind, seemingly out of nowhere. A man strode through, but Ellia swiftly realized that he wasn't a man. Ellia had heard that the Faerie never left their woods, but there could be no doubt as to what this person was. He stood at least a head taller than all of the guards. His face slightly resembled Ellia's, but the lines were much sharper and harder, with a look of pride and scorn that seemed fixed permanently on them. His ears, unlike Ellia's, ended in points. His eyes were ancient, completely inhuman, filled with a sort of wild, savage freedom, and yet also very cool and calculating. Ellia drew back into the passageway in wonder. Even the twins, who never stopped talking, were silent. Ellia had already seen many Faerie in the Shadow Woods, and she saw elvish features every time she looked into a mirror. However, this one was different. He seemed to radiate power. Just as the wind had blown open the gates, his presence seemed to blow people out of his way. He swept past in silence, never glancing to either side, so that he never saw Ellia, staring at him out of the doorway. She remained like that for many minutes after he had disappeared, her thoughts whirling. She only dared to move once the swish of his footsteps had completely faded.

They spent all day roaming around in the palace. Ellia was eager to learn as much as possible, especially about the Faerie in the palace, but heard nothing other than exclamations of astonishment and surprise at such an event. Nevertheless, she didn't give up, and didn't stop poking around and eavesdropping until she noticed the twins yawning, and beginning to complain that they were hungry. She finally relented and they trekked back to the twins' rooms, where dinner was waiting for them. Not only dinner, Ellia realised as she stepped through the door.

Two royal guards in full armor were leaning yawning against the walls. They had clearly been waiting for a very long time. At the sight of her, they jumped to attention, and the one on the left cleared his throat officially. Ellia's mind raced back to something that the Nursemaid had said early that morning.

"Um... Does the King want to see his children?" She asked hesitantly, wondering how she was supposed to get the twins to look presentable on such short notice. However, the guard shook his head.

"Actually, His Majesty wishes for Her Majesty's new Starfall to be present at his council tonight. That would be you. We are already very late, so I suggest we go immediately." Ellia gaped at him in surprise.

"What about the twins?" She demanded indignantly. The guard shrugged.

"They'll have to manage on their own for a bit. We shouldn't be too long." He offered her his arm, but she ignored it, and they left to see the King.

Chapter Eight

In Which Politics Get Rather Complicated

***

"To appear wise, it really doesn't matter what you say, only *how* you say it. If you use words so long that no one understands you, they assume that *they* themselves are the stupid ones."— High Philosopher in Chief, Stephanio.

***

The door to the council was closed, but even through it they could hear the sounds of an argument.

"I won't have it!" a deep voice bellowed. Ellia guessed by the looks on the guard's faces that this was the king. The voice that answered was very soft, but deadly and hard as iron.

"I'm afraid I didn't ask your permission."

The room fell deadly quiet just as Ellia entered. The guard had wisely decided to stay outside. The king was glaring daggers at someone. Not just someone, but the very same Faerie that Ellia had seen enter the castle earlier that day. He stood in the middle of the room, facing the king with cold defiance etched into every muscle in his body. The king was leaning forward in his throne, his face dark red with rage, his knuckles white against the arms of his chair. The various nobles and servants in the room were staring from one face to the other, looking as if they wished to be somewhere far away.

The Elf's clothes were very simple, mostly dark forest colors. His only ornaments were several silver beads in the braids of his hair, and a silver leaf design on his sword sheath. However, the king, in all his extravagant finery, seemed to pale by comparison. When Ellia entered, the King's eyes flickered towards her, and then stopped on her face. He blinked several times in surprise, and the Faerie twisted around to follow his gaze. He looked her over coolly, then smiled triumphantly as he turned back to the king.

"You see, your Majesty? She isn't one of yours."

The king snorted in derision. "Nonsense. A few differences in her facial structure prove nothing. If she were Elvish, she'd have pointy ears and freaky eyes like the rest of you creatures. Her eyes aren't green, they're gold. That makes her a Starfall, and all Starfalls belong to me. The Kurdu can't have my Starfalls, and neither can you Faerie Devils. Go back to your woods where you belong." He settled back into his chair, as if confident that the argument was over. The Faerie glared at him.

"Her Father was Elvish. She was one of ours long before your disgusting human smugglers did this to her. The star they used to do it was in our woods. They stole both her and the star from us. If you return her now, we will forgive you that crime."

The king's face paled, but he set his jaw.

"Lies. You can't prove any of that." He growled. The Elf just smiled.

"Actually, I can." He strode over to Ellia, placed one hand on her shoulder, and with the other pressed his fingers against the side of her neck, just under her left ear. She felt a tingling shock go through her, and nearly fell over.

A Pale arm, raised as if in farewell... A soft

chanting... The child stirs in her sleep... the boat rocks.

Ellia's head swirled with the memory. Black spots danced before her eyes, and the skin under the Faerie's fingers burned with a prickling pain. He took his fingers away, but the pain remained. The room was silent. All eyes were fixed on the strange insignia glowing on Ellia's skin, under her ear, as the Elf turned her to face the King.

"You see? She is marked. We marked her as your smugglers stole her from us. What more is there to say? I will take her with me to my realm, and I will forget this slight against my people. She was never yours." He was telling the truth. He knew it. Everyone else in the room knew it. Ellia could even see the truth of it echoed in the King's eyes. However, his face had a look of mulish stubbornness on it.

"What sort of proof is that?" He scoffed. "You say that you marked her long ago, but we all saw that the mark wasn't there until you put it there just now. No more of this. It's just an excuse to steal my only Golden Starfall from me. Well, you can't have her. No one can. Go back to your woods. You're lucky I don't have you run out of the castle for the thief that you are. Get out of my sight."

The Elf at first just stared at him in astonishment, and then his lips curled into a sneer. Although there were no windows, a wind began to pick up in the room, growing steadily stronger.

"You won't get away with this, Human. We will have what is ours. No puny mortal king can stand against us." He turned and swept out of the room. The wind howled after him, knocking over the table, ripping the door off its hinges, and bowling over the statues in the hall as he strode down it.

Ellia went to bed in a daze. She forgot all about dinner. The nursemaid took care of the children during the night, so she didn't bother returning to their rooms, but instead went straight to her own room and collapsed on the bed. Her thoughts whirled in a thousand different directions, trying to make some sense out of this gigantic mess she'd stumbled into. Had she really stumbled into it, though? Or had it always been following her? She'd known that she was valuable, and that both the King and the Kurdu wanted her. But the Elves too? It was too much. Not only that, but her father was Faerie. That explained her face, her build, and her enhanced physical abilities. However, it created more questions than it answered. The faerie seemed to know how Starfalls were made, and also who her father was. This was very strange. Men had been killed for less. The method of turning an ordinary baby into a Starfall was a carefully guarded secret, but everyone knew that the babies were always stolen. So how would the Elf know who her parents were? She needed to talk to him. With so much on her mind sleep seemed impossible, and yet she was so tired from the day that she slipped swiftly into oblivion.

It wasn't night this time. She was glad. Unlike most creatures, she couldn't hide her glow in the night. She hid better in the day, and right now she needed to avoid notice. She crept through the forest, careful, silent. Her quarry wasn't stupid like most humans, and by now he probably knew she was coming. The idiot had tried to hunt her. Her, the Greatest Huntress the world had ever known. Naturally, he had failed to slay her. Hadn't even scratched her. However, he had managed to escape with his life, after such an impudent action. That couldn't be allowed.

He was setting a fire in a small clearing. Perhaps not so smart, after all. She crept forward, wings folded, with murder in her cold, proud heart. She was no small beast, and made no small noise when she pounced.

The Hero spun around, sword out, his face fierce and alive with the knowledge of his imminent death. He leapt in close to her, too close for her to burn him with her breath. It was a brave move. As he slashed upwards at her throat, she actually felt a slight tickle of fear. However, his blade was as mortal as it's owner. It wasn't one of those that had been forged deep in the fires of the earth, those that might actually be able to wound her. Instead, it glanced harmlessly off and flew out of his hands. She turned to face him, and watched his hope fly. He was out of options, and fear filled his eyes. He turned to run. He actually made it a few yards before her tail came whipping round, and struck with the force of a tidal wave. The Hero died on impact, and his body was catapulted far over the trees. It was so swift, so sudden. One moment he was there, then he wasn't. The world went on. The forest was filled with a silence that could almost be called peaceful. One human wiped from the earth without a trace. She congratulated herself on a successful kill. Thus to all my enemies, she thought gloatingly. With that thought, she settled down in the clearing and took a nap.

Ellia stood in the clearing. The dragon was gone. She remembered what had happened here, and wasn't sure whether to be violently sick or to cry. Instead of doing either, she rushed into the forest. She found him on the ground, where he had fallen. He was surrounded by branches that had cracked in his fall, and she laid them over him. His body was broken, and he was very dead. His face was blank, empty of that fearless courage that had shone out of him in life. She closed his eyes, wishing she could bury him, but also knowing in some part of her mind that this was a dream, and she wouldn't have time.

Then she really did cry. She knelt in the forest, over the body of the nameless Hero, and wept like she never had before. She cried for his death, but also for the fact that it was meaningless. He had been killed for no reason, with no warning. No one would ever know his name. No one would ever bury him. Nothing would mark his passing except the tears of a girl who wasn't even there. She cried because such things were even possible, that men died for no reason, that other men killed them and suffered no consequences. Children were stolen from their families, and given powers they would never be able to use, but would always be used by others, the same ones who stole them from their families in the first place. Families lost their children and never found them. Children who had parents were neglected by them. People died, people were buried, People starved, people were used, sold, stolen, and neglected, but no one cared. How could they not care?

She was roused from her tears by soft footsteps. Someone was coming through the woods towards her, from the direction of the clearing. She got up swiftly, and slipped behind a tree. Seconds later, the boy from the alley came into the clearing, and stopped short at the sight of the body. He glanced around in bewilderment.

"That can't be. Nobody dies in a dream. So who's dream is this, then? Nobody else is here." He began to slowly retrace his steps, calling out hesitantly,

"Lady Myth?"

"What an odd name," Ellia thought. She was still shocked by what had happened, and didn't want to talk to anyone this soon after crying. However, she remembered vaguely that she had questions for this boy. She stepped out from behind the tree.

"Stop! I need to talk to you."

The boy spun around. He wasn't wearing a cloak this time, and she was able to get a good look at him. He was definitely Elvish. Also very handsome, but she pushed aside that thought. He was tall, with a typical

Faerie build and features. His eyes had that same ancient and yet young look that she had seen in all the other elves she had met. However, where all the other elves had possessed very fair or even white hair, his was black, and curly. His skin was also much darker than most Faerie. When he saw her, his face turned pale though.

"No. You shouldn't be here. What are you doing here?" He demanded, rather as if he knew the answer but didn't want it to be true. Ellia began to grow annoyed. All these secrets and riddles were driving her crazy.

"I could ask the same of you." She shot back. "This is my dream, so I get to ask the questions. You'd better answer them straight, too, because if you don't, I swear I am going to find you in the real world and permanently mess up your perfect face for lying to me." The boy's eyebrows shot up. "You're a feisty one aren't you?" He asked with a grin. Ellia just glared at him. "I mean it. You stupid elves are always showing up everywhere, sneaking into my dreams, with all these mysterious warnings and hints, then disappearing. If someone doesn't tell me what's going on, I am going to lose it." By the time she finished this rant she was so frustrated she was practically stamping her feet. The boy's grin just got bigger, and his eyes danced with amusement.

"All right, your highness," He said mockingly, "I'll answer your questions, maybe, if the answers aren't forbidden, but you might have to pay for the knowledge. Fire away." He settled himself cross-legged on the ground and assumed a slightly more serious expression. Ellia felt silly standing, so she sat down as well.

"Okay, why are the elves "watching me", and why did they mark me as a child, and why do they want to take me back now, when they could have years ago?"

She asked. "No, wait, first, what is your name, and why are you in my dream at all?"

The boy smiled. "Those first two questions are free. My name is Rowan, and I'm a Dreamwalker, which means that I can be in any dream that I choose. I'll answer your other questions, but you will have to give me something in return. Knowledge is never free." It sounded simple enough, but Ellia smelled danger. You should never bargain with an Elf. Everyone knew that. However, her curiosity was burning her up. "What would I have to give you?" She asked warily. Rowan gave her an innocent smile. Much too innocent. "That depends on the question. For the ones you've already asked, you will have to pay with your deepest, darkest secret." Ellia thought about that. "Nope." She decided. "I have a better idea. You answer one of my questions, and in return I'll answer one of yours." At that, Rowan frowned. "You drive a hard bargain."

"It's a fair trade." Ellia argued. Rowan cocked his head and considered that.

"Yes, I suppose it is fair. Fine, I'll do it. What's your first question?"

"Why are the Elves following me around and why did they put the mark on me?"

"That's not fair. It's more than one question."

"Okay, fine. How and Why have the Elves been involved in my life so far? That's one question." She smiled innocently back at him, watching him realize that he had been outsmarted, and that he now had to answer all of her questions at once.

Rowan at first looked as though he was about to argue, then like he wanted to smack her. Finally, he just laughed dryly. "Yes, I suppose it is one question. A very big one, though. I don't even know the whole answer to it, but I'll tell you what I do know. The Faerie have always been drawn to beautiful things. I suppose you *might say they collect them. They do not associate much with the world of Men, since it is ugly and unmagical. However, they still watch that world, since there are occasionally both beautiful and magical things that come out of it. They consider all beauty and all magic to rightfully belong to themselves. When you were born, you were more beautiful than most human children. You also looked more Elvish than Human, which roused the interest of the elves, and caused quite a scandal among the higher Courts. Your mother was definitely Human, so they knew that your father must be Elvish, and they were all looking at each other, wondering who had betrayed their blood and actually stooped so low as to mix with a common Human Baroness, who wasn't even beautiful. No one wanted to admit it, and so no one wanted to claim you." Rowan spoke in a matter-of-fact tone of voice, but Ellia's cheeks flamed in anger and shame at the way in which he was describing Humanity, as if it were some sort of ugly disease. She opened her mouth to object, but Rowan held up his hand. "I'm just explaining how they felt about you, not how I do. They are quite proud about their blood and race." Here his voice turned bitter, but he took a deep breath and went on with the story.*

"They fell to arguing amongst themselves, and then, while they were distracted, you were stolen by a band of Smugglers. They turned you into a Starfall. Not just any Starfall, but from a gold star. No Gold Starfall has been seen in over a hundred years, and they are said to have great power. Suddenly, all of the Faerie Lords were claiming to be your father. They all wanted you, but wouldn't accept anyone else's claims, so finally the High Lord Iberus put a mark on you, and declared that no one should have you, but that they should all wait to see how you turned out, so that they might properly determine who your real father was. However,

after sixteen years they still have no idea. You don't have any similarities to any of them. They sent me to watch you, especially your dreams, to see if you had any memories that might tell us something. That's why I'm here." He stopped talking, as if done, but Ellia sensed that there was something he wasn't telling her.

"If they don't know who my father is then why did that Faerie come to the castle to take me away?" She demanded. Rowan frowned.

"What did he look like?"

"A tall Faerie, with a really hard, chiseled face and long braids that had pieces of silver wrapped around them. He had a wind that followed him around and blew people over." As she described him, Rowan's eyebrows creased in confusion.

"That's the High Lord Iberus. He came to the castle? But why... Oh." His eyes grew dark with a sudden realisation. Ellia felt her frustration growing.

"What?" She asked. Rowan shook his head, and stood up, as if he were in a hurry for the conversation to be over. Ellia stood up with him, determined to get her answer.

"You haven't fully answered my first question yet. You know something. What is it?"

"Nothing. Maybe they decided that palace life is influencing you too strongly." Rowan shrugged. *"I really don't know. My turn for a question now."*

"No it isn't."

"What do you mean, it isn't? I answered your question, so I get to ask one."

"You already did."

"No, I didn't."

"Yes you did. You said, 'What did he look like?' That's a question." Ellia smiled impishly up at Rowan. She expected him to get angry, but he didn't. Instead, he just looked astonished, as if he were really seeing*

her for the first time. His face slowly lit up into a delighted grin. "Well played, Lady." He said, with a bow. "Your bargaining skills are worthy of the craftiest Elf alive. I'm afraid I underestimated you. I assure you, it won't happen again." With that, he turned and walked away. He had barely taken two paces before the wood around him seemed to warp and he was gone.

Ellia woke up.

Chapter Nine

Stick Rafts and a Sneaky Snake

***

"I don't believe in monsters. No creature could possibly be as dangerous as it looks. It's only our blindness to their good side that makes us afraid of them."— Dalmoni Carrica, a young man who sadly was eaten by his pet Ice Creeper.

***

Was it just a dream? Ellia wondered, as she hurried to the Twin's apartments. Perhaps her head had been so full of questions that it had caused her brain to merely conjure up answers to them. She didn't think so, though. She had only met the boy from the alley once, and so there was no reason why her brain would have included him in the dream unless he really was a Dreamwalker, like he said.

So what was she going to do? She had the answers to most of her questions. However, that information did her no good if she didn't use it. Despite the fact that she was a Starfall, bound to serve the Queen, Ellia wasn't resigned to that role. Deep down, she longed for other things. Her brief taste of freedom on the road had made her determined to taste it again. Someday soon, she was going to get out of here.

Something that looked vaguely like a plan began to form in her mind. Despite the telltale cuff on her wrist, there had to be a way to get out.

The twins were restless when she arrived. The Nursemaid looked like a wreck. She didn't even bother to greet Ellia, just shuffled past her down the corridor, head down and hands shaking. In the room, the twins both had gleeful grins on their faces. Ellia sighed.

"What did you do?" She demanded. The twins' smiles disappeared as they reluctantly met her eyes.

"It wasn't me!" Myrgen yelped, widening his eyes in pretend innocence. "Myria was the one who bit her!"

"That's not fair!" Myria squealed indignantly. "It was you that mixed the soap into her breakfast. Also you threw her ring out the window. That's why she was crying." She glared at her brother. He just stuck his tongue out at her. She promptly kicked him, and he pinched her. They flew at each other, and Ellia had to jump in to pull them apart.

"Stop fighting! Look, I know you're both bored, but making people cry is not okay. Pranks are only allowed if the person is horrid. I need you to stop picking on your nurse, okay?" The Twin's reluctantly agreed. Ellia gave them both a tired look, and dropped into a chair.

"Great. Is there any breakfast without soap for me?"

After she had eaten, Ellia took the twins out into the gardens. They didn't use the window this time, but went through the palace to a side door, where a guard gave them a strange look, but let them out.

These gardens were very well-kept, and had more people in them. Ellia noticed, with some disappointment, that there were no gates leading to the City. She led the children down to an artificial stream and fountain. They wanted to plug the pipes with mud, but instead she showed them how to make stick-rafts, and float them down the stream. They decided to build an Armada, and then sink it with rocks. Ellia left them to it, and sat down on a bench where she could see them, but still have some space to think. The sound of the water and the wind in the trees gradually lulled her into a half-sleep. Her thoughts were slow and dreamy. *If I'm going to get out I'll need outside help. I wonder if Tuck is still in the city. No, Tuck wouldn't help me. I need to try to be less scary and maybe make some new friends...If I fall asleep right now, I wonder if Rowan will come back and talk to me.* A hand on her shoulder jolted her from her dreamy thoughts about Rowan, which, if she had been fully awake, she would have never allowed herself to think. A voice in her ear brought her back to reality.

"Hello, Love," Jasper purred. Ellia had completely forgotten about him. At the sound of his voice, her memories rushed back, and her face burned with shame. She felt nothing but revulsion for this idiot whose hot breath was brushing the back of her neck. How could she have acted so unwisely around him earlier? He sat down beside her, and started to put his arm around her, but must have seen the way she tensed, ready to strike, because he took it back.

"What's wrong, Sweetheart? I missed you at dinner Yesterday. Where were you?" His voice sounded concerned and pained, but Ellia didn't trust him for an instant.

"Get away from me!" She snarled, turning to glare at him. That was her mistake. The moment her eyes met his silver stare, a headache crashed into her head. Her glare softened. Why was she glaring at Jasper? He was so nice. She smiled at him instead. "Nothing's wrong. I wasn't at dinner because I had a job to do." Even in her hazy state, Ellia's old habits of concealing information kicked in. She didn't tell him about the King, or the

Faerie. Deep inside her, a little voice whispered, *He won't like that.* She wanted him to like her. Something told her he wouldn't be pleased to find out about the Elves' interest in her, so she lied to him through an innocent smile.

"I'm taking care of the royal twins now. Their father wanted to see them." Jasper frowned slightly, but seemed to believe her.

"Great." His smile was fake and sweet, and it made Ellia feel dizzy. "I've been wanting to talk to you, alone, but I never got the chance." Somewhere in the back of Ellia's mind, a warning bell clanged, but she ignored it.

"What about?"

"About *You.*" Jasper's smile got bigger, and he leaned closer. "See, Sweetheart, I know almost nothing about you. What's your ability? Where did you come from? Are you... Faerie?" He said the word carefully, almost as if it might explode. "I don't mean to be rude. Being Faerie is completely fine. Elves are beautiful, and wise, and... *Powerful.*" His voice turned greedy. "I think they're wonderful. I didn't ask that because you look strange, or anything. It's just that, well, your face is really... different. In a good way. You look Faerie, but not quite. And yet you're a Starfall. How can that be?" He was leaning towards her, his face barely inches away, his silver eyes taking up her whole vision, compelling her to speak. The warning bells were louder now, but Ellia's mind refused to listen to them. Instead it was clamoring for her to obey Jasper. *Just answer him. Make him happy. You like him, don't you? You want to make him happy? So tell him!* Ellia knew she shouldn't, but the voice of Reason was rapidly growing quieter. Her mouth seemed to open of its own accord.

"I..." She began, but just then a yell shattered the stillness.

"Hey!"

Jasper jumped, looking around for the source of the noise, and her headache disappeared. Myria was standing in the middle of the stream, her little face scrunched up in anger as Myrgen threw a rock at some stick rafts that were floating around her legs.

"Those are mine! You sink your own stupid boats!" She picked up a raft and threw it at him. They jumped on each other with howls of rage and began to fight in the middle of the stream. With a huff of irritation, Jasper turned back to Ellia.

"You were saying?" But Ellia wasn't paying any attention to him. Concern for her charges flared up inside her. If someone didn't stop them, they were going to hurt each other. She jumped up. Jasper tried to grab her arm, but he hadn't anticipated her speed. His hand closed on empty air, as she dashed down to the stream, peeling the rock from Myrgen's grip before he could hit Myria on the head with it. By the time she'd sorted out their squabble, she was soaked, and Jasper was standing on the bank, looking very irritated.

"Ellia, you're covered in mud. What are you doing?" He demanded, as if her wet and bedraggled state were a personal insult. Ellia scowled at him, but some strange impulse kept her from meeting his eyes.

"These are my charges. I had to stop them from fighting!" She protested. He snorted.

"These monsters? You'd just as well try to stop an earthquake. They were born fighting. Just leave them. I was *talking* to you." He acted as if his conversation were the most important thing in the world. Ellia began to be fed up with this self-centered idiot.

"Look here," She snapped, sloshing through the stream toward him.

"You can take your *talk* to someone else, because I'm tired of hearing it. I don't have time for idiots." Jasper's eyebrows went way up in surprise. His astonished silver eyes met her angry gold ones. She felt a head-achy feeling pushing into her brain. Along with it came thoughts. *You like him so much, wow, he's so nice.* However, Ellia was angry. Jasper had made her look like a fool, swooning over him all the time. She was beginning to suspect that he was *doing* something to her. There was nothing she hated worse than people who messed with her thoughts. The mushy, swooning thoughts that pushed into her brain were so different from her actual mood that she could recognize them as foreign invaders. Something unlocked inside her. A burning fury roared to life, burning up all other thoughts. Jasper seemed quite unaware of her mood. His eyes were confident as he gave her a sticky sweet smile.

"See here, Sweetie, you don't have to be angry at me. I was only looking out for you. All I want is to take care of you. I can't if you won't listen to me." He gave her a wounded, pleading look. Ellia sneered at him.

"Sure." She said sarcastically. "Like anyone would actually look out for a Starfall, without wanting anything back. I know a greasy power-monger when I see one." Jasper gaped at her. However, his astonishment quickly turned to anger. His face turned red. His smile was gone, and his eyes glowed brighter than ever, as he strode forward and grabbed her arms.

"Look at me, Sweetie." He hissed. "You don't think that. You love me. Terribly. Now, say you're sorry, and promise to obey me from now on." The thoughts in Ellia's head echoed his words. However, she wasn't listening to her thoughts anymore. She laughed. It was a strange sound, halfway between a laugh and a snarl. Her anger surprised even herself. It seemed as if something that wasn't her had pushed it's way through into her mind, enhancing her anger beyond anything she had ever felt before.

"I don't obey anyone. And if you call me Sweetie one more time, I'll rip your tongue out." She growled. Her thoughts were scary, but coming from the mouth of a slight, bedraggled girl, Jasper evidently didn't find them frightening. Instead he just smirked. "You may not obey me now, but you'll learn to eventually. I'll tame that smart mouth of yours. No one says no to me." He leaned down, and Ellia realized with a kind of hysterical astonishment that he was going to kiss her. *He really is full of himself, isn't he? He doesn't think I'm serious.* She almost laughed. Then she slammed her forehead into his nose.

Jasper stumbled backwards, his eyes wide, blood running down his face. He just stood there for a second, staring at her, and then he turned and ran from the garden. Ellia turned, anger still burning, to see both the twins staring at her with open mouths. She shoved her anger away. It didn't want to go, almost like some other creature, locked inside her, that wanted to get out. With a conscious effort, she pushed it down and locked it back where it came from. She ducked her head in the stream to rinse the blood away, then smiled at the twins. She could feel a bruise forming on her forehead, but consoled herself with the knowledge that Jasper was definitely feeling a lot worse.

"Sorry about that. That's the kind of person I was telling you about, the type you can play pranks on." She explained. Myrgen snorted.

"Yeah, he's pretty nasty. He hates us because we don't like him like everybody else does. He calls us Little Animals." Myria nodded.

"Did he just try to *kiss* you?" She demanded. "Ewww." She wrinkled her nose. Ellia laughed.

"Yeah." She agreed. "Ewww. Forget about him. What do you guys want to do now?"

The twins seemed to do as she said and forget

about him, as they tried to climb an old, twisted tree. However, Ellia couldn't get Myrgen's comment out of her head. *We don't like him like everybody else does.* She realised that she didn't know what Jasper's ability was. Could it maybe be... To make people like him? It made sense. She never trusted people, or let them get close to her, until Jasper. She always acted so stupid around him. Ellia suddenly felt a stab of panic. If she was right, and that was his power, then he could do it again. She wouldn't be able to trust her own emotions, and he might be able to get her to do almost anything for him. *I need to get out of here.*

Chapter Ten

In Which Ellia Breaks the Ceiling and Saves the Day

* * *

"The only way to win is to cheat. The honest ones never get anywhere."
— Rudolfus Podge, owner of the Golden Chance Gambling House.

* * *

That night, Ellia lay down on her bed. Then, when the voices outside had disappeared, and the torches had been extinguished, she got back up again. She'd spent the entire day watching the guards on the walls, and had concluded that there was no escaping that way. Although she'd been able to get into the City to catch the twins, she'd learned that that part of the city was sort of an extension of the palace, where Nobles lived. It was separated from the *real* City by much higher walls, with more guards. If she was ever going to get out of the palace, she needed to do some snooping.

She crept out of her room, and eased the door closed behind her. With one hand trailing the wall for guidance, she headed off down the passage on silent feet. Three doors down, a slice of light slanted across the floor from a half-open doorway. Jasper's room. She could hear voices inside. She was just considering turning the other way, to avoid Jasper, when she heard something that made her creep forward and stop to listen outside the door.

"What happened to you?" The voice was incredulous, and Ellia recognized it as belonging to Burke.

"Did you run into a wall, or what?"

"I don't want to talk about it." It was Jasper. His voice sounded clogged through his broken nose. Roy's nasal whine drifted through the door.

"You can tell us, Jasper. You know we won't laugh. Come on, just tell us what happened." Jasper let out a rueful laugh.

"She's stronger than I thought."

"Who?"

"Ellia. I tried to get her to spill her secrets. There's something really fishy about her, with her weird Faerie face, and some secret ability that nobody has been able to figure out. It was going fine, I had her hooked like a fish, and she was about to tell me everything, but then those stupid Royal Rats interrupted me."

Burke laughed.

"The Monster twins did that to you? How'd they reach?"

"No, not the twins." Jasper snarled. "It was Ellia. Something's wrong with her. She suddenly turned on me, with this creepy look in her eyes, like she'd suddenly changed personalities and turned murderous. Even her voice sounded different. She threatened to rip my tongue out, just 'cause I was flirting a bit, and then she smashed my nose in with her head."

"Wow." Burke sounded impressed. "She must really hate people messing with her." Jasper laughed dryly.

"You should've seen her. She was practically spitting flames."

Burke snorted.

"Funny, she didn't seem to mind all those other times."

Ellia leaned back against the wall. She felt as if the wind had been knocked out of her. *Practically spitting flames*. Those words sounded so familiar. Hadn't she done that before? She could almost remember the taste of fire in her lungs, rushing out of her... She shook her head. No, that was stupid. The only thing she'd ever spat was ice, that one time in the woods. *That* was her ability, if she could only figure out how to do it again. She stood up, and crept off down the hall before anyone could come out of the room and find her.

Even during the night, the palace was full of life. Servants preparing the next day's meal, guards yawning against the walls, sleepless Nobles wandering about aimlessly. Ellia skulked in the shadows, but it was hard to avoid notice. She needed to observe the guard's shift patterns, so she couldn't use the side passageways where there were no guards. When she reached the Banquet Hall, she was relieved to be able to slip behind one of the tapestries and climb the secret stairs to the catwalks above. She climbed across beams and walkways, until she'd been all around the entire hall. She'd been hoping for a way to get around the castle by using the catwalks. However, after circling the hall several times, she finally had to admit that there was no way out of the hall besides the way she'd come in. Nothing interesting was happening below. There were a few guards, but they seemed bored, and were engrossed in a card game. The problem was, they had decided to play it in front of the secret stairs. Their backs were to the tapestry, but Ellia couldn't get down until their shift ended.

Ellia finally leaned back against a pillar and gave

up. She was sitting there, miserably watching the guards, when she caught a flash of movement out of the corner of her eye. At a nearby corner of the room, above a pillar on which she'd walked only a few moments before, a roof tile was moving. It swung up, revealing a square hole, through which Ellia caught a glimpse of stars, before a shadow blocked them out. Heart pounding, Ellia scurried backwards and hid behind a stone Siren. It was leaning out over the room, holding a chandelier on a chain above the Hall. Ellia peered out through it's snaky mane of stone hair to see a figure drop down onto the pillar. It was a short, agile man, dressed all in black. His skin was also dark, except for a feathery lock of very pale hair escaping from his hood. Ellia sucked in a breath. She recognised that hair. The raiding parties who had tried to capture her when she was living with Baron Opulus had had the same hair and build. *A Kurdian spy! How did he get in here?* She wondered, as the figure prowled along the catwalks as if he owned them. He passed so close to her that she could see the green flecks in his hazel eyes. She quickly closed her own, in case he might see them shining in the shadows.

His soft footsteps faded, and she dared to look again. He was walking along the ledge closest to the far wall, running his fingers across the wall panels. There was a soft click, and one of them swung inwards. The man disappeared into it. *Oh.* Ellia realised. *The passageways are hidden behind the panels. Why didn't I think of that?* She was just about to slip from her hiding place when the man backed out of the passageway again. After him came another man, also Kurdian. Two more dropped through the roof trapdoor. *they're going to find me.* Ellia thought in a panic. Keeping as low as possible, she wiggled backwards along the beam. It was easy to stay hidden from people below, but much harder to hide from people on the catwalks. She backed into the far wall, then slid along the ledge against it until she reached a corner. There were at least ten men inside now, and more were coming. They crawled out of the passageway and dropped through the roof like an invasion of shadows.

In perfect silence, they spread out, all heading in Ellia's direction. She frantically backed as far as possible into her corner. Suddenly, there was a soft *click,* and she fell backwards into a passageway. The panel swung closed behind her, leaving her in darkness. The only thing she could see was a dim circle of light. It was a knothole in the panel. She crept forward and pressed her eye to it.

The silent men were coming towards her. Her heart seemed to stop, and she held her breath. Then, with a swish of black cloaks, they passed her panel, and continued on, towards the secret stair into the Dining Hall. Then they were gone, and she couldn't see anything. Suddenly, she heard the tapestry rip. The guards shouted in surprise. There was a brief scuffle, a thud, a gurgle, and then silence. Ellia felt sick. *The Kurdu are here, they killed the guards. What am I going to do?* She thought for a minute, then turned and crawled down the passageway.

She took turns aimlessly, not really caring if she got lost, just wanting to get as far as possible from the invasion. The floor she crawled on was riddled with knotholes and spy holes, looking down into all sorts of rooms. She was beginning to suspect that you could get almost anywhere in the palace without being seen if you knew where you were going. At first, she didn't bother looking at anything, but as she became less panicked, her interest grew, and she began to peer through the holes. Most of the rooms were quiet, or had people snoring in them. After a while, Ellia became bored.

Nothing was happening. No amount of spying told her what she wanted to know, which was why the Kurdu were in the palace. Finally, she crawled out into a very oddly shaped room.

It was round, with a domed ceiling. However, a second, matching dome rose up out of the floor, so that there was only a little room to walk around the outside of it. The smaller dome was wooden, and had many round holes in it, always in pairs, like eyes. Light came through them. Curious, Ellia peered through a pair of them. The room below was also round. Across from her, on the other side of the dome, Ellia saw a painting of a deer, leaping away from some wolves. Their eyes were dark... No, they were holes. Ellia realised that all the holes in the dome were the eyes of a wolf pack. The room below had a domed ceiling, with a mural of wolves chasing down a deer on it. To the people below, the holes must just seem like black painted eyes. It was ingenious. She smiled as she looked down at the room, wishing she could meet the architect of this place. However, her smile swiftly disappeared.

In the room below was the creepiest man she had ever seen. He was old, with a thin, sallow face. He was looking up at the mural, with his hands clasped behind his back. Ellia had the terrifying feeling that he saw her, even though he shouldn't be able to. His eyes were horrible. The irises were completely white, so that she couldn't tell them apart from the whites of his eyes. In the exact center of that creepy whiteness, his pupils stood out like tiny black bugs. They looked so weird in his still, grayish face that Ellia had trouble thinking of them as eyes at all, more like some child had pushed white marbles into the eye sockets of a statue. *He's a White Starfall.* She realised. She knew that there were plenty of white stars in the sky, and they fell quite often, but she'd never thought of how it might make a Starfall look.

She heard a door open and the Starfall turned away.

"What would you like me to listen for tonight, your Majesty?" He asked politely. The King's gruff voice echoed through the room.

"The usual, Chadwick. Treason." The Starfall bowed. Then he stood up, opened his eyes wide, and the tiny black dots of his pupils blinked out altogether. Ellia suppressed a shudder. The Starfall stood like that for a long time. Then his mouth opened, and he spoke in a voice that wasn't his.

"...Treason? Aren't you afraid of being found out?" Another voice answered, also coming from the Starfall's mouth.

"It's worth the risk, Kerra. Imagine how greatly they'll reward us!"

"The Kurdu, my lord? Aren't they poor as dirt? What will they pay you with?"

"They aren't poor. Or primitive either. That's a lie our king has fed us. I've spoken with their king. He has more gold hoarded than you would believe. All he wants is Starfalls, or information on how to make them."

"But surely you don't have that information, lord?"

"No, of course not! But I have other information, such as I know of the secret Spy network of passages throughout this palace. I told them of it, so that they can send their spies and assassins straight into the heart of the palace, without attracting notice. It's worth a lot of gold, especially since this way they can steal the King's own Starfalls right out from under his nose. Don't you think I will receive a great reward for that?"

"Undoubtedly, my lord. Hadn't we better leave soon?"

"Yes, but that's the best part! I have a vacation planned in a few days, so no one will be surprised when

I leave."

"Very clever, lord. I'll just pack your bags, then."

The Starfall's mouth snapped shut, and his pupils reappeared. During the strange discussion, the king had come into view, drawing closer to the Starfall, as if hypnotized. When the Starfall was done, he was practically jumping up and down with excitement.

"It's Lord Hawthorn, I know it is! That's his voice, and doesn't he have a servant named Kerra? Wonderful work, Chadwick. We must stop him immediately! Oh, this is wonderful! A real treasonous plot against me! won't he be surprised when I catch him. Oh, I can't wait. This will teach everyone not to plot against Rudbeck the Mighty! For this, Chadwick, I'll make you my Master of Spies. Quickly, go tell the guards to go arrest that sneaky piece of worm bait." He chuckled with glee.

Meanwhile, Ellia was struggling with her conscience. *It won't do you any good to meddle. You'll just get yourself in trouble, and ruin any chances you have of escape.* Her reason argued, but if she didn't do anything, people would die. Servants, guards, anyone who was standing unsuspecting in the hallways right now, unaware of the assassins in the palace. *Your fault if they die.* That was too much. With a deep breath, she stepped back, then ran forward and slammed herself, shoulder first, into the painted wooden dome.

The wood broke under her, and she felt her arm break as well. She flipped downwards through the air in a cloud of splinters, landing in a heap in front of the two men. All three of them yelled, her in pain, and the other two in surprise and fear. Chadwick pulled out a knife with a metallic shriek. Ellia heard it and raised her good arm just in time. The knife glanced off of her gold cuff. It must have been the intricate gold of it that sparked the King's memory, because he yelled,

"Wait! That's my wife's Starfall." Chadwick

lowered his knife. Ellia swallowed her pain, and rose into a kneeling position.

"Your Majesty, listen to me, there's no time to waste. The Kurdu are in the palace already. They entered through the roof, and are probably all over by now. They killed the guards in the banquet hall. You have to stop them before it's too late." She gasped. The king and Chadwick both stared at her.

"How do you know that?" The king demanded. "And how did you get into the ceiling?"

"I saw them." Ellia said, deciding to improvise a story. "I... knew about the secret tunnels because... I was having an affair with one of the guards stationed in the Banquet Hall, and we used the secret stairs behind a tapestry to... meet in private." She pretended to be embarrassed. "So that's what we were doing, but then the Kurdu came, and I hid, and they..." She choked out a sob, which actually sounded very convincing, since her arm hurt so unbearably. "Then they killed him, my Sweetheart, and the other guards too, and then I couldn't escape through the Hall, since they were there, so I used the passages to get here." Ellia figured it was a pretty safe lie, since no one could ever question the dead guard to see if he had a sweetheart. The King and Chadwick seemed to be convinced, as well. It was expected, around the palace, for pretty girls to flirt with guards, and to hide when anything dangerous happened.

"Good girl, coming here to warn me!" The King exclaimed. "Kurdu in the palace! Great Firth, it's miles to the border! How did they get all the way here? No matter. To arms! Call the guards! Chadwick, you stay here and protect the girl. If it's my Starfalls they want, they shan't get them. My guards will protect you both. Guards!" He charged out of the room, robes flying out behind him, bellowing for the guards. Ellia was left alone with Chadwick.

The Starfall turned his strange eyes on Ellia. She couldn't help but flinch. However, when he smiled it seemed genuine.

"I suppose I should thank you, Starfall. You saved all of us from capture, at considerable cost to yourself." His face turned serious.

"I'm not just talking about your arm. I think we both know that you weren't originally in those passages to warn the king."

Ellia's skin crawled.

"What do you mean?" She demanded. Chadwick just smiled.

"I hear things. Just now, I thought about you, and heard several conversations throughout the palace about you. Judging from what I heard, I would wager that you're not the type to have a sweetheart, or to run to the king with your problems. Whatever you were really doing in those passages, I think it cost you quite a lot to tell the king about them. So why did you do it?" Ellia stared at him.

"Well, I couldn't just let people die!" She exclaimed. Chadwick frowned.

"Yes, you could've. But you didn't. Why? What did they ever do for you?" He seemed genuinely curious. Ellia just looked at him blankly.

"Because... I don't know. They're *People*. With their own lives and everything. To walk away, I'd have to be... heartless." Ellia tried to explain. Chadwick was staring at her with an unfathomable expression on his face.

"Up until this moment I would've sworn that that's exactly what anyone with your features was." He said quietly.

"And the rest of us might as well be, the way we treat each other. I think you're too good for palace life."

He seemed to be thinking of something else, because his pupils disappeared. Ellia wondered if she should leave, but then his pupils reappeared, and he looked down at her with a slight frown.

"If I don't say anything about what I think you were really doing in those passages, would you accept that as a thank-you?" He asked abruptly. Ellia nodded. She couldn't do much else. Her arm was on fire with pain, and spots danced before her eyes. Chadwick's frown deepened, and he strode out of the room without another word.

Ellia vaguely heard him yelling at the guards outside the room. There was the sound of someone running away down the corridor, then silence. Gradually, the quiet murmur of conversation between Chadwick and the remaining guards drifted through the doorway.

Ellia was about to drift off to sleep when Chadwick came in again, along with several guards and a bunch of other people. Before she knew what was happening, they were putting Ellia on a stretcher and rushing her off down the hall, as if she were mortally wounded. Ellia tried to tell them she wasn't, but the bouncing of the stretcher kept her from doing anything other than hissing in pain every time they bumped her arm.

The doctor's rooms were overflowing with people. Some of them had been wounded by the assassins, but most were just spectators, roused from their sleep by the commotion. There were a few long, covered shapes in the corner which Ellia didn't want to think about. When Ellia's entourage entered, the room was filled with noise. The moans of the wounded, the clamouring of confused onlookers, yells of servants and, worst of all, the occasional scream of someone who was being treated by the doctor and his helpers. The doctor was in a hurry, and did not seem to be very gentle with his patients.

       The moment Ellia entered the room, the servants carrying her began to yell.

"Make way! We need a doctor immediately! The Queen's Starfall has been wounded!"

As soon as the doctor heard the word "Starfall", he dropped everything he was doing and came running over. Ellia felt quite nervous, as she'd seen the way he'd been treating the other wounded palace staff; However, she needn't have worried. He treated her as gently as if she'd been made of blown glass. It hurt a bit when he set her arm, but not as much as she'd expected. After her arm was splinted and in a sling, the doctor insisted that some patients be moved so that she would have a bed. Ellia thought that was entirely ridiculous. Why would she need a bed for a broken arm? However, no one would listen to her. Starfalls were incredibly valuable, and so must be treated with care, but they were also slaves, and were often treated somewhat like ornaments. No one ever listened to them. Ellia sat on her bed willingly, but, as soon as people stopped paying attention to her, she got back up again and left the room to go see what was going on.

       Outside, she ran into a guard who was headed for the doctor's rooms with his shirt wrapped around his arm. She stopped him and quizzed him as to what was happening outside. He smiled tiredly, which she supposed was good news.

       "We've got them good. They surprised us at first, but then reinforcements came from the king, and we were able to push them back, away from the other Starfalls' rooms. We've got them cornered in the far end of the North Wing now, with guards outside the windows so they can't get out. Hardly anyone lives near there, so that should minimize casualties until we can get rid of them altogether." He chuckled cheerfully. Ellia was about to smile back at him, until a thought struck her. "Wait, did you say the far end of the *North* Wing?" She demanded in a panic. The guard nodded, his smile slipping into a look of confusion. Ellia's blood froze.

"You *fools!* No one lives there because they don't want to live too close to the Prince and Princess!" She choked out. The guard stared at her with a look of horror.

"Wait. Do You mean that Their Highnesses are in with the assassins, unprotected?" He gasped, but Ellia was already gone. She completely forgot about her arm, and her lack of a weapon. Adrenaline pumping, she sprinted down the halls, going faster than any ordinary human could have. She careened around corners, using walls and statues to make sharp turns. Servants and Nobles dived out of her way and yelled, but she didn't listen. A thousand different images of what she might find flashed through her mind. She hadn't known Myrgen and Myria for very long, but the idea that they might be dead tore her heart.

When Tuck had turned his back on her, she'd thought she had left her heart behind for good, and would never trust anyone again. However, when she saw the backs of guards blocking the hallway ahead, she realised that she did, in fact, have a heart, and wished that she didn't. Her guess had been right. The sound of clashing swords came from the hallway leading to the Twin's rooms, which meant that the twins were alone behind enemy lines. Had they hid, or had they been killed? She didn't want to know, but she had to.

The guards turned in surprise when she skidded into their midst. They started to draw their weapons, but stopped when they heard what she was gasping.

"The twins! They're in there! Let me through!"

The guard's faces drained of color. They stared at each other in horror, and then one of them finally voiced what they were all thinking.

"The King is going to kill us." He said gloomily. The guards immediately began yelling and blaming each other. Ellia began to be frantic.

"Let me through!" She half cried. A guard finally took notice of her.

"I'm sorry, miss, but there's no way that's happening. The Assassins are after you, remember? Also there's a big fight going on, and it's far too dangerous for a girl. You'd be killed in seconds." He turned away, and Ellia felt like kicking him. A tornado of emotions whirled inside her, and she felt like she was flying apart. Suddenly, she had an idea. She turned and ran the other way.

She intended to go back to the Banquet hall, then use the tunnels to try and find her way into the North Wing. However, she had barely started on her journey before she saw something and stopped short. The nooks in the hallway were all filled with statuary. However, one particular set of statues in a large nook had caught her attention. It was a depiction of the Great God Firth, creating the first Humans. His hand was outstretched, and under it was a bunch of smaller statues in various stages of emerging from the dirt. She didn't see what was so special about it, until she realized that this exact same image, with people in the same positions, was depicted on the tapestry covering the secret stairs in the Banquet Hall.

Heart pounding with a desperate hope, Ellia squeezed into the alcove behind the statues. There wasn't much room, and she began to think that she'd made a mistake. However, as soon as she had pressed her back against the wall directly behind Firth, something behind her clicked, a secret door swung inwards, and she stepped backwards onto a set of stairs leading up.

Chapter Eleven

Ellia Falls Through Yet Another Ceiling

***

"In regards to culture, language, and Hierarchical structure, the kingdoms of Dalia and Kurdu are really very similar. The only difference is that we hate them and they hate us."
— Pete Lirricies, a Dalian who was stoned for his heretical beliefs.

***

The men seemed bored. In the distance, swords clashed, but the men in the room were just strolling around, kicking over furniture and grumbling.

"A thousand curses on that idiot Lord Hawthorn!" One of them finally burst out.

"It's his fault we're trapped in here. If he'd given us an actual map of those rat-tunnels, instead of vague directions, we could have grabbed the Starfalls and been out by now." He aggressively kicked a chair, then yelled in pain. Looking down through the boarded ceiling, Ellia was vaguely surprised that he spoke the common tongue. From what she'd heard of the Kurdian Tribes to the north of her country, she'd expected them to converse in some sort of guttural grunts. Only the curses he used were unfamiliar to her, as he hopped around on one foot, glaring at the chair. Ellia was in a panic to get down, but the boards she lay on, looking down through a crack, were far too thick to break. What had become of the twins? The door to their chambers was open, the assassins were everywhere, but there was no sign of the children. Were they dead already? For as long as she'd known them, they had never stopped making noise. The fact that she couldn't hear them sent a spike of dread through her.

Suddenly, a commotion in the twins' room answered her question. A guard came stumbling out, holding his head, and another one followed, dragging Myrgen and Myria.

"Guess what I found?" He drawled. "Found them on top of a dresser. Pushed a rock down onto Amon's head. What should we do with them?"

"Kill them" Snarled the man called Amon. "The little rats deserve to die."

He took a step towards them. However, another man reached out his arm and stopped him.

"No, wait. Maybe we can use them for leverage. Maybe someone in this cursed palace will care enough about them to let some of us go free." He crouched down in front of Myrgen and reached out to put a black-gloved hand on his shoulder.

"What say you, little boy? Does anyone care about you?"

Myrgen's quivering, tear-streaked face changed immediately at those words. His eyes burned with fury and hurt. He let out a yelp of rage, lunged forward, and bit down hard on the Assassin's outstretched hand.

The Assassin yelled a vulgar curse and struck Myrgen with lightning speed across the face, so hard that his head snapped back and he slid to the floor, unconscious.

"Little demon!" He cursed, pulling out a knife.

He never had a chance to use it.

The moment the man struck Myrgen, something like a thunderclap sounded in Ellia's chest. All the furious love of a Lioness for her young roared up inside her. *No one hurts MY children*. The boards which had only moments ago supported her easily, suddenly broke under her weight. She landed in a crouch in the room, with a scream of rage, towering over the Assassin. He spun around in astonishment, starting to bring his knife up in defense. Too late. With one swipe of her paw, she sent him flying across the room into the wall. *Wait, Paw? What?* She suddenly realised that the assassin hadn't somehow gotten smaller. She'd grown bigger. Her body felt completely different as well. She was suddenly aware of her paws, her lashing tail, thick fur, coiled muscles, and something else, on her back... *Oh.* If she could have smiled with her strange new muzzle, she would have.

The Assassins were backing away from her, eyes as round as marbles, weapons clattering from nerveless fingers. The man holding the twins had dropped them and was fumbling for his knives. Ellia's claws unsheathed. In a single bound, she leapt over the twins and knocked him away. He crumpled to the floor against the far wall, chest slashed with five claw marks. Ellia turned to face the rest of the men, her heart burning with fury. Some of them seemed to be recovering from their shock, eyeing their dropped weapons and reaching under their cloaks for knives. With a shriek like an eagles', but many times louder, Ellia spread her wings. They swept out like great sails in the small chamber, bringing down more chunks of the ceiling when she beat them. She leapt forward to protect the children, but there was no need. The assassins were already running. With yells of fear, they raced away down the passageway. Some even leapt out the window, onto the swords of the waiting guards outside.

Ellia didn't try to chase them. She didn't care about anything but the children. Instead, she turned and wrapped them in her wings, her long, furry body vibrating with purrs.

Myria's eyes were wide with wonder and fear, her face red and puffy from crying. Myrgen was still unconscious. Gradually, Ellia's fury faded, replaced with concern at seeing them this way. She grew rapidly smaller, the room telescoping around her, and embraced them awkwardly with her uninjured arm, tears of relief leaking down her face. Myria stared at her in astonishment.

"Ellia?" She exclaimed, then her face broke into a huge grin.
"You saved us!" She threw herself at Ellia and tackled her in a hug. Then her face screwed up into a worried frown.

"Will Myrgen be all right? Also, why were you a monster?" Ellia drew back in surprise. *Monster.* Something inside her reared its head in recognition of the name. She pushed the feeling away and smiled.

"Myrgen will be fine. How was I a monster? What did I look like?" She asked, pretending to be amused. Myria looked slightly embarrassed.
"Well, not *really* a monster. You were like a big huge lion with wings. *I* wasn't scared, though."

Ellia frowned. *A Gryffon? How is that even possible? Why can I spit ice then?* She shook her head, confused. She didn't have time to dwell on it, however, because just then Myrgen woke up. At the same time, a whole troop of guards came storming into the room, weapons drawn. When they saw Ellia and the children, they stopped short in complete confusion.

"Umm... Miss?" One of them finally stammered. "The assassins... What happened?"

Don't tell them the truth. If they find out you're a monster... Her subconscious whispered. Ellia gave them a blank look.

"I have no idea. I fell through the roof," She pointed at the hole. "And all the assassins were gone. She looked hard at Myria, to see if she would speak up, but she didn't. She just looked back at Ellia with wide, curious eyes. Myrgen was in no danger of telling. He was looking around dazedly. The guards frowned, confused.

"But... What were you doing in the ceiling?" One of them asked. Ellia just frowned at him. She recognized him as the same guard who had blocked her in the hall. "Trying to get to the children, obviously, because *Someone* wouldn't let me through the hall." She was pleased to see his face flush red, and he asked her no more questions. The other guards tried to question her, but she skillfully headed them off as she guided the children out of the room, with the excuse of getting Myrgen's head checked.

Despite all of Ellia's evasions, the palace was soon awash in rumors. Barely an hour had passed before the whole palace was buzzing with the news that the Queen's Golden Starfall had defeated the entire Kurdian invasion single-handedly. Literally, as she had had one broken arm. This led, of course, to wild speculation as to how she had done it, despite Ellia's protests that she hadn't. The King, Queen, and almost everyone of importance in the palace wanted to see her. However, she wasn't required to obey anyone except Their Majesties, so she carefully avoided the many demanding Nobles. When she had to offer an explanation to the King and Queen, she was careful to divert their attention onto other matters. During her interview with the Queen, she deliberately steered the conversation towards the Children, and filled the Queen with worry by exaggerating the tale of Myrgen getting hit on the head. Queen Priscilla was not a caring mother; However, she was resentful at her husband for taking the children into his domain, and so she easily became engaged with railing about her husband's complete failure to protect his own children, and forgot about questioning Ellia.

With the King, Ellia took a very different approach, according to the type of person she judged him to be. Like most powerful people, he was greedy for still more power. To her surprise, however, he had so far made no move to enlist her into his services, but instead had glared at her suspiciously. Ellia had been quite confused until Chadwick quietly explained to her about the King's obsessive distrust of Elves. He apparently hated them because they were a powerful People which lived in *his* forests, and yet no one could find their cities unless they wished to be found. This infuriated him. He hadn't allowed the Faerie Lord to take Ellia simply to spite the Elves. However, that didn't mean he wanted her around. He was strongly prejudiced against her Elvish appearance, and hated her all the more now that she seemed powerful. With this new knowledge, Ellia had to think quickly to find a way to keep him from discovering the truth.

When Ellia was called into his presence, she behaved much as she had the first time she'd met him, as if she were an emotional and distraught young maiden. She whimpered about her dead lover, then about how she had been so worried that poor Myrgen was dead too. When he asked her straight out if the rumors were true, she protested that she had had nothing to do with such things, but had simply gone to see about the children, and found the Assassins gone. She then bemoaned her injured arm, complaining that she could do nothing with it, which seemed to put the

King's suspicions at rest. Before he could ask anything else, Ellia meekly inquired as to whether he had apprehended the traitorous Lord Hawthorn and his servant. This put the king into a very good mood, and successfully distracted him. He was very proud of having caught a traitor, and so he proceeded to brag about his greatness for the rest of the conversation.

Feeling very pleased at having dealt so neatly with the king and queen, Ellia was convinced that she had solved the matter. Her only regret was the destruction of the Tunnels. Terrified by the threat of another invasion or assassination, the king had ordered at least a hundred guards up into the tunnels and passageways, where they proceeded to collapse and block off every door leading out of the palace. *There goes my chance of escape.* Ellia thought gloomily. However, she was confident that at least her accident of turning into a Gryffon had been undiscovered and forgotten. Little did she know the extent of palace gossip.

Ellia had barely ventured down a few hallways the next morning towards the twins' rooms before she was accosted by a nobleman. He was short, with a wide, flat nose and squinted eyes. He strutted up to her, with his chin in the air, then stopped and peered at her suspiciously. At first, Ellia attempted to just walk past him, but he blocked her path.

"Ehm... Excuse me!" He demanded shrilly, "But I simply *Must* speak with you about the events of yesterday!" Having commandeered her attention, he took a deep breath and began launching a barrage of questions and demands into her face.

"What is your ability? Were you in league with the Assassins? Is it true that you broke your arm punching through a solid rock ceiling? Did you really create tunnels through the walls by burning holes with your eyes? You must use this skill to create tunnels for me. I want one connecting my rooms to those of the Baroness Frisia."

"You're in my way." Ellia protested, but he pretended not to hear her.

" Did you battle the assassins in the tunnels? Or did you let the assassins into the palace in the first place? Who were the assassins? Were they spies for your Elvish friends? Is there really a love affair between you and the Elvish Lord who was here a few weeks ago? Are you close to the Faerie council? If so, I must demand that you mediate a trade agreement between myself and the Faerie Kingdom. It is of utmost importance. I also must ask..." He barreled on, listing still wilder theories and demands, without giving Ellia a chance to answer. When he finally stopped to catch his breath, she looked at him with as cold of an expression as she could muster, attempting to copy the look of the Faerie Lord himself.

"If I burned tunnels through solid rock with nothing but the power of my eyes," She said in a bored tone, "What's to prevent me doing the same to you, mere flesh and bone, who are standing in my way?" She fixed him with a piercing stare, her face a mask of cold annoyance, although inside she was quivering with anxiety. *Please don't let him see through this!* The man's eyes bugged out with astonishment. Evidently, he had never before been addressed in such a way by someone who he obviously considered to be little higher than a Gutter Rat.

"You wouldn't dare!" He spluttered. "The King would have you killed instantly!"

"Really?" Ellia remarked dryly. "I rather think he'd thank me for ridding him of a traitor. How do you think he'll react when I tell him of your traitorous schemes to establish a trade agreement with his enemies, the

Faeries?"

The nobleman blanched. His face, recently red and round, suddenly turned bleach-white, seeming to sag and droop in dismay like a melting candle. With a gibbering whine of half-audible protests, he plastered himself to the wall, and shook like a leaf until she had passed him by. Although she didn't show it until she was beyond his sight, inside, Ellia was shaken up almost as badly. *They didn't buy my innocence. They're still talking about me, still suspecting me. How long are my lies going to hold before they figure out the truth?* Ellia wasn't sure which truth would be worse, if they should discover her to have a monster inside, or for her to be unable to master an ability, and for them to decide that she didn't even have one. She was half afraid of that herself. Deep inside, she still suspected that the strange happenings had simply been some sort of strange curse or accident, that in reality she was a freak, a strange phenomena with Starfall looks but no Starfall abilities.

Chapter Twelve

Something Comes Up

***

"The worst thing a woman can possibly be is a Gossip. Women who gossip are only bringing bad luck on themselves. Take Duchess Haile for example. She gossips all the time, and only last week I heard she was kicked by her horse." — Sharla, kitchen maid of Duke Haile.

***

During the next few weeks, Ellia began to obsessively avoid everyone except the children. Her encounter with the nobleman had scared her far worse than she was willing to admit. It meant that, not only did people remember her role in the Assassin attack, but they were talking about her, and making up stories that wildly expanded her abilities. The less they knew, the more they made up. Ellia was afraid of being pulled into the elaborate political machinations of the palace, and yet, it seemed she was being sucked in despite everything. Her lies were slowly closing in on her. Sooner or later, someone was going to demand an actual demonstration of her powers, and she would be unable to do anything. Either that, or she would transform into a monster and kill someone. A third danger was also surfacing. This one scared her more than any of the others. The more Ellia was noticed, the more likely it was that someone would try to kill her, either because of their fear or their hate. Jasper hated her, she suspected. The Kurdu most likely did as well, because of what she had done to their spies. Many of the noblemen and people in the palace feared her because of her supposed Powers, also her Elvish looks. Some of them probably feared her enough to want her dead.

In order to avoid them, Ellia began using the tunnels to get around whenever she didn't have the twins with her. Although the tunnels leading outside had been closed off, the rest were still usable, and Ellia slowly learned to navigate them.

She never saw Jasper anymore. In truth, he was the one she was most afraid of. Not because he was the most likely to kill her, but because she couldn't trust her own thoughts around him. If he *were* to try to harm her, she wouldn't be able to stop him. Worse yet, he could probably just tell her to kill herself, and she would do it.

She always had meals with the twins now, since she didn't dare face Jasper and his cronies in the Starfall's dining room. Several times, he had slipped a note under her door, or left a gift outside of it on his way to serve the King each morning. However, she always waited until he was long gone before daring to emerge and dart to the nearest Tunnel entrance. The gifts and notes seemed harmless. Simply what one might expect from an admirer or sweetheart. The notes usually began with a declaration of love and loyalty, followed by a plea for her forgiveness, and a request for her to meet with him alone in a certain place. The gifts were usually flowers or jewelry. The latter surprised her at first, since Starfalls seldom had money with which to buy such things. However, she soon realised, as the gifts grew more expensive, that he must be using his Ability to persuade the noblewomen of the court to give them to him. She didn't dare keep these, but instead dropped them down through peepholes and grates as she crawled through the tunnels each morning.

The notes, however, she kept. She couldn't explain why. She told herself that it was probably because of her desire to collect information. The notes might reveal something about Jasper that might be useful to know later. In reality, though, she kept them because she couldn't bring herself to destroy them. Despite what she knew about Jasper, despite the fact that the rational part of her was scared of him, she couldn't bring herself to hate him. She tried, but some of Jasper's power still clung, and at the thought of him her treacherous heart still flipped over.

When she wasn't hiding in the passageways, she was with the twins. The children had a terrible reputation, and when they were by her side, everyone gave her a wide berth. Even the most persistent and demanding noblemen would turn tail when they caught sight of the twins' mischievous grins.

Myrgen and Myria likewise stuck to Ellia like leeches. Despite their horrible reputations, the two were becoming sweeter by the day. They still played nasty tricks on the other inhabitants of the palace, but to Ellia they showed nothing but admiration and loyalty. At first she couldn't understand it, but soon realised that it was because she was the only person they had ever known who loved them openly despite their mischievous pranks. Probably the only person who loved them at all.

There was only one other person who Ellia was not afraid of speaking to. Chadwick, like Jasper, served the King, but he was only ever needed during their nightly sessions, when the King would give Chadwick a word, usually a variation of the word Treason, and Chadwick would use his ability to see if anyone in the palace was using that word. This was Chadwick's only job, so he spent the rest of his days either in his rooms or walking in the gardens. He explained, somewhat awkwardly, that many people found his eyes very creepy, so that he preferred to go places where he could be alone and avoid the stares. Ellia didn't trust the old man, but she did sympathize with him. People stared at her, too. Because of this, she went to see him whenever she wasn't needed to look after the children.

Chadwick was the only person who didn't seem interested in Ellia's role during the Kurdian attack. She suspected that he already knew. He knew a great many things. It was the nature of his gift, to hear many things, and he had a good memory. Ellia found herself enjoying his company more and more as the days passed. Even his eyes no longer seemed as frightening. She dropped in sometimes through the ceiling of his room, but more often she met him in the gardens, usually a set of overgrown, untended ones near the East side of the palace.

It was during one of these outdoor excursions that it happened. They were walking through the overgrown trees, discussing the history of strife between their kingdom of Alissaria and it's neighbours, Kurdu and the Faerie Kingdom. Chadwick knew a great deal about this because of his closeness to the King. Chadwick was telling her of the fluid borders between the Faeries and themselves; the impossibility of going to war with a country which seemed to have no borders or entrances. They really knew nothing about the Elvish borders, he explained, except that they always lived in forests.

Normally, Ellia would have been fascinated. However, she was tired, and she found her attention wandering to the trees around them. She found herself thinking that she understood the Elves' choice of home. Trees were so beautiful.

Suddenly, she stiffened with shock. A face was looking back at her through the leaves of a Whispering Elm to her left. Not just any face. *Rowan.* He didn't look like the Elf she had come to know. He looked like the dirty Guttersnipe she'd first taken him for, only less dirty, and dressed in a soldier's uniform. She still recognized him, though. Something about his eyes, and the way he stood there, leaning against the wall. The fact that he was trying to look like a guard on duty somehow made it all the more clear that he wasn't a real one.

Confused, alarmed, but also excited, Ellia quickly looked back at Chadwick. He had stopped talking and was frowning at her.

"What's wrong?" He asked.

"Nothing." Ellia replied. Too quickly. Chadwick's brow furrowed in concern.

"You're lying." He stated.

"No I'm not." Ellia argued lamely. She was too busy wondering about Rowan to think of a good excuse.

"I... Just remembered something. I have to go. Bye!" She dashed away, leaving Chadwick standing there, looking puzzled.

When she reached the place where Rowan had been standing, he was gone. She stopped short, and looked around. She was about to walk away when a soft *"Pssst!"* sounded from above her. *Whispering Elms say Shhh. They don't say Pssst.* She glanced up, and there he was. She looked carefully around, then, using her good arm and both her legs, carefully climbed up to join him.

High in the green foliage, Ellia reflected that it would be almost impossible for anyone to see them. *Smart.* He was perched on a branch above her, swinging his feet.

"Rowan." She greeted him. He looked surprised, then his Human features faded away, so that he was once again the Elf from her dreams.

"You recognized me then?" He asked with mild annoyance. Ellia suppressed a snort.

"Of course I recognized you. Anyone with one eye and half a brain would have known at once that you weren't a real Guard. What are you doing here? Why aren't you in my dreams anymore?" Ellia stopped, and blushed. She hadn't intended to say that last thing. Rowan broke into a grin.

"Did you miss me?"

"No."

"Are you sure?"

"Yes. What are you doing here?"

"Talking to you."

"That's not what I meant. Why are you here? Also, how did you get in?"

"The soldiers have their laundry done in the City. I snagged a uniform and got a ride in on a cart under the clean laundry. They left the laundry in a storeroom near the barracks so I just crawled out when no one was there." He flipped upside down and hung by his knees from the branch, bringing his head level with Ellia's. It seemed to her that he was much more relaxed and cheerful than he had been before. However, his evasion of her questions was really starting to annoy her.

"Can you just answer me already?"

"Okay, but each answer will cost you ~"

"No."

"What?"

"No more bargaining. No more games."

"You want information for free?"

"It isn't for free. You're wasting my time. This isn't a dream. I could be doing something useful right now, if I weren't listening to you. So, in return for my patient attention, you tell me why you're here."

Rowan gave her an upside-down smile.

"Okay, fine. Have it your way. I'll answer both your questions. One," He held up one finger, or rather, held it down, depending on perspective.

"I'm here because I was charged with the job of looking out for you. Some Elves in high places are concerned for your welfare, especially when the news of recent events reached them." He looked significantly at her broken arm. "Also, some rumors reached us that you had single-handedly defeated a troop of Kurdian Spies and Assassins. Naturally, that needed looking into, so here I am. In answer to your second question, Why I wasn't in your dreams anymore..." He paused to give her a long, flirtatious glance, enjoying her discomfort as she blushed. Eye's twinkling with amusement, he finally went on.

"Some new things had come up, and I was forced to ride in haste to inform the Elvish council of my discoveries. Once there, I was very busy and every waking minute was spent trying to deal with a new crisis which had arisen. You know, it's funny." He mused thoughtfully. "I can only Dreamwalk when I'm awake. It's very strange. Anyways, I was very preoccupied, so I had no time to walk your dreams, although I'm sure it would have been a pleasure." He smiled, but then he looked at her and his smile suddenly faded, becoming serious.

"Speaking of dreams," He said urgently, flipping right way up again. "Have you been having any more... Disturbing dreams? Nightmares, maybe, similar to the ones I found you in last time?"

Every night. Ellia thought, remembering her dreams of chaos and carnage, which had been becoming more and more frequent. Always, she would witness these events through the eyes of the beast, or monster, who was responsible for creating the destruction. It always seemed to be the same creature, too. A great flying, fire-breathing golden monster. Ellia had never heard of or seen anything like it. These dreams scared her even more because of the creature than the violence. How could her mind come up with an animal so completely different from anything she had ever seen? She hated it, hated that her mind was so disturbed as to conjure up such gruesome images at night. The scariest thing, though, was the nagging thought that they might be more than just dreams. *Why would Rowan be asking about them if they were just dreams? What if that creature isn't just my imagination?* No. They had to be dreams. The idea that they might have some truth in them made her heart clench in fear and horror. It was too much to accept. She felt almost as if just to admit out loud that she had them would cause them to come true. She didn't dare.

"Not... really, no." She said instead. Rowan sighed in relief.

"Good. Then there's nothing to worry about. You're safe." Rowan smiled again, unaware that at his words Ellia's face had drained of color, as her heart filled with dread. *No, wait, I lied. there IS something to worry about. Why am I not safe? What do the dreams mean, and why would they put me in danger?* It was too late to say it aloud though. Ellia was committed to her lie.

He was still smiling, so she choked down her dread and pretended to smile, too.

"So..." Rowan trailed off, looking curiously at her. "Care to explain what you've been doing recently that's sparking so many rumors?"

Ellia thought fast. She carefully scanned the surroundings, then leaned forward.

"I... Haven't told you this before, but I don't actually have an ability. The Queen bought me because of my gold eyes, without even asking for a demonstration. Everyone assumes that I have marvelous powers, and a lot of them hate me for it. If they ever found out the truth, I'd be dead." She whispered. She didn't have to fake the look of fear on her face, because most of it was true. Rowan's eyebrows slanted down into a quizzical look, but he didn't interrupt. Ellia took a deep breath and continued.

"I've been taking some risks. People were starting to wonder, so I had to stage a display of power to quiet them. I bribed a merchant to smuggle some Firepowder into the castle. When the assassins attacked, I used the ceiling tunnels to get above them, and then dropped two sticks of the stuff on their heads. It made such a big explosion, with so much heat and force that the Assassins fled in fear. Some of the guards saw the bright lights and heard the explosion so that they thought that someone must be doing powerful magic. Unfortunately, the shock wave damaged the ceiling, so I fell through and broke my arm. That's all, but everyone is convinced that I have incredibly unusual abilities. You wouldn't believe how fast rumors travel around here." She shrugged and grinned ruefully. Rowan's face was unreadable. His smile had disappeared, and he was looking at her intently. Ellia's grin faltered as those hard, ancient eyes stared into hers, seeming to pierce right through into her mind. Finally, he settled back and shook his head, as if clearing it of cobwebs, then looked back at her. He opened his mouth as if to say something, but then stopped, frowned, and snorted in surprise.

"You're lying." It was a statement, not a question. Ellia was at a loss for an argument, so she just settled on denial.

"What?" She gasped. Rowan laughed dryly.

"I don't know how it took me so long to see it. Usually I can tell instantly when someone switches from the truth. Either you're a very good liar, or you're mixing truth and lies so thoroughly that they can't be picked apart from each other."

Ellia faked a laugh.

"That's ridiculous. What would I have to lie about?"

"Exactly what I was wondering."

"I told you what happened. If you don't believe me, that's your problem."

"You didn't bribe a merchant."

"What do you mean?"

"Think about it. You're a Starfall. Where would you get the money?"

Oh. Ellia hadn't thought of that. She didn't have an answer, so she was silent. Rowan looked at her for a while, then sighed. He got up, swung onto her branch and sat down beside her.

"Look, Ellia. I know you don't know me very well, and you have no reason to trust me. I understand that in a place like this you have to lie a lot to survive. Humans, especially City Humans, are a thieving, backstabbing bunch."

Ellia's chin shot up defiantly, and he hastily put a soothing hand on her arm.

"I'm not saying Elves aren't. We have a lot of flaws, too. It's just that we don't really lie like you do. We might be evasive, or misleading, or twist words to our own advantage, but we mean the things that we say. I know it's probably hard for you to trust anyone, but when I tell you that I'm here to protect you, and that I'd never betray you or your secrets to anyone who would hurt you, I promise I'm telling the truth."

Ellia didn't trust him. She didn't trust anyone, not even herself. However, when she felt his strong, steady presence beside her, and looked into his serious eyes, she believed him. She sat there, wrestling with her caution, wondering what she dared tell him. When she didn't say anything, Rowan went on.

"I don't know what you've been hiding from me, but if I'm going to protect you I need to know who I'm protecting, and what you need protection from." He looked so earnest, determined, and caring that it was all Ellia could do not to sob into his chest and tell him everything. Her desolate, lonely heart was aching for someone to trust, to confide in, to turn to. However, her common sense wouldn't be silenced. *Remember Tuck.* It hissed. She sighed.

"I... wasn't telling the truth when I said that I had no abilities. The truth is, I have been able to do some strange things. I was able to defend myself from an Ice Creeper in the Shadow Woods, and defend my charges from Assassins in the palace. The issue is that I have no idea how I did it, and I can't do it anymore, no matter how hard I try. It never works when I want it to, and it always works differently so that I still have no idea what it even is. *That's* the problem. I would almost be better off with no ability at all, since now people expect me to accomplish feats I have no idea how to do." She didn't tell him about the dreams, which seemed to be the most dangerous secret, and her common sense was satisfied with that compromise.

Rowan considered that for a moment, and then he nodded.

"*That's* the truth." He seemed to regain some of his earlier good humor, and flashed her a smug smile.

"There, that wasn't so hard, was it? I still don't believe that you're powerless, though."

"I am. I can't do anything!" Ellia insisted. Her eyes filled with bitterness. The unfairness of it made her feel like crying or yelling.

"Every other Starfall has some kind of amazing ability, but all I have is an unusual face. My eyes are a lie."

Rowan looked thoughtful.

"You can't be sure of that. After all, you *are* half elvish." He brightened.

"As a matter of fact, I wasn't able to use magic until I was fifty winters older than you are." He gave her an encouraging glance. However, Ellia just looked at him. Suddenly, her lips twitched, and she burst out laughing, much to his confusion.

"What?"

"Oh, nothing. I was just thinking that, for an old guy, you aged pretty well." She stated, completely straight faced. Rowan looked confused, and a smile tugged at the corners of his eyes. He tried to look reproving.

"Actually, Faerie count age differently than Humans. I'm considered a Youngling in my community. I'd rather you didn't call me 'old guy'."

"Whatever you say, Ancient one."
Rowan looked slightly annoyed.

"You still haven't explained what exactly happened with the assassins." He said, clearly attempting to change the conversation.

"Also, I need to know about your situation here. You mentioned people who hate you. I need to know who they are."

He glanced at her expectantly. She was about to answer, but then he suddenly cocked his head, stiffened, and put a finger to his lips.

"Later." He hissed. "That man you were walking with earlier is looking for you. He's standing about a meter away from this tree."

Ellia didn't hear anything, but she guessed that Rowan's ears were much sharper than hers. He stealthily rose to a crouch on the branch, then began sliding noiselessly down the far side of the trunk.

"You can tell me tonight. I'll find your dream." He

whispered, before dropping out of sight. Ellia climbed down more awkwardly after him, not really caring if Chadwick saw her. She couldn't help smiling to herself. *You can find my dream tonight, Rowan, but I won't be sleeping in my castle bed. Thanks to you, I have a way out of this place.*

She dropped down the last few feet next to a surprised Chadwick. The fact that she couldn't stop smiling while she explained her tree-climbing habit to him and then bid him a hasty farewell left him even more mystified.

"Elves." He finally muttered to himself, shaking his head as he wandered off into the gardens alone. Ellia looked back and watched him walk away, feeling an unexpected twinge of guilt for lying to him. *What am I doing, lying to a lonely, friendless old man? He's my friend, and he's always been honest with me.* She felt a sudden desire to go back and tell him goodbye. If her escape worked, she would likely never see him again. She shook off the impulse. *No. I can't trust Chadwick with the truth. He might tell the king, and I can't risk that.* She turned away, determined. Nevertheless, it still felt like a betrayal of Chadwick's trust, as she set off towards the Guardhouse.

Chapter Thirteen

Sweaty Clothes Are Not the Worst That Can Happen

***

"The secret to happiness is… Something. I don't know. Go ask someone else." — Gazzania the Prophetess, a wise and virtuous but somewhat frustrating woman.

***

Ellia hadn't considered the difference between Rowan's method of entering the castle, and her own method of escape. She thought that she had her entire escape planned out perfectly. The guards who weren't on duty were constantly going in and out of the Guardhouse, talking and laughing. However, there was one time of day when they all left it at the same time. She waited behind a tree near the Guardhouse until the dinner bell sounded, then ran in once all the guards were gone. As she crept through the main room and into the back room where the laundry carts were stored, she realised her mistake. Rowan had ridden the *clean* laundry cart into the palace. To leave, she would have to hide underneath the clothes in the dirty one.

When she'd talked to guards around the castle, she'd never noticed them to smell like much. However, they had been wearing armor. Ellia quickly realised that guards who had to stand at attention all day in the hot sun, wearing full suits of armor, sweated a *lot.* The pile of sweat-soaked laundry in the cart had been sitting there for several days, growing more and more foul-smelling. When she opened the door, she was hit by the overpowering stench of Sweaty Man. She faltered for a moment, gagging. *Why am I doing this? My life isn't that bad, I could just go back, take care of the twins, sleep in a clean bed...* For a second, Ellia couldn't decide if it was worth it. Then she remembered what it was to be free. Strangely enough, it wasn't the journey with Tuck which came first to her mind, but the many dreams of flying in the night on great golden wings, glowing with power, cutting through the silent air. Despite the fact that the violence in her dreams frightened her, they always had that feeling in them, of wild freedom, with no one to bow to, no master, no obligations. It was mesmerizing. Ellia longed to feel that type of freedom more than anything. *Yes, it's worth it.* She thought. *I'm going to be free. That, or die trying.*

With that noble sentiment, she took a deep breath and buried herself in stinking laundry.

It was the most torturous experience Ellia had ever endured. Not even a beating - and she'd had plenty – was quite as unpleasant as this. At least a beating was over quickly, and after that the pain subsided. As Ellia lay under the stinking, sweaty pile, waiting for someone to take the cart away, she felt as though she were being suffocated. The weight of the cloth was smothering, but she still tried not to breathe, because inhaling the stench was almost worse than suffocation. It made her feel as though her lungs were molding. *If I don't get out soon, I will spend the rest of my life smelling like dirty laundry.* Eventually, she began to hear the muted sound of the guards returning, but still no one moved the cart.

Finally, when she was about to give up hope entirely, she heard footsteps, the cart lurched forward, bumped over the door frame, and rolled away. Ellia heard two different voices grunting with effort, but they didn't seem to be the talkative type, and so she had no idea what was going on. The cart turned and stopped so many times that she quickly lost all sense of direction. Abruptly, the sounds of the castle gave way to the loud, unmistakable clamor of the City. The laundry cart was apparently a common sight, because no guards detained them. *They're smarter than I am.* Ellia lamented. *They know to stay clear of something that smells this gross.* There was a lot of shouting, the sound of horses snorting; the cart tilted backwards, stopped for a while, then started again, only this time it lurched in time to the clopping of a horse's hooves, and a man's curses.

Ellia was almost unconscious from the stench by the time it finally stopped again. She groggily listened to a very loud conversation being carried on outside. One voice she recognised as that of the cursing man, and the other was that of a young woman.

"See here, where's the old hag who usually takes this stinking load? She ought to be paying me, instead if the other way around, on account of how nasty it smells this time around."

"The Head Wash-woman is out, sir. I was instructed to ask for the usual twenty pieces."

"But that's not the usual. That's twice as much as she asked for last time!"

"This is a large, stinky load, as you said yourself. Besides, prices rise. Inflation, you know."

"Liar! You're keeping the rest of the money for yourself, aren't you? I see how it is. Well, I'm giving you ten, and if you don't accept it nicely, you're going to be sorry."

"If I don't receive twenty, the washing won't be done." Her voice was stubborn.

The man proceeded to curse and swear at the top of his lungs, calling the young woman all manner of vulgar names. Her voice rose shrilly in protest, finally resorting to swearing as well. Ellia lay there, listening to the swearing match drag on, until finally there was the sound of running footsteps, and the slamming of a door. The man, now left alone, began to mutter angry threats under his breath. He stomped up to the cart. Suddenly, the cart was violently shoved onto its side. Ellia nearly screamed in surprise, but she restrained herself, only emitting a soft groan as she landed on the ground.

With the cart on its side, Ellia was fully exposed among the fallen laundry. The only thing between her and the man was the fallen cart, still attached to the patient horse. If he walked around it, he would see her. Ellia froze, heart pounding. *This is it. He's going to find me, and that will be the end of my freedom.* She heard the man laugh, so close that she caught her breath in fear.

"Ha! Let's see how she likes *that.* Nice and muddy now. Hopefully it stains them. Stupid girl. I hope that old hag gives her a good beating for this. Firth knows she deserves it. Maybe I should stomp on some of them, too, just to make sure they're good and dirty." His footsteps began to scuff around the back of the cart. As soon as he came around the edge, he would see her. Ellia braced herself, stealthily drawing her legs up so that she could kick him in the face as soon as it appeared. Maybe she could knock him out, and still have time to get away...

There was a soft hiss, and the footsteps stopped. The man made no sound except a wheezing huff, as air escaped his lungs. Ellia was getting ready to kick out, sure he had seen her, when he suddenly fell against the cart with a crash.

Ellia jumped up in confusion, nerves on edge. Then she saw the man and stopped short. He was dead. An iron crossbow shaft was buried in his back. *That was the hissing sound. There's someone with a crossbow watching this alley.* Ellia's heart began to pound in terror as she realised what that meant. She couldn't see anyone, but she knew that they could definitely see her. The angle of the shaft meant that hiding behind the cart would do her no good. She was alone, in a darkening alley, with no cover. In a panic, she crouched low and darted over towards the horse, which was stomping and blowing nervously.

Suddenly, there was a sound. If her ears had been that of a normal human, she wouldn't have heard it at all. However, her Elvish ears quickly recognized the sound of soft boots landing behind her. She turned, just in time to block a slim metal club that was swinging at her head. Her broken arm was almost healed, but she was still wearing a thick wooden brace. The club cracked the brace, but luckily her arm was unharmed. The man was wearing a dark cloak, hood, gloves, and mask. His face and hair were hidden from view. However, the skin of his wrist was a dark mahogany color, so Ellia guessed that he was Kurdu. In a flash, he pulled out a long knife, letting out a yell as he stabbed at her.

It was a slow stab, and she dodged it without much difficulty. *If he's a Kurdu Assassin, why would he yell when he strikes? Aren't they supposed to be completely silent?* Too late, she realised that both the yell and the strike were a feint, to distract her from the sound of another pair of boots hitting the ground behind her. Faster than a striking snake, she spun around.

Not fast enough.

The club clipped her squarely in the back of the

head, dropping her like a stone. Darkness closed in.

Chapter Fourteen

The Problem of Untying a Bloody Knot Is Addressed

***

"Some people do not ride the Wheel of
Fortune.
They get run over by it." – The Honorable
Bruce Ballekin, A Bald Bard and a Beggar, who
speaks from personal experience.

***

The first thing that Ellia was aware of when she woke was a burning pain in her wrists. She was lying over the back of a horse, hands and feet tied so thoroughly that she couldn't move them. *I've been kidnapped. Again. How did they know I would be in the cart?* She wondered. Her cast was off, but her arm was healed enough that it no longer hurt. It was night-time, and they were no longer in the City, but were riding through the countryside. The horse was trotting, making her stomach ache every time she bumped down on it's back. She didn't fall off, though, because she was tied to it with a thick rope that connected her arms and legs under the horse's belly.

She gradually became aware of all of these things, as well as the fact that she was hungry, thirsty, and the back of her head hurt. Through it all, however, the most powerful sensation was that of the pain in her wrists. Two circles of pain burned on her skin, as though she were being branded. The source of the pain were two metal manacles which, in addition to the ropes, were clamped around her wrists. They were unremarkable, except that where they touched her skin the metal glowed slightly, and seemed to be somehow burning her skin. *What kind of metal burns like that, though? Is it poisoned?* She wondered. She could feel a warm, sticky substance sliding down her hands from her wrists, soaking the ropes, and realised that it was blood. *This is a lot worse than my last kidnapping. I shouldn't have tried to run away.* Her stomach flipped with fear as she thought of all the rumors she'd heard about the Kurdu, and their cruelty.

The horses kept up the agonizing trot for more than an hour. They were no longer on a road, but were striking straight across the Wild country. Several times they had to ford small streams, or push through thick bushes. Ellia was hanging level with the bushes, so she was smacked on the head and arms by every passing twig. She hadn't seen a house or any sign of civilization for a very long time.

When the last of the three moons, Sorbus, had sunk behind the hills, tingeing them red, they finally came to a halt.

Both men tethered their horses, then walked a few paces away and began building a fire. Ellia was left hanging head down over the horse, feeling miserable. She couldn't see much except her own arms and the horse's belly. The men talked in clear, accent-less voices, obviously not caring if Ellia heard them. She wasn't listening, anyways. The pain clouding her mind made it hard for her to think straight. Eventually, one of the men came over to unsaddle the horses, and noticed her. He took the saddle off, then reached over to untie her from the horse, but stopped and exclaimed in surprise.

"Hey Cerris, come look at this."
The other man stood up and shuffled over, chewing on a piece of dried meat.

"What? The Starfall? I know what she looks like."

"No, not the Starfall, you idjit. Look at the bloody ropes."

"Look like ropes to me. What about them?"

"I just told you! They're soaked in blood! I can't even untie them."

"Oh. That. I just thought you meant 'bloody', as in, 'Wow, Cerris, what nice ropes you've got there. Wish I had ropes like that to tie up my prisoners.'"

"No one uses 'bloody' like that."

"Where I come from they do."

"We come from the same place, you moron."

With considerable effort, Ellia managed to turn her aching head, and looked up at the men through pain-laced eyes. Both of them were definitely Kurdu, but they were considerably taller than the average Kurdian. They had their hoods off. The one on the left, who had first noticed the bloody ropes, was slightly shorter, with darker hair, and amber eyes. The one on the right, who appeared to be called Cerris, wore his hair longer, with the ragged, white-blond ends brushing his jaw. He also had a pale scar that snaked between his eyebrows and curved down to his left nostril. Despite these differences, however, Ellia noticed that they bore a startling resemblance to each other. *They're brothers. That explains why they argue so cheerfully.* The man on the left noticed her movement. He frowned slightly, took out a small knife, and began sawing through the blood-encrusted knots holding her to the horse, all the while still talking with his brother.

"Are you saying you knew she was bleeding, and didn't do anything about it?"

"What was I supposed to do?"

"You could at least have told me you'd wounded her. I didn't see you do it. I thought you missed with that knife. If she dies, it's on your head."

"She won't die, and the blood isn't from my knife."

"What do you mean-- Oh." The man pulled aside a bloody knot, and caught sight of Ellia's wrists.

"Great Firth, what did you do, line the cuffs with spikes?"

"No. They're Lava-Forged. The cuffs are specially created to contain magic, so they keep the wearer from using it."

"But she's bleeding."

"That just proves that she needs to wear them. If she weren't a magical creature, the cuffs wouldn't hurt her. See, I can touch them perfectly fine." He stepped over beside his brother, reached out, and slid a finger under the edge of one of the cuffs. It came away bloody, and he wiped it off on the horse, which shied away. He looked down at his smeared finger and shook his head.

"Faerie and other Starfall would usually get an itchy rash or a small burn from touching these. This girl is literally dripping blood, and the cuffs are glowing underneath as if they were red-hot. The fact that they burn her so badly just shows how dangerous she is. Do you really want to unchain the Starfall who supposedly defeated the whole Shadow Squad by herself, Terrius? Really, I thought you were smarter than that."

The other man, Terrius, looked uncomfortable.

"No... Just, isn't there some way to make it less painful?"

"We could knock her out again."

"I mean like bandage her wrists or something."

"No. They have to be touching skin to work. Get

her off the horse and feed her, that's about all you can do." He continued to munch his piece of meat, which he had speared on the end of one of his throwing knives, and wandered away back towards the fire. Terrius continued working on the ropes in silence. When the last knot parted, Ellia had no strength to cling to the horse. She found herself slipping head first off it's back, and didn't even try to stop herself. Terrius cursed quietly, dropped the knife, and caught her. He carried her closer to the fire and propped her against a small tree. She just slumped there, blinking dazedly through the pain. She knew she should be planning an escape, but her mind felt all fuzzy. Cerris brought her some food, but she couldn't work up the strength to eat it for several minutes. Holding a slice of bread with bound hands, she brought to her lips, only to put it back down again, because the lifting of her arms made the cuffs shift, which hurt.

With the piece of bread still clutched in one hand, she found herself slipping into an exhausted sleep.

It might have been a forest, or it might not. The landscape did not hold to the laws of physics, and distance appeared to be relative, since objects were distorted, and all the wrong sizes. Fuzzy trees swam in and out of focus, disappearing into a purple fog. Among the trees colored lights drifted through the air, leaving glowing trails. Rowan was waiting for her, his face tight with irritation.

"Where have you been all night?" He demanded. "Your dream wasn't here, and that means you were awake until now, when all sensible people have been fast asleep for hours. Also, why is your dream so..." He gestured around him,

"... Wrong?"
His eyes suddenly narrowed, and he looked closely at

her.

"You haven't been eating Smokeweed, have you?"

Ellia threw up her hands in protest. She noticed with interest that her dream-hands were flawless, with no bleeding sores around the wrists.

"Of course I haven't. I'm not stupid."

He didn't look convinced.

"Then why?"

"I had an unfortunate run-in with some Kurdian assassins, and got kidnapped." Ellia finally admitted.

"WHAT?" Rowan exploded. "How did they get into the palace?"

"Um... I sort of ran away. They found me in an alley." Ellia said sheepishly. Rowan groaned and put his head in his hands.

"Of all the stupid things to do! Didn't you know that those walls were your strongest protection? After what you did, the Kurdians have been trying to get into the palace for weeks to capture you. I was focusing on protecting you from your enemies inside the palace, because I thought you were safe from the Kurdu. But then what do you do but just walk right out while I'm not there. For Firth's sake, I only left you for a few hours!"

"You could have told me."

"I thought you knew."

"How was I supposed to know?"

"I don't know! You're the one who made a whole group of their Assassins look like helpless fools. Didn't it ever occur to you that they might be your enemies?" Rowan kicked a blurry blue tree in frustration. It uprooted and bounced away though the air without the slightest regard for the laws of gravity. He stared at it moodily, then sighed.

"You've explained why you were up late, but you still haven't told me why everything in this dream is so *strange. Did they drug you?"*

"No. I just... My phythical body... I mean, my physical body has lost a lot of blood, and also got hit in the back of the head with a metal club-stick thing." Ellia found it hard to concentrate on words, and Rowan was clearly alarmed by her slurred and confusing speech.

"Where are you?"

"Here." Ellia replied listlessly. Something in the real world was tugging her mind away from the dream. Rowan's face was tense with worry, and he caught her hands to keep her from leaving.

"No, I mean your physical body."

"I don't know. I was unconscious, and then we were trotting past some houses."

"What kind of houses?"

"Um... I remember a big tent. It was yellow."

"The Spring Carnival. Okay, you're traveling North. What else?"

"Not much. Just hills and trees and wildlands. We stopped at around Moonset, for the night." The tugging was growing stronger, pulling Ellia away from sleep. Noises from the real world began to seep through into the dream, so that the murmur of far-away voices began to fill the purple mist. Rowan looked desperate.

"Moonset? Wait, which one? Stay with me Ellia!"

"Red."

"Sorbus?"

"Yes."

"Which side did it set on?"

"In front of us, I think."

That seemed to tell Rowan something, because he nodded, looking determined.

"Hold on. I'll find you."

Something touched her hand – her real hand – and she was yanked from the dream.

Terrius was checking her pulse. From the grim look on his face, it was clear that he didn't really expect to find one. When he saw her eyes open, he breathed out a long sigh of relief. Over by the fire behind him, Cerris was watching. He feigned indifference, but his shoulders were tense, only relaxing when he was certain that she was really alive.

"I *told* you she wasn't dead." He said calmly, pretending to be unconcerned.

"She's close enough." Terrius retorted hotly. "You and your stupid cuffs. If we don't take them off, she's going to be dead within the hour. Her pulse stopped completely a moment ago."

"We can't take them off. She's dangerous." Cerris protested. Terrius snorted.

"Look at her. She's about as likely to attack us as that tree right there. I'm at least going to bandage her. If she's dead she's no use to us."

Cerris, obviously unnerved by Ellia's reputation, wouldn't back down, insisting that she would kill them both in their sleep if they let down their guard. Terrius tried to persuade him, but he set his jaw and refused to listen. Ellia watched the brothers' previous camaraderie dissolve as their argument became more heated, the cold, deadly look of the trained assassin becoming clear on both faces. Cerris was passionless and scornful, his scar twitching between his eyebrows as he glared at his younger brother. Terrius was more passionate, but he didn't let his anger get the better of him, instead using it to his own advantage. Ellia had the feeling that, if it came to a fight, Terrius would be the more deadly. Cerris was older, and therefore a more skilled assassin with carefully honed abilities, but Terrius's passion gave him an extra edge of determination. Ellia could see it shining in his eyes now, as he refused to back down, adamant in his belief that the cuffs were cruel and unnecessary. This fact didn't seem to bother his brother, so Terrius resorted to pointing out the practical problems of the cuffs.

"If they kill her, we lose a fortune in gold, not to mention what it will do to our reputation."

Cerris snorted. "Rather our reputation dies than us. If it's a choice between her possible death and mine, there's no question as to which is the wiser decision."

Terrius looked stubborn.

"I don't care. I'll do it if you won't." He said, standing up. Cerris stood up as well, his hand sliding towards his knife. His face was amused, but his eyes were cold.

"I'll duel you." He challenged calmly. "I don't want to kill you, but I will if it keeps you from sending us both to our deaths through your stupidity."

Alarmed, Terrius raised his hands in surrender.

"Alright, fine. We'll do it your way. Don't say I didn't warn you, though."

The brothers sat back down and settled into an uneasy silence. Ellia feigned sleep, but inside her newly-awakened mind was whirling. *They're divided about me. How can I use this?* She wondered. The only thing she could think of was to continue to look sickly, thus reinforcing Terrius's conviction and dividing them further. It wasn't hard. She was having trouble staying focused as it was. Giving in to gravity, she let herself slump sideways onto the ground, pretending to be unconscious. Sure enough, a few moments later she felt Terris crouching over her, carefully checking for a heartbeat. Through slitted eyes, she could see the concern on his face. *Good. Should I moan a little bit? Or would that be overdoing it?* She didn't know, so she decided not to, instead acting completely unresponsive. She figured that complete stillness would alarm him more. Fighting the urge to shift herself off of a bumpy tree root, she lay there, trying to look dead. The throbbing pain and a nagging itch in her back were hard to ignore, but her patience payed off. After a while, Terrius checked her pulse again, then again, each time looking more concerned and frustrated. Ellia expected him to restart the argument with his brother, but to her surprise and disappointment, he didn't. Instead, he sighed, walked away, and lay down by the fire, his breathing quickly slowing into the soft rhythm of sleep. *Rats.* Ellia thought.

Once he was certain that his brother was asleep, Cerris also lay down, apparently not worried about keeping a watch on Ellia when she was wearing the manacles. Sighing inwardly, Ellia resigned herself to her fate, and settled down in an attempt to get a few more hours of sleep before morning.

Cerris's breaths also slowed down into a sleeping rhythm. Ellia was just about to fall asleep herself when Terrius's soft snores abruptly cut short. With a careful glance at Cerris, he rolled silently to his feet and stole over to Ellia, face set with a dogged stubbornness as he pulled a bandage from the saddlebag nearby. He wasn't very gentle, but he was quick, and after a moment he had deftly wrapped her wrists in snug bandages. He folded them carefully so that they were almost completely hidden by the cuffs. Then, to further hide his work, he removed his cloak and carefully covered her with it.

Ellia opened her eyes then, and caught him looking at her with a gentleness that she would never have expected in the eyes of an assassin. He gave her an apologetic smile, put a finger to his lips, then slipped away.

Chapter Fifteen

The Way Out

***

"The funny thing about people is that you can never tell what their breaking point will be. Some will die in a week from the damp, while others are tough as rocks. I remember one old guy who was supposed to die by starving, but after two weeks, when we came to collect his body, he jumped up and ran for it." — Robur, a prison guard.

***

Apparently confident that they had eluded all possible pursuit, the assassins didn't get moving until late the next morning. Ellia was grateful for the extra sleep. Thanks to the bandages, her wrists were no longer hurting, and she felt wide awake when the Assassins were ready to move on.

She awoke to the sound of another argument between the two men. Cerris had just discovered that they were several miles off course, and he was in a savage mood. He evidently wanted to take out his frustration on something. He had caught sight of the cloak covering Ellia, and was ridiculing his younger brother for it.

"You've grown soft." He sneered. "Look at you, going mushy-eyed over the prisoner just because she's acting all weak and helpless. What happened to all your killer instincts?"

Terrius's eyes flashed, but he said nothing. Cerris followed him as he stalked away, clearly not willing to let the matter drop until he'd had a reaction from Terrius.

"Really, Terrius. How many people have we killed together? Plenty of those were weak and helpless. You didn't care about them, did you?" He waited for an answer, but Terrius was busy with the saddles, and didn't seem to be listening. Cerris looked disappointed. He stood there for a second, and then decided to play both his last cards at once.

"It's because she's beautiful, isn't it? You're *attracted* to her. Or is it just because she's the only woman you've seen in this country who isn't taller than you?"

That last comment about his height was what did it. It was evidently a touchy subject with Terrius, who was shorter than his brother. Cerris knew it, and his eyes glinted with malice as he said it.

Faster than thought, Terrius whipped around and lashed out at his brother, a knife glinting in his hand. Cerris laughed and dodged it, pulling out a knife of his own. Within seconds, they were sparring around the fire, circling each other warily, slashing and dodging with insane skill. Ellia watched in astonishment. The Kurdu men had a very different style than any other fighters she had ever seen. They used their feet, hands, and even their elbows to fight, not to mention any piece of their surroundings that proved useful. She was caught up in the fight for a moment, before realising that this might be exactly the chance she had been waiting for. Time to try an escape.

Terrius kicked burning coals at his brother, who

dodged, but came up coughing from the smoke in his face. Seizing the opportunity, Terrius darted at him while he was distracted. Cerris recovered just in time, kicking Terrius in the chest. However, he seemed surprised, and a little worried. They were no longer just sparring. Terrius's eyes were blazing, and he was attacking ferociously. Cerris seemed to realise this, because he looked frightened. He fell into a defensive position, and began deflecting blows carefully, face concentrated with the sudden realisation that this wasn't just a game anymore; Terrius might actually be trying to kill him. Between strikes, he began trying to reason with his brother.

"Terrius, stop this. I'm sorry, okay? I didn't mean that." Terrius kept attacking blindly, his face murderous. He was no longer in control of his anger. Cerris kept talking, face grim.

"Listen, Terrius, be reasonable. What good is fighting me going to do? If I kill you, what good will that do your precious Starfall? You might kill me, but not without getting wounded yourself, and then what would you do, all alone? The girl won't help you. You might like her, but believe me, she'd kill us both without a thought. We kidnapped her, remember? The whole reason we're here is so that we can take her to Kurdu and the King. That's our duty. Are you going to betray your king for a random prisoner?"

That seemed to get through to Terrius. His anger cooled, and he stopped attacking, backing off warily.

"I'm not going to betray the King." He stated sullenly.

"I'm still going to take her to Kurdu. I just want you to stop being cruel. She's a girl, for Firth's sake, and we may be killers but we're not monsters. These Dalians already think that we're barbaric and heartless. You can see it in her eyes when she looks at us. I don't want to prove them right."

He looked mulishly at his brother, daring him to argue. Cerris didn't, so he went on.

"This girl isn't just another target, Cerris. She's important. The Wood-Demons want her, the King wants her, the Dalian King also wants her. She's the only Gold Starfall in ages, so she's practically like royalty, and we should treat her with some respect. It's not just that I feel badly for her, it's also that we might get into big trouble if we deliver her damaged or dead. Please, Cerris, don't be so pig-headed!"

Cerris chewed his lip uncertainly. Finally, he shook his head and snorted a laugh.

"Look who's calling *me* pig-headed! Fine, little brother, we'll make a compromise. The cuffs can come off during the night, if we take turns keeping watch, but they stay on during the day. If she bleeds too badly we'll bandage her. Deal?"

Terrius nodded. Cerris smiled.

"Great. Let's get moving. We've wasted enough time. Grab the girl and... Wait. Where's the girl?"

Both men turned, but Ellia was no longer lying beside the tree. The rope that had bound her feet was untied, and she was gone.

Heart pounding, Ellia crouched in a ravine. The thick underbrush and trees lining the bank gave plenty of cover, but it was hard going. A small stream ran over most of the ravine floor, so that Ellia had to hop from rock to rock, hugging the side of the bank. She didn't intend to get her sandals wet, as that would mean blisters. With her hands bound, she couldn't catch herself if she fell, so she had to test each rock before stepping on it. The Wildlands were crisscrossed with streams like these, but the problem was that they twisted and turned, so that Ellia had no idea which way she was going. *If I actually manage to escape, how will I ever find my way out of here?*

Several times, she heard shouting, and had to crouch down close to the bank until it passed. Once Cerris crashed through the bushes almost on top of her. He was busy peering into the trees, so he didn't seem to notice the fissure where the ground dropped away into the ravine. He may have been a skilled assassin, but he wasn't much of a tracker. After slashing at the bushes with a sword and swearing for a bit, he gave up and stalked back the way he had come. Ellia let her breath out slowly. This was a much more high stakes game of hide-and-seek than any she had ever played.

After around half an hour of trekking awkwardly over the slippery rocks, the sounds of pursuit finally faded into the distance. Vastly relieved, Ellia climbed up out of the gully and began making much better progress. *Progress to where, exactly?* An inner voice criticized. Ellia was suddenly confronted with the one gigantic flaw in her brilliant plan. She had managed to run away, but now she was stranded deep in the Wildlands. She was a Great House slave, alone, without a weapon, and completely lacking survival skills. Silently cursing her Aristocratic upbringing, she looked around cluelessly. *I can eat plants!* She thought brightly, only to realize that she didn't know anything about the plants surrounding her. She recognized some of the trees and bushes, but knew nothing about them save their names. No one had ever bothered to teach her which, if any, were edible. With an inward sigh of despair, she trudged onward. Her last hope was to somehow reach civilization, or Elves, or *anyone* who would help her. Feeling stupid, weak and helpless, she wandered through the underbrush, hoping she wasn't walking straight over the border into Kurdu.

Despite its hardships, Ellia couldn't help noticing that the country was beautiful. The jagged hills, split by gullies, were a light orange in color, with purple and green underbrush overhanging their steep cliffs. Little waterfalls and streams trickled between them, under thick stands of dark green trees. Every now and then, the sound of water would be joined by the twittering of birds, or occasionally the yelp of a Barking Mouse. Once Ellia heard a cacophonous mewling, and saw a pack of Hill Cats pouncing around under the bushes, tackling each other and tumbling down the gully banks.

By now, she had been traveling for several hours, and was facing utter exhaustion. It had been hard enough to simply escape in the first place in her fuzzy state of mind. The thrill of being hunted had cleared her head somewhat, but now the drowsiness was returning, stronger than ever.

In the end, it was the Whispering Elms that did it. There were groves of them dotting the countryside, their pale bark and leaves standing out in sharp contrast to the dark green of the other trees. Late in the afternoon, Ellia stumbled into a large grove of them without realizing what they were. Under their spreading shade, the hot, whining shrill of Summer insects disappeared, replaced with a cool hush. Even with no wind to speak of, the soft whisper of the long, silvery leaves filled the air. It was a beautiful, calming sound, like waves breaking on soft sand. Ellia had barely ventured a few paces into the wood before the sound soothed all the urgent desperation out of her body. *Why would I need to stay awake? It's so nice here...* The surrender was sudden, total. Her muscles turned to mush as she collapsed ungracefully to the ground, fast asleep long before she hit it.

"Oh dear, this won't do. Not at all." Ellia was

awakened by the nudge of a toe in her side. Her head was full of the leftover cobwebs of a deep sleep.

"What?" She slurred, rolling over slightly, but not bothering to open her eyes.

"Well, don't you see, some strange human creature has fallen asleep on all my Wormwood plants! A body on my plants. Much heavier than a mouse. Much more damaging. Get up, you big oaf, can't you see you're crushing them?" The strange, scratchy voice penetrated through the cobwebs, accompanied by sharp toe nudges. Ellia became fully awake with a jerk. She scrambled to her feet and backed against a tree, heart pounding. Despite her lack of food, plus numerous cramps and itches resulting from spending the night on her face, with her hands bound under her, she felt surprisingly well. Well enough to take on the odd creature across from her, anyway. At first, the thing in front of her resembled nothing so much as a gigantic hedgehog. Then it straightened up a bit, and Ellia saw that it was in fact an old man. He was medium in height, but stooped under a very large basket, loaded with branches, sticks, plants, and a great many other things. He wore an overlarge black cloak, with the hood drawn up over his face. The only thing Ellia could see of him was his small, beady eyes, a large dirty beard which covered most of his face, and a pair of very large, steel-capped leather boots poking out from under his cloak. He was looking at her irritably. He didn't seem very dangerous, so Ellia relaxed slightly.

"Who are you?" She inquired warily.

"Ha!" cackled the man, rather suddenly. "Slept on my Wormwood, stomps on my Wormwood! Now she asks me who I am. Who are *You*, you should ask, and I would tell you that. Who *I* am is not your business. A strange creature indeed. A stomper too. Nosy! And a trespasser!" The old man stopped his disjointed speech abruptly and glared at her. *Right. A crackpot. Just what I needed. At least he's not asking dangerous questions that any sane person would, seeing me here, like this.* Ellia regarded the man with some astonishment. At the sight of this odd personage, her unquenchable curiosity flared to life, drowning her alarm. The old man was now down on his knees, carefully inspecting the soft, whitish plants which she'd been sleeping on. He gave several grunts of disapproval, and glared at her again, making a complicated shooing gesture with his hand. Ellia backed away carefully, following the wiggling course his hand had traced in the air in order to avoid several odd-looking plants. This seemed to have been his intention, because he looked satisfied, and went back to the Wormwood inspection.

When he was finished, he broke a few leaves off for his basket, then stood up and brought his attention back to Ellia. His eyes widened slightly as he took her in.

"Oh my." He mused. "Not just any Plant-Stomper, this one. Not just human, either. Many mysteries, you are. That chain, for one thing. that's *Magic.* I feel it in my teeth. Smell it too."

Ellia doubted that he could smell anything at all over the mix of nasty aromas which clung to her blood and dust spattered clothes, but she didn't point that out. Instead, she seized the opportunity of his attention.

"Mister, Um... Sir, Could you perhaps help me to find food and direction? I'm not sure where I am, and I need help." She wasn't sure how sane or helpful the man was, but she figured that it couldn't hurt to ask. The old man cocked his head thoughtfully, then seemed to come to a conclusion.

"For free? Not my help. Most humans in these parts need a good rock to the head, and that's all. Not help. But you aren't a most human are you? Very full of mysteries. Solving mysteries brings Wisdom. Wisdom is a Hermit's gold and diamonds. Yes. You, I will help. This is my offer. You will get food and rest and hiding from your pursuers." He nodded his head wisely, and Ellia gave a start, alarm jolting through her. *How does he know I'm being pursued?* The old man cackled, and pointed to the manacles on her wrists.

"Your chains, my payment. Interesting magic, and I want it. Then you will get my help." He eyed the chains greedily, and Ellia almost laughed out loud. *Thank Firth. I was so sure I was going to die in the wilderness. Who knew a weird old crackpot would be my way out?* She smiled gratefully at her strange source of salvation, and nodded.

Chapter Sixteen

In Which Our Heroine Battles the Forces of Evil and Nasty Soup

✳ ✳ ✳

"The key difference between sanity and insanity is whether or not one is aware of one's own strangeness." — Alium Thesaida, a surprisingly philosophical Beggar.

✳ ✳ ✳

The old man introduced himself as Ham, the Hermit. His house turned out to be a kind of sandy cave or tunnel in the side of a large hill. The door to his house at first looked like merely a large boulder propped against the hill; However, it had some sort of invisible hinges that enabled it to swing out with a mere touch, and even lock. It was logically impossible, and Ellia stood for several minutes staring at it in consternation when Ham pushed it open. Seeing her confusion, he laughed.

"Magic. Like your bonds. Can't you smell it? Got the Spell-metal off an old wizard. He didn't need it, being dead. Hunger got him. No spells that make food. Nope. Only wild magic and spells trapped inside metal. Got to forge it in the Earthfires, you see. Hinges and locks are metal." He wandered inside, and Ellia cautiously followed him, feeling that she was making a big mistake.

Hams' "house" was shaped more like a mouse nest. There were sticks and branches woven into the walls and roof to hold back the sandy soil. Every twig that jutted from the wall was laden down with all manner of strange things. On most, there were herbs, mushrooms, and vegetables drying. However, near the back, the roof bristled with hanging bits of metal. Ellia guessed that they must be "spell-metal", given the old man's apparent obsession with the stuff. The strangest thing about Ham's house, however, was that there was no furniture of any kind. No bed, table, or chairs. His only normal possessions seemed to be the large pot hanging over a fire-pit outside the house, and a collection of cooking utensils hanging on one wall.

Ellia looked around curiously as he ushered her in. Without a word, he dumped his load on the floor, grabbed what seemed a random handful of objects and dried foods off the walls, then headed back out again. Ellia followed, getting the feeling that her host was not one for conversation. Hermits rarely were. Ham was shoving a stack of sticks underneath the big pot in front of his dwelling. He stared in consternation into the empty bottom. With a hand he waved Ellia over, and heaved the pot into her arms, which she caught with difficulty.

"Stream behind the hill." He grumbled, glaring at the pot as if it's emptiness was a personal insult. Ellia considered pointing out that her hands were still tied, and that she wasn't his servant, but she decided not to when she realized that the chore would give her a chance to wash the grime and blood off her arms.

She found the stream with no problem. Even filling the pot was not overly difficult. The only irritating thing was that once she had washed her arms, the rest of her body suddenly felt much more dirty.

When she returned and hung the pot back on its

hook, she was surprised to see that Ham made no move to light the fire under it. Instead, he tossed random handfuls of dried plants into it, then went back into his house. Ellia choked down a slightly hysterical laugh. *This guy is supposed to help me survive? He doesn't even know how to cook a meal!*

Ham came back out, carrying a long metal stick. He pointed it at the pile of sticks. Ellia, amused, was about to ask him if he needed help, when all of a sudden a ball of fire exploded from the end of the stick, knocking Ham backwards onto his rear. The heat and smoke struck Ellia like a physical blow, and she backed away, coughing. The fire was crackling nicely now. The only sign of the strange event was the blackened, smoking, grass all around it. Ellia gasped for breath.

"What *was* that?" She demanded indignantly, backing away from the fire. Ham, still sitting down, cackled with glee.

"Spell-metal! You wouldn't believe all the things it can do if forged properly. This is just a little one. Simple spell. I don't have any really strong ones, like the Heroes of old. *Those* were powerful weapons. Not nearly as practical as this fire starter, though." It was his most coherent speech so far, and Ellia was vaguely impressed. *I want a fire-starter.* She decided. Ham stood up, dusted himself off, and wrinkled his nose at her.

"The dinner will be a while. Time enough for you to wash the stink of the road off of you. If you don't get yourself clean, the smell will wither the grass." He handed her a knife to cut her bonds with, then went back to stirring the pot.

Ellia wasted no time. The knife failed to pry the shackles off, but the ropes were easy. She hurried down to the stream behind the hill and had a bath, clothes and all. The water was frigid, but she didn't mind. It was late morning, so she expected her clothes to dry quickly in the blazing sun, as she stretched out on a rock to take a nap.

She was awakened suddenly by a metallic crash that echoed across the countryside. For what seemed miles around, birds rose in clouds from the trees. Ears ringing, Ellia jumped up and sprinted back to Ham's house, certain that some some kind of disaster had struck. She rounded the hill, only to find the old hermit standing there, grinning from ear to ear. He stood next to the pot, and had a large metal spoon in his hand. As she came around the corner, he swung back the spoon and dealt another mighty blow to the side of the pot. Ellia covered her ears.

"Hey! Stop! What are you doing?" She yelled. Ham beamed at her.

"The birds were too quiet. If you don't wake them up, they'll sleep all day. Lazy slug-a-beds." He gestured cheerfully to the screaming flocks still rising from the trees.

"I woke them up." He sounded so sincere and earnest that Ellia refrained from pointing out that there were many sayings based on the fact that birds were known to rise early.

"You can't do that!" She begged. "It's too loud. You'll let everyone for miles know where we are, which is bad, since there are people hunting me."

Ham looked sullen, but finally agreed to cease his bird-waking ritual for the duration of Ellia's stay. With a sigh of relief, Ellia sat down on a rock and accepted a bowl of food from him. She hadn't noticed bowls in the house, but figured that the crazy old hermit probably kept them buried in the dirt or something. The food was very strange, with many bitter herbs in it, and some objects floating around in the soup that she didn't want to identify. Nonetheless, she was hungry, so she choked it down, and thanked him sincerely. The old hermit looked embarrassed by her gratitude, and shuffled off quickly.

Ham brought a spike and hammer out of his house. Ellia was momentarily alarmed, until she remembered the manacles still clamped unrelentingly onto her arms. Once she realized what he wanted, she eagerly stretched her wrists apart over a large rock, ignoring the pain when her blisters reopened. Having a crazy person pounding a spike so close to one of her major arteries made her more than a little nervous, but she clenched her teeth and endured it.

They were both sweating, he from exertion and her from fear, when the last cuff finally broke apart. It clattered, somewhat bent and dented, to the ground. With a huge sigh, Ellia stood up and stretched, reflecting on how strange it was that Ham had demanded the manacles as payment, instead of the incredibly ornate and valuable Starfall cuff openly displayed on her arm. The thing was probably more expensive than the King's own crown. Then again, she thought wryly, nothing about Ham made sense. Her thoughts were cut off abruptly by Ham's sudden yelp of surprise. He stumbled back a few steps, staring at her, jaw slack. Ellia instinctively glanced behind her. Nothing.

"What?" She faltered.

"How did I miss this?" Ham gasped. "The magic! You *reek* of it. Makes my teeth hurt just being this close!" Ellia wasn't sure how to react. The old man was telling her that she reeked, which wasn't a compliment. She didn't feel offended, though. Just surprised, and more than a little curious. *I have magic? Real magic! Maybe I'm not an impostor after all.*

"What do you mean, I smell of magic?" She pressed eagerly.

"Is it something I'm wearing, or actually *me*? What kind of magic?" The old man didn't pay any attention. His eyes were somewhat unfocused, and he seemed to be thinking very hard. His expression was becoming more and more agitated.

"No, no. This is not good. Don't you see, this deep in the Wild-lands, who knows what might smell you and be drawn here? Powerful magic causes reactions. People feel it. *Things* feel it." Ham dived down and scooped the chains off the ground, shoving them at her. His eyes were wide with fear.

"Put these back on, quick! I don't care about my payment anymore. I only care about keeping dangerous things away from my house."

Frightened and shaken, Ellia gingerly took the manacles. They burned her fingers, and she dropped them immediately, backing away.

"No… I can't. Nothing's going to come get me. I've been in the wild before and nothing did." The moment she said that, she realized that it was a lie. She remembered the terrifying crossing in the Shadow Woods, how the Darkwings had chased them, and the Ice Creeper had seemed to focus on only her. *Could he possibly be right? Does magic call to magic like that?*

"Um… what kind of magical creatures live this far out in the Wild-lands?" She asked tentatively. She wasn't sure she wanted to know, and was almost relieved when Ham ignored her question.

"Put those back on!" He snapped. "I don't care if they hurt! They blocked your smell, and without them you'll have the attention of every magical creature for miles. Believe me, you don't want to find out what lurks out there." Strangely enough, in this crisis, the old man's voice seemed to steady, and his sentences actually made sense. He seemed lucid and serious enough that Ellia was swayed into obeying. She reluctantly allowed him to snap the horrid things back on. Strangely enough, one of the warped and scraped ends still clicked together and held. The other wouldn't attach, so she just left that end swinging free. It seemed to block the magic well enough, though, because Ham let out a sigh of relief.

A high, clear laugh cut the sigh short.

"No, you don't want to find out what lurks out there. Things like me, for example." Ellia's blood ran cold as Cerris rose like a shadow out of the bushes, sword in hand.

"I suppose I should thank you, old man, for all the help you've given us. Finding our quarry, putting those cuffs back on her, and making a tremendous racket to let us know where you were." He drawled cheerfully. He cocked his head to the side, eyes glittering with cold triumph as he looked at the two of them.

"But you know what?" He smirked with false cheer, turning his feral grin on Ham. "I really don't *want* to thank you. What I'd really like to do is kill you instead. I'm in the mood for killing people, and *some* people," He eyed Ellia with dark longing, "Are too *important* for me to kill." He sauntered forward into the clearing. Ellia turned to run, but Terrius was slinking into the clearing from the other side. They were trapped. Before she had time to panic or plan, all possible escape routes had been cut off. Terrius wore a furious scowl. His gaze was focused on Ellia's face, and something like betrayal flashed across his face when she met his eyes. Cerris, however, wasn't looking at Ellia at all. His bloodthirsty gaze was fixed on the clueless old man, who just stood there, blinking in astonishment. Suddenly, Cerris leaped forward, slashing his sword downwards at Ham's head. Ellia gasped, and stumbled backwards as the sword whistled down.

"Oh dear." Ham said blandly. One moment he was standing there, directly in the path of the sword blade. The next instant, he was gone. He moved so fast that for a moment Ellia thought he had fallen. No old man should be able move that fast. In an instant, Ham had dodged the sword, and the fire-stick was in his hands. Without a shift in stance or expression, he brought it swinging up into the side of Cerris's head. It was so fast that Cerris, the trained assassin, didn't have time to block. He crumpled, and before Terrius could intervene, Ham dashed into his house and slammed the door.

There was a moment of stunned silence. Ellia suddenly realized that she needed to run. She had barely taken a step away before Terrius pounced on her. Instinctively, she dodged sideways and used the only weapon she had. As Terrius stepped towards her again, she wrapped the chain of her manacles once around her hand. Heart pounding, she swung the broken end hard around, sending it whipping into his surprised face. It was a lot more dangerous than it looked. The twisted metal end was sharp and heavy. It slashed viciously across Terrius's face and his arm that he brought up in defense. It was the first time Ellia had ever used all of her strength in violence against another human being, and the impact shocked her.

She paused for half a second, her attention fixed in surprise on the jagged gash dripping blood down his cheek. Too late, she swung the chain again in defense. With a snarl, Terrius snatched the chain from the air, letting it wrap around his arm. She couldn't let go, and he yanked her off balance. Before she had time to react, he knocked her down with several ruthless and well-placed blows. He punched her hard in the stomach, then brought his elbow down on the back of her head when she doubled over. Sparks swirled before her eyes as her face was shoved into the dirt. She choked out a wordless cry of agony as Terrius drove his knee into her back, yanked her head back, and pressed a knife to her throat.

"Don't you dare try anything." He rasped in her ear. "Give me any excuse to kill you, and I will." Ellia silently cursed herself. *You idiot, this is all your fault. You made a fool of a man who can't control his temper. You turned on him and ran away while he was fighting his own brother for your sake. Now he's going to kill you, and you led him to this.* Terrius's hand was shaking slightly with the emotions raging inside him. The shivering knife edge bit into her skin. Ellia caught her breath and held perfectly still, feeling a single drop of warm blood slide down her collarbone. Her world narrowed down until she was only aware of two sensations: Terrius's harsh breathing and the cold feel of the knife pressing against her skin. *This is the end.* She thought, her heart sinking in despair.

Cerris woke up. He rolled over with a groan, barely a foot away from where Ellia herself was lying. His bleary eyes locked onto hers. Then his gaze shifted to the blade at her throat, the unsteady hand holding it, and his eyes snapped into focus. His whole body tensed on the ground.

"Terrius." He said the name softly, calmly, but his tone held a warning.

"Think about what you're doing."
Terrius stiffened at the unspoken rebuke. His knee pressed down harder into Ellia's back, and he jerked her head back by her hair. However, after a moment, he lessened the pressure on the knife, so that it hovered a hair's breadth away from her skin.

"She deserves to die." He growled. "Look what she did."
There was a moment of silence, as Cerris looked at his brother, and Ellia held her breath. Then Cerris laughed.

"You mean your face? I'd say it's a big improvement! After all, everyone knows that nothing fascinates the ladies like a mysterious scar. Makes you look almost handsome!" He grinned, and despite the knife at her neck, Ellia couldn't help the smile that tugged at her lips. Cerris may have been a bloodthirsty, heartless brute, but his lighthearted humor was very contagious. Terrius, however, was not amused. If anything, it made him more angry.

"I don't just mean my face!" He exploded. "She's a freaky witch! She made both of us look like fools, with how she pretended to be dying. She should have been, too, with how much she bled! No one heals that fast, that they can get up and run away right after being drained like that. She shouldn't have been able to *Stand,* let alone run for miles. And then she somehow eluded two trained assassins, like a shadow. She isn't human, Cerris. She's a witch, and we should kill her." His voice shook slightly with emotion. Cerris sat up, looking bored.

"Really, Terrius, You're not being rational. We should kill her because she heals too fast and tried to escape us, her *captors*? She's a Starfall. They're not human. We *know* this already. She's even less human than the rest, since she looks like a Wood-demon. We didn't capture her because she's Human, we captured her because she's supposed to be the most powerful Starfall in over a century. Of *course* she heals fast. that's no reason to kill her."

"But she just disappeared..." Terrius protested weakly. He was losing the argument, and everyone knew it. He didn't even sound very convinced himself. Cerris sighed.

"You're not exactly the best Tracker, Terrius. Neither am I. Stop this nonsense. We only have to put up with her a little longer, then we can just collect our reward and leave." He stood up and brushed his coat off dismissively, as if assuming that the conversation was over. Terrius seemed to think so too, because he huffed in annoyance as he stood up, pulling Ellia to her feet with him. Ellia's hands still weren't bound, but she didn't even consider escape. Terrius had trapped her arms behind her back, and she was pinned against him by his arm and the knife. The blood from his arm was soaking into her shirt, and she had some small satisfaction in the fact that keeping her pinned was probably hurting him more than he had hurt her. Cerris tossed him a piece of rope with a disdainful expression.

"Hurry up and tie her, we need to get moving."

They were only halfway down the hill, headed towards the horses tied in the trees at the bottom, when there was a roar behind them. A burst of flame struck Cerris violently from behind, sending him pitching forward. He screamed in agony, and tumbled down the hill, beating madly at the flames licking his clothes. Half of his cloak had been blasted away, and the shirt beneath it was burning too. At the top of the hill, stood Ham, framed in a halo of smoke. There was a wild look in his eyes, his beard was singed, and he clutched the Fire-stick like a sword.

"Foul Kidnappers!" He roared. "Murderers! Plant-Smashers!" He sent another fireball down the hill, and Terrius cursed. He dodged sideways and dashed down towards the horses, dragging Ellia with him. She tried to plant her heels in a last desperate bid for escape, but the dirt was dry, and her feet skidded in the dust. Terrius just cursed some more, threw her over his shoulder, and kept running. Blasts of fire struck against trees nearby, but he dodged them as he ran. Below them, Cerris rolled to his feet. He was hunched in pain, and the back of one arm seemed to be badly burned, but his eyes were murderous. He bared his teeth, drew a knife, and flung it up at Ham with surprising strength.

Ellia gasped as it stabbed into Ham's thigh. The

old man stumbled back, blinking down at the handle. Cerris laughed wildly, pulling out another knife. There was an answering laugh from the top of the hill.

"Ha!" Ham cackled gleefully. "You missed! This is only a scratch! Die, Fool!" Another burst of flame blasted down the slope. Cerris rolled to the side, still clutching his knife. He looked as if he wanted to charge the old Hermit head-on and stab him.

"Let's get out of here!" Terrius yelled as he reached the horses with Ellia. "Leave the madman, Cerris. We have to go!"

Reluctantly, Cerris turned away and sprinted towards them. He vaulted onto one of the horses, then bent backwards and held out an arm. Terrius tossed Ellia up to him, and then swung onto his own horse so smoothly that Ellia was sure it was a well-practiced drill. Only it usually wouldn't have been a real person they were throwing around. Ellia's breath was knocked out of her as Cerris caught her and swung her around onto the horse in front of him. Her own self-pity vanished, though, when she heard Cerris's groan of pain, and remembered that his arm was badly burned. She knew she shouldn't pity the bloodthirsty villain, but her vivid imagination immediately assessed what he must be feeling, and she couldn't help but wince in sympathy.

They kicked the horses into a gallop, and thundered away over the hard-packed earth, without a care for the branches that whipped by. As Ham's furious shouts faded into the distance, Ellia finally accepted that her escape had failed, and her heart sank in despair.

Chapter Seventeen

A Bird Sings in the Night

＊＊＊

"Although many philosophers assume that the dragon Myth was the one who brought magic to the earth, the truth is that there were many ancient magics and sacred places here long before she came." — The True History of Allaria, by the council of Philosophers.

＊＊＊

The soft whistle of a songbird woke her. She was lashed firmly to a tree in a small wood where they had stopped for the night. Cerris was on guard duty, moodily watching her with his back to a tree a few feet away. It was night, and the fire had dulled to nothing but a few flickering coals. *Wait, why was a Songbird whistling at night?* Ellia was instantly wide awake. She looked around carefully, curiosity burning, but didn't dare ask Cerris. Both the brothers had been irritable and bad-tempered the day before. They both hated Ellia for all the trouble and pain she had caused them – specifically the pain. Terrius had calmed down after his wounds had been bandaged, but Cerris's burns had only become more painful, making him increasingly miserable as the night wore on. He seemed determined to inflict that misery on anyone or anything that caught his attention, so Ellia thought it wise to keep silent. He saw her eyes open, and scowled.

"Why aren't you sleeping?" He demanded suspiciously.

"Because..." Ellia began to answer, but was suddenly distracted by a very odd sensation. Her ropes were moving. Very slightly, almost imperceptibly, they were shifting back and forth on her arms, growing slightly looser and then tighter by turns. She trailed off in her explanation, wracking her brain in an attempt to place the sensation. *Someone – or something – is cutting my bonds, but holding them together so they don't fall off.* She realized. The answer came to her suddenly, clearly, and she struggled to mask her emotions. *Someone is trying to rescue me! Ham, maybe?* Her heart beat fast in her throat, and she immediately ignored the sensation, focusing back on Cerris. He was looking at her strangely.

"What are you doing, little witch?" He asked warily. "You'd better not be planning another escape."

Ellia realized that she had been staring vaguely off into the distance, her mouth slightly open as she tried to figure out what was happening with her ropes. She immediately schooled her expression into an appropriate, slightly sleepy look.

"No, I wasn't." She defended herself. "I was just... trying to remember my dream. It was very strange... and... and violent. It woke me up." The lie sprang easily to her lips, as it was very close to the truth. She *did* have strange, violent dreams, and they *did* wake her up most nights. From behind her in the dark, her mysterious rescuer drew in a sharp breath. Ellia's heart hammered, but a small pop from the fire masked the sound, and Cerris didn't seem suspicious.

"Well, go back to sleep." He said gruffly. "We all have nightmares, and they never mean anything, except that you've done too many bloody deeds to sleep quietly." He went silent and stared into the fire, evidently reliving his own nightmares. It was the first time Ellia had ever seen him betray anything like remorse, and she was stunned. Suddenly, a bloodthirsty, heartless monster had been transformed into merely a broken Human. The ropes stopped moving. She took that to mean that they were cut through. Her thoughts went back to the strange person on the other side of the tree. *Why did they gasp when I mentioned my dream?* She wondered. *Why would Ham care if I had a violent, strange… Oh.* Suddenly, she knew who her rescuer was. *It's not Ham.* Only one person had ever shown an interest in her dreams, and she'd lied to him, told him that she didn't have any strange, violent dreams, in order to calm his fears. *Well, now he knows that I lied to him. Whatever danger those dreams would put me in, I'm in it. Knowing Rowan, he'll probably be more concerned about that mystical danger than about the fact that I'm kidnapped, my wrists are bleeding, and I'm tied to a tree.* She sighed, leaned back, and pretended to be falling asleep.

Cerris was watching the fire, looking bored. All of a sudden, the ropes went slack. Ellia held her breath. For several moments, nothing happened. Then a sudden hiss split the silence.

An arrow sailed from the darkness on the opposite side of the fire, and buried itself deep in the soft ground. A small scrap of paper fluttered from the handle. Cerris was on his feet in an instant. He dove behind a tree and pulled out a throwing knife.

For a long moment, nothing happened. Terrius let out a soft snore. Finally, Cerris crept back towards the fire and plucked the paper from the arrow. Holding it close to the glowing embers, he squinted to read it.

"You have… Tres... Trespassed… within the

Faerie Sacred Grove. The punishment is… Death." Cerris swore so loudly that he woke Terrius, who leaped to his feet.

"Wood-Demons!" Cerris hissed, his face filled with disgust. "No matter how bad things are, they keep getting worse! Get behind cover!" He dove for the nearest tree, and Terrius followed, demanding in a loud whisper to know what was going on. At the same instant, Rowan reached out of the darkness and grabbed Ellia's arm, yanking her backwards into the night.

Ellia was bursting with questions, but she held her tongue. As soon as she got her feet under her, she ran as fast as she could, holding Rowan's hand tightly between her two bound ones as she stumbled blindly into the night.

He seemed to have much stronger night vision than she did, because although she couldn't see a thing, they didn't once run into a tree. Once the assassin's confused shouts had faded completely into the dark wood, Rowan slowed to a walk. Ellia was panting. She had rarely met anyone who could outrun her, so she wasn't prepared for the challenge of running with someone who more than matched her in speed and strength. At the sound of her labored breaths, Rowan stopped and turned to face her.

"Are you alright?" He sounded concerned. "I'm sorry I couldn't find you sooner. The Wildlands stretch for miles. Finding one person in all of that is… almost impossible. Not to mention you were moving around." He motioned for her to sit, knelt down in front of her, and began untying her bonds. Despite her exhaustion, Ellia's heart raced at having him so close. She was glad of the darkness to hide her blush as his knuckles brushed her wrist. Casting about for something to distract herself with, she started asking the questions that had been burning on her tongue.

"How did you find me?" She demanded. Rowan didn't answer for a long moment. His face was in shadow, so she couldn't see his expression.

"It was pure luck, really." He said at last. "I wish I could say I found you with my wonderful tracking skills, but the truth is I was miles off track. I hadn't seen a sign of you for days, and I was starting to give up hope, when I heard a really loud noise, kind of like a metal crashing sound. It was really faint, but I could hear it because, well, I'm an elf. So anyway, I would have ignored it, but then all of a sudden I felt this odd, tingling sensation, like static. Anyway, it was coming from a long way off, but it… Well, I know this will sound stupid, but it called to me." He sighed and ran his hand through his hair.

"A moment later it was gone, but I had the location, so I kept going. Then the next night I saw the fire." He grinned mischievously. "Those Kurdu kidnappers will probably hide behind trees for hours before they figure out that they're not going to be shot." He laughed, and Ellia couldn't help smiling with him. Then she frowned.

"Wait, I thought Faerie didn't lie."

"They don't, usually. But that doesn't apply to writing. Otherwise no one could ever write a story. I can *write* about a Faerie Sacred Circle, but I wouldn't *say* it." He pulled the last of her ropes off. In the dark, the red-hot glow of the Spell-metal where it touched Ellia's skin was clearly visible. The unbroken manacle was still clamped onto one wrist, and Terrius had wrapped the broken chain end around her other wrist. Rowan reached his hand toward it.

"What… Ow!" He touched it, then suddenly jerked his hand back and sucked on his burned fingers.

"Ellia, what *is* that?" He gasped. "Does it burn you like that too?" He looked horrified. Ellia realized that she could see his face now, which meant morning was fast approaching.

"No, It doesn't." She admitted with a tired grimace. "It actually hurts me worse. It's based on Magic, see. It contains magic, and the stronger the magic is, the more it hurts. Cerris, one of the kidnappers, said that it would give Faerie a slight burn, but because I'm a Gold Starfall, it gives me these bleeding sores. That's why I was acting all weird in my last dream. From loss of blood… It's not as bad now that I've formed a scab." She quickly added, seeing the look of cold fury on Rowan's face.

"I'll kill him." He hissed through clenched teeth. "I'll kill both of them. How *dare* they do this to you, the dirty barbarians!" He looked ready to jump up and run back in search of the Assassins. Ellia put out a hand to stop him. The gray light of morning made Ellia's arms visible, and with them the dark stain of dried blood around her wrists. The sight seemed to shock Rowan out of his vengeful mood. He shook himself.

"First, though, we need to get that off. Come on, let's go find a sharp rock."

The first rays of sunlight were lancing over the tops of the tree-clad hills when they finally found a suitable rock. Rowan also insisted that it be near water, since they would need to wash out the wound before bandaging it. They came at last to a secluded valley, with a clear, gurgling stream lined with rocks.

Ellia knelt with her wrist against a large rock while Rowan found a smaller one. He started to steady her wrist with one hand, but then cursed and dropped it. A faint burn showed red against the paler skin of his palm. He thought for a moment, then pulled off his shirt and wrapped it around his hand like a glove. Ellia was surprised at first, then intrigued. While he was busy pounding at the lock on her cuff, she stole a glance at his bare torso. He was lean, well-muscled, and quite good-looking, but she found herself somewhat disappointed at how *normal* he looked. She'd seen plenty of shirtless men and boys in her life. The blacksmith and his sons in the village near Baron Opulus's mansion never seemed to wear shirts at all. However, Ellia had for some reason expected Rowan to look different, since he was Elvish. He didn't. Other than being slightly taller than average, his physique was indistinguishable from any other athletic Human boy's. *Oh well.* Ellia thought. There was a sharp crack as the cuff fell apart. Rowan straightened and Ellia looked away, embarrassed.

"Well, that's done." He said cheerfully. He gingerly picked up the broken cuff and flung it with all his strength away into the trees. His face turned serious as he turned back to her.

"No one will ever do something like that to you again, Ellia. I promise. You'll never have to suffer through such pain again, as long as I'm here to prevent it."

He looked earnestly into her face, and his eyes glowed with sincerity. Caught in his warm gaze, Ellia's heart did a flip, and for a moment she forgot all her pain.

"Um…" She said stupidly, a blush creeping up her cheeks. Rowan grinned widely.

"I'll just assume that what you really meant to say was, thank you, Rowan, for heroically rescuing me from a bunch of murderous Assassins, I missed you so much." He smirked. Ellia snorted.

"I could have rescued myself. I already did, once. But then a crazy old hermit banged a pot with a spoon and… oh, never mind." She gave up, seeing Rowan's bewildered look. His lips quirked in amusement.

"No, really. Keep going. I could use a distraction while I clean out your wounds, and so could you. No offense, but it's a nasty job. It'll be painful for you, too. Just keep talking, and you'll be okay." He set to work, and Ellia racked her brain for things to talk about.

"Where are we going to go, after this?" She asked finally. "I'm not going back to the palace. I ran away for a reason."

"No. Not to the palace." Rowan mumbled, shredding a bandage off of the bottom of his shirt with his teeth. "I'll take you to the High council. If anyone can protect you, they can. It's not far from here. We just have to find a patch of Deep Woods. They're all connected, and they all have doorways leading to Alestromaria. Which reminds me." He looked up with a frown.

"When I was rescuing you, you mentioned a strange, violent dream. You told me you weren't having any more of those. Did you lie?"

Ellia was silent for a moment. Under his piercing gaze, she finally caved.

"Yes." She whispered, hanging her head. "It's just that... You looked so concerned, and I didn't want to worry you." Her defense was weak, even to her own ears.

"I've been having them almost every night." She admitted. "What does it mean?"

Rowan's gaze was very troubled, as he bit his lip in thought.

"Maybe nothing." He said uncertainly. "But it could mean that you've... inherited the powers, or at least the memories, of a very dangerous creature. It's... oh, never mind. You don't want to know. Suffice it to say that a lot of people want that power, but others would do anything to keep those powers from coming back."

"What do you mean, coming back?" Ellia demanded. Rowan sighed.

"See, Starfall powers are usually linked to the

history of the star they came from. Almost all the stars have stories about what they represent. Some are true, some aren't. However, when that star falls from the sky, the Starfall usually has powers that are linked in some way to the legend of the star."

His explanation left Ellia with more questions than ever, but he clearly wasn't willing to say more. Frustrated, she dropped the subject.

"What about your abilities?" She asked curiously. Rowan didn't answer, his mouth set in a hard line.

"Let's talk about something else." He sounded annoyed. Ellia found herself getting annoyed, too. He was breaking her scab open to clean out the wound, and it hurt a lot, making her still more irritable.

"Um, no. I want to talk about this. Now." She snapped peevishly. "You keep avoiding my questions, or giving vague answers. Can't you just stop being so… *Elvish!* It's annoying!"

Rowan laughed. "I *am* Elvish, in case you haven't noticed."

"Yes, but you could stop acting like it." She shot back.

This brought another laugh from him. He raised his hands in surrender. "All right, fine. I'll tell you, but you can't laugh."

"Okay." Ellia quickly agreed. He sighed and, after a pause, reluctantly began.

"The truth is, I'm kind of an embarrassment to my family. A long time ago, one of my ancestors had an affair with a Human. It doesn't show in most of my family, but I turned out with curly hair and too dark of skin to be fully Faerie. My abilities are… not as strong as they should be. Most Elves can master basic illusions as children. I've never been able to do any of that, except make myself look like a cat occasionally, and change my features to be more Human. Also, I can't cast any spells, or use Nature Magic. Most Faerie can do all of these things. The High Lords have all mastered certain Elements, like Lord Iberus with Wind, that you saw at the palace. All I can do is Dreamwalk, which isn't even supposed to be an Ability. It's quite useless. Most of the Elves consider me to be a failure." His voice was flat, but Ellia could see the pain behind his bland expression.

"They were even considering banishing me." He continued. "But then you came along, and one of our oracles foresaw some very important events, and she declared that you were tied up in it somehow. So one of the lords had the wonderful idea that I might make a good spy, so instead of banishing me, they sent me to Thalis to keep an eye on you. I was also supposed to be on the lookout for… someone, some*thing* else, but it never showed itself. The oracle finally decided that she must have been mistaken, and that the… creature, wasn't actually coming back." He frowned. "But if you've been having those dreams…" He shook his head. "No. It can't be you. I *know* you. You would never be… that." He stopped talking abruptly, mouth clamped shut. His eyes sought Ellia's uncertainly.

"I shouldn't have said that. You're not supposed to know." He finished his work, tied off her new bandages neatly, and stood up. Ellia was burning with curiosity, but Rowan wouldn't meet her eyes. Instead, he headed off to find dry wood for a fire. He was gone for a long time, and came back with two squirrels as well as the wood. After a quick breakfast of Spitted Squirrel, which wasn't very good, but still better than Ham's soup, they set out again. They traveled for a long ways in an uncomfortable silence. When the silence stretched too thin, Ellia was careful to break it with innocent small-talk, and Rowan seemed relieved that she wasn't pushing him for answers he couldn't give. Gradually, the guarded look faded from his eyes, and the silence became more companionable.

It was late afternoon when they finally reached a patch of what Rowan called "Deep Woods". To Ellia, they just looked like ordinary trees. They looked slightly older than the others, but she didn't see much of a difference, until she saw that the underbrush died away abruptly into soft, pale grass, and there were no leaves on the ground. A soft curl of unnatural shadow twisted lazily around a tree trunk. Ellia stopped short.

"I'm not going in there, Rowan." She hissed. "Darkwings hate me. Last time they attacked my whole group and nearly killed us." Rowan gave her a strange look.

"They shouldn't have. I mean, sure, they're attracted to magic, but it doesn't make them angry. Were they actually attacking *you*, specifically, or just your companions?" he asked. Ellia considered that.

"I don't know, actually. At first they just followed us, but then as we were nearing the edge of the woods they attacked us. I didn't get bit because Tuck was shielding me with his body." Her breath hitched, and she struggled to mask her emotions. The memory of Tuck still ached. A strange expression flashed across Rowan's face. It looked almost like jealousy. Then it was gone, and he nodded thoughtfully.

"Yes. That's to be expected. They would have wanted your magic to stay in their woods, so they attacked the people who were taking you away. You don't have anything to worry about. They shouldn't attack you if you go in." Ellia wasn't convinced, but she reluctantly allowed Rowan to lead her into the trees.

From the outside, the small wood hadn't looked more than a few meters across. However, after a few steps into the trees, Ellia felt something shift. She couldn't see to the end of the trees. Instead, they

seemed to stretch forever. She looked back, and saw
nothing but Deep Forest in every direction.

"What just happened?" She asked in a hushed
whisper. No birds sang, and the solemn hush felt almost
sacred. Ellia was afraid to break the silence. Rowan,
however, seemed to have no such feelings. He smiled
down at her, eyes sparkling with excitement.

"I suppose you've heard that no one can find the
Faerie Kingdom unless they're invited? Well, this is why.
If we weren't welcome here, we would have simply
walked out the other side of that little forest. However,
we're expected here. The Deep Woods became a
gateway Home."

"Home?"

"Alestromaria. The First Wood. that's where we
are. It's where most of the Faerie live. It's the biggest
Kingdom on this Continent, and yet it's impossible to
find." He looked proud, as if Alestromaria had been his
own invention. Ellia looked around, and some of his
excitement leaked into her. The trees stretched
majestically up into the dreamy twilight. High above, the
leaves formed a silver canopy, shivering in an unseen
breeze. The pale grass and flowers were also slightly
silvery, and the flowers glowed with a faint light, echoing
the stars that glimmered through the leaves above. The
tall, straight, tree trunks seemed much more elegant to
Ellia than the pillars of the King's palace.

"Is it always night time here?" She asked. Rowan
laughed softly.

"No. It's just that we traveled a long way with that
one step through the Gateway. Over here, the sun
hasn't risen yet. Also the trees filter out most of the light,
so we don't get a lot of strong sunlight. That's why most
Faerie are pale, except those who spend a lot of time
among Humans." He started walking forward into the
trees. Ellia started to follow, but then she remembered

something, and stopped short.

"Wait. When we came through the gate, you said that we were *expected* here. How is that possible? How would they know that I was going to be kidnapped, and end up here?" She asked, confused. Rowan's face went blank. For a second, Ellia saw guilt flood his eyes, plain as daylight. It was immediately wiped away, and he gave a noncommittal shrug.

"The High Lords know a great many things. We have a lot of oracles." He took her hand. "Come on. I want to show you my City." He started off, and Ellia followed numbly, a hard seed of doubt gnawing at her insides.

Chapter Eighteen

The High Court of Alestromaria

"Nowhere else can I breath so free,
Nowhere else can I laugh so free,
Nowhere else can I love so free,
as in the deep forest green*."
— An Ode to Alestromaria, by a mediocre Elvish poet.

*Some critics argue that the 'n' should be left off of 'green', so it would rhyme, but others say that it would make no sense.

They walked for a long while, and the woods gradually began to whisper with the sound of voices. Shadows slipped back and forth under the trees. Those who passed nearby revealed themselves to be Faerie Folk, tall, beautiful, and dressed in the same soft grays as the woods around them. Ellia was wondering where they lived, when she suddenly realized that the random clumps of trees in the wood were not random at all. Somehow the Elves had caused the trees to twine and lace together into intricate walls and pillars. The trees themselves formed the City of Alestromaria. Once she knew what to look for, Ellia could see that she was in fact walking down a sort of street, surrounded by houses. Each Elvish dwelling was different, but they were all formed of the same white, pillar-like trees, and they all stretched upward many floors like the spires of a castle.

At first, the inhabitants payed no attention to them. However, gradually, Ellia's brown hair, human ears, and Rowan's black curls began to stand out among the silvery heads of the rest of the Faerie folk. As they drew nearer to the city, they passed more Elves, and they began to draw curious looks. The dark color of their heads drew contemptuous frowns. Some of them seemed to recognize Rowan, and they turned disdainfully away. At first, Ellia instinctively ducked her head, wishing she had a hood. However, the moment the thought entered her head, another one drowned it out. *If you accept their contempt, they'll never treat you any other way.* The thought made her feel more determined. She lifted her chin and glared at the elves. The sight of her glowing golden eyes caused their bored, disdainful expressions to suddenly change. Looks of shock, fear, and then keen interest flashed across the face of everyone who met her eyes. Ellia expected the fear to feel better than the contempt did, but instead the attention just made her uncomfortable. The Elves had ancient, piercing eyes, and when they all began to turn away from Rowan to stare at her, she wished she had a deep hole to hide in. She tugged on Rowan's hand, and they hurried through the growing crowds toward the city.

The trees and houses on either side of the path grew thicker and thicker, growing so close together that Ellia could no longer tell them apart. Then she saw it. In front of them, the path ended abruptly. The trees gave way suddenly to a wide clearing, on the far side of which was the city. A wall of gigantic trees towered over them, growing so close together that they seemed to be a white cliff of wood, in the centre of which gigantic gates were set. They were made out of the same wood as the trees, and were ornately carved. Several hundred feet above them, the straight walls branched into a leafy canopy, which stretched across the clearing and melded with the forest on the other side. Ellia could see sentinels perched with crossbows on the branches, feet swinging over empty air far above the ground. They seemed unnecessary, since no enemy could possibly find Alestromaria in the first place, and also arrows wouldn't be able to do much damage from such a distance. Nevertheless, it was very impressive, and she let out a gasp of wonder.

Suddenly, there was a creaking sound like trees in the wind, because it was. As they watched, the great gates began to swing open on their own. Wind ruffled the grass in the clearing. A soft breeze swirled around Ellia, almost like a caress, and she felt the hair rise on the back of her neck. The gates opened to reveal the most intimidating group of people Ellia had ever encountered. There were at least twenty of them. Every single one of the women was breathtakingly beautiful, and the men all had dangerous good looks. All of them were dressed in sleek, simple finery. They wore few ornaments, but their clothes glinted with silver designs in the cloth. In the center stood the High Lord Iberus, his hands outstretched. When the doors were fully open, he let them fall and the wind ceased.

"Come forward, half-breed." He said. It was not a command, nor was it a request. It was simply a statement, as if he could not possibly imagine that she would disobey his wishes. Ellia stepped forward. Although her temper flared against such an attitude of ownership, it was as natural to obey this man as it was to breathe. When she was close enough to touch him, he motioned for her to stop.

"Do you know why we brought you here?" He asked. Ellia shook her head mutely. *Brought you here... as if the kidnapping and escape were all a part of the elves plan... Was it?* Ellia wondered. One of the other Elvish women stepped forward. She threw back her hood, and Ellia saw that her face was covered in strange, looping designs.

"We brought you here because I had a wonderful dream." She declared. "I foresaw that the Mother of our race would return. The Lady Myth, the great Dragon, who gave us our powers and raised us far above the mere mortals we once were." Her eyes shone with a strange fervor as she spoke, and Ellia found herself taking a step backwards.

"But what does this have to do with me?" She asked in a small voice. She was strangely afraid to speak up among this crowd, as if she were interrupting a prayer or a Royal council. The oracle didn't seem to hear her.

"This I foresaw; that the Dragon would return without fire, and that she would live among us silently until her return to glory. She will regain her fire, strike down the arrogant mortal king, and lead us, the faithful, to a new era, when we will rule at her side over all the land. We will bring peace to the puny, squabbling mortals. This I saw."

At her words, a hush fell over the crowd that had gathered. The Faerie's eyes all filled with the same strange fervor. All except the other High Lords, that is. They remained impassive during the oracles' speech, and some looked Ellia up and down skeptically.

"But what does this have to do with me?" Ellia asked again, somewhat louder. Lord Iberus turned to her, then eyed the listening crowd of elves.

"We will discuss this in private." He said. "In the

Silver Hall. Come." He turned and swept away, traveling deeper into the city. The others of the High council followed him, as did Ellia, reluctantly. Rowan was nowhere to be seen.

The Silver Hall turned out to be a large, circular chamber nearby, formed out of delicate, interwoven silver trees. The council members filled the room, every one of them scrutinizing Ellia as she came in. She felt as though they were peering into her soul. Iberus stepped closer, so that Ellia had to crane her neck to look him in the eye as he spoke. It was annoying, this habit of standing too close to people, and it made her feel very short and intimidated.

"Glinda was not the only one who has dreamed of the Dragon." He told her. "Our other oracles have also been having strange dreams. This does not concern us. We have long suspected that the Lady Myth was not dead. However, the concerning thing is that the oracles have also seen you in their dreams. Llirian especially, has dreamed of you almost every night." He gave her a long, searching look. The other elves were also looking at her, curiously. Ellia struggled to breathe. A part of her felt completely lost and confused. However, a small voice was whispering, *Isn't this what you suspected all along? Sooner or later, you knew they were going to find out that you are a monster.*

"Why?" She whispered.

Lord Iberus smiled. It was the smile of a sea serpent just before it devoured a boatload of juicy sailors – cold, smug, and hungry.

"We asked ourselves that exact question." He purred. "Our best guess is that you are to be the Firstborn of the new elves the Lady Myth will bless with immortality when she comes. Either that, or she will use you as her host to channel her power and provide her with a body to return to. Seeing that you are a Starfall –

and, most importantly, a *Gold* Starfall – I believe this to be the case. Because of this, we thought it best that the Lady Myth should come here while she was trapped in a weak human host, that we could… *protect* her by keeping her close." The High lord stepped still closer, until she could feel his warm breath on her face.

"Also," He said, lowering his voice. "Because you are my only daughter, and I couldn't bear the thought of leaving you among those dirty, heartless slime that call themselves Nobles." Ellia's mind reeled. *Ha!* A voice hissed in her head. *And you pretend as if you Faerie are too perfect to lie.* It was a very familiar voice, but it was not Ellia's. In that moment, she knew, with absolute certainty, that, while Iberus had obviously been lying about everything else, he had been right about the monster living inside her. She suddenly became aware of it as a separate presence lurking within, a dark, angry pit of churning power that smelled like Madness. All this happened instantly as Lord Iberus was speaking. She was so overwhelmed, she barely registered the Elf's attempt to claim her as a daughter. She snapped back into the present just as he reached out his hand and gently caressed her face, his eyes showing no feeling whatsoever except power-hungry greed.

At the touch of his hand, every fibre of her being reacted in revulsion, and she jerked away from him. In that one, tiny motion, something very strange happened. Wind and flames surged past her, the world telescoped, and next thing she knew she was standing against the far wall of the room, feeling strangely off-balance. Suddenly several meters away, the group of elves were gaping in astonishment. Ellia met Lord Iberus's eyes warily. His hard, chiselled face was impassive, but his eyes glowed with triumph. Her heart sank. Even though she didn't know what had happened, she knew that if it pleased the Faerie lord, it was not good. He turned and addressed the rest of the Faerie council.

"You see?" He asked softly. "Does anyone doubt me now?" There was a sullen silence. Several of the hooded oracles were muttering and shaking their heads. Finally, a tall, white-haired woman spoke up.

"Aye, Iberus. We doubt you. What proof have we that what you say is true? Yes, the girl sprouted fiery wings and launched herself backwards a few feet. But what does that prove? She is a Starfall. They wield the magic of the stars, and their abilities defy all reason. Golden stars in the past have always granted wondrous abilities to their bearers. Fiery wings are but a small thing." Lord Iberus opened his mouth to argue, but she waved her hand to indicate she wasn't done.

"You think that she is the dragon? Then you do not remember Myth. Few remember things so long ago, but I was her Firstborn, and I remember. The dragon did not have fiery wings. She breathed fire, yes. And she had wings. But her wings were golden, and so huge that they could not unfold in this hall. The girl is a Starfall, nothing more. When Myth returns she will likely be the first killed or the first Changed. That is why the oracles dreamed of her. You see? Do any of you doubt *me*?" Her sarcastic echo of Iberus's earlier words caused him to wince. She stared at each of the gathered elves one at a time. They all reluctantly nodded agreement. Lord Iberus's eyes flashed with annoyance.

"Perhaps you are right, Lady Eaglenda." He said stiffly. "But nevertheless the coincidence is rather strange. Myth's star disappeared very near the same time that this girl was Gifted. Who is to say that it did not fall to the earth? I, at least, am not fool enough to ignore all the obvious connections." He turned and stormed out of the room, sending an angry gust of wind blasting ahead of him. Lady Eaglenda thoughtfully watched a few silver leaves drift down from the trees.

"The High Lord needs to learn to control his temper." She gave a disdainful sniff. "If he does not learn to act his age, he will soon strip our trees bare."

The other elves looked uncomfortable. Some gave nervous chuckles, while others looked offended or embarrassed. Clearly, they respected Lord Iberus far too much to be comfortable with insulting him as the Lady Eaglenda was doing. She didn't seem to notice, though. As Ellia stood there against the wall, carefully thinking through everything she had heard and trying to make sense of it, Lady Eaglenda snapped her fingers and ordered everyone out of the room. Strangely enough, they all left without argument.

Ellia stayed. The old faerie lady hadn't told her to go, and, besides, she didn't like following orders. The Lady glanced briefly at Ellia, then started walking through the Silver Hall, jerking her head in an indication that Ellia should follow. She was walking straight towards a blank wall of trees. Ellia decided to follow, simply because she was curious about how the lady intended to get through a solid wall. Her question was soon answered. With a wave of her hand, the lady caused the trees to twist and bend until there was a gap between them. She stepped through the makeshift doorway, and Ellia hurried to follow.

The sun was rising. Patches of grass and some occasional tree branches glowed orange with sunbeams, but most of the forest was a dull gray in the light of day. The glowing Night Flowers had all closed up and withered. Without the moonlight, the trees were rather plain, and the silver leaves were the color of old cobwebs.

"Don't let my son's wild ideas infect you." The lady plopped unceremoniously to the ground and leaned against a tree. Ellia was somewhat confused.

"Your son?"

"Yes. My son. Iberus. They call him a High Lord now. Practically a king. It's clear he wants to be one. He always was power-hungry. He cared nothing for our prophesies until they started involving a powerful Starfall who he thought he could use."

She looked up at Ellia suddenly, a fire in her eyes. "You *aren't* the Lady Myth. Reborn or otherwise." She said emphatically. "The great Dragon would *never* choose a frail, mortal, half-human as her body. She is a proud creature, and I can see no reason that she could possibly have for doing such a thing. Even for her to make you her Firstborn… well, her second-born, really. I was first. But even if she were to do that it would be an unusual honor for such a young, puny human as you. No. Iberus is trying to poison your mind with self-important ideas. I don't know why, but you shouldn't trust him."

Ellia began to grow annoyed. Human Nobles always seemed to treat her as if she were incapable of forming her own opinions or making decisions. The elves, it seemed, were no different. They were also constantly trying to manipulate her, and she found it very frustrating.

"I don't intend to trust *anybody*." She snapped. "I don't intend to stay here, either. I thought you Faerie would be different from the Human Nobles, wiser, since you've lived longer, but you're all the same. Self-centered, conniving, snotty, and judgmental. Hasn't it occurred to any of you that I might actually have an *opinion* about all of this?" Ellia knew that yelling at an ancient, powerful elf was probably not a good idea, but her frustration and anger was overcoming her caution. Seething at the stupidity of the world, she turned and stormed away into the woods.

She had barely taken a few steps before she was stopped short by a warm, scratchy laugh from behind her. Lady Eaglenda's laugh was rough, as if from long disuse, but her eyes sparkled with genuine amusement. It didn't dissolve Ellia's annoyance, but it did cause her to stop and turn around.

"I appreciate your honesty." The Lady struggled to keep a straight face. "I appreciate it so much that I am inclined to forgive the blatant insults that you have just heaped upon me and my people. Sadly, we have a terrible shortage of hot-headed elves in Alestromaria. We have all outlived our short tempers, I'm afraid. I haven't been insulted to my face in over a hundred years." As her anger faded, the realization of what she had just done hit Ellia full in the face. Shivers of apprehension coursed down her spine. Despite the Faerie's smile, she was not reassured that she wasn't in for a swift death. *Great going, Ellia.* She silently cursed herself. *You had to pick the time when you were facing the most important person you've ever met to throw a tantrum.* She met Lady Eaglenda's eyes, and was slightly relieved by the flicker of warmth that she saw there.

"Frankly, I find it refreshing." The lady declared. "So, tell me, Starfall. What *are* your opinions about 'all of this'?"

Ellia hesitated. Since entering the King's court, she had grown into the habit of withholding information and evading questions whenever possible. However, this woman genuinely wanted to know her opinion. It was such a rare opportunity that Ellia couldn't bear to pass it up. She cautiously sat down.

"I don't think I'm what everyone assumes me to be." She admitted. "Everyone assumes that I'm important because of my eyes, but I think they're wrong. I do have powers, but they're completely erratic and useless. Every other Starfall I've ever met is far stronger than I am. So, really, I think that you all should just leave me alone. I don't want to be a part of any political scheme."

The Lady Eaglenda was looking at her thoughtfully.

"Hmm…" She hummed. "What *do* you want, then?"

The question brought Ellia up short. What *did* she want? She had no idea, except some vague feeling that it wasn't what she had.

"I want..." She hesitated. "I don't know… Freedom?" She suggested, somewhat helplessly. Lady Eaglenda frowned.

"You already have that. While you are here, at least, you are no one's slave. What will you do with that?"

"I don't know."

"Then I suggest you find out."

Lady Eaglenda stood up and brushed herself off.

"I don't particularly care what you choose." She said, suddenly grave. "But others do, and will try to influence your path to suit their own ends. *This,* I care about. If you don't make your own decision soon, someone else will make it for you, and you could become a very powerful weapon in certain Faerie hands. Not because of your own power, but because of your reputation, and supposed 'Destiny'. I don't want that to happen, and neither, I think, do you." She looked Ellia hard in the eye.

"Don't let them make you their weapon, Starfall. Don't let them make you a threat, or I will be forced to destroy you. I can't have anything dangerous threatening the peace of my forest." Leaving that last ominous warning hanging like a dark cloud in the air between them, Lady Eaglenda turned and walked away.

Chapter Nineteen

In Which Ellia Finds an Old Man

***

"A lot of people think that living in the woods is easy. That might be true, except for the fact that the woods are full of trees. Trees are hard to live with."
— Balliol the Squirrel Hunter.

***

Left to her own devices, Ellia wandered through the Faerie city. She intended to do some exploring, and perhaps find Rowan. However, she barely begun to explore when she was apprehended by a troop of Lord Iberus's servants. Claiming that it was "The High Lord's orders", they quickly hustled her off to the upper floor of a large tree-castle. There she was fed, bathed, and well taken care of, but she couldn't shake the feeling that she was being imprisoned. The feeling intensified when a young elvish woman led her to her room, instructing her to get some rest. The room had no windows, and there were several guards posted in the hallway outside. *I'd better do something about them.* Ellia thought, as she flopped down on the bed to think, head whirling with all that had happened that day.

Next thing she knew, she was waking up to dim sunlight glowing through her eyelids. She got up sleepily and looked around for the source of the light. The room had no windows, but she was delighted to discover that the entire roof was made from the shifting canopy of the forest itself. She reflected that there couldn't be much rain in the area, if the elves didn't even bother to roof the top floors of their houses. *Good news for me, though.* She thought, climbing up onto the headboard of her bed, and from there pulling herself up into the canopy.

The soft thump of a spear handle against wood told Ellia that there were still guards outside her door. She considered trying to brazen her way past them, but they would doubtless alert Lord Iberus, and she had no desire to see that man again. Despite what he had claimed, Ellia was certain that he was not her father. He was simply another person who wanted control over her, and she didn't intend to be anyone's slave anymore. With that thought, she crawled away through the leaves.

The sun was just rising when she finally managed to climb down to the ground. She stopped for a moment, confused. The sun was in the same place in the sky as it had been when she'd fallen asleep. *I've been sleeping for a whole day.* She realized, feeling slightly panicked. She stood there for some time, trying to come up with a plan. She felt very confused, and alone. She felt desperate for someone to talk to, but everyone in the forest was a stranger... Except one. *I need to find Rowan.* She decided. The goal made her feel calmer. She took a deep breath and marched off into the trees.

This is ridiculous. Ellia thought, for the hundredth time that day, as she tripped over yet another root. She had been searching through the woods for several hours, having spent the entire time tripping over roots and running into awestruck elves, who always insisted on having long, awkward conversations about her "Destiny". She found herself becoming more and more annoyed at the inhabitants of Alestromaria. They mostly seemed to be proud, stuck-up snobs, with long, difficult names which she immediately forgot. Also, they treated her like a sacred object, or occasionally a detestable Half-blood. Most of all, though, they were annoying because they were so quiet, and silvery. This would not have been a bad thing in itself, except that the woods were also quiet and silvery, and so she was unable to spot them among the trees. More than once that day, she had run smack into an elf who she hadn't been able to see.

Ellia had decided quite quickly that she hated living in a forest. Having spent all her life in cities and towns, she was used to walking on flat ground. The elvish paths, however, were not much different from the rest of the forest, and there were large, hazardous roots everywhere.

She hadn't seen any sign of Rowan, either, which only added to her bad humor. *Why would he want to spend time with you?* A tiny, annoying voice nagged. *He's probably got a powerful, beautiful, elvish sweetheart here. Why would he want a powerless, half-human slave girl?* Irritated, Ellia told the nagging voice to shut up. It didn't, of course, since it was only in her head to start with. The thought was childish, she knew. However, she finally had to admit to herself that the real reason for her worry was much more serious than some imagined Faerie girlfriend. She kept replaying in her head the look of guilt on Rowan's face when they first arrived. At the same time, she thought back to how the Kurdian Assassins had kidnapped her the moment she found her way out of the safety of the palace walls.

How had the assassins known that she would be concealed in the cart of dirty laundry? Rowan was the only one who had known about that particular escape route. In fact, he was the one who had placed that idea in her head in the first place. The more she thought about it, the more likely it seemed that Rowan had betrayed her. But why? She was determined to find him, and confront him about it. The only problem was that he seemed to be avoiding her. *How do you find an elf in a forest full of them?* She wondered hopelessly. Not to mention that quite a few of the elves were shape-shifters. Many of the younger elves would change their appearance constantly to show off their abilities, especially when they knew she was near.

Fuming with grouchiness, she rounded a corner – and came face-to face with an old man. At least, at first glance she assumed that he was an old man. He had a short white beard, and his face was creased with lines of age. The strange thing, however, was that he was also clearly an elf. The beard masked his slanted, elvish features, but his pointed ears were clearly visible. Like all elves, he was physically in his prime, with a strong, healthy body and clear skin, which contrasted sharply with his obvious age.

Ellia stopped short in astonishment.

"Hello. Who are you?" She asked curiously. The man looked up, startled.

"Hello, little girl. An answer for an answer. I'm Fenwick. Now, who are you?"

"Ellia."

"Very nice to meet you, Ellia."

"You too..." Ellia paused, dying to ask, but sure that it was a rude question.

"Um... What are you?" She finally blurted out. The old man's eyes narrowed.

"You mean, how is it that I have a beard and a gray head, since I'm a Faerie?" He chuckled. "Everyone asks that question sooner or later, although most are too polite to ask for several years at first." He paused thoughtfully.

"Yes. I will tell you the great secret to my aging. But only for an answer of your own. It's been too long since I've had any news from the outside, and you are clearly an outsider."

He waited for Ellia to nod assent, and then continued.
"The truth is, all elves can grow facial hair. For several hundred years, it has been the fashion to go beardless, and so outsiders have assumed that we can't have beards at all. You assumed the same, I see. Why would we not be able to? I personally don't care for fashion, at my age, and so I have a beard. As for my age, however, *that* is not something the Faerie come by naturally. We grow quickly to adulthood, but there we are frozen, staying youthful and in our prime for the rest of our *very* long lives.
In truth, it is something of a curse, for wisdom only truly comes with old age."

Ellia was confused. "But then, why are you..."
"Old?"
"Yes."

"A very good question." The old/young man smiled, relishing the suspense.
"You see, I was not born an elf. I lived to old age as a human before I was Changed. Because of this, I kept the look of an old man, even though I lost my weakness and frailty. In some ways, this makes me far better than my fellow elves. I have had many more Mortal experiences, and so I am much wiser."

He gave Ellia the cheerful grin of a toothless old man, but with a mouth full of strong white teeth. Ellia found it very strange.

"That's... Nice." She managed to say, unsure of how to respond to this strange person. He seemed to accept the response.

"Indeed it is. Now, your turn. What are *you*? A

half-breed? If so, how did you manage to get in here, without immediate banishment for your tainted blood? Also, please explain your eyes. They are a very unusual color, even for humans, if I'm not mistaken."

He raised his eyebrows curiously. Ellia found it hard to believe that he didn't know the answers already, since most of the elves seemed to know more about her than she knew about herself.

"I'm a half-blood human, and a Starfall." She explained. "I only came here because I was trying to escape from slavery."

The old elf's eyes narrowed. "Slavery? You consider yourself a slave?"

"Ye-s." Ellia was confused. "All Starfalls are slaves, in Allaria, at any rate. They're created, bought, and sold like magical artifacts."

"So you call yourself a slave, because you belong to someone?"

"Yes. Isn't that what slavery is?"

"No. You are wrong. All humans belong to someone. Only the king belongs to himself. It's what we Faerie call a feudal society. No one is completely free, but most of them don't mind." He cocked his head slightly. "You belong to someone rich, yes?"

"Yes. The Queen." Strangely, the admission made Ellia feel somewhat ashamed. She thought she could see where the old man was leading the conversation.

"So, you're saying that despite the fact that I was physically bought and sold, I'm no different from the rest of the King's subjects?"

"No… You are different. But you are not a slave. Slavery is a horrible concept, and it was abolished in its true form long ago, thank Firth. Slaves back when I was born were beaten, abused, starved, and overworked. You, on the other hand, are educated, pampered, protected, and valued. Therefore, what right have you to complain, and call yourself a slave?"

Ellia felt her face flush in shame. He was right, she knew. She had been favored by the queen far more than any commoner of the kingdom could ever have hoped.

"Um, well…" She stammered, longing for a change of subject. She suddenly remembered her original goal, and grabbed for it like a life-line.

"I hate to interrupt such a fascinating topic, but have you seen a dark-haired elf anywhere around here?"

The old faerie laughed. "Dark hair? Here? No. All Faerie with questionable blood are banished. We only keep the pure and proud in our special little forest." His smile was touched with bitterness.

A sudden howl of pain slashed through the forest stillness, causing both of them to jump. Every nerve in Ellia's body tensed. Her immediate impulse was to run to the rescue of whatever was making that horrible noise.

"Right. Bye then." she yelled absently over her shoulder, already sprinting through the trees toward the sound. It was several seconds before she remembered that she was completely weaponless. She didn't stop, though. Blood was pounding hot in her ears, making it difficult for any logical thought to get through. The trees were thinning ahead. At the same time, another howl of pain reached her ears. It was very close now. Desperately, Ellia put on a burst of speed and dashed blindly forward. Her foot caught on yet another root, sending her tumbling out of the trees and into the clearing in a cloud of dirt and leaves.

She sprang to her feet, oblivious to the scratches on her face, knees and elbows. The scene in the clearing almost made her fall back down in shock.

There were a lot of elves in the clearing. Ellia recognized Lord Iberus, Rowan, and several members of the High council. Most of the elves were staring at Ellia in surprise, but she was not looking back at them. Because there was an elf in the clearing who was not staring at her. He was pulling a long, silver sword out of a body on the ground.

Ellia's mind froze in horror. She knew that body. *No.* She stood there, frozen, mouth open in disbelief. The clearing was completely silent. In that silence, the elf with the sword moved on to the other bound figure lying on the ground. Cerris looked up at the sword hovering over him, his eyes dull and emotionless. Ellia suddenly found her voice.

"Stop!" She screamed. The elf stopped. Now every eye was fixed on Ellia. At the sound of her voice, the dullness faded from Cerris's eyes, and they narrowed with suspicion.

Lord Iberus broke the silence.

"Starfall." He smiled thinly. "I did not expect to see you here. I thought you were still recovering from your journey."

"Locked in my room, you mean." She growled. "With your guards posted outside to keep me from escaping."

The High Lord's smile faltered. "I'm sure you were simply misunderstanding the situation." He sounded distinctly uneasy. "My guards were merely protecting you."

"Then what's this?" Ellia demanded, gesturing at the scene in the clearing.

"Do you call this protecting me, too?" her voice shook with shock and anger.

"Why, of course not. This is..." Lord Iberus began smoothly, but Ellia wouldn't let him finish.

"You killed Terrius!" she accused, barely able to

contain her fury. The other elves shifted uncomfortably. Lord Iberus laughed.

"Of course we did, child." He said, his tone condescending. "We caught these wicked human Assassins prowling about near our wood. Naturally, we could not let them live, especially not after they so brutally kidnapped and abused one of our own."

"Oh, really." Ellia's tone was bitingly sarcastic. "You just *had* to kill them, these horrible Assassins, because, for the first time in their careers, they actually *didn't kill anyone?* They're *assassins.* They kill people. They didn't kill me. Why does that deserve death? Not to mention you're killing them after they're tied up, and defenseless. How *Noble.*" She met the eyes of each and every elf in the clearing, one by one pining them with a withering glare. She no longer found their perfect features intimidating, but instead saw them as spineless hypocrites. Many of the elves winced. Rowan's dark skin was flushed white with shame and guilt.

"Ellia..." He began hesitantly. "Are you actually *defending* these murderers?"

"I wouldn't go throwing that word around, if I were you." she replied darkly. "Seeing as you're all dipped in the blood of that man on the ground. And, yes, Rowan. I am defending him. Because he didn't deserve to die on my account. Yes, he was a killer. He was bloodthirsty, and unstable. His brother is also a killer, heartless and cruel. But they were just doing their job. They don't deserve to die because of me. If anyone is to blame, it's whoever sent them."

A tiny muscle twitched at the corner of Lord Iberus's eye. At the same time, a similar wince passed over the face of Rowan, and several other Faerie. It was very fast, one might almost have missed it. But Ellia didn't miss it. She saw it, and she saw the truth. *Not another betrayal.* She turned to look at Cerris, as icy tendrils squirmed down her spine and wrapped around her heart.

"Cerris, who told you that I would be escaping the palace in that laundry cart?" She asked, her voice cold and flat. "How did you know where to find me?"

Before Cerris could answer, Lord Iberus moved like lightning. In one swift motion, he drew his sword, stepped forward, and slashed downwards at Cerris's head.

The silver blur of steel was stopped mid-slash by Ellia's arm. There was a clang of metal on metal as his sword met her slave bracelet and caught on the golden engraving. A single, tiny golden bird snapped off and fell to the ground.

Ellia didn't even look up. Her eyes were locked on Cerris's. He stared up at her without speaking. However, his eyes shifted for a moment, and he glanced over at the person standing behind Ellia. It was enough. She turned slowly around, her heart feeling like a dead, frozen lump in her chest.

Rowan, too, had seen the glance, and he was already protesting as Ellia turned to look at him.

"No, Ellia, look. You don't understand. It isn't what you think. It wasn't me..." He trailed off when he saw the look in her eyes.

"You should work on your lying, Rowan." She said softly, her voice colder than an Ice Creeper's fangs. "There's guilt written all over your face."

Rowan's mouth opened in protest, but no sound came out. Ellia turned away. Lord Iberus still had his sword out. Ellia ignored him and knelt by Cerris. She reached out towards the ropes binding his arms, but was stopped by the touch of cold steel at the nape of her neck.

"Step away, Starfall." He murmured. "If you insist on continuing with this foolishness and making a scene,

I shall be forced to confine you to your room again."

Ellia didn't move. Her emotions had condensed into a cold, hard ball of anger in the pit of her stomach. She would not, *could* not, give up now, and let Iberus win. She was done with being a meek little slave. Instead, she mentally reached out, down, down, inside of herself to the place where she could feel that other presence lurking. She reached out for something, *anything…*

and something came. Far too eagerly.

The clearing grew dark. Shadows swirled through the trees and condensed around Ellia's kneeling form. Iberus stepped back, as did all the other elves. He eyed Ellia nervously, clenching his hand and summoning the wind. Ellia also clenched her hands, which were starting to feel very strange. Something like panic was rising up inside, howling around in her mind, scratching to get out. The darkness was becoming solid around her, now. Wisps of it were whirling around her and connecting to form wings at her back.

She looked down at Cerris. His eyes were open, and the corner of his mouth was twitching with an odd little smirk.

"Witch." He breathed softly, but it wasn't an accusation, and there was no anger in it. Instead, a small, teasing light was dancing in his eyes. That was the last thing she heard, because then the howling panic broke loose.

The world suddenly changed, and all she could see was shadow. Her entire body seemed to be made of nothing but shadow, pain, and terror. Worst of all, she couldn't feel her heart beating. In a panic, she rose up into the air, wings beating. All around her, she could see the dim, shadowy shapes of elves, gaping in astonishment and yelling.

"It's a Darkwing!" She heard an elf gasp, and

others echoed him. "But how did it get in here? What happened to Myth's Vessel?" It was the voice of an oracle, thick with panic and confusion as she gazed up at Ellia.

Suddenly, before Ellia could gather her own confused thoughts, there was a roar, and she was thrown violently backward. Lord Iberus was advancing towards her, and the clearing howled with the force of a rising hurricane. She tried to flap away, but was trapped in a powerful funnel of wind. Lord Iberus's eyes were narrowed.

"You're not going anywhere, Starfall." He hissed. "I don't know what this new power is, but it won't change anything."

Ellia struggled desperately, but the wall of wind on all sides held her immobile in the air. She could feel herself growing bigger. Around the clearing, many of the shadowy elves seemed to be oozing a dark substance from their open mouths. The wisps of oily black vapor was drifting from their bodies and joining onto Ellia's dark wings, making them wider, and stronger. Lord Iberus's face grew tight with concentration.

"Do not be afraid!" He yelled to the gaping Faerie around him. "Your fear only feeds her!" His commanding voice seemed to snap the awestruck elves into awareness. Several of them clapped their hands over their mouths, blocking the oily wisps, while others raised their hands and began to chant. Vines crawled upwards out of the ground, reaching for Ellia's immobilized feet. *...No. Not feet. Claws. I have claws?* Ellia thought stupidly. Her mind was shutting down in panic, and she knew she could not hold out much longer.

Below her, she was dimly aware of Cerris rolling over. He drew himself together and then lashed out violently with his legs. Lord Iberus, being a Faerie, was naturally very fast, but nothing could have prepared him for the lightning quick strike of the Kurdian Assassin. Before he or anyone else in the clearing knew what was happening, Lord Iberus's legs were whipped out from under him, and he toppled to the ground. The wind dissipated. Ellia felt her wings suddenly released from the funnel. Letting out a shriek, she dove downward towards Cerris, her claws closing on the ropes binding his arms to his sides. With a mighty heave, she dragged him into the air.

Cerris was heavy. Far too heavy for her new, small frame to support. She drew more shadows in towards her, making herself bigger. Her wings swept out many feet in either direction, churning the air as she turned and swept out of the clearing. Behind her, Lord Iberus sprang to his feet.

"Stop her!" He yelled. "Close the portals! Don't let her leave the Deep Wood!"

He was suddenly cut off by a shout. Lady Eaglenda stormed into the clearing, backed by a small troop of oracles and soldiers.

"What is going on here?" She demanded, eyes flashing. "Who do you think you are, giving orders like that without my agreement? You're no king."
Iberus turned toward her, distracted. Ellia seized the opportunity to begin flapping away into the trees. Lord Iberus caught the movement. Raising his hands, he sent wind blasting towards her. The darkness in the clearing was swept away, and shafts of sunlight stabbed through to the forest floor. Somehow, Ellia knew that those shafts were deadly to her. She needed to leave. Flapping frantically, she shot deeper into the woods, until not a single ray of sunlight could reach her. Up ahead, she could see a patch of trees which seemed different from the rest of the wood. They were older, and darker. She dove towards them.

Halfway through the grove, the air shimmered,

and their surroundings suddenly changed. They were no longer in Alestromaria, and it was no longer day. *A portal!* Ellia thought distractedly, and then her claws gave out to the strain of carrying Cerris. She dropped him on the top of a moonlit hill, near a grove of slender willows. She severed his ropes with a slash of her claws, then flapped backwards warily, flexing her tired claws and wondering what he would do.

"My thanks, Witch." He said with a soft laugh, and a wave. Then he turned and strode cheerfully off down the hill. Ellia hovered for a moment over the hill, utterly confused. She tried to sort out her thoughts and feelings regarding him, but before she could, the human part of her mind shut down entirely, and the darkness swept in. Without Cerris's calm, amused presence nearby, she was suddenly overcome with pain and panic. She fled through the night, in and out of the trees, leaving little wisps of shadow in her wake. She darted in and out of several Faerie portals, finding herself in different places every time. The panic drove her onward. Finally, she burst through a grove to find herself flapping frantically down a back alleyway in Thalis. The sun was starting to rise, driving back the sheltering darkness. Terrified, Ellia threw herself into the closest patch of darkness she could find – the inside of a garbage can.

Chapter Twenty

In Which King Rudbeck Takes a Trip

* * *

"The garbage bins of Thallis are one of the wonders of the world. You can find all sorts of strange things in the City's trash. I once found my grandmother's shoe. Even stranger, my grandmother was still wearing it."
— Riccardo, a trash picker.

* * *

She was frozen in time, looking down. Everything had faded, over the years, until nothing but her consciousness remained. Nothing but her consciousness, and her power. She hovered there, lacking a body, trapped in the sphere of her own power, which kept her alive but caged her. She hated cages. She looked down on the earth, far below, where once she had reigned. Now, no one even remembered her. What a tragedy. She would have wallowed in self-pity, but she was too busy watching the little drama being played out on the earth.

She was watching a man bury his wife.
The woman was old. Her wrinkled face was peaceful in death. Her husband's face was not peaceful, and it was not old. As he scooped the last shovelful of dirt in place, he raised his agonized face to the heavens. His slanted,

elfin face was hard and chiseled, crisscrossed with scars. Those who had known him before would hardly have recognized him now, with his Faerie build and ancient eyes. But those who had known him before were all either very old or dead now, so it wouldn't have mattered.

"What have you done to me?" He screamed, glaring up at her with a heart full of hate. She didn't reply. She was too busy enjoying his pain.

He looked back down at his wife's grave, and his eyes darkened with the pain of it – that he would never grow old and be laid to rest beside her. He pulled out his sword and looked at it. High in the sky, She was practically wriggling with anticipation.

Oh yes, Gilead. Do it. End your miserable life, so that I don't have to look at you anymore. Don't have to look at the one who destroyed me, prancing around down there on what used to be my kingdom. Please do it.

But the man didn't do it. He ran his thumb down the sharp, glistening edge, then sighed and lowered the weapon. He looked back up, and met her questioning gaze with a defiant one. He laughed grimly, as if he could read her thoughts.

"No. I'm saving this for you, monster. When you come back, I'll drive it through your stinking hide. And this time I'll do it right."

Ellia woke with the lingering image of the man's face in her mind. For some reason, he seemed vaguely familiar. She tried to place his face, but her tired mind refused to work. Instead, it shut itself off, and plunged her back into a dreamless sleep.

It was Captain Gwylan, a city Guardsman, who finally found her – shivering and crying and hiding in a garbage can. He was, naturally, a little surprised, but, being a shrewd man, he realized the importance of his discovery, and recognized the possibility of a promotion.

Luckily for him, the rest of his Patrol were absent, having come across their favorite tavern in one of the city backstreets. The lack of discipline in the city guards was astounding, Gwylan reflected, letting out a snort of scorn as he surveyed the empty street. Especially since many of the patrols consisted of palace guards who had been ordered out onto the streets to search for the missing Starfall. palace guards, were, naturally, a snobbish, lazy lot, and they resented being forced to do manual labor. Hence, the detour to the nearest tavern to drown their woes in cheap wine. Gwylan shook his head in disgust, then went over to peer into the trash can, wondering what he should do. Evidently, a rough week on the streets had been too much for this palace-bred Starfall. She had clearly lost her sanity; Nevertheless, a Starfall was a Starfall, and that meant dangerous. Her eyes were open. He could see them glowing golden up at him from the shadows. The soldier decided to try persuasion.

"Um… Ma'am?" He gave a slight cough to get her attention. Unfortunately, the action caused him to inhale the smell from the garbage can, which set him to coughing still harder. Tragically, the good captain was allergic to dust and mold. He hacked and wheezed for a good few minutes, bringing tears to his eyes. When he finally looked up, the girl was standing beside him, looking concerned. He hadn't heard her move.

"Captain? Are you all right?" she asked hesitantly, as he had another coughing fit. *Great Firth.* Gwylan thought, as he finally straightened up and looked at her. He'd seen Starfalls before, but none as unsettling as this girl was. She was pretty, in a scary, striking sort of way, but her features were far too fine and sharp to be human.

"Um, Miss Starfall, Ma'am." He stammered, unnerved by her steady golden gaze.

"I'm so glad you're safe. The city guard has been searching for you for weeks, with no sign. The King was furious. He's certain that the Elves are behind it."

He glanced at her searchingly, hoping for some inside information which he could flaunt to his peers.

Something dark and bitter flashed in the Starfall's eyes.

"Yes." She said softly. "The Elves are behind it. And the Kurdu. And everyone. Everyone is treacherous." She laughed, a little wildly. "You can't trust anyone."

"Ye-s..." Gwylan agreed uncertainly. She was clearly more than a little crazed.

"Well, Miss, if you'll accompany me to my horse, I'm sure we can have you back safe at the palace very soon, among people you can trust."

"No. You don't understand." She pleaded, desperately. "*No one* is trustworthy. They're all treacherous."

A troubled frown crossed the soldier's face. Ellia knew she was unsettling him, but she couldn't help herself. With all the loneliness and emotion bottled up inside her, she had to let it out in some way. It was either laugh like she was crazy or burst into tears. The captain was clearly struggling for a reply, so Ellia sighed and rescued him.

"Where's your horse?"

They were almost halfway to the palace before Gwylan spoke again.

"Ma'am... Miss, I mean..."

"Call me Ellia." She groaned.

"...Right." He paused. "Well, Ellia. I hate to disagree with you, but what you said before is wrong. People *aren't* all treacherous. Not even close. I'm not. Most of my soldiers aren't. Most of the people I know are good people at heart, and I'm not a bad judge of character."

Ellia was surprised. *He's been silent this whole time because he was thinking about that?*

"You don't know many people then." She retorted. Captain Gwylan frowned. Then his face cleared.

"Oh. I see. That's because you lived in the palace, isn't it? With the Nobles? The Nobles are a slimy bunch, true. But that's because no one can ever get that kind of power without resorting to slimy means. I think you'll find that the common folk are a different breed altogether."

Ellia snorted. The soldier's naive optimism was starting to annoy her. It contrasted too sharply with her present mood, so she decided to ignore him.

A few minutes later, as she waited nervously outside the throne room, she began to wish that she had some of that optimism herself. She was going to be in so much trouble.

The great doors swung open slowly. Ellia held her breath. The room was massive. Gold, tapestries, and statuary littered the walls, but the floor was completely bare except for the massive, gilded chair in the center. Lazing in the center of the chair, with her gigantic hairdo and voluminous dress making it seem much smaller than it was, sat the Queen.

Ellia blinked in surprise. What was the Queen doing in the King's wing of the palace, sitting on his throne? And why were all of the Queen's attendants standing around, where the King's should be? She was so surprised that she almost forgot to give the royal salute. At the sight of Ellia, the Queen's mask of makeup crinkled at the corners in an attempt to smile.

"Ah, my little missing Starfall. What a pleasure it is to see that you aren't dead." She purred. "too bad you didn't return a day earlier. My *Husband,*" she said the word like it left a bad taste in her mouth, "only just rushed off to bang on trees and yell at the Faerie to return you. He should be gone a while." She allowed herself a tiny smirk of pleasure, then leaned forward and locked eyes with Ellia.

"So, child. Tell me where you've been. Who kidnapped you? Why did they free you?"

Ellia gaped in shock. *I'm not in trouble? How am I not in trouble?* Then she remembered the way in which the queen always looked at her, and she realized the truth. *Of course. I'm just a pretty ornament to her. An ornament couldn't possibly even consider running away, so how could I? The thought probably never occurred to her, so she just assumes that I must have been kidnapped.* Ellia decided to leave it that way.

"Your Majesty." She paused, dramatically, guessing that the queen didn't want facts, she wanted drama and entertainment.

"It was the Kurdu." She pronounced ominously. The queen's eyes widened, and the room filled with gasps.

"Oh, how *interesting.*" The queen gave a little shiver of pleasure, confirming Ellia's earlier guess.

"This certainly thickens the plot, doesn't it? The Kurdu! After those assassins in the palace, this is almost enough to start a war!"

Ellia's stomach dropped.

"Your Majesty, wait… there's more." She said hurriedly. Starting a war was definitely not a good idea, and she attempted to undo the damage.

"The Kurdu assassins kidnapped me, but they were working for someone else!" She paused, certain that she had the attention of everyone in the room. A plot twist was always interesting.

"You see… There was a Faerie Lord, who wanted to abduct me, but the other elves would not permit him to. So… He stealthily went to Kurdu, and persuaded two Kurdian assassins to do the job for him. Then, when they had kidnapped me, and were headed back to their own land, the treacherous elf waylaid them. He stole their prize, and then, when they tried to get me back, he killed them."

There was a collective gasp of horror throughout the room. Her audience was riveted now, and Ellia hoped that she had successfully prevented a war through throwing the blame onto the Elves, who were beyond the King's reach.

"But how did you escape?" Gasped one of the attendants, stepping forward. The queen shot her a glare, and she shriveled back into her place. Clearly, Her Majesty wished to be the one asking questions.

"Yes, Starfall, how *did* you escape?"

Ellia considered this. *Tell the truth? Or lie?* She decided to be ambiguous.

"I am a Starfall." She pronounced simply, standing up straight and allowing her eyes to flash golden at the crowd. There was a confused silence. The queen blinked in surprise, obviously realizing how little she knew about this golden eyed girl she had bought. Ellia could see the confusion on her face. She was clearly very curious about Ellia's powers, but she was also unable to ask, without revealing how little she knew about her own possession. That would be very embarrassing, and the slimy vultures of her court would pounce upon such a display of ignorance, seeing it as weakness. Ellia knew all this, and she could see that the queen knew it, too. *Good.* She thought to herself in satisfaction. *Now hopefully she'll leave me alone and stop prying for details.*

The queen swiftly came to a decision, and wiped away the confusion on her face.

"Of course." She agreed knowingly. With a wave of her hand, she dismissed the court. Ellia turned to leave.

"Everyone *except* you, Starfall."

Oh rats. Ellia thought gloomily, as she turned back around. *It seems the queen is smarter than she looks.*

Chapter Twenty-One

In Which the Queen is Smarter Than She Looks

***

"Never underestimate a Queen. If she's smart enough to get there in the first place, she's smart enough to outwit any of you dumb commoners."

— King Circo the First and Last, who ruled for several years after he was dead, thanks to the ingenuity of his queen, who wanted to stay queen, and had no wish for another king to be crowned.

***

"I do not appreciate being lied to, Starfall." The Queen said in icy tones, once the room had emptied. Ellia slowly met her eyes.

"I did not lie to you, your Majesty."

The Queen's eyes narrowed. "Perhaps not, but you did not tell the whole truth, which I count as the same thing."

"How so, your Majesty?" Ellia asked warily. She was keenly aware of the emptiness of the room, and yet knew that the Queen's most trusted guards and supporters were definitely present, but unseen. An intelligent queen would never let herself be caught alone, and unguarded. Nevertheless, the certain presence of others was even worse than being alone with the queen, because it meant that Ellia was outnumbered, with no friends among her audience. "You withheld information as to how you freed yourself. Please expand upon that subject. I find it fascinating." The queen leaned forward onto her elbows. Ellia felt a shiver of apprehension at the ruthless intelligence in her eyes. *I underestimated her,* she realized.

"Well… I had help." She started, wondering how much she had to confess to appease the queen. Her Majesty nodded encouragingly. Feeling slightly shaky, Ellia took a deep breath and began her narrative, carefully avoiding the details of her powers, the Elves' suspicion that she might be Myth, and the fact that she could hear another presence speaking in her head occasionally.

"You see, I was treated as more of a guest in Alestromaria." She explained.
"They wanted me to believe that they had rescued me from kidnapping, so I was allowed some freedom within their city. However, I found out that they were in fact responsible for my kidnapping. I caught them killing my kidnappers, and one of them helped me to escape because I prevented his execution. It wasn't hard, though, because like I said, I was treated as a guest."

She held her breath, praying that the queen didn't see the gaping holes in her explanation. The queen was silent for a moment, and then her eyes suddenly lit up with excitement. Ellia waited anxiously.

"Wait. Am I to understand that you are claiming to have been in the Elvish Capital?" She demanded. Ellia felt her breath leave her in a huge whoosh of relief.

"Yes. Yes I was." She affirmed, glad for the change of subject.

"And you know how it is that they can enter and exit this realm, while no human can find it?" The queen was getting excited now.

"Yes… Through Portals in the Deep Wood." Ellia thought that she could see where this was going. The queen's next words confirmed her suspicions.

"Could you find these portals again?"
Ellia's heart sank, but then a tiny voice whispered in her head. *Why would you care about selling out the elves? Don't you hate them? Didn't they kidnap you?* Ellia realized that, for once, she agreed with that voice. *Yes. They did. And Rowan, of all people, was the one who sold me out to the Kurdians.* Her heart flared with anger.

"Yes, your Majesty." She said out loud. "I think I can."
The queen's eyes were practically glowing with excitement.

"Wonderful." She purred. "From now on, you are excused from your duties in caring for my children. Instead, I want you to report to my Master of spies early tomorrow morning, in the room behind the tapestry of King Circo in my Receiving Hall."
 She sank backwards into the King's throne with a relaxed smile.

"Yes, your Majesty." Ellia saluted. "Is that all?"
The queen didn't answer. She seemed to be lost on her own thoughts, and Ellia cautiously turned to go, hardly daring to hope that the interview was over. She was halfway to the doors when the queen's voice stopped her.

"No… Wait." A slight frown tugged at the queen's carefully sculpted eyebrows, and she sat back up in her chair.

"You still haven't said how you were captured in the first place. How did the Kurdian Assassins find their way into the palace?"

Ellia's heart sank down to the toes of her soft leather boots, and her mind scrambled frantically for an answer. If she admitted to an escape attempt, her life would be ended before she could finish the sentence. Running away was one of the worst crimes a Starfall could commit, and the punishment was always a swift death. Starfall were so powerful that the idea of anything even remotely resembling a rebellion was terrifying to all Starfall owners, and any signs of it were crushed instantly.

"I… I was in the garden." She stammered desperately. "It was after the dinner bell sounded, and… they must have come over the wall while the guards were distracted. One moment I was simply walking towards the dining hall, and the next moment someone hit me on the head." She tried to sound sincere, and found, to her surprise, that the lie came as easily to her lips as truth did. *I've been lying too much.* She thought ruefully. The queen pursed her lips.

"Hmm." She hummed thoughtfully, then glanced around at the empty room. "Can anyone else verify this tale?"

There was a soft rustle in the room, and several dozen people stepped from concealment behind statues, carvings, and the throne itself. Some of them of them were guards, but most of them wore the muted, unassuming colors of servants, but without the servant's standard green armband. Ellia guessed – correctly – that they were spies.

"I can." A soft, slightly scratchy voice sent shivers of horror down Ellia's spine. She knew that voice, and she also knew that it belonged to the one person in the palace who could ruin her with what he knew. She slowly raised her eyes and met the creepy, white ones of Chadwick, the King's master of spies. *Wait. Chadwick is the King's Starfall! Why isn't he with the King?* Clearly,

Chadwick was not what he seemed. Ellia felt cold dread grip her heart. She had counted on Chadwick's absence when she told her tale, because he was the only person in the palace who had been with her in the gardens, and he knew that she hadn't stayed there until the dinner bell. She looked him in the eyes, and her mind calmed with a quiet acceptance of her imminent death. Chadwick stepped forward, knelt, and saluted the queen.

"Your majesty, I was in the gardens with Ellia. She was with me until the dinner bell sounded, when she left to go to dinner. I stayed behind for a short while before following her. However, when I reached the spot where she should have been, she was nowhere to be found. There was, however, several broken branches, and some soft, black fabric caught on a bush. Ellia was not wearing black." He looked around to make sure that everyone understood the significance of this statement, then stepped back into line with the rest of Her Majesty's spies. Ellia stared at him with uncomprehending shock. *Wait, I'm not going to die? He didn't give me away. Why did he lie for me?* She stood staring at him for several seconds, but he refused to meet her eyes. The queen looked at them both for a moment, then sighed and waved her hand dismissively.

"Very well. That will be all. You are excused. Someone see her out and find her a new room in my wing of the palace. Oh, and someone open those doors and let back in those simpering idiots waiting outside." She adjusted the many flounces of her voluminous skirt and fixed her eyes regally above Ellia's head as the great doors swung open.

Someone caught hold of Ellia's arm as she made her way out of the room. She did not even have to look to know who it was.

"Why did you do that?" She demanded once they

were past the crowd of nobles surging back into the throne room.

"Hush." Chadwick replied, increasing his pace. "Not here."

Chapter Twenty-Two

Ellia Finds a Truth

***

"Lying is a bad practice. It keeps growing and growing until eventually someone ends up dead."
—Demitrius Scallop, the highwayman, who failed to take his own advice and is now dead.

***

Chadwick didn't speak until they had left the castle, and were walking in their usual meeting place – an untended garden full of concealing trees and shrubs.

"You were going to ask me something. What was it?" He finally asked, sitting down on a worn bench and motioning for her to do likewise.

"Why did you lie for me, in the great hall?" She demanded, too shaken to sit.

"You knew that I left the gardens much earlier in the day. Why did you pretend that I didn't?"

Chadwick looked mildly surprised.
"You expected me to betray you, and condemn you to certain death? What kind of a friend would that make me?" He smiled teasingly, but Ellia just looked at him, uncomprehending.

"You're a spy for the queen, aren't you?" she stammered, confused.

"Yes. But what does that have to do with anything?" Chadwick seemed equally confused himself, until his eyes suddenly lit up with understanding, and he sighed.

"Oh, Ellia. I'd forgotten how mistrustful you are. You never thought of me as a friend, did you?"

"Of course not. I don't have friends." Ellia found herself saying, and even as she said it she realized how sad it must sound. Chadwick winced.

"So you expected me to betray you?"

"Yes. It's the only logical thing to do. What could you possibly gain by lying to the queen on my behalf?" She looked at him searchingly, longing for him to provide some logical answer that might clear up her confused emotions. He looked pained.

"Not everything is about gain, Ellia. Or logic, for that matter. I would never betray you for the same reason, I think, that you wouldn't betray me. Because it would be wrong. I stood up for you because it was the right thing to do."

He met her eyes and she read the truth there. Suddenly, those strange, white eyes with the tiny, black, bug-like pupils seemed to her to be the kindest eyes in the world. She remembered the words of Captain Gwylan earlier that morning. *People aren't all treacherous. Not even close.*

Somewhere deep inside her, a tiny crack formed in the hard, cold ice of her heart. She sat down hard with the shock of it. Chadwick gently put his arm around her, and she could not stop the tears from spilling. He was silent for a long time, and there was no sound except for the sound of her hiccuping sobs, and the wind rustling in the trees. Eventually, her tears dried up, and he handed her a handkerchief.

"Ellia," He said gently, a frown furrowing his brow. "How many people have betrayed you?"

She stopped sniffling to think for a moment.

"Everyone." She said at last. "Or at least, everyone to whom I've given the chance… Except Myrgen and Myria." She realized, remembering how the twins had kept their mouths shut about her transformation into a Griffon. Chadwick sighed, looking very old and weary.

"I thought as much. Your eyes have that look in them. Like you've buried your emotions because they hurt too much. You weren't always this way, were you?" Ellia shook her head.

"No. Back when I was a slave of Baron Opulus, I was… foolish. I trusted unwisely, and it got me into a mess of trouble."

"Hmm." Chadwick hummed thoughtfully, and his fingers patted her shoulder absently.

"Do you want to talk about it?" He asked at last. Ellia did. There was nothing she wanted more than to unburden her loneliness onto him, and get rid of the horrible, frozen ache in her chest. But her caution held her tongue-tied. *Don't trust him. How do you know he isn't going to betray you?* She sat there, silent and frozen, until Chadwick broke the silence.

"You're wondering if you can trust me, aren't you?"
She nodded.
"Very well." He was silent for a moment. "Do you know how Starfalls are made?" He asked at last. The question startled her.

"No. No one does. It's a carefully guarded secret."

"Yes. It is. I'm going to tell you something that no one else knows, and that I could be killed for knowing. Do you understand?"
Ellia started to shake her head, but then stopped as she saw what he meant.

"You mean that you're going to give me a weapon that I could use to kill you, to prove that you trust me?"

"Yes." Chadwick said simply. "And to prove that you can trust me."

Ellia was stunned. Chadwick began speaking softly, easily, as if he were merely sharing the time of day.

"The secret of Starfall magic is really quite simple, and it's all in the name." He began. "All magic that we know of comes either from the stars, or from the fires of molten rock deep beneath the ground. The Lava Magic in the earth cannot be harnessed by living things, although if it is used to smelt iron, the metal produced has magical properties. Nevertheless, any human who touches the lava will simply die. The magic of the stars is similar, but with one crucial difference. When a star falls to earth, it forms a pool of magic. Like the earth-fires, this magic will kill any grown human who touches it. However, long ago it was discovered that if a child is very young, it does not always die. Instead, sometimes, it is *changed.* It absorbs the magic of the star, and is able to wield that magic. Thus the Starfall Black Market was formed, with smugglers stealing babes and throwing them into stars, then selling them as powerful servants to the rich. This is the closely guarded secret. Not even the king knows it, or he would declare all the fallen stars to be his property."

He looked into her eyes, and once again she knew that he was telling the truth.

"Yes." her eyes widened with understanding. "And the Starfall's powers are connected to the legend of the star from which they came. Or the constellation."

Chadwick frowned.

"How do you know that?"

"The Faerie told me."

"Interesting." Chadwick chewed his lip, thinking,

then raised his eyebrows.

"So does this mean you trust me?"

"Yes." Ellia said, and the answer surprised her, as she realized that she *did* trust him. Completely. It was a strange new feeling.

The ice around her heart shattered, and suddenly she found herself pouring out her story. For the first time, she didn't leave anything out. She felt that, after revealing his own secrets to her, Chadwick deserved to know the truth. In reality, though, she told him everything because it hurt to keep it all inside for so long. As she talked, she felt as though she were slowly spilling light into the dark emptiness inside.

Chadwick was silent for a long time. When he finally spoke, his voice was grave.

"It seems to me that you're wrapped up in something far bigger than you. There is something going on here that we don't understand. Something dangerous."

"My thoughts exactly." Ellia sighed. "And I don't know what to do."

"We need to find out more." Chadwick decided. "And, above all, we need to keep you safe. This Lord Iberus, is he likely to come after you?"

"Probably." Ellia admitted. "He's very determined. And he's used to getting his way."

"Then we need to keep you safe, and away from trees." Chadwick eased himself to his feet. "Come. I think it's time we find you your new quarters. I know the perfect place."

The tower was very tall, and made of solid stone. It formed the corner of the queen's wing of the palace, overlooking a courtyard where the palace guards marched and drilled. Ellia sat in her room at the top of it, looking out to where the palace walls met the city, and the view disappeared in a sea of sun-baked tiles. She was glad for the safety of the solid walls, but she found herself missing the twins. Without their hectic, wild company, she felt rather lonely and bored. She sighed, and poked around her new room for a bit. The room had very little in it, other than a wardrobe for her clothes, and a bed, so she quickly tired of that. With nothing better to do, she finally curled up on the bed and gave in to the sleep that she'd been putting off for so long... Sleep came. And so did the nightmares.

The town was warm and dusty. The sun had set, but the heat of the day still seeped from the stones. It was the time of day when the townsfolk would usually take naps on their porches, or chat leisurely with their neighbors. They were doing neither. Instead, they were gathered in the square, throwing rocks at a young woman.

Ordinarily, the people of this particular town were quiet and pleasant. However, this particular woman was an outsider, and she had rudely refused marriage to the baron of the town, so they had no objection to stoning her. It was the baron himself who had, in a rage, ordered her execution.

The creature looking down on this scene was only mildly interested in the events. However, just as she was about to turn her eyes elsewhere, she saw someone at the town gate, and she was instantly riveted. An elf was walking up the street, nonchalantly swinging a huge sword. He was tall and weather-beaten, with scars all over his face and arms. He noticed the crowd in the square, and turned in the opposite direction. He was just passing through, and by this time he had learned to avoid large groups of humans.

Then the woman screamed.

The Faerie froze, then turned and looked hard at

the crowd in the square. When he realized what they were doing, he instantly sprang forward and sprinted into the square, yelling. The quiet, pleasant townsfolk were, naturally, quite shocked by the sight of a furious, scar-covered elf bearing down on them. The sight of his large, wickedly sharp and rune-scrawled sword waving in their faces was enough to make them pay attention. They stopped throwing rocks, and turned to face him. He halted, and stared at them with dark, dangerous eyes.

"What," He asked softly. "Is the meaning of this idiocy?"

The townsfolk shuffled their feet, and no one spoke. When he didn't get an answer, the elf advanced towards them, flicking the edge of his sword at anyone who didn't immediately get out of his way. He reached the woman, and, kneeling down, gently helped her to her feet. They gazed into each others eyes for a long moment, then conversed together in tones so quiet that the creature in the sky, even with her incredibly sharp ears, could not hear what they were saying. The elf put an arm around her shoulder, then turned to face the crowd.

"If any of you so much as think about hurting this woman again, I will personally chop off your head." He said calmly.

Followed by the shocked crowd and the awed woman, he then marched to the baron's manor and hammered on the door. A moment later, the angry, red face of the owner poked out of the doorway. At the sight of the woman he had ordered killed still alive, his complexion changed from red to purple.

"What is the meaning of this?" He roared. "Didn't I tell you useless peons to kill her? Must I do everything myself?" He stepped out into the street, and the Faerie chopped off his head.

For a moment, the town was utterly silent, as everyone failed to grasp what had just happened. Then the silence dissolved into a chorus of shocked gasps, cries of outrage, and the sound of several women fainting.

"You killed our Baron!" One of the men finally gained his courage enough to yelp. The faerie glanced at him coolly.

"Yes." He agreed. "But I have given you a new Baroness. See, here she is." He gestured at the woman who they had been stoning a few minutes prior. "If any of you do not accept her, please step forward."

The townspeople were wise enough to stay where they were, so the elf smirked, took the new baroness's arm, stepped over the body, and led her into her new house. The watcher in the sky turned away, snorting in disgust at the romance sparking between the pair. Secretly, though, she was pleased. In all his efforts to kill monsters, Gilead was gradually becoming a monster himself. Her influence was growing on him, causing him to be more ruthless and violent. If she had had a face to smile with, she would have smiled.

Just wait, little Hero. Sooner or later, one of us will win this fight, and it won't be you.

Ellia sat up fast. Too fast. She hadn't noticed the shelf over her bed when she'd fallen asleep, but now she noticed it with the full force of her forehead.

"Ow." She groaned, cradling her bruised head. With some astonishment, she realized that the pillow was black and charred where her head had been. *What is wrong with me?* She wondered, remembering her strange dream. The face of the scarred elf hovered in the front of her mind, nudging at her memory. There was something very familiar about him, but her mind was too preoccupied with pain to think about it.

The soldier's training grounds outside were eerily quiet. All throughout the palace, not a sound could be heard. In a panic. Ellia thought for a moment that her keen elvish hearing had deserted her – until she realized that it was the middle of the night.
I really need to start sleeping during normal hours. She thought. But her mind was wide awake now, and the cool night outside was beckoning, so she climbed out the window.

The stones were rough and cool under her fingers as she climbed down the outside of the tower, towards the training grounds below. *This tower isn't as safe as Chadwick thought.* She reflected as she scooted along a ledge and lowered herself carefully onto the roof of what appeared to be the stables. *If I can get down this easily, then any elf could climb up.* The roof of the stable slanted upward to another roof, and from there it was only a small jump across to the roof of the dining hall. Ellia tripped on a small, loose panel, and she quickly recognized it as the one through which the Assassins had descended into the palace so long ago. Doubtless it was under guard, but she hopped down anyway.

The guards were there, but they were tired, and they were looking down, not up. Ellia almost laughed at the utter lack of security in the palace. *Won't they ever learn?* She wondered, as she climbed down a tapestry hanging from the ceiling and jumped onto a table. Being a loud, clumsy race, the Dalians did not seem to realize that both the Kurdu and the Faerie were far more silent than they were, and so could easily slip past the king's halfhearted attempts at guarding the palace. She briefly wondered if she should suggest it to the king. He needed to change the palace guard. She slipped out through the doors of the banquet hall, and none of the guards so much as turned their heads. *What a bunch of slobs*. Ellia thought, slightly irritated. If it wasn't for the constant vigilance of the city guards, out on the palace walls and patrolling the streets, the palace would have been overrun with invaders long ago. The Dalian King was not very friendly, and most of the surrounding countries hated him. She strolled down the palace hallways, reflecting on all the ways that assassins could slip past King Rudbeck's imperfect guard system.

She began to feel nervous. *I shouldn't go for walks at night.* She thought, feeling slightly panicky. *It's quiet enough for me to hear my thoughts, and my thoughts are never something I want to hear in a dark place, by myself.* She stopped walking suddenly, because her thoughts were no longer the only things she could hear. She was standing outside a large, dark library. The door was open, and a small fire in the fireplace was casting strange shadows on the walls. A soft, muttering voice floated from behind the bookshelves to Ellia's ears. She recognized it, and quickly stepped out of the doorway. Somewhere in the room, Jasper was talking to someone, or perhaps to himself, since there was no answering voice.

Ellia was about to sneak closer and eavesdrop, when something stirred in the room, and she froze. It was not so much a *thing,* as it was a presence. The light moved oddly on the walls, and the entire room seemed to *breath* in a sinister way. Ellia felt a jolt of recognition shoot down her spine, and something dark seemed to be tugging at the inside of her rib cage, trying to get out.

Ellia did not like books. Reading was a chore she generally avoided. She did not like Jasper, either. Most especially, though, she did not like the dark presence rearing it's ugly head inside of her, and in the room. She turned and fled, heart pounding in fear.

Chapter Twenty-Three

The Sun's First Light

"The worship of Firth, bringer of Life, is carried out in many ways across the world. Most people pray first thing in the morning, thanking Him for each new day. However, some are slightly more fanatical. One small cult in Kurdu jump off tall ledges every day, thanking Firth for catching them. Strangely enough, some of them actually survive."
— High Philosopher Stephanio.

It was not until she passed the fourth group of sentries, near the kitchens, that Ellia began to suspect that something was wrong. Not a single sentry had so much as blinked when she walked past. Most of them were tired, but some were wide awake, and should have noticed her slight form slipping through the shadows. *They can't be that blind.* Ellia thought uneasily, as she skirted yet another group of guards. She looked down at herself, and could not restrain a gasp. The guard's heads immediately snapped up, and they peered into the shadows suspiciously. Ellia held perfectly still, her heart pounding with terror. Her body was coated in shadow. As she lingered in the darkness, little wisps of the stuff were clinging to her arms and swirling around her lovingly, making her blend in with the shadows far better than she should have. Wisps of the terror that she had felt as a Darkwing also clung to her. She edged carefully along the wall until she was out of sight of the guards. As soon as she was out of sight, she scrubbed desperately at her arms, trying to get rid of the lingering shadows. *How is it still sticking to me?* She thought frantically. *Am I going to turn into a Darkwing permanently?* Spooked, she raced through the corridors, searching for a way out. She finally found a courtyard, climbed the wall, and made her way back onto the palace roofs.

Morning found Ellia huddled on the peak of the highest roof in the palace, shrouded in darkness, like a sad gargoyle. She stayed that way for a long time, until the edge of the sun finally broke the horizon. As soon as she saw it, she stood up straight and spread her arms wide, waiting, hoping, praying. The first ray of sunlight washed over her, bathing her in warmth and peace. All lingering shreds of the fear and darkness shrank away from the light, vanishing like dew in the desert.

Ellia sighed in relief and stretched out her tired, sore muscles. Somehow, she knew that the danger was past. *I am never, ever, going to turn into a Darkwing again.* She silently swore. *That was horrible.*

Ellia didn't know it, but the rising sun had set her ordinarily brown hair on fire with colors, and her entire body was glowing in the golden light, contrasting sharply with the gray slate of the roof under her feet. Down in the courtyards and gardens of the palace, where everything was still blanketed in dull, gray light, early risers stared in astonishment at the fiery, golden girl standing on the highest peak of the palace. No ordinary Dalian could have balanced with such poise on such a sharp peak, and so rumors immediately began circulating. People began to whisper that the Queen's Starfall could fly, while others claimed that she was so fanatically devout that she risked death every day to worship Firth with the rising of the sun. Still others maintained that she was simply crazy, and had a death wish. All of these rumors Chadwick laughingly narrated as they had breakfast together in his room. Because of his gift, he could listen in on almost all conversations in the palace, as long as they were about the subject that he himself was thinking about.

"They don't think you're human." He said, his amusement fading. "They didn't think so before, and now they're sure of it. You should be more careful about demonstrating your agility in public, or they'll start cursing you for a Faerie Devil."
Ellia nodded seriously.

"I think they might have good reason to fear me, though, Chadwick." She confided. "*I'm* even afraid of me. I don't know what's happening." And she told him about her dream, the charred pillow, and the lingering wisps of darkness. He frowned.

"We need more information. I'll do some reading on Darkwings in the library today, while you're speaking with Her Majesty's master of spies. I'll also see if I can find out anything about this scarred elf… Gilead, you said?"

Ellia nodded, and thanked him before hurrying off to the Queen's wing of the palace.

The master of spies was a tall, spidery man with a face like a bat. He had large ears, a flat, wrinkled nose, and very pale eyes. Ellia felt very uncomfortable every time those moist, disturbing eyes landed on her, which was very often, since she was sitting in a small, bare room with him directly across from her. He proved to be a very sharp and inquisitive man, and asked many questions which Ellia would rather not have answered. The more she told this man about the Elves and their secret doorways, the worse she felt. Guilt gnawed at her stomach, even though she told herself that the Faerie had it coming. *They betrayed me, didn't they?* But it didn't make her feel any better. To her relief, she was unable to give the man any helpful information on the exact location of the Elvish Portal in Thalis, since all she knew was that it was in an alley near a garbage can. That could have described thousands of places in the city, so the man finally sent her away in disgust.

Ellia wandered the palace in a daze. Her thoughts were warring with each other, shouting accusations and denials inside her head.

She was so busy fighting with her guilt that she didn't notice the familiar figure stepping out of a doorway in front of her. When she finally did notice him, she didn't recognize him, and glanced up in annoyance to see who was blocking her path. By then, it was too late.

"Hey." He said softly, and it was all he needed to say, because his silver eyes did the rest.

The effect was immediate. All her caution was swept away in an instant, and she smiled.

"Hi." She replied, somewhat breathless with happiness. The force of his eyes was ten times stronger this time, and his brows were creased with concentration. When he saw the blissful smile on her face, he relaxed somewhat, and laughed softly, running a hand through his hair.

"It's nice to see you, Ellia. I confess, I was a little worried, because of how you treated me last time, but we're going to get along fine this time, won't we?"

"Yes." Ellia agreed eagerly. Then she frowned, trying to remember how she'd treated him last time. The memory made her cringe. How could she have been so rude and insulting to someone she liked so much?

"Sorry..." She offered, a little helplessly. Jasper didn't seem angry. Instead, he smiled.

"Forget about that, Sweetie. I'm just glad you're back. Someone said you were kidnapped?"

"Yes. By Kurdians, and then Elves. But I escaped, and came back here accidentally." Her narration clearly didn't make a lot of sense to Jasper, but he didn't seem to care enough to pursue the subject.

"Listen, Ellia. Someone said you can fly. Is that true?" He asked nonchalantly, but his eyes flashed with urgent interest.

"No-" Ellia began, but then stopped as her memory bombarded her with images of flight. Fiery wings, golden wings, shadow wings, elegant, feathered wings and claws, Sweeping Cerris up into the air, and hurtling through the trees…

"Ye-es." She said slowly, trying to concentrate through the foggy headache Jasper's gaze was giving her. "But only when I have wings. Which I don't most of the time."

"Really?" Jasper looked intrigued. "Is that your only power?"

This was a harder question, and Ellia frowned.

"No." Jasper's eyes begged her to go on, but something was telling her it was a bad idea. She hesitated, and he began to grow impatient.

"Come on, Ellia. You can tell me." He pleaded, taking her hand. "What else can you do? I need to know. It would make me happy. Don't you want to make me happy?" She did, and her caution shrank away under the onslaught of his gaze. Luckily for her, however, the strength of the power he was pouring over her was so great that it interfered with her ability to speak coherently.

"I can also dream things which are true, but maybe not, but also horrible, and I think they already happened, but to someone else, who isn't a someone because she's a star in the sky." Ellia explained, staring dreamily up at him. Jasper cocked his head.

"Um, *What*?" He demanded.

"Yes. And also I can maybe turn into something sort of but I don't know what. It's always different except it doesn't always work and also I'm like a dragon, maybe. Or the elves think so at least. And once I spat ice. Also I sucked in darkness and flew and then I was very scared, and so was everyone else."

Jasper looked as if his eyebrows were about to throw a seizure. His face twitched, and his stare grew more piercing.

"Sorry, what? Are you saying that you don't know what your powers are?" This seemed to be the most logical solution he could come up with, from Ellia's rambling.

"Sort of." Ellia winced slightly, as the headache grew stronger. It was almost too much to bear. "But mostly I just can't control them."

She thought about telling him about the darkness, nightmares, and the evil, angry presence inside her, but decided not to, because it might upset him. *I like him and want him to be happy. Telling him the truth would not make him happy. He would just be scared.* So she let him think what he wanted. Jasper's eyes were sparkling with interest and excitement.

"So you can't control them at all? They just happen randomly?"
Ellia didn't bother answering, and he took her silence as a yes. He pressed his lips together in thought. His hand absently moved up to her wrist, and he rubbed his thumb against her cuff, eyes sparking with a sudden idea.

"Listen, Sweetheart." He said, his face taking on a crafty look. "I know exactly what your problem is.

You've never looked into the Mirror of Souls."

Ellia blinked. "The mirror of what?"

"Souls." Jasper looked knowledgeable. "It's an ancient mirror in a cave, and it's magical. All Starfalls go there to truly master their powers. I couldn't use my powers until I went there."

Ellia struggled to comprehend this, and the fog in her mind lifted somewhat.

"But how does a mirror help?" She asked. She was no longer just eager to learn this because of her liking for Jasper. This time, she actually wanted to know. Her interest was kindled.

"You just look into it?"

Jasper nodded earnestly. "Yes, and then it shows you who you truly are inside. For ordinary mortals, in merely shows them their own shallow souls, but for us Starfall, it shows us the true nature of our powers." His eyes glimmered oddly, and the way in which he was speaking sounded strange. Ellia thought that it reminded her of someone else, but in her foggy state she couldn't remember who.

"That's it?" She asked incredulously. Jasper chewed his lip thoughtfully, then shook his head.

"No. There's one other thing. The final challenge. When you look into this mirror, you release the Monster in the Mirror. This monster takes the shape of your own power, and then you have to fight it. If you succeed, then you master your power. If you don't, well..."

Chapter Twenty-Four

The Mirror of Souls

***

"The worst part about caves is the darkness. And the smell. And the creepy crawly things that live there. Actually, everything about caves is equally bad. Just steer clear of them."
— Glaed Stinger, author of *a Guide to Allaria and How to Stay Alive in it.*

***

That night, the fog finally cleared from Ellia's mind, but for some reason she was still excited. One part of her mind woke up, and began chanting *This is a bad idea. This is a bad idea.* But Ellia ignored it. Her mind was on fire with curiosity. *Could this really be true?* Of course, she didn't trust Jasper, but still she could not give up this new idea. If it were true, and there really was a mirror, and a monster, would it solve her problems? Maybe. She was scared of the darkness inside her, but what she really hated the most was the uncertainty. She didn't know what was happening, so she was constantly scared and confused. If this mirror were real, then at least she would know. She would know everything about herself, and be able to control it. Maybe. But it was worth a shot, wasn't it? She knew she was being rash, but she also knew that if she didn't take the chance, she would go mad wondering what might have happened.

In the end, she couldn't take it anymore. She got up, put on her traveling clothes, and climbed out the window.

Jasper was waiting for her. Roy and Burke were with him, both trying to suppress grins. Ellia paused uncertainly at the edge of the courtyard, but Jasper caught her eye and beckoned her forward. Her uncertainties vanished.

When she reached them, Jasper handed her a dagger.

"You'll need this. For the Monster." He said seriously. Ellia took it and slid it into her sash around her waist. Roy sniggered.

"Oh how romantic. Why don't you just slay the monster *for* your girlfriend, Jasper? Isn't that how it's usually done?"

Jasper glared at him. "You know I can't do that, Roy. You know the rules. She has to face it herself."
Roy gasped dramatically. "Oh, Of course. The rules. I'd forgotten about that."

Burke cleared his throat and scratched his head. "Um, where are we going, again?"

"To the Mirror of Souls, of course." Jasper winked exaggeratedly at Burke, but Ellia didn't catch it. The headache was back, and she was too busy admiring Jasper's handsome profile. Burke frowned.

"But isn't that like a children's story or something? I heard it was a myth."
Jasper sighed. "No. It's not a children's story. It's where we all went to gain control over our powers, remember? Now we're taking Ellia there because she can't control her powers and doesn't know what they are."
Burke frowned for a long time, then his brow cleared.

"Ohhh! *That* mirror. Where is it again?"

"In that old cave up on the mountain behind the city. The one with the statues, remember? But you have to go deep, deep, into it until you find the mirror at the very bottom of the mountain, way past where everyone else dares to go, because it's too dark." Jasper's sarcasm was lost on Ellia's achy head, and somewhat lost on Burke as well.

"Oh." He said. Jasper was impatient.

"Let's go. It will take us all day just to get there." As she was being pulled along toward the gate by Jasper, Ellia's tired mind suddenly seized on this last thought.

"Wait..." She stopped. "What about the Queen? And your master, the King? How will we get out of the palace, anyway?"

Jasper smirked. "The King is gone, and I had a little talk with the Queen. She *Likes* me, you know. Everyone does." Roy chuckled darkly, which caused Jasper's smirk to widen. "So anyway, I told her you were a little shaky after your kidnapping, and it had messed up your ability to do magic, so we needed to take you on a little retreat for your nerves. She won't mind if we're gone a couple of days."

"Oh, okay then." Ellia agreed, slightly confused. She allowed Roy, Burke and Jasper to lead her away. As they walked, Burke flicked his hand, and all the torches dimmed. Any guards or servants they came across instantly melted under Jasper's warm smile. No one stopped them.

Long before they reached the cave, the scenery began to take a dark turn. Many years ago, hundreds of monks, myth-seekers, and philosophers had gathered to the area, and a small town had grown up around the mouth of the cave. However, those monks and philosophers had never found anything, and eventually they all died out, leaving a skeletal graveyard of worn marble in their place. The very air seemed to smell of lost hope and dead dreams. They trekked over the cobbled path, passing more white marble chapels and graveyards than Ellia could count. All of them were ornately carved and crumbling.

At first, Ellia thought that the place was inhabited, but then she realized that the people she thought she saw were in fact statues. Roy, for some reason, had decided to animate every statue they passed, and they were soon surrounded by a silent crowd of stone men and beasts. It was with this disturbing procession in tow that they finally reached the cave.

It was a tall, dark slot in the side of a cliff face, flanked by two gigantic statues of what appeared to be Elvish oracles, both wearing hoods and holding, for some reason, animals. The one on the right was cradling a raven, while the one on the left held a baby pig at arm's length. Ellia paused between them, feeling very small. Roy, Burke, and Jasper were talking about something, making jokes about the strange statues, but she didn't hear them. Her whole attention was captured by the steep descent in front of her, where the cave stretched downwards into impenetrable darkness, like the throat of a gigantic snake.

Jasper came to stand behind her.

"There's your path, Ellia." He said, handing her a torch. "All the way down, until you hit the bottom… If there is a bottom. Then you'll find the mirror."
Ellia took a step forward, then stopped. The darkness had cleared her head somewhat, and she backed up slowly.

"This is a bad idea." She turned to leave, but Jasper stopped her, putting his hands on her shoulders.

"No, no. It's not." He took her head in his hands, and stared deep into her eyes.

"Listen to me, Love. This is the only way. I wish it were easier, I wish I could go with you, but I can't. You have to do this on your own."

Ellia drew a shaky breath.

"Okaaay…"

Jasper smiled.

"Great. Just promise me you'll be careful, all right? Come back safe. I couldn't bear to lose you." Something false flashed in his eyes, and Ellia frowned, suddenly uncertain. He saw the look. Before she could pull away, he leaned forward and kissed her. Everything was suddenly all right again. Worries forgotten, Ellia sighed, leaned her face against his palm, and smiled up at him. He smiled back, his silver eyes gleaming with triumph. Behind them, Roy gagged.

"Just get on with it already!" He pleaded. Both Ellia and Jasper turned and glared at him. Then Jasper sighed reluctantly.

"Roy's right, Ellia. It's time to go. We'll wait out here until you're back."

So Ellia went. One foot in front of the other, she descended cautiously into the darkness, with nothing but a torch and a dagger. The sunlight quickly faded, leaving nothing but the dim circle of her torch as she walked deeper. Behind her, there was a sudden noise, like a mountain sneezing.

Ellia whirled. The two gigantic oracles had awoken, and were busy wedging themselves into the mouth of the cave. Behind them, hundreds of Roy's smaller army of statues were climbing over each other, using arms, legs, and bodies to block the entrance. Ellia's headache cleared, and she sprinted back, but it was too late. Where once there had been a high, vaulted doorway, there was now nothing but a woven wall of intertwined stone bodies. They were once again frozen and lifeless. Not even a hint of sunlight pierced the barrier.

Ellia screamed. She threw herself against the wall, howling curses and threats through the barricade, using every foul and nasty bit of street slang she had ever heard to insult the Starfalls outside. Through the stone, she could hear the sound of raucous laughter.

"Serves you right, idiot!" Jasper sneered. "You're not even really one of us. You're a fraud, a fake! You can't even use your powers! And yet everyone seems to think you're so *special.*" Even through the stone, Ellia could clearly hear the bitter jealousy in his voice.

"They all ogle and adore you like you're really something. Well, you're not. And now, with you out of the way, maybe they'll finally realize that the *truly* powerful one is me."

Ellia said something very dirty, and Roy howled with laughter.

"Oooh! The girl's got a real sharp tongue on her, at any rate! That's almost enough to make me want to let her out!"
Jasper growled at him.

"Shut up, Roy. Ellia, I was planning to just leave you trapped for a few days, to teach you a lesson, but since you're being so nasty, I've decided to just let you rot in there. Come on, guys. Let's leave. I don't want to listen to her anymore."

But Ellia had stopped swearing. She sat with her back pressed against the stone, listening to the sound of the boys' voices fade, and blinking hard to keep back the sudden flood of hopeless tears. *I shouldn't have let my temper get away from me.* She thought gloomily. *I should have swallowed my pride and convinced them to let me out. But I didn't, and now I'm stuck. So what am I going to do about it?* She sat there for a while, and then got up. She was still miserable, but her hopelessness had faded into cold, hard determination. After some thought, she carefully felt her way along the barricade, making sure that there were no loose statues or holes she might be able to squeeze through. There weren't. Roy had done his job well, and the wall of statues was as solid as the rest of the cave walls. With a sigh, she finally admitted that it was pointless. Her only hope now lay in finding another way out. Hefting her torch, she set off deeper into the cave.

At first, it was only the darkness that worried her. It seemed to push in on all sides, held at bay only by the feeble, unsteady light of her torch. The walls were smooth, with not even the smallest cracks or crevices. The tunnel continued to descend for what seemed like hours. Not once was there a branch or side tunnel that might have led to a way out. The floor was dusty, and littered with all sorts of nasty things – Bat droppings, dead bugs, the ancient, fur-covered skeleton of a mouse, and broken stalactites from the ceiling. As she progressed, however, the utter stillness began to worry her more than the dark.

The air was very stale. Except for her passing, there was no breeze, and Ellia felt as though she were breathing air that had never before been breathed since the dawn of the world. This was worrying because there should have been *something*. An occasional drip of water, an echo, or a light breath of wind, would indicate that, somewhere, there was an opening to the outside world. However, there was nothing. Even the small carcasses of cave dwellers were beginning to dwindle, giving place to nothing but dust and silence. Eventually, even the dust disappeared, leaving only the empty tunnel of rock, the silence, and Ellia.

It was then, when she was miles under the earth, so deep that even the dust no longer collected on the ground, that Ellia's torch burned out.

She froze, suddenly feeling the weight of the darkness crush down on her. It was very, very cold, and she couldn't even tell if her eyes were open or closed. Slowly, cautiously, she edged sideways, until her palm was pressed against one wall. She breathed deeply, pushing the panic away. *Think, Ellia.* She silently encouraged herself. *You can't give up, and you can't go back. That leaves forward. With one hand on the wall, you should be able to tell if there are any side passages. And if the tunnel branches, the sound of your feet will change, and you'll know.* With that thought to bolster her courage, Ellia continued on, straining all her senses except her eyes.

Time became meaningless. Ellia was about to give up, or simply sit down and cry, when suddenly the wall under her hand disappeared altogether. The sound of her footsteps echoed, and she knew that she had entered a very large, open space. Ellia suddenly stopped, and blinked her eyes several times. She could see something. At what she assumed was the far end of the chamber, two very faint points of light shone.

With a cry of relief, Ellia stumbled forward, heedless of the uneven, invisible floor under her. Light meant that there must be a tunnel – two tunnels – and they must lead to the outside. She was only about halfway across what she thought was the length of the chamber, when she ran into a wall.

She stumbled back, rubbing her eyes and staring. When she rubbed her fist across one eye, one of the lights disappeared. *Oh.* Her heart plummeted in disappointment. There wasn't a tunnel after all. It was simply some sort of reflective surface, and the lights that Ellia was seeing were her own eyes. *Wow, I look creepy.* She thought, stepping close to the mirror and staring into her own, disembodied eyes, hovering golden in the darkness.

Suddenly, the eyes winked out. In their place, a galaxy of stars sprang into view. In their dim light, Ellia could suddenly see the chamber. It was huge, and vaulted, the ceiling and walls sparkling with crystal. In front of her, most of the wall was taken up with a mirror. It was roughly the shape of an arch, it's edges seamlessly blending with the wall, and it was filled with stars which could not possibly be there. *The Mirror of Souls.* She realized. *But I thought Jasper just made that up!* The image in the mirror changed. Ellia saw an ocean, dark waves crashing against a rock. A shape broke the surface, and she found herself staring into the impossibly blue eyes of the most beautiful creature she had every seen. It was a girl, of sorts, but her skin was slightly transparent, and her hair was a kind of stormy blue, like the sea itself. Her entire body was covered in tiny, slimy scales, which glittered like the sun on waves as she moved. Ellia leaned forward, captivated by the wild, stormy depths of her eyes. She pressed a palm against the glass, but then the image changed again, and she found herself instead looking into the panicked, flat darkness of a Darkwing's eyes. Before she could react, the Darkwing was replaced by a Ice Creeper, then a Griffon, then something with fiery wings and red feathers, all in quick succession. In the darkness at the bottom of an ocean, something huge, with many fins and teeth, uncurled.

The images faded, and Ellia found herself again looking into a pair of golden eyes. This time, however, they were much larger, farther apart, and completely without pupils. Also, they were filled with a dark, burning anger. Ellia backed away. One of the eyes winked, and the remaining eye became a star. This star was then surrounded by five other stars, each of them a different color, and all connected to the center star by thin lines of light, like spokes on a wheel. The stars changed again.

The night sky behind them vanished, and cages appeared around each star. The constellation shrank, until Ellia could see herself in the mirror, with the constellation of caged stars gleaming where her heart should be.

Ellia stared at it for a long time, and then moved sideways, so that the cages no longer covered her heart. The image of Ellia in the mirror did not move. Instead, she simply faded, talking everything else with her, until there was nothing left but darkness. Not even Ellia's eyes reflected back at her anymore.

All of this had happened in moments, and in complete silence. However, as Ellia began to turn away, there was a sudden sound, like the crunching of ice under a boot. In the mirror, a single crack appeared. It spread across the glass, branching out from the center with a sound like the crackling of a fire. A golden light was gleaming through the cracks, lighting the room. Then the mirror shattered.

Chapter Twenty-Five

The Monster in the Mirror

"Many people try to explain Magic. They give it rules, and try to define where it is, and how it works. The truth is, Magic makes no sense. Those who try to explain it just drive themselves mad."
— Gazzania the Prophetess.

Ellia was hurled backwards by the blast, and she crashed into the far wall. She sat up slowly, aching all over. The cavern was no longer dark, and it was no longer empty. Crouched in the broken glass was a great golden dragon. It reared back it's head, spread it's wings, and roared, bathing the ceiling in flames.

Ellia stood up shakily, and then immediately wished she hadn't, because the movement caught the dragon's attention. It turned, scraping chunks of rock off the walls. Ellia scrambled backwards, but found herself pressed against a wall, as the dragon nosed closer. It's scaly nose stopped within inches of her face, and it sniffed. Hot air blew Ellia's hair back from her face. The dragon stared at her for a moment, then growled.

The sound alone was enough to send a vibration

through the floor. The creature opened it's mouth, revealing row after row of shining, black, knife-like teeth. It sucked in a deep gulp of air, then spat a torrent of flames at Ellia.

But Ellia was no longer there. Instead, she was running up the beast's nose. As it reared back in confusion, she grabbed hold of a large spine between it's ears. The monster roared. It shook it's head, and Ellia hung on for dear life. The dragon lowered it's head and swung Ellia toward a wall, intending to crush her. Heart pounding, she unlocked her knees from around a second spine near it's nose, then, seconds before impact, she kicked the dragon in the eyes and let go.

The shock was horrible. Ellia hit the wall and landed in a heap on the ground. Her head rang with a headache and the dragon's roars. The creature was staggering around the cavern, smashing chunks of rock off of the walls and cracking the ceiling. It was letting out a screeching, glass-shattering noise that set Ellia's teeth on edge and shook the cavern. Then the sound stopped, and it turned bleeding, hate-filled eyes on Ellia.

Oh rats. Ellia thought, then jumped to her feet and sprinted away. The creature lunged after her, it's wings beating the air and walls, creating a hurricane of wind that sent her tumbling. The cavern was not big enough to outrun the monster. Ellia dived to the side as it's teeth and claws slashed past.

The next few moments were frantic. Ellia dashed back and forth between the dragon's legs, trying to avoid it's claws and teeth, while the dragon whirled and stomped in furious circles, trying to smell her out. Fortunately for Ellia, the cavern was not big enough to give the dragon full range of movement, and it was partially blinded. Unfortunately for her, she had forgotten to watch out for it's tail. She dodged a claw, jumping backwards to avoid being slashed to bits, and was suddenly struck across the ribs by the tail. It hit with the force of a falling tree, sending her skidding across the floor. She groaned and tried to roll over. The dragon heard the groan. It couldn't see, but it could hear perfectly well, so it turned and blasted her with flames.

Ellia could feel her skin begin to crisp from the heat. The curtain of flame swept towards her, blistering the stone. Then it was on her. A little voice inside whispered, *You should let me take over now.* Before she could realize what had happened, something inside her rib cage broke free and exploded outwards. The light in the room doubled, and Ellia let out a blast of flame that boiled the rock, and pinned the other dragon against the wall with it's force. She sprang forward, slashing and biting. The other dragon responded in kind, but it's movements were off, due to it's blindness. For what seemed forever, the two dragons grappled in the cave, shaking the very foundations of the mountain with their struggle. Ellia was seeing through a red haze of anger, but gradually the anger turned to desperation. She slashed and bit frantically, blindly, as chunks of the ceiling rained down, and the walls shook. With every blow, she knew that her claws were dealing damage to the other dragon, but she could feel her own skin tearing at the same time from it's teeth and claws. Blood splattered the ground, hissing as it hit the cold stone.

Suddenly, the ceiling gave way. Ellia hurled herself backwards, as a thousand pounds of rock suddenly collapsed on top of the other dragon's head. Her teeth and claws disappeared. Ellia found herself lying on the ground, bruised and bleeding and Human. The ground was almost too hot to touch, and there was blood everywhere. The ceiling was still collapsing. Somehow, with strength she didn't know she had, Ellia managed to drag herself a few feet into the tunnel mouth. The next moment, the entire cavern was nothing but a pile of rubble.

Ellia closed her eyes.

She hung suspended in a fog of white light. There was no ground, no surroundings of any kind, just foggy white light. For a long time, nothing happened. She didn't want anything to happen, because she knew that to come back to herself would mean pain, darkness, and all sorts of problems that she didn't want to have to face.

The white fog shifted. A small blob solidified and came toward her. It seemed to be trying to talk to her, but she couldn't hear it.

"Go away." She told it, but it didn't. Instead, the muffled voice emanating from the dim blob became more agitated. It was yelling something. She ignored it, but the calm, painless fog couldn't last forever. Eventually, a door opened up to Reality. She reluctantly drifted toward it. As she passed through into the pain and darkness, the blob reached out, took her hand, and walked through the door with her.

Ellia awoke to pain, darkness, and someone talking. It was Rowan.

"Oh, Ellia." He said softly, and his voice was choked with pain. He bowed his head, and Ellia felt something warm splash onto her hand. Ellia was vaguely annoyed. *I'm the one in pain, you moron. Why are you the one crying?* She thought. Ellia then realized that she was also crying. There were tears trickling down her cheeks and into her ears, making it hard to hear. She drifted back into the white fog.

The second time Ellia awoke, she was still in pain, but it was not dark. There were several candles in the cave now, stuck to the floor of the tunnel and melting into little pools of wax. Rowan was gently washing blood from her face with a wet cloth. She squinted up at him.

"How did you get in here?"

Rowan rinsed the cloth out in a basin of water, then started bandaging a cut on her face before he answered.

"I'm not entirely sure. I Dreamwalked to you, then followed you out of your dream when you left it, and ended up here. I can't normally do that, only with… Only with people I…" He trailed off. Ellia looked at him curiously.

"People you… What?"

"Care about." Rowan winced and looked away.

"I know." He burst out, before she could say anything. "I know I don't have the right to make that claim, not after what I've done." He sighed, and ran his hands through his hair. Ellia stared at him incredulously, then groaned and closed her eyes.

"Did you tell the Assassins where to find me?" She asked flatly.

"Yes." He replied, sounding miserable. "And it was the worst decision I've ever made."

Ellia sighed. Then, "How did you bring candles and bandages and a basin of water in?"

"I made several trips." Rowan gave a hollow laugh.

"I can always return to Alestromaria after my dreamwalking. And I can always return to you because, well, I love you."
Ellia didn't say anything, and she didn't open her eyes. Rowan finally broke the silence.

"Look, Ellia. I know you can't forgive me." He burst out miserably. "And I don't blame you. I can't forgive myself. But I love you, and if we ever get out of here, I'm going to spend the rest of my life making it up to you."

Ellia opened her eyes.

"That's a pretty big claim, coming from an Elf.

The rest of your life could be a very, very long time.”

“I mean it.” Rowan held her eyes. She looked at him for a long time, then shook her head and turned away. She wanted to feel angry, but all she felt was tired.

“I believe you.” She said slowly, thoughtfully. “Or at least, I believe that *you* believe what you’re saying, but it’s not enough. I can’t forgive what you did. Not now, and not for a long time. You acted like dirt, Rowan, and that’s what you are. If I didn’t need you, I would tell you to get out of my sight right now. But I do need you, so I’m going to try to forget it for now.”
Rowan’s face flashed with disappointment, then acceptance. He took a deep breath, his emotions disappearing from his face. There was a long silence. One of the candles guttered, and Rowan suddenly seemed to remember that Ellia was still only half bandaged, and bleeding. He turned away, digging through a pile of bandages, and finally pulling out a needle and thread.

“Hold still, I need to stitch a gash on your leg.”
Ellia gritted her teeth as he pulled the first stitch through.

“How bad is it?” She asked at last. Rowan sucked in a breath.

“You don’t want to know.”

“Yes I do. Besides, I need something to distract me from the fact that you’re stabbing me with a needle.”

Rowan grimaced

“Bad.” He admitted. “It’s astonishing that you’re alive at all. What did you do?”
She told him, briefly and in a monotone, wincing as she got to the bit involving Jasper. Telling it out loud made her realize how stupid and gullible it made her sound. Rowan, however, didn’t seem to notice. He was more interested in the part about the Mirror. When she had finished, he was silent for a long time. Finally, he let out

a sigh, looking troubled.

"Well, I don't know what you are, but your powers are like nothing anyone has ever seen before. I'm starting to think that maybe the Elvish oracles are right, and you're connected to the dragon, Myth. The thing I'm worried about, though, is that if Myth really does return, what will that do to you?"

"Don't worry about it." Ellia growled, suddenly feeling the need to defend herself. "My powers are none of your business, and besides, I can't be Myth, because I've changed into a lot of other things as well as a dragon."

Rowan didn't look convinced. In his preoccupation, he pulled a stitch too tight, and Ellia yelped.

"Sorry." He hastily apologized, flinching away from her glare. "Ellia, If you really have inherited the powers of Myth, or something like that, there's something I need to tell you. Just after you left, a man showed up in Alestromaria. He's an ancient elf, who's lived in the darkest part of the wood since before anyone can remember. He almost never comes near the other elves, but this time he did. He marched right into the center of Alestromaria, and wanted to know if anyone had seen Myth. He's looking for you. And he's dangerous."

A bell rang in Ellia's memory. She frowned.

"Does he carry a big sword? And have scars all over his face and arms?"

Rowan looked perplexed. "Yes. How did you – "

"I dreamed about him. He's named Gilead, and I think he has a grudge against Myth. She ruined his life, or something like that." Ellia explained. Rowan bandaged another cut.

"We need to do something about him."

"Later. We have more important things to worry

about." She reminded him grimly. He nodded, then grinned ruefully.

"We're in so much trouble, Ellia. Remember my promise? Well, the rest of my life might not be such a long time after all."

Ellia was about to protest, but he cut her off with a shrug.

"Oh well. At least it'll be interesting."

Chapter Twenty-Six

A Book is Desecrated For the Sake of Art

***

"A wise man can do anything if he puts his mind to it. However, it might take a really long time and a lot of effort. An even wiser man gives up after the first few tries and finds someone else to do it for him."
— Diggory Drudge, an even wiser man who never does anything for himself.

***

The wall of statues was still just as impenetrable, but now, with candles to drive away the darkness and Rowan beside her, the situation didn't seem quite so hopeless.

The two of them stood facing it, both holding candles. The journey back up the tunnel had been hard, but as time passed they had made more progress. Ellia's wounds were completely healed now, although several gashes in her stomach were still tender and made it hard to move faster than a slow walk.

"Well," Rowan remarked after a moment. "You were right about it being solid. Moving even one of these statues would be like trying to untie a stone knot. We'll have to smash them."

Ellia turned to stare at him.

"*What?* How on earth are we supposed to do that?"

Rowan grinned. "Not us. You. There's no way *I* could break those."

"I can't." Ellia instantly protested. "There's no way. How would I do that?"

Rowan shrugged, then sat down, crossed his arms, and leaned against the wall. Ellia gave him a quizzical look.

"What are you doing?"

"Waiting." Rowan opened one eye. "You *can* do it, and I'm just going to sit here until you do."

"I can't!" Ellia's voice rose in desperation, but Rowan didn't react.

"Then I guess you're going to die in here. And I'm going to stay here and die beside you." He looked into her eyes, and she felt stronger at the sight of the determination shining there.

"So either you master your powers and bust us out of here, or we both die, Ellia. Your choice."

Ellia took a deep breath, and faced the wall, willing it to fall down.

Nothing happened. She glared at it, as though she might bore holes in it with her eyes, but the statues stayed there, as though mocking her.

Several minutes passed. Ellia became increasingly frustrated. Rowan shifted a few times, but said nothing. Ellia finally sat down and tried to think. *I need something big, and strong.* She thought blankly. *Where would I find that?*

High on the wall, one of the statues looked downward, wearing a very smug expression. Ellia stared at it for a moment, and realized that it looked just like Jasper did. She jumped up, feeling irrationally angry at the statue, and filled with an intense desire to crush it's head.

The next second, she was crushing it between her teeth. The taste of the crumbling stone was immensely satisfying. She spat it out, and realized that her head was only inches from the roof of the tunnel. She felt huge, and incredibly powerful, but also very dry. The air felt wrong in her lungs, and the dirt under her was strange. She reared up, and felt the entire length of herself shift, trailing a long, long ways back into the tunnel.

I'm a snake! She realized, suddenly gleeful. *But… a HUGE snake. With fins and spines. Wow. I feel like I could crush an island with just my tail.* She twisted to look down at herself, and saw Rowan. He was on his feet, and his eyes were huge. He stared, mouth hanging open, and then a wild grin spread across his face. He reached out, somewhat hesitantly, and tapped a scale on her shoulder. It was the size of a large shield, thicker and harder than armor. It was a deep, deep blue in color. Rowan's eyes lit up.

"That's more like it!" He cheered. "Now get us out of here!"

Ellia nudged him back out of the way, then coiled herself and slammed the wall.

Heads and limbs of statues crumbled to the ground. On the second blow, the cave shook. By the third, she could see small rays of sunlight slanting through the cracks. On the fourth, the mouth of the cave exploded outwards, and Ellia flew out with it.

She landed as a human and tumbled down the slope, scraping her knees. Rowan followed, climbing out of the rubble.

"Well." He said after a long moment, coming over to sit beside her on a rock.

"That's the first time I've ever seen a Sea Serpent on land. In fact, that's the first time I've *ever* seen one."

"What's a Sea Serpent?" Ellia wanted to know.

Rowan looked at her in surprise.

"You don't know? Haven't you ever read any of the old stories?"

"Not if I could help it." She admitted. "I don't like reading."

Rowan clicked his tongue. "Well, you'll have to change that if you're ever going to figure out what you really are. Once you get back to the palace, you need to visit the library.

Ellia shuddered, remembering the dark presence she had felt in the library the last time.

"Okay." She agreed reluctantly. "But you have to come with me."

"But I can't." Rowan objected. "I'll get caught. I can come with you back to the palace, but I'll have to remain in hiding outside of it, in the city or the gardens. There's no way I'm going to be allowed to just march into the palace to look at the library."

Ellia felt a sudden flash of panic, realizing that she would have to return to the palace alone.

"I don't want to go back." She said suddenly, urgently, thinking of all the hostility and deception that went on in the royal court. Rowan looked sympathetic, but determined.

"You have to." He gently reminded her. "It's the safest place for you right now, with Gilead hunting you, and Lord Iberus determined to get you on his side, no matter the cost. I'll check in on you often, and keep watch from within the city, if that makes you feel any better."

"It doesn't." Ellia complained miserably. "Remember Jasper, the guy who tried to kill me? Well, he's in the palace, and he'll probably try again. And the worst thing is, there's no way to guard against him. One glance into his eyes and he could get me to walk off a cliff."

Rowan frowned. "Maybe I will come with you, so I can stab him while he's trying to mesmerize you." He looked as though he were relishing the idea. "Yes, I think that might be the best thing. The issue would be how to get into the palace. They're going to be guarding it even more carefully now." His eyes lit up with a sudden idea.

"Here's what we'll do. I'll wait outside the palace until nightfall, then dreamwalk into the palace as soon as you fall asleep. Or you could pretend to be sick and take a nap as soon as you get inside. Then, once I'm in, I can pretend to be a cat. No one will notice if there's an extra cat running around the palace."

Ellia was doubtful that it would work, but it seemed better than no plan at all, so she reluctantly agreed. They stood up and started back toward Thalis. Behind them, the mountain groaned as yet another section of the cave collapsed.

It wasn't until they had descended from the mountain, and were reaching the outskirts of Thalis, that they realized something was wrong. Ellia was leaning on Rowan for support as they trudged around a bend and the city walls came into view. Her injuries were aching from the long walk, and so she was relieved when Rowan suddenly stopped. Then she saw the smoke.

The city itself was not on fire, but in the distance, the villages to the north of the city were sending thick columns of black smoke into the cloudless sky.

"What on earth?" Rowan wondered. "Why is someone burning Dalian villages? Do you think it's the Kurdu?"

Ellia didn't answer. Injuries forgotten, she was already stumbling down toward the city as fast as her tired legs could carry her. Rowan hurried to catch up, and caught her arm.

"Ellia, wait. What are you doing?" He demanded.

"You can't run like that. You'll kill yourself. You're not healed yet. Why do you have to get to the city so fast, anyways? It might be dangerous, so you should stay here until I go down and find out."

Ellia shook her head and tried to pull away from him, irritated.

"People I care about are down there." She insisted stubbornly. "Chadwick and the twins might be in danger, and I'm not just going to stand here when I might be able to help."

She held his eyes, her own glowing with determined fire. Rowan finally blew out a breath and looked away.

"Fine. But You're not running anywhere. You'll tear open your scars. Either you walk like a normal person, or I carry you." He let go of her arm, and she tried to follow his orders, walking slowly. But then she imagined the mysterious attackers reaching the city before she did, burning it to the ground, and she broke into another sprint. Rowan sighed, picked her up, and the next thing she knew, he was sprinting down the slope with her over one shoulder.

When they reached the city, they found chaos. Guards were everywhere, buckling on armor and yelling at each other, while merchants, citizens, and street rabble were running about in a panic. Several guards were trying to close the gates, but were having trouble due to the packed stream of people trying to flee the city, and village refugees trying to get in. Rowan put Ellia down once they were inside the gates, and she stood in front of him while he ducked his head and changed his face to look Human.

Ellia spotted a familiar face among the guards, and she hailed him. It was Captain Gwylan, running past with a sword belt in his hand and a slice of bread clamped between his teeth. He jogged over at her wave, looking confused.

"Ma'am – I mean, Ellia. What are you doing here? You're supposed to be dead! The King's other Starfalls brought in the report on how you'd tried to explore a cave and were crushed by a cave-in. We even held a funeral for you, since the royal twins were very upset, and demanded one. What happened?" His eyes flew to the new, pink scars visible on her face, arms, and shoulders, and his brow darkened with concern.

"There wasn't a cave-in, was there? Those are blade-scars, if I've ever seen one."

"Teeth and claw scars, actually. But never mind that." Ellia cut him off. "What's going on here?"

Gwylan grimaced.

"It's a mess. Half the army is still with the King, who won't be returning for at least a couple days. The rest of us were busy looking for an Elvish portal in the City, on the Queen's orders. Then the Kurdu suddenly decide to attack, while we're all distracted and unprepared. No one expected it, and by the time we realized what was happening, they were already almost to the city. And of course, all the Nobles have withdrawn their Starfalls to their private villas in order to protect themselves, so we don't even have magic on our side. The best we can hope to do now is to hold Thalis until the King returns." He shook his head in disgust, then hurried off in response to a shout from the gates.

Ellia turned to Rowan.

"What now?" She asked. His eyes were dark with thought.

"You should go back to the palace." He decided. "It looks like we're going to have a siege, so you should start trying to solve the puzzle of your powers. Right now it's not really a question of whether you can use them, but more of whether they're safe to use at all, isn't it? Go to the Library, and find out everything you can there. Look through the old stories and myths, maybe you'll find something that might help. I'll try to come with you, but if I get caught, find that Chadwick guy, and stick close to him. You said you trust him?"

"Definitely." Ellia confirmed. "He's the wisest person I know."

"Good. Then maybe he can protect you from Jasper, if you run into him." Rowan looked doubtful. He took her arm, and they started off down the street, dodging panicked people.

The palace gates, when they finally reached them, had few guards, but those guards were alert and watchful, carefully inspecting anyone who wished to enter. Ellia suddenly had a better idea, and dragged Rowan to the side before the guards could spot them. He didn't protest, just gave her a quizzical look as they hurried through side alleyways, keeping the palace wall in sight. As Ellia had suspected, the guard was stretched thin, since most of them were barricading the city. The garden gates were not guarded, but only had a rotating guard strolling the wall above them. They waited until the guard had passed, and then made a quick dash through, Rowan practically carrying Ellia.

The garden beyond was occupied.

"Ellia!" Myria squealed, catapulting across the grass, with Myrgen close behind. They threw themselves at Ellia, knocking her over.

"You're not dead!" They cheered. Ellia grunted, trying in vain to protect her injuries from their sharp knees and elbows.

"I will be if you don't get off me." She complained. The two twins reluctantly backed off, Myria bouncing in place with excitement. Rowan glanced nervously up at the wall, where the guard was returning. Following his gaze, Ellia quickly herded the children into the cover of some trees. Rowan followed, ducking low.

"We need some way to get Chadwick to meet us in the library." He muttered to Ellia in a low voice. She looked around, her gaze landing on the twins.

"Yes, we do." She agreed. "And we also need a distraction so that we can get you into the palace unnoticed."

Ten minutes later, everyone in the west side of the palace was shocked by an unnatural scream, so loud that it seemed to shake the tapestries on the walls. Some hurried in the direction of the scream, but most, guessing the source, simply turned and discreetly slipped away in the opposite direction.

Myria stood in the middle of a courtyard, her face a bright, burning red, mouth open so wide you could see her tonsils, and making a noise so horrible it would wake the dead. Ellia and Rowan ran through the now-empty corridors, hands over their ears.

Chadwick was already in the library, as was Myrgen. The older man was trying to prevent the young prince from dumping books off the shelves, but he turned to greet Ellia when she entered.

"Ah look, It's my little hot-headed friend, come back from the dead. When Myrgen told me you needed me, I thought he was joking, or planning a prank that would send me to the same place." He embraced her, then turned to Rowan, his strange eyes taking him in.

"You're Rowan." He said at last. It was an accusation. Rowan hesitated, then nodded. Chadwick's eyes were hard. He looked at Ellia, and then back a Rowan several times. Finally he asked,

"You've forgiven him?" He sounded incredulous. Ellia shook her head.

"No... but he's sorry and, well, we need him."

Chadwick reached for the door.

"Not right now, we don't." He pinned Rowan with a glare.

“Out.”

Rowan didn’t argue, and Chadwick closed the door behind him.

“So… What did you need me for?”

Ellia didn’t answer. She was staring around the room, relieved that she could feel no trace of the dark presence she had sensed the last time.

“Books.” She finally said, eyeing the many leather bindings with distrust. They sat there, looking all innocent in their neat rows, but Ellia couldn’t shake the feeling that they were waiting to jump out at her, thrusting their pages of boring, unnecessary knowledge into her already overcrowded brain.

“I need you to help me find information. I’ve never been very good at reading.”

Chadwick snorted. “So I gathered, from the way you’re looking at the books. They don’t bite, you know.” He laughed softly to himself, then turned serious.

“What kind of information?”

“Legends, history, anything to do with Myth.” As quickly as she could, Ellia explained what she had seen in the mirror, what the Faeries believed about her connection to the dragon, and her transformations in the cave. Chadwick looked grave.

“That would be in the back section.” He hummed to himself, striding off into the far recesses of the library. While she was waiting for him to find something, Ellia glanced around and noticed a writing desk. She wandered over thoughtfully, picking up the pen and dipping it into a bottle of blue ink. There was no paper. With considerable pleasure, she tore a few blank pages out of the back of a book, and began to draw on them.

When Chadwick returned, bearing a stack of books, he looked horrified. However, his shock at the ripped pages quickly faded when he saw what she had drawn.

"Why are you drawing the constellation of Myth?" He asked with interest. Ellia's heart sank at the now-familiar name.

"Of *course* that's what it's called. I should have expected that. Everything has something to do with Myth." She grumbled bitterly. She glanced down at the paper, where she had drawn several images from the Mirror of Souls, including the mysterious circular constellation. Haltingly, she explained where she had seen them. Chadwick looked fascinated.

"Yes, this makes sense. You see, the middle star of that constellation vanished something like sixteen years back. A *gold* star." He sat down beside her, his face taking on the look it always did before he launched into a history lesson.

"There are many legends surrounding these stars." He began, tracing the stars on the page with something like reverence, which Ellia didn't like.

"However, it is generally agreed that the middle star is Myth, a legendary dragon, and the surrounding stars are the six creatures that she changed into magical beings. The Siren, Ice Creeper, Griffon, Darkwing..." He pointed out the first three stars, then stopped on the fourth star.

"You know, in reality, the Darkwing star doesn't actually exist. There are only five stars, and one blank gap, around the center star, although legend says that there is in fact a sixth star in the gap, only it's black, like the Darkwing. These other stars are supposed to be the Sea Serpent, the Siren, and the Phoenix, although those creatures are thought to be legend. No one's ever seen them."

Ellia stared at him, entranced. As he spoke, she could feel everything he said filling holes in her mind, clicking into place. Suddenly, everything made sense.

"Yes." She whispered, staring down at her

drawing. "But if I've inherited the powers of the middle star, how can I turn into the other ones too?"

Chadwick frowned, then finally shrugged.

"It's *magic,* Ellia. You can't explain it. Everyone who tries just goes mad. Maybe you've inherited Myths' transforming powers, only instead of changing other things, as she did, you can change yourself? Or maybe you're just extra special. I don't know."

Ellia sighed.

"I hope you're right, and the elves are wrong. Because I'm actually kind of scared of what I might be capable of."

With reluctance, she finally turned to the stack of books.

"What about these? Did you read them? Find anything useful?"
Chadwick snorted.

"Read them? No. Not yet. I just picked out the ones I thought might be relevant and brought them over. These are all about Myth, and also some just about magical creatures in general. Most of them are by a philosopher called Glazgo, who I find to be quite interesting. Want to read them?"

Ellia let out something like a squeak of fright and jumped out of her chair, eyeing the formidable stack.

"No thank you. I think I've learned enough for now. Why don't you read them instead, then tell me what you find?" She looked pleadingly at him, and he relented with an amused chuckle.

"Fine. I'll read them. It looks like I'll have plenty of time, anyway, with the expected siege and all. Don't worry, I won't torture you with these letters. Go ahead and run off." Immensely relieved, Ellia kissed him on the cheek in thanks and then turned to go. Then she stopped short and turned back, remembering something.

"Chadwick, wait. Can you promise me something?"

Chadwick looked up from a book, amused.

"What is it now?"

Ellia took a deep breath, knowing that she was about to request exactly the type of thing that she herself would hate to be asked.

"Could you please try to stay in the castle, out of danger, and away from the fighting, when it comes?"

He laughed softly.

"You don't have to worry about me, child. I'm far too old to participate in the fighting as it is. As the king's Master of Spies, my place is in the council chamber, not the battlefield. You're the one who should be promising to keep safe, but I'm not going to ask it. I know it will just annoy you into doing something reckless and dangerous. All the same though, be careful out there."

Ellia nodded, trying not to sniffle with a sudden flood of emotion at the sight of the old man's earnest, careworn face.

"I'll try." She promised, before dashing out the door so he wouldn't see her tears.

He actually cares about me! She thought, overcome with the knowledge. *And not because of any selfish ambition. He knows what I am, how scary I can be, and he still cares!* She caught sight of Rowan, standing in the corridor, and instantly banished her tears. Embarrassed, she glared at him, daring him to comment. Rowan wisely decided to pretend he hadn't seen anything.

"So… Now you're sure your friends are safe, I don't suppose I could convince you to flee the city before the siege?" He asked with an odd half-smile. Ellia marched up to him and shoved her face up close to his, eyes burning with a furious fire.

"No, Rowan. I am *not* running from danger

anymore. I'm tired of you trying to keep me safe. If this city isn't safe for me, it isn't safe for those I love, and I'm going to stay and protect it." She was deadly serious, but Rowan just smirked.

"Yes, that's what I assumed you would say. Shall we go throw ourselves into danger then?" He looked resigned to the idea, even slightly amused. Ellia hesitated. She suddenly realized that she was so tired she could barely stay on her feet. She suddenly reconsidered the idea of rushing off into another dangerous situation. At the thought of rushing *anywhere*, in fact, she felt slightly nauseated.

"Actually, I think I'll take a nap first." She admitted somewhat sheepishly.

Chapter Twenty-Seven

A Cat Makes Strange Faces

***

"It is well known that the people of Dalia are rubbish at making biscuits. Nevertheless, they still persist in making great quantities of them, though they never get any better. At the very least, they are useful for throwing at one's enemies."

— Selman Smiles, an exasperated Kurdian baker.

***

When Ellia had decided to sleep in the secret passageways, she hadn't thought of the dust. When she awoke the next morning, her nose and lungs were full of it. She stumbled and crawled out of the nest of stolen blankets, coughing. The dust was inches thick in some places. Rowan was nowhere to be seen. The other nest of blankets in an adjoining passageway was empty.

She staggered sleepily through a hidden panel, out into the rafters of the Dining Hall. Hidden behind a cluster of statues, she coughed, then spat a lungful of mud out over the edge. She watched with considerable delight as it splattered onto the polished, gilded helmet of a passing royal guard. He started, looking around, but

Ellia ducked out of view. Choking on a giggle, she headed off in search of breakfast.

The palace was hushed. It was a waiting silence, as if everyone held their breath. It was also quite empty. Most of the lords and hangers-on at the palace had packed up and left at the first hint of trouble, taking their servants with them. Many of them had well-fortified towns of their own to stay in, while others' homes were far away and out of danger. The King's wing of the palace, especially, was empty. The king had taken almost all of his servants with him, and those left behind were staying with relatives in the city. Ellia raided the pantries in the kitchen, then headed out into the city herself.

Thalis, in stark contrast to the palace, was bustling with life. In addition to the normal inhabitants, all of the villagers and farmers from the surrounding country were seeking shelter within the city walls. Ellia was glad of the large, hooded cloak she had chosen to wear. She jostled through the huddled, nervous-looking crowds and made her way to the city wall. Still gnawing on an old biscuit from the pantry, she jogged up the stairs. Her body felt full of energy after the nights' rest, and she relished the feeling as she strolled along the wall. The Kurdian army had not yet arrived, although the smoke and dust from their passing was much closer. If Ellia strained her eyes, she could begin to pick out the shapes of men and horses within it.

"Hey!" A guard's sharp voice broke her concentration. "Only fighting men allowed on the walls. This isn't a spectacle, so get down, woman!"

Feeling vaguely offended, Ellia restrained herself from giving the guard a tongue lashing. She wasn't sure that she wanted people to know she wasn't dead, just yet.

"I'd be more useful in battle than you would." She

muttered to herself as she reluctantly retraced her steps. She paced about beneath the wall, growing increasingly impatient. Danger she could handle, but she hadn't expected for it to take so long to arrive. The army from Kurdu was moving too slowly, in her opinion. The city seemed to mirror her feelings. Everywhere, people gathered in nervous, huddled clumps, exchanging gossip and breakfast biscuits. There was a storm on the horizon but it, too, seemed to be holding its breath. Slowly, a wind began to pick up. Instead of relieving the nervous tension, however, it only added to it. Ellia paced. And paced. Finally, she gave up and went in search of a distraction.

Rowan was reclined on a high cross-beam above the empty great hall. It seemed too narrow to hold him, and yet he didn't even look troubled by the fifty foot drop beneath him. In fact, he was reading a book. At the sight of it, Ellia felt her old, irrational hatred flare up. She could almost feel the malice emanating from those innocent looking pages.

"Rowan!" She barked, hoping he would drop the book in surprise. He didn't, but his whole body tensed at the sound of her voice, and he looked up carefully.

"Put down the book and come teach me to fight." She said. A flicker of a smile crossed Rowan's face, but he looked back at his book.

"No."

Ellia stood there for a moment, waiting for an explanation. It didn't come, and she became annoyed.

"Why not? Surely you know how. Don't all Faerie boys know how? Or do you all just wear those swords for decoration?"

Rowan touched the hilt of the slender, elegant sword in question, and looked up again.

"I can use it."

Ellia nearly stamped with frustration.

"Then why won't you teach me? You can use this as a first step towards winning my forgiveness."
Rowan laughed. "The morning before a battle, Ellia? You can't be serious. Besides, it wouldn't do you any good."

"Why not?"
He sighed, and finally met her eyes.

"Ellia, if you're going to be in a fight, you're going to be fighting in the form of some kind of magical creature. You won't be able to wield a sword."

It was a very logical argument, and Ellia found herself struggling for a response.

"But what if I can't change?" She asked softly, a hint of doubt creeping into her voice. She immediately regretted it. She hated to let her insecurities show, especially in front of Rowan, who she no longer trusted with her feelings. He looked at her sharply, then vaulted the empty space between them, landing in front of her. His eyes glowed with concern.

"Look, Ellia," He began, taking her hands. She instantly snatched them away, and a flash of sorrow clouded his eyes. He put his hands behind his back.

"Look, Ellia. You're done with the powerless stage of your life. When you need the magic, it will come. You looked into the mirror, didn't you? There's nothing blocking your power now, I can tell, just by looking at you. I mean, the air around you *shimmers*. Not even Lord Iberus radiates power so visibly." His eyes pleaded with her, as though he meant to give her confidence through his willpower alone. She relented.

"Fine, so I don't need to learn to fight. But you should still teach me anyway."
Rowan looked confused. "Why?"

Ellia ran out of arguments, so she admitted the truth.

"I hate waiting. I need a distraction."

For a moment, the old Rowan shone through, and he flashed her a flirtatious grin.

"I could give you that."

Against her will, Ellia's heart did a flip, and she scowled.

"Not *that* kind. It's just that… Oh, never mind. You're useless." She turned and stalked off. In moments, she could hear his soft tread beside her, as they crossed the rafters.

"I'm sorry." He said after a moment. "I shouldn't have said that. I know how you feel about me and I am, indeed, the lowliest scum of the earth, but won't you come back and talk to me anyway? I'll try my best to help you, it's just that you really shouldn't be tiring yourself out with a fighting lesson right before battle. If there's anything else you need, I'll try to help."

Ellia stopped and turned to face him, failing to hide the grin on her face.

"What?" He faltered.

"Did I just hear what I think I did?" She asked in mock amazement. "You, a high and mighty Faerie, admitted to being scum?"

Rowan's face flashed with momentary irritation, but he saw the smile in her eyes and it changed to a grudging grin.

"You shouldn't be so disrespectful of my kind." He said mildly, but the typical Elvish pride was absent from his eyes. Ellia was momentarily caught off-balance by an unexpected surge of fondness for him. To hide her confusion, she turned quickly and headed down a set of stairs to the floor below. There was a pause, and then she detected Rowan's soft tread behind her.

There was no one in sight when she peered out through the sliding panel at the base of the stair. She carefully slid it open and crept out. She took a step into the hall, then stopped short. Her foot was ankle deep in water. With a soft yelp of annoyance, she hopped over the puddle, then glanced around. There were puddles everywhere. Little trickles of water ran between floor tiles, and under doors.

"There's a roof leak." Ellia called softly, just as Rowan stepped out and soaked his own feet. She smirked, and he glared at her. Then she drew the knife Jasper had given her and gestured around with it.

"Look. This hall is empty. We should-"

"No."

"Please?" Ellia made her eyes wide and innocent.

"No."

"What about if you just show me some blocks and parrys?"

Rowan sighed in frustration, running his hand through his hair.

"Fine."

Half an hour later, the hall was still deserted. They stood facing each other. Rowan held his sword out for the hundredth time, and performed a complicated wrist flick. Ellia held out her own dagger and attempted to mimic him. To her eyes, the motion was exactly the same. Rowan groaned. Biting her lip, she tried again.

"Like this?"

"No… *this*."

"*This*?"

"No! This… no... No. This. *Look* at what I'm doing!"

"I *am* looking!"

Rowan huffed out a frustrated breath and slammed his sword back in it's sheath.

"You're hopeless."

Ellia felt annoyed.

"I don't see why it has to be so complicated. I know how to stab someone. Isn't that what the dagger is for?"

Rowan laughed.

"Yes, but what if the other person is also trying to stab you? Then what would you do?"

Ellia had no answer. Rowan grew more serious.

"Just try to use your powers instead, okay? We're done here for now. I'm going outside."

He left the hall, and Ellia hurried to catch up.

 The passages outside the hall were dry. As they emerged from the deserted west wing, thunder rumbled overhead. The overgrown grass shivered in the wind. Ellia frowned, glancing around at the towering trees.

"Huh. I thought this gate lead to an open lawn." She looked around, searching for a familiar landmark. Suddenly, a distant crash echoed through the air. Rowan drew in a sharp breath.

"That's not thunder."

For a moment, Ellia wasn't sure what he meant, until she heard the rising, panicked shouts from the city. She turned to Rowan, eyes wide.

"What in Allaria makes a noise like that, besides thunder?" She asked in a shocked whisper. Rowan's mouth was a grim line.

"You've never seen a siege, have you?"

He turned and looked out towards the city, eyes narrowed. Suddenly, he was gone. A black cat streaked past Ellia's legs and through the garden gate. She stood there for a moment, then followed at a run. As she broke the cover of the trees and passed through the gate, she heard a sharp yell of surprise.

"Halt!" A man's voice called, but Ellia ignored him. She couldn't see Rowan, but the towers on the city walls were within sight. She ran toward them. The sound that was not thunder crashed over the city again. The street down which she ran was, for some reason, overgrown. Thick grass clogged the gutters, and young trees stretched up from between the cracked paving stones.

There was water here, too, but Ellia no longer cared about wet feet. In the distance, the top of one of the guard towers had suddenly exploded, showering the city below with stone. The crash shook the city, sounding a bit like thunder. Ellia stopped short, unable to comprehend what she was seeing. The people around her murmured with fear, huddling closer together. Mothers clutched their children so hard they squirmed in discomfort. A stone the size of a small horse sailed over the wall. Ellia couldn't see it fall, but she heard the crash. *What sort of creature can throw a stone that big?* She thought in horror. The murmurs around her seemed to echo her thought. One man started praying. Ellia started forward again, dread clutching her stomach. *How can we fight such things? How can we even hope to survive long enough for the king to arrive?*

The streets were in chaos, but up on the wall the guards were grim and silent. They waited behind the battlements and the barricaded gates, weapons ready. No one seemed to notice Ellia. She edged closer, listening to the archers curse.

"Darkwings take these rat-faced midgets. They're just sitting back there, throwing stones but staying out of arrow-range, curse them." One snarled.

Ellia couldn't believe her own ears.

"But how could they throw stones so large?" She asked, pulling her cloak close about her face and hoping no one recognized her voice. The archer didn't even turn around, but he chuckled darkly.

"The Kurdians aren't nearly as brutish and barbarous a lot as King Rudbeck would have you believe. What they lack in Starfalls, they make up for with ingenious devices that do incredible things. They haven't even come close enough to shoot at, and already they've knocked out two of our towers. Sneaky little beasts."

Curious despite the danger, Ellia found a clear stretch of battlements, crept up, and peeked over. The Kurdian army stretched below. Hundreds and hundreds of short, dark men in light armor swarmed over the ground, strands of pale hair peeking out from under their round leather helmets. They had quite a lot of horses, Ellia noted, and also several gigantic, wooden, tower-like things which they set up facing the walls. Even as she watched, a team of horses dragged another large rock up one of the towers, and men began rolling it into a strange, spoon-shaped thing.

"Quite a sight, isn't it?"

Ellia started as a large black cat leaped onto the wall beside her.

"The Kurdians learn to fight as children. Their full army is not something to scoff at."

The face of the cat contorted strangely as it fitted it's mouth around Rowan's human speech. Ellia watched it in fascination. It smiled Rowan's smile at her, and that was even stranger. Ellia struggled to swallow a laugh. The effort made her hiccup.

"But why isn't anyone *doing* anything?" She finally managed, once she had recovered herself.

"Are they just going to stand here and let the wall get knocked to pieces under them?"

Rowan laughed. The cat looked as though it were choking on hairballs.

"They're waiting." He explained. "The Kurdu would never just sit back and throw rocks for long. That's not how they fight. To them, battle is about manly prowess, and they can only prove that through hand to hand combat. They'll throw a few rocks, but then they'll come close and start trying to bash the gate down. *That's* what these men are waiting for."

Another rock sailed over the wall, pulverizing a house within the city.

"Someone *do* something!" Ellia hissed, her muscles tense with urgency. Suddenly, a cloud of flame hissed over the battlements from within, streaking out towards the Kurdian army. Men yelled and screamed as the ball of fire swept toward them, singeing Kurdian soldiers and sending the horses stampeding. Ellia glanced sharply to her left. Burke was standing not twenty paces away, the corded muscles in his neck standing out as he concentrated. Behind him was Jasper, leaning against a flag pole with a bored look on his face. They didn't seem to see Ellia. Roy was nowhere to be found, but Ellia heard a crunching noise, and looked down to see the statues from the king's entrance hall marching down the street. Roy marched behind them, directing them to join the ranks of soldiers waiting behind the gate. The soldiers looked somewhat bewildered at the sight of the weaponless stone men and women, scantily clad in artfully draped stone bed-sheets, but they made no comment.

The ball of fire flew back and forth through the Kurdu, finally launching toward one of the wooden towers. As it sped further from the walls, however, it grew smaller. Burke's face was red, his eyes bulging with effort. His hands clenched and he strained, but the ball of fire fell short of the wooden tower, going out. Burke growled.

"It's no use. I need more fire." He complained. "I already sucked all the fire out of this part of the city. Someone get me more."

"Get it yourself." Jasper drawled, crossing his arms. Burke's thick brows drew together in a scowl.

"Why are you even here if not to help? Why can't you get it?"

Jasper's eyes glowed.

"Come on, Buddy." He sounded annoyed. "You really don't expect me to *work,* do you? That would make me sad, and it would make you a bad friend."

Burke's scowling face became slack and complacent.

"Oh… Yeah. I think I'll go get some fire." He lumbered off down the wall.

Another crash sounded. This time, the rock struck a flat section of the wall. Ellia watched the rock buckle, the stones fly. She watched two men fall screaming from the wall, while another died instantly in the impact. She watched, and her heart froze.

"Any time now…" Rowan muttered beside her, his cat body tense. "Any time now and they'll stop throwing rocks."

"No." Ellia whispered, softly, but with utter conviction. "We can't wait for that. *I* can't wait for that."

She started forward. Instantly, Rowan was a man again, standing next to her, reaching out.

"Ellia, wait. Think about what you're doing."
She paid no attention, flinging off her cloak and stalking passed astonished guards, shouldering her way towards the front of the wall. Rowan muttered a curse and stretched his pace to stand beside her, snatching a bow and arrows from a dumbstruck archer.

"I won't stop you." He said miserably. "But please be careful."

Thunder rumbled overhead as Ellia reached the very edge of the wall and looked out over the sheer drop beyond the battlements. The flat, scrub-covered ground seemed miles below her. She looked across the gap to where the Kurdian army crouched, readying yet another missile. Any moment now, that rock would strike a deadly, crushing blow. Smashing rock, smashing people… *No.*
Without another thought, Ellia stepped forward and threw herself off the wall.

Chapter Twenty-Eight

In Which Some Catapults are Forcibly Dismantled

***

"The tradition of kissing in a thunderstorm was allegedly started by the famous lovers Martha and Prog. This is probably not true, but Dalians like to believe it anyway, as it is a tradition the younger generations heartily approve of. This is also why modest, disapproving old grandmothers like to stay indoors during thunderstorms. (this is probably not true either, but reader be charitable. I can't help lying.)"
— The historian/poet Philip the Bold.

***

By the first step, she was already changing. As she stepped up onto the battlement, the hand that grabbed the wall was edged with thick, curving talons. She launched herself, and great feathered wings exploded outward in a blaze of light. She hung there for a moment in the air, wings flapping slowly, taking in her new dimensions. Then she gathered her strength, her eagle's eyes narrowing, focusing on her target. With a roar, she streaked towards the Kurdu, her body narrowed into a comet of fur, feathers, and flashing teeth. The men, even the strongest soldiers, quailed at the sight. They knew lions, knew what they could do, but lions did not have wings, and were never larger than a horse. This was something different, and it filled them with fear.

Ellia ignored the men. Instead, she swept over them, scattering them like leaves, then angled herself upward toward the nearest rock-throwing contraption. It was very strange, and she could not fathom how it could be possibly used to do the things that it did. However, it was made of pieces that she understood. Rope, wood, metal, these she knew how to deal with. She crashed into the thing, slashing, biting, and tearing through all the ropes she could get her teeth on. Cries of dismay rose in a chorus from the ground as she flew up and sank her claws into the peak of the tower. She threw her full weight against it, and felt the wood splinter. With a groan, a whole section of the frame peeled away from the tower under her weight. Wood creaked, rope snapped, nails screamed as planks twisted apart. The rock rolled free of the spoon-like thing as the whole structure buckled.

Ellia destroyed another tower before the Kurdu gathered the courage to start shooting at her. The first to try it fell dead almost immediately, nailed between the eyes by an arrow, launched an impossibly far distance from the wall of Thalis. This caused the soldiers to fall back in confusion long enough for Ellia to destroy a third tower. Then they rallied and began shooting in earnest. Arrows kept coming from the wall, but they came only one at a time, and did little to stop the Kurdu. A hail of small, sharp crossbow darts whined at Ellia. She spun, but many still embedded themselves in her wings. Sharp pain flared. Ellia faltered. It hurt too much to fly. Finally she folded her wings and dived at the ground.

The moment she hit the ground, the Kurdu soldiers swarmed her, knives and swords flashing. They were afraid, but they weren't cowardly, and they attacked without a care for their own safety. Ellia struck them off with her wings, then wrapped the thick, tawny feathers around her body like a shield. She felt many blades pierce her wings, heard the shouts of triumph, saw death in the eyes of the soldiers as they slashed at her. *You fools. It's not my death you'll be seeing.* She was reluctant to attack them, but eventually the pain in her wings became too great. With a snap, she unfurled them, sending men flying. Her wings hurt too much, so she simply got rid of them. They disappeared, and suddenly she was an Ice Creeper. A freezing cold gale poured from a bottomless pit inside of her. Opening her mouth, she let out a long, drawn out scream. Spinning in place, she encased everyone and everything around her in ice. Before anyone not imprisoned in ice could recover from their shock and react, Ellia leaped over the wall of ice and charged through the crowd, spitting icicles in front of her like arrows.

When a person finds icicles flying at their head, their immediate response is to cover their face. No one can attack while blinded, and so Ellia reached the final tower with only a few minor scratches. She stopped at the base, considering it. The Kurdian army stretched all around her. They were wary now, taking a moment to draw together and organize themselves. They approached slowly, moving forward at a crouch from all sides. They held swords at the ready, shields protecting their faces.

Ellia looked at them. Then she looked back at the tower and *stretched.* Her hindquarters stayed on the ground, but her head zoomed upwards until she was as tall as the strange contraption – taller. The gigantic rock was suddenly small enough for her to swallow in a mouthful. She was huge, powerful, deadly. Her scales, made to withstand the deepest sea pressure, were far too thick for swords to pierce.

The Kurdu soldiers didn't even try. At the sight of her, they screamed, cursed, and backed away. Ellia knew that she could not remain a serpent for long. Already her skin was drying, and her gills burned from the lack of water. She swiftly coiled herself around the final tower and crushed it to splinters, fins churning the air. Then she let go of the magic.

The ground greeted her with an unwelcome, solid embrace as she fell onto it. She stood up slowly, feeling frail in her tiny body. Trying to hide her sudden weakness, she squared her shoulders and lifted her chin. A circle of bulging, terrified eyes watched her, the way a mouse watches a Hill-cat just before it becomes breakfast. Several of the soldiers whispered prayer to Firth to save them from devils. Others raised their swords in nerveless fingers, a last attempt at bravery.

Ellia met their eyes, one by one, slowly. She tried her best to convey coolness, power, and scorn through her gaze, although all she felt was her own frailty. Then she smiled. It was the wicked, teeth-baring grin of a hill-cat when it sees a mouse, and the soldiers trembled. Then she said,

"Scram."

And they fled.

Ellia also fled, but in the opposite direction. As soon as a path began to clear, she made a dash for the palace walls. Arrows whistled one by one from the city wall, arcing over her head and covering her retreat. As she approached the walls, the arrows flew faster as more archers joined in, picking off those who, seeing how she fled, had decided to pursue her. The first raindrops began to fall, and the storm broke in earnest as she drew up to the wall. Above her, soldiers began shouting at each other, suddenly seeing the problem.

"Unbar the gates!" They cried, while some yelled for a rope. Ellia ignored them. Approaching the rain-slicked wall, she carefully touched the stones, sized up the crevices between them, and began to climb.

Gradually, the voices above fell silent as they realized what she was doing. Bit by bit, foot by foot, she scaled the wall, as the rain poured down, and the watchers gaped. It was a longer climb than she had ever made before, and a harder. However, the tiny cracks and crevices presented themselves to her fingers when she needed them, and she was not afraid.

When she reached the last few feet, many eager hands reached down to help her up. The men's eyes were shining, their voices wonder-struck. It was Rowan who pulled her up, wrapping a supportive arm around her as she stepped shakily down from the battlement, soaking wet and shivering. He had stopped shooting, giving the borrowed bow back to it's awestruck owner. The other archers were watching Rowan with the same stunned respect in their eyes as he walked away from them to help Ellia over the wall.

"That was you shooting, wasn't it?" She asked him softly. He nodded. She was silent for a moment, thinking over what she wanted to say. A beaming soldier offered his cloak, and Rowan took it, wrapping it around her soaking shoulders.

"You, ma'am, are the most amazing creature any of us have ever seen!" The soldier enthused, his eyes shining.

"I've never seen anything like what you did out there, to those blasted barbarians. You scared them witless! They'll be a whole lot more hesitant to attack us now!" He clutched his helmet to his chest and gave her a deep bow.

"Lady, you have our eternal gratitude." The men around him muttered their agreement. Ellia accepted their words distractedly, then twisted to look up at Rowan, tugging on his shirt to get him to meet her eyes. He looked down at her, eyebrows raised. She took a deep breath.

"Rowan," She dropped her voice and spoke in a low tone, not wanting the soldiers to hear.

"You saved my life several times out there with your arrows. You're..." She swallowed, breaking eye contact and looking down in sudden shame.

"You're a better man than I took you to be. I'm sorry-" She breathed in slowly. This was hard. Harder than she thought it would be. She hated apologizing.

"... Sorry that I didn't see that before now. Sorry that I refused to trust you, even after you protected me, took care of me, and saved my life when I was dying in the cave."

Rowan caught his breath. She felt him let it out again, and it was ragged with suppressed emotion.

"Then you forgive me?" He asked in wonder, hardly daring to believe it.   She nodded, meeting his eyes shyly. For some reason, she felt a bit embarrassed. His eyes were glowing with joy.

"I'll never forgive myself." He said softly. "But if you forgive me, that's all that matters." He smiled hesitantly at her. Ellia nodded, smiled back. Somewhere further down the wall, a soldier started singing a loud, off-key victory chant, and someone else joined. Ellia and Rowan smiled at each other for a moment.

Then, because her nerves were still singing from the adrenaline of the fight; because her heart was flipping over at being so close to him; because she was cold and wet; because he was warm; because she had always been impulsive, and because he looked so uncertain in that moment, Ellia tugged his head down and kissed him.

The soldiers hooted and cheered. Rowan looked stunned. A corner of his mouth quirked into a small smile, and then gradually grew into a delighted grin. He kissed her back, to the absolute delight of the gleeful guards. Ellia pulled away after a moment, a bit embarrassed by the audience.

"This isn't going to become a regular thing, you understand." She said, trying to look stern, but failing.

"That was just for saving my life."

Rowan nodded seriously, but his eyes were dancing. The rain still poured down, and everyone was soaking, but no one noticed. Ellia allowed Rowan to guide her, still shivering, off of the wall. They turned, and the soldiers parted to give them a path.

Jasper was standing in the middle of a small group of soldiers near the edge of the wall. Rain dripped off the end of his nose, and his clothes were plastered to his tall, thin frame. He was staring out over the wall at the wreckage of the wooden towers with a disbelieving expression on his face. As the people around him moved aside, he turned, scanning the crowd for the source of the disturbance. His eyes landed on Ellia, and his face turned dead white.

"Ellia?" He whispered. She met his eyes, and he staggered backwards as if she had punched him in the gut. He looked out at the wreckage on the plain, and then back to her, his eyes growing wide.

"No. No! It can't be you!" He gasped. "You don't have any powers, and besides, you're… You're dead."

Ellia just looked at him. Beside her, Rowan was rigid. His eyes were narrow slits of fury, fixed on Jasper with such intensity that Ellia half expected the Starfall to melt under it. Jasper, however, didn't seem to be able to tear his eyes away from Ellia's face.

"How did you survive?" He asked at last, his eyes taking in the faint scars tracing her face and neck. Ellia still didn't answer, feeling a hard, cold knot of anger tie itself into her stomach.

The silence hung between them. When she didn't do anything, or change into a strange creature, Jasper's confidence began to return. He noticed Rowan's arm around her shoulders, the rain on her face, and the sight seemed to reassure him that she wasn't, in fact, a ghost.

"Well," He said at last, plastering a fake attempt at a smile onto his wet face, "It's a great relief to see that you're not dead. You can't believe how worried I was."

His eyes began to glow, and he took a step forward. Rowan drew his sword. The soldiers around them looked at each other uncertainly. Those nearest to Jasper edged away from him, giving him distrustful looks and reaching for their own weapons.

Except for one wary glance which he shot at Rowan, Jasper kept his eyes on Ellia. She fought against the power of his gaze, setting her teeth against the warm, mushy thoughts that attempted to shove their way into her mind. Rowan's arm tightened around her shoulder and she drew strength from him.

"Shall I kill him for you?" He asked, his voice hard. The fake smile dropped from Jasper's face. His eyes darted to Rowan with the look of a trapped rodent. Ellia drew a deep breath, and shook her head.

"No." She said, her voice full of a newfound certainty.

"I can deal with him."

Jasper laughed, but it was too high. His face twitched nervously.

"Deal with me? Why would you want to deal with me? Me, your closest friend and most devoted sweetheart? Remember how you loved me, Ellia? Would you desert me so fast?" His voice grew whiny.

His eyes were glowing so brightly now that some of the soldiers around him began to be affected, muttering in halfhearted agreement.

"Awfully coldhearted girl." One mumbled, his eyes unfocused.

Encouraged, Jasper took another step forward.

"You still feel that way about me, I know it." He said, his eyes bright. "Deep down, you haven't forgotten."

Ellia felt an odd, prickling sensation slither its way up her spine, and she stood up straight in the rain. The warm whispers of Jasper's power fell silent in her mind.

"I've forgotten nothing." She said, her voice as dark as the ocean. She held Jasper's eyes, and her own changed from gold to a deep, swirling blue. Her skin glittered, and it wasn't from the rain.

"What about you, Jasper? What do you remember?" She asked softly, and her voice was like the ripple of a thousand tides. It was the most musical, captivating sound any of them had ever heard. Jasper gasped, struggling to break away from her gaze.

"What are you doing to me?" he choked like a drowning person, his face filled with desperation.

"The same thing you do to other people." She replied evenly. "Now, why don't you answer my question and tell me what you remember?"

It didn't matter what she said, merely speaking was enough. The musical tone of her voice and the fathomless depths of a Siren's eyes would have drowned much stronger men. Jasper's face slackened, and he gave in to his own poison.

"I remember hating you." He murmured, his face tilted to the side and eyes dreamily fixed on her face.

"I can't remember why though." he frowned slightly, as if straining to hear something no one else could.

"I remember luring you to… a cave. And blocking you in, then leaving you to die." His face turned woeful, and tears trickled out of his eyes.

"You weren't so beautiful then." He said desperately, almost pleading. "I would never have done it if I had known."

He fell to his knees and turned tragic eyes to her face.

"You have to believe me!"

Ellia saw how far gone he was, how easily his mind was bent to her will, and she felt sick.

"Yes, yes. I believe you." She said, hating herself. "What else do you remember?"

He frowned, struggling to think through the fog of emotions. Then his eyes lit up, and he gave her a dopey grin.

"I remember kissing you."

Ellia felt her face flush at the memory. Jasper was coming closer, that same dopey smile on his face. Ellia suddenly realized that everyone else on the wall within hearing range, except Rowan, was tilted toward her like sunflowers to the sun. Frightened, she instantly dropped the magic.

"Well, there you have it, men." Ellia said to the guards, hoping she didn't sound as shaken as she felt.

"He confessed to trying to kill me, and thus betraying his Queen."

An angry mutter rippled across the crowd. The guards gave Jasper unfriendly glances, but none of them seemed confident enough to arrest him. Suddenly, a voice barked,

"Seize him." Captain Gwylan strode forward, flanked by four of his men. As they grabbed his arms, Jasper suddenly seemed to come awake.

"How did you do that?" He demanded incredulously, staring at Ellia. She said nothing, amazed at how no one else seemed to object to what she had done. It made her feel worse about herself.

As they dragged him away, Jasper began to struggle and yell.

"Wait, you can't do this!" He cried, eyes wide. He tried to catch Ellia's gaze, but she looked down.

"You need me, Ellia!" Jasper insisted. "You need my power on your side! Without me, you're just another Starfall slave. But with me by your side, we could rule this land! I could make you queen."

Ellia shook her head.

"Treason!" An archer growled, and others took up the cry. They dragged Jasper off the wall in an angry mob and marched him toward the palace. Captain Gwylan remained behind for a moment. He looked at Ellia, a question in his gaze.

"How..?" He started, but Rowan cut him off.

"You should bind his eyes." He advised quietly, nodding towards Jasper. "And put him in the dungeon where he can't work his magic on people."

Gwylan nodded his thanks and hurried off. Rowan watched him go unhappily.

"I wish you would have just let me kill him." His voice was bitter. Ellia glanced at him sharply.

"Gwylan?"

"No. Jasper. That treacherous snake who treats you as though he owns you. It would give me great pleasure to kill him."

Ellia stared at him, raising her eyebrows.

"Are you jealous?"

"No." Rowan instantly denied, his face hard. "I would just like to kill him for what he did to you."

Ellia saw a flicker of a look she recognized in his eyes, and she sighed softly.

"That's what Myth took from you." She realized. "Your empathy. She gave your race so much, but as well as magic, she also gave you her disregard for mortal life."

Rowan looked at her, astonished.

"What are you talking about?" He demanded. "Myth took nothing from me."

"Not you specifically." Ellia amended. "Your race. The Faerie. Myth never cared about human life, and neither do they. They have her same arrogance, and anger. I don't think it's an accident, and I don't want you to succumb to her poison, either."

Rowan frowned.

"But I have empathy for Humans."

"Yes, but you're not fully Faerie, either." She reminded him. He was silent for a long time, thinking. Finally, he let out a long sigh and nodded.

"You're right. I don't know how you knew, but we're a broken people, Ellia. We live for so long, but we live only for ourselves. It leaves us empty. My people practically worship Myth, despite the fact that she was a monster."

He looked troubled. Ellia nodded in understanding.

"Sometimes I think that I'm becoming a monster." She admitted. "Something feels very wrong about my powers, about all of this. What I did today, the way that I can manipulate Humans like that… It's wrong. I *stole* Jasper's mind, Rowan. He was powerless against it. I shouldn't be able to do that."

"He deserved that." Rowan growled.

"That doesn't make it any better, though." She whispered, staring at her feet. He looked at her for a long moment, then sighed and pulled her into a hug.

"What's broken can be fixed." He said gently. She leaned her head against his chest, letting a tear slide down her face and mix with the rain.

Chapter Twenty-Nine

In Which Trees Pose a Problem

*** * ***

"There is a myth which says that once upon a time, snakes fell from the sky, and bit people. However, it was invented by a drunk sailor, and has no credibility whatsoever. People still believe it, though. This only proves that people will believe anything. Therefore, everything else that people believe is probably also false."
— High Philosopher in Chief, Stephanio.

*** * ***

The place where they were standing wasn't deserted, but it felt that way. The wall was silent. Drenched, somber archers leaned against the wall at regular intervals, watching the equally silent Kurdian camp below. The rain still fell, and both sides seemed inclined to settle down and wait.

Ellia eventually stopped crying and looked around, feeling tired but comforted. She watched the archers for a while, then looked down at the gate below, where wet statues and soldiers waited out the rain, watching the gate. *Something's wrong here.* The thought tickled at the back of her mind, and she frowned.

"Rowan, what happened to the Assassins?"

"What do you mean?" He caught her tone and followed her gaze out to the silent army on the plains.

"What's wrong?"

"Well," Ellia took a moment to consider. "Kurdu's most powerful fighting force is it's Assassins, right? They're trained from birth to fight, and they're impossibly fast and strong. It's why, even with Starfalls, Dalia has never dared to attack Kurdu."

"Yes."

"So... where are they?"

Rowan frowned.

"You saw none out on the field?"

Ellia shook her head. "No. Those were all just ordinary soldiers."

Rowan thought for a moment, then spoke slowly.

"If I were Kurdian, and I wished to successfully invade Dalia... I would not leave the King to be dealt with later, when he returns. I would send out an ambush of elite fighters to kill or at least detain him so that he does not return to break the siege."

They were both silent.

"I don't think we can count on the King's intervention." Rowan said at last. His voice was calm. Ellia nodded resignedly, but still something was bothering her.

"It's not just that, Rowan. Something else is horribly wrong, but I don't know what."
She turned and looked out over the city. Water ran down the roofs, soaking the streets, swirling around the roots of the trees. *Wait a minute... Trees?* She gasped. Rowan saw it the same moment she did, and he sucked in a breath. The city was full of trees. Some parts were so overgrown that the houses could no longer be seen. Rowan dragged a hand through his hair and groaned.

"Of course. The water in the hall, the overgrown

garden, grass in the gutters, the wind… the storm. Great Firth above, why didn't I see it sooner?" He cursed.

"See *what* sooner?" Ellia demanded, although she thought she knew the answer, and didn't want it to be true.

"My people. The Faerie. They're coming." Rowan's eyes were dark. "Not just coming, they're *invading.* I've never seen it happen, but I've heard of it. It's only allowed in the most extreme circumstances. How on earth did the council agree to this?"

Ellia descended swiftly towards the city, feeling dread clutch her heart. Other than the thunder rumbling, the city was filled with an eerie, oppressive silence. Puddles of water swirled on the streets, but it swirled upwards from between the paving stones, not from the rain. Trees and grasses crept upwards with it, shivering as they grew. The citizens of the city were all indoors because of the rain. Ellia saw with horror that there were vines creeping up over the doors and windows of the houses, trapping the occupants inside.

"We have to get the guards." She whispered. Rowan shook his head.

"It's no use. They won't hear you. The oracles have cast a Silencing spell on all humans in the city."

Unwilling to believe, Ellia dashed up to the nearest guard, seized his arm, and began shaking. He turned towards her, his eyes glazed. When she continued shaking, he glared at her, shoved her hands away, then turned his back and continued watching the gate. The other guards behaved the same way. Frustrated and close to panicking, Ellia turned and ran toward the palace. Her footsteps made no noise as they splashed through the puddles. Neither did Rowan's, following her, but he always walked silently. She flew headlong down the main street, holding her wet, torn skirts in one hand and dodging trees. The wet grass scratched across her bare calves, and the branches whipped at her face.

She was so caught up in her desperation to protect her friends, she didn't hear the sound until Rowan caught her arm and stopped her. He pushed her behind a stand of trees, his eyes wide, and then she heard it too. It was the soft clinking of chain mail, coming from an alleyway ahead.

"They're here already." Rowan hissed, for the first time looking slightly scared. They both held still as the sound grew closer. Suddenly, there was a flicker of movement, and a group of elvish soldiers marched out of the alley, lead by a hooded oracle. They moved silently towards the palace, glancing carefully into every alleyway as they passed.

A cold wind twisted through the streets, as if it were a living creature. Ellia waited a few seconds, then dashed out of her hiding place and continued after the soldiers. The street was still silent, but the city rustled with the soft, almost imperceptible tread of Faerie. The alleyways were full of them. Ellia flattened herself behind an abandoned merchant stall just in time as yet another group emerged from an adjoining street. They were also headed toward the palace. Ellia felt her heart pounding in her throat. She braced herself, feeling ragged wings begin to take shape on her back. Beside her, Rowan nudged her hand. When she looked at him, he shook his head vigorously.

"I have to save them!" She insisted through clenched teeth. He shook his head again.

"You can't just go charge in and fight them, Ellia. Elves are very resistant to magic. It's why your Siren spell didn't affect me, and neither did Jasper's persuasion. If you try to fight them, they'll just kill you."

Ellia sighed.

"Fine. I'll just fly over them, then, and rescue my

friends.”

“They’ll shoot you down.” He pointed out. Ellia was close to screaming with frustration.

“Let them try.” She growled. Rowan sighed, then pointed upward.

“There is another way.”

For the first time, Ellia was glad of the trees. Although she found their roots very annoying, she was thankful for the branches as she followed Rowan onto the roof of a nearby house. The flat clay wall would have been impossible to climb without them. Once they were on the slanted, rain-slick tiles of the roof, the trees also provided cover, so that Ellia’s crouching form would not be visible from the street. Rowan shifted into a cat for better balance, and they started off across the rooftops, keeping low.

After several death defying leaps and scrambles, they neared the walls. The houses were taller here, and there was no cover from the trees. Rowan stopped, crouching behind a chimney.

“We need a plan.” He said, with typical caution. Ellia felt a flash of impatience.

“We have one. Rescue the twins and Chadwick. Oh, and also probably Gwylan.” She added with sudden alarm.

“He’s probably still escorting Jasper through the city, right into the thick of trouble.”

Rowan gave her an exasperated look.

“That’s not a plan. That’s an end goal. We need to really *think*.”

“I’m terrible at planning,” Ellia replied defensively, “and at carrying out orders. An end goal will have to do.”

She stood up and headed for the next chimney. Rowan put up a hand to stop her.

“Wait. Just think for a moment. Lord Iberus will expect you to be in the palace. He’ll be looking for you there. He won't expect you here, so you're safer here. We need to figure out the least risky way to get in and extract your friends."

A cold wind lashed around the chimney. Ellia felt a prickle of apprehension. A spot on her neck, just behind her ear, began to warm up. Her stomach plummeted.

"You're wrong, Rowan." She whispered, feeling sick with dread. "Lord Iberus knows exactly where I am."

The roof collapsed.

One moment they were crouched behind the chimney, the next moment every tile and stone of the building was ripped apart by a blast of wind so violent it flattened the houses on both sides. Ellia and Rowan tumbled onto the small hill of rubble, him landing in cat form while she tumbled and landed painfully on her knees.

Standing several feet away, Lord Iberus regarded her coolly. He was flanked by a large troop of armored elves, as well as several reluctant-looking oracles, two council members, and his mother, Lady Eaglenda. She stood slightly behind him, glaring daggers at his back. He looked Ellia over calmly, then glanced at Rowan. His eyes flashed with momentary fury, but he hid it quickly.

"Well." He said softly, his harshly beautiful face betraying nothing. Ellia stood up, fists clenched and eyes glowing like two coals with anger.

"You monster!" She snarled, practically spitting fire. "How could you? Do you have any idea how many people were in the house you just destroyed? There was smoke in the chimney! And you just *killed* them. Someone's family. Someone's *kids.*"

Lord Iberus looked amused.

"It's nice to see you also, daughter."

"I'm not your daughter." She spat.

"No?" He raised his eyebrows. "Doubtless you

believe you belong to one of these human *families* you think so highly of?”

“I belong to no one but myself.” She declared, chin high. Rowan, once again a man, came to stand beside her. Lord Iberus raised his eyebrows.

“And that is as it should be.” Lady Eaglenda interjected suddenly before he could speak, stepping forward.

“For surely the future Lady Myth, ruler of our Golden Age to come, should bow to no one? *Especially* not you, dear son.” She gave him a malicious smile. Many of the oracles nodded their agreement. Lord Iberus, however, gave her a smooth smile of his own.

“Certainly, Lady. But, as the dragon’s chosen host happens to be my daughter, I am responsible for caring for the girl until the Golden Age has come. Is this not so?” He turned to the other members of the council and they reluctantly nodded, like puppets on a string. Lady Eaglenda looked from them to her son, with deep resentment in her eyes.

“I see no resemblance.” She said. Iberus smirked, finally turning to look her in the eyes.

“Yes, but *I* do. And over half the council agrees with me.” He turned back to Ellia.

“Come, child. You have spent far too much time among these mortals. Their poisonous presence has started to affect your mind, as we can all see. The council has agreed that you must be removed from this harmful atmosphere. Come here, and I will take you home.” His tone was gentle and condescending, as one might speak to a feral dog that looked as if it might bite. Ellia was about to spit in his face, but then she remembered the twins, and she checked herself.

“If I come with you,” She started warily, “Will you leave this city and it’s inhabitants alone?”

Iberus’s mouth twisted into a thin line.

"Regretfully, we cannot. The human queen has violated our borders by sending spies poking about our doorways, and the human king has set fire to one of our ancient groves. An act of war. Unfortunately, we must retaliate. He burns our forest, so we will flood and choke his city."

The armored elves cheered grimly, their eyes alight with a vengeful fire. Ellia felt ready to fly at them and tear their throats out, she was so furious.

"What, so they burned a few *trees*, and now you're going to massacre thousands of innocents?"

Lord Iberus sighed.

"Very well, dearest. If you feel so strongly about it, we will not mete out our vengeance on the innocent. For your sake, we will only execute the fighting men, the spies, and the royalty."

Ellia started forward, her outrage burning so brightly that her eyes cast a faint glow on the lord's face. Rowan put a restraining hand on her arm.

"We can't solve this like that, Ellia. It would only end in blood."

"It would end in blood either way. The only difference is who's." Ellia objected, but she relaxed slightly at his touch, and restrained herself from attacking. Rowan looked at Lord Iberus.

"You can't do this thing, sir. Have not the people of Thalis suffered enough? Already they are besieged by the Kurdu. They fight with each other, and eventually they will kill each other. There is no need for us to intervene."

Lord Iberus looked wounded.

"So, you would even turn traitor to your own lord? I, who took you in when everyone else wished to exile you? Where is your loyalty?"

"My loyalty is to Ellia." Rowan replied evenly. "As should yours be, if what you claim about her is true."

The lord looked at Rowan's face, and then at his hand on Ellia's arm, and he sneered.

"Spoken like a traitor and a thief, Rowan. You have even turned my own daughter against me! We are done talking. You either come willingly, or we will take you by force. The girl's decisions cannot be trusted any longer, since her mind is so clearly corrupted."

Ellia made her decision. Without a word, she threw herself at Lord Iberus. She meant to transform at the last second and attack him unawares. Unfortunately, her transformation was accompanied by a flash of golden light. Lord Iberus's eyes widened at the sudden sight of the snarling lion's mouth bearing down on him. A tendril of wind lashed out, twisting her aside just in time. She crashed into his entourage, bowling over soldiers and oracles. She landed on all fours, tail lashing for balance as she skidded around to face him again. She leaped, but he was ready for her this time. His hands clenched, and the wind caught her great, torn wings in an iron grip.

"*Fascinating*." He whispered, his eyes gleaming. Then she became a girl again, and dropped. Halfway to the ground, she changed again into an Ice Creeper. She was already launching a spray of icicles as she hit the ground. Lord Iberus's normally impassive facade disappeared. An icicle struck him in the thigh and he staggered, astonished.

"How is this possible?" He gasped. Around them, all order had dissolved. Many of the soldiers could not seem to bring themselves to attack the girl they believed to be their destined leader. Some moved to attack, but several oracles threw themselves bodily in front of the soldiers, arms out in Ellia's defense. Rowan drew his sword and launched himself into the mayhem, causing utter chaos. Several Faerie drew their bows, sighting on Ellia. She heard the creak of wood, and Lord Iberus's cry.

"Don't kill her! I need her alive!"

The oracles had withdrawn themselves, while the council members raised their arms. Rain and lightning lashed down. Vines sprang up from between the stones. The ground heaved and shook like a flea-bitten dog. Lady Eaglenda stood in the middle of it all, looking around. She saw Ellia, facing off against Lord Iberus, and Rowan, struggling to reach her, his eyes full of desperate love. Lady Eaglenda saw that love, and her eyes softened. She turned decisively, and attacked the other council members.

Ellia scampered sideways to escape the vines tangling at her paws. She jumped over a fallen soldier, and was suddenly sent hurtling skyward. The wind tore at her throat and screamed in her ears. The earth whirled and spun through her vision as she tumbled through the air. Becoming a flying creature only made it worse, as the wind wrenched her already torn wings in opposite directions. She gave up and allowed herself to be flung about like a leaf. Then the wind stopped. She reached the limit of Iberus's power, and hung there. For an instant, everything was still. She saw the city stretched below her. It was broken, overgrown, flooded in parts, and on fire in others.

It was also swarming with elves, and every one of them was converging on the spot where Rowan and Lady Eaglenda still fought. For an instant, Ellia saw all of this, and her heart seized in terror. Then she was falling.

For the first time, Ellia knew what it was to be utterly frozen with fear. She was falling, and the city seemed a mile below. Her wings were dislocated, torn, and bleeding. She knew that they could not hold her if she summoned them.

Her heart stopped, then started again when the certainty of her own death settled in. She saw Lord

Iberus's upturned face rushing up at her, his hands spread. He was waiting for her to open her wings, she knew, so that he could seize control of them and, through them, her. So she didn't open them. Instead, she became a serpent. *I'm going to take you down with me.* She thought grimly. *One snake to cut off the head of the other. With you dead, at least this city might be saved.* With the sudden weight of her vast, armored body, she plummeted downward at Lord Iberus with all the deadly force of the falling star she came from. She saw his mouth open, and knew that he understood. He screamed, lifting his hands in one last, desperate attempt to save himself and her.

All throughout the city, running elves stopped short in astonishment at the sight of a mighty Sea Serpent falling through the sky. They were still more astonished when, at the last moment, the creature slowed, stopped, and finally, seconds before impact, hung twisting in midair.

On the ground, Lord Iberus had been driven to his knees. His skin was white as bone, and sweating, but his face was alight with triumph. Straining, he slowly got to his feet, every muscle trembling.

"You cannot beat me with this magic, Starfall!" He cried, his voice hoarse.

"I am more powerful than you will ever be, and I will always win!"

Ellia turned into a human, dropping through his grip.

"Who needs magic?" She asked, and stabbed him.

Chapter Thirty

In Which Lord Iberus Passes Into the Realm of the Deceased

***

"Die, nasty plant-stompers!"
— An old hermit named Ham who lives in the Hills.

***

Lord Iberus froze. He looked down with disbelief at the dagger handle sticking from his chest. Slowly, he slid to his knees.

"How…?" He whispered, trailing off in shock. Ellia pulled the dagger out of him. He gasped, and her heart throbbed with sympathy despite how much she hated him.

"Sorry." She said, "But I have to protect my people."

He stared at her, his expression dumbfounded.

"How can you be sorry," He asked, "When you hate me?"

Ellia shrugged.

"I hate to see pain more than I hate you. I'm Human. It's the way we're made, though some of us forget it."

Lord Iberus blinked. His pain-clouded eyes filled

slowly with a look of dawning comprehension. Then the light behind them went out, and he died.

Ellia stepped back. There was a shocked silence. None of the Faerie seemed able to comprehend the fact that their lord had really died. As more and more poured into the street from other parts of the city, they too stopped and stared. Ellia turned to face them.

"Release this city." She said. She tried to sound commanding, but her voice shook with exhaustion. The oracles, standing to the side in their huddled group, murmured among themselves. They finally raised their hands, and the silence lifted. Ellia could hear terrified screams and shocked yells all over the city, as people awoke to what was happening around them. She relaxed slightly. The water splashing around their feet began to recede back into the ground.

"No!" One of the council women whirled on the oracles, her face a mask of fury.

"We must purge this city!" She cried. Springing forward, she drew a long knife and stabbed one of the oracles. At that, everyone in the street instantly sprang into action, taking one side or the other. Lady Eaglenda began rallying the soldiers to her side. Ellia felt a hand catch hers, and looked up to see Rowan.

"We have to get out of here." He tugged on her hand, his face urgent.

"This is fast becoming chaos. We don't want to be caught in the middle of an Elvish civil war."

Ellia relented. Dodging swords and thrusting people out of their way, they ran from the turmoil and down a side street. Ellia's muscles screamed. Her breath came in painful gasps as they ran, their feet sloshing through the receding water. Rowan was practically dragging her now, with her arm across his shoulders as she stumbled along beside him. Although she no longer had wings, she felt sore across her shoulders where they might have been. It seemed as if they had been running forever, although they had only turned a few corners. Ellia heard a few shouts and sounds of pursuit. The sound motivated her to run faster, although her muscles protested.

The footsteps behind grew louder, and Ellia knew that they were being gained upon. Rowan sucked breath in through clenched teeth. He gave up on matching his pace to hers, and instead just took off, dragging her along with him. Her feet barely skimmed the ground as he sprinted around yet another corner, past an abandoned Faerie portal. No elves emerged from it any longer, but by the fresh forest air which blew through the branches of the trees, Ellia could tell that it was still open. They ran past it and around another corner. Their pursuers followed, and then suddenly all sounds of pursuit stopped. There was a yell, and then utter silence.

Rowan pulled Ellia through a broken doorway, and stopped. They ducked into the shadows and waited, straining their ears. The only sound was Ellia's ragged breathing, and the skitter of a rat in the corner.

When she could no longer bear the silence, Ellia pulled away from Rowan and peered out the door. The twisting alleyway was empty. Cautiously, she stepped out, looking back the way they had come. Rowan stepped out beside her and took her hand, his stance full of nervous tension. No pursuers rounded the corner. After a moment, Rowan let out a sigh of relief.

"We should go find your friends-" He began.

Then a man stepped from the shadows. They peeled back and fell away from him like a dark cloak, and he stepped into view.

He was tall, even taller than Lord Iberus. His face would have been young, save that it was streaked with a myriad of scars, crisscrossing his face and arms like a snarled spiderweb. His eyes were deep, and layered with countless years of dark, bitter hatred. It was a poisonous hatred, and, looking into them, Ellia could see nothing but that twisted darkness. And pain. His whole face was ravaged with the aftermath of a prolonged, intense pain. The very lines between his brows spoke of heartbreak in a way no words could. Across one shoulder, he had casually slung a long, wicked-looking sword, its wide blade etched with hundreds of strange runes, its sharp edges gleaming.

"Gilead." Ellia said. It was not a question. At the sight of him, the small, angry voice inside of her had suddenly grown much louder, screaming his name with hate and hunger. *Let me out! Let me out NOW! Now is the time!* Ellia pushed it away, back into its cage inside her chest. *No.*

At the sound of his name, the tall Faerie's eyes snapped to Ellia's golden ones. His eyes widened in recognition. He strode forward, sliding his sword from his shoulder. Rowan stepped in front of her and drew his own sword.

"You." His eyes narrowed, and he looked up at the ancient elf without a trace of fear.

"Stay away from Ellia."

Gilead looked down at him, his eyes blank.

"Who is Ellia?" He asked, mystified. Ellia placed her hand on Rowan's shoulder, suddenly afraid for him. The last time she had seen that sword, it had been cutting off the head of a baron.

"I am." She said softly. "Now, please, would you put away that sword and tell me why you're here?"

Gilead smiled. It was an ugly thing, that smile, in a face in which all joy had long ago died.

"Ah. I see." He eyed Ellia, as though actually seeing her for the first time.

"So the monster has hidden herself inside the

body of a human child. A clever disguise, but a mistake, as it makes her more vulnerable." He looked at Rowan.

"She has fooled you, boy. That creature which you are protecting is not a girl, but a terrible dragon, the murderer of thousands. If I allow her to live, she will emerge and kill thousands more. She must be stopped. Now, please step aside so that we may finish what we started."

Rowan stood his ground.

"Don't, Rowan." Ellia pleaded softly. Over his shoulder, she met Gilead's eyes.

"I never started anything with you that needs finishing." She told him, her voice steady. He stared, and his dark eyes welled up with an immense bitterness.

"Never started anything?" He growled. "What about when you cursed me with this broken form, to live forever, knowing I had failed to avenge your victims? When you caused me to outlive my family, everyone I had ever loved, and watched me bury them?" His voice shook, rough with anger. "What about when you poisoned the minds of those townspeople, urging them on to kill Lillium, my only joy in this poisoned life? No, Dragon. You started many things. And I am going to finish them with my sword in your murderous heart."

Ellia took a deep breath. She had seen most of those things happen, and she knew that Gilead had good reason to feel bitterness.

"I am sorry for what Myth has taken from you," She whispered, "but I am not the dragon."

She instantly realized her mistake, but it was too late. Gilead's eyes gleamed.

"Then how do you know the dragon's name?" He hissed. His sword came whipping forward, but Rowan was instantly moving to intercept it, his own blade slashing upwards. They clashed, with a sound like a scream. The runes on Gilead's sword glowed hot, and

Rowan's blade shattered like ice. He yelled as the handle clattered from his numb hand.

"Move aside, boy." Gilead growled. Rowan set his jaw.

"Never." He drew his knife. It looked tiny in his hands as Gilead brought his huge blade slashing down. He swung it for Rowan's head, but the younger elf dodged to the side.

The next few moments were a blur of movement. Rowan dodged in and out of Gilead's deadly swings, sometimes as a cat, sometimes as a man. Whenever he could, he slashed at Gilead, but seldom connected. Eventually, he ducked under a swing and succeeded in slicing the former hero's arm. Gilead roared. With deadly accuracy, he swung his sword at Rowan's head, simultaneously wrapping a curtain of shadow around him. Blinded, Rowan faltered. He became a cat just as the sword connected, dropping beneath its swing. He stumbled forward inside his prison of shadow, and Gilead kicked him.

Ellia cried out as the cat flew through the air, crashing into the alley wall opposite with a horrible thud. It slid to the ground in a tiny, crumpled heap. In that moment, Ellia felt her heart shatter, and she knew that she loved him. She fell to her knees, all the strength that she had borrowed from him suddenly draining away. Gilead was approaching, sword in hand, but she couldn't take her eyes from Rowan's crumpled form, which was now lying there in his true shape. His head was flopped backwards, and blood trickled down the side of his face.

Gilead followed her gaze, and his brow creased in perplexity.

"You really cared for him?" He asked, dumbfounded. Then he shrugged.

"I'm glad I crushed him, then. Perhaps it made

you feel a touch of the pain you caused me." His voice was once again full of hate.

Ellia didn't reply. She watched the blood trickle down Rowan's beloved face, and her bones ached with the deepest weariness she had ever known.

Gilead raised his sword. Inside her mind, the voice was screaming. *Let me out! You stupid girl, stop holding me back! He's going to kill us! Why are you just sitting there? LET ME OUT!* Ellia slowly raised her head and met Gilead's eyes. All her sadness and exhaustion showed there. He paused. A slight uncertainty flashed through his eyes, and he frowned. Stepping back, he held his sword out so that the point hovered between her eyes.

"Come out, dragon." He commanded. "Face me in your true form. Stop hiding inside a little girl. You think I wouldn't kill a girl to get to you? I would do anything, *anything*, to stop you from returning and wreaking havoc on the world again. So come out."

The thing inside Ellia strained and grew. She set her teeth, knowing what would happen if it emerged. The thing pushed.

"No!" Ellia gasped. Gilead frowned. The bars imprisoning the thing inside of Ellia's chest suddenly gave way, and it flared up with a power so immense, her own will shredded like paper before it. She arched her back and screamed, golden light pouring through her skin, eyes, and mouth. Gilead let out a shout of fury and stabbed at her, but he was knocked back by a sudden blast of force.

The dragon emerged.

Chapter Thirty-One

In Which Magic Makes No Sense

*****

"Revenge is pointless. I once knew a man who stole my mop bucket. I did nothing to retaliate, and the next day he tripped over it and broke his foot. Firth watches over those who mop the street, so we have no need to avenge ourselves."
— Bob, a street washer.

*****

"Hello, little hero." Myth said. "That was quite noble of you, to challenge me like that. Last time, if I recall correctly, you hid behind a rock and attacked me when I was weak and drained of power." She spread her wings, knocking the shacks on either side of the alley flat. Her gigantic form glowed with power, the glittering, gem-like scales on her chest shining with the fire inside. She was incredibly beautiful, and terrifying, with a long, hawk-like face and angry golden eyes.

"You're not so lucky this time."

Gilead gripped his sword with both hands.

"I have no need of luck." He growled. Without a care for his own safety, he charged at her, sliding under her snapping teeth. His sword pierced her impenetrable scales like butter, and she roared, rearing back before he could reach her heart. She swiped at him with her claws, and he smashed into the narrow alley wall. They were both bleeding now, Myth from a ragged slice just over her left foreleg, and Gilead from a gash in his arm. He staggered forward, regained his balance, and charged again.

She opened her mouth. White hot flame poured up from her stomach and roared from her jaws. Gilead threw himself aside, hair singed. She turned her head, still flaming, after him. He sprinted along the side of the alley, and the walls behind him melted. Everything – stones, wood, metal, and clay – exploded in the heat, leaving a field of slag where the houses and alley walls had once been. In a desperate move, Gilead threw a cloud of shadow into the dragon's face, at the same time rolling under her. She felt a sharp pain slash across her stomach, and screamed, struggling to see him in the darkness. Gilead emerged on her other side, and she felt her wing shred all the way down it's great length. The pain was unbearable. She turned, catching sight of him through the shadows. A great heat rose into her throat, and she opened her mouth to blast him into a smoking crater. He stood, hemmed in by her tail on one side and a wall on the other. Rowan's body lay near him. The young elf's hand twitched. Myth, with fire filling the hole where her heart might have been, could care less about the boy. However, the tiny flicker that was Ellia saw him, and screamed. With everything she had, she wrenched Myth's head away, so that the dragon's fire spilled into the sky.

Myth's anger blazed.

"What are you doing, girl?" She screamed at the sky, struggling to bring her head back down.

"Release me!"

Gilead, seizing the chance, leaped forward and

drove his sword into the joint between her scales, crippling her other foreleg. She wrenched her head down, shattering Ellia's fragile hold on her mind. Liquid fire spilled from her heart through the hole in her armor, melting the ground. Gilead strode forward, and she dragged herself backwards in a clumsy retreat, suddenly afraid.

"Really, Gilead." She attempted a confident tone, but it came out with a slight whine of fear.

"I'm surprised at you. Would you really kill your own daughter to conquer me?"

Gilead's face was black with hate.

"I have no daughter. Your lies cannot deceive me."

"Is that so?" Myth's tone suddenly became very smug. "Do you not recall a certain beautiful young woman… One who you saved from an angry mob and made into a baroness over her town? What was her name again? Lillium, wasn't it?"

Gilead grew very still at the name, and his face blanched with fury.

"You killed her." He whispered. "I know you did. The townsfolk would never have done so on their own initiative."

"Yes." Myth agreed, her voice impassive. "But before that, she had a child. Guess who's?"

Pain flashed through the elf's dark eyes.

"That's not true." He hissed. "The child died at birth. She told me so."

"She didn't want to cause you pain with a false hope." Myth grinned. "Sweet woman. But in truth, the child was stolen. By human smugglers. On the night they took her, I threw myself down from the sky. It was the most perfect revenge I could imagine, to take the only child of my enemy as my host. Of course, I didn't expect her to be so strong. And there was the small issue of her power failing to mature in her half-blooded system. But those were easy things to solve. She's mine now. And, to kill me, you'll have to kill her as well. But, to make my revenge even sweeter, I killed her mother as well. When her newborn child disappeared, I whispered a rumor among the townspeople that the unnatural woman had sacrificed her own child to the heathen gods of her Faerie husband. They were furious." She chuckled, despite her wounds. Gilead's face twisted with pain.

"You're lying!" He screamed, raising his sword to strike the wounded dragon. Even faced with that shining blade, she continued laughing.

"Am I?" She suddenly released Ellia. The dragon disappeared, and Ellia crouched in its place. The girl was huddled in on herself, shaking as she battled against the ancient, overpowering will of the dragon. She raised her eyes to look at Gilead, and the hero froze. Ellia stared back at him, her exhaustion momentarily forgotten. She suddenly realized why he had seemed so familiar in all of her dreams. Those same features had stared back at her every time she looked in a mirror. She had his slanted, skeptical brows, his sharp cheekbones, the same tilt to her chin. Even her faint scars, silver against her tanned face, were similar to his own. Both had been caused by a dragon's claws.

Gilead stared at her, and his eyes gradually filled with recognition. His breath caught in his throat, and his face crumpled with agony.

"No." He whispered. "How could you do this to me?"

Ellia stood up painfully, swaying on her feet as she faced him.

At the other side of the alley, next to the one untouched wall, Rowan awoke. He slowly looked up with unfocused eyes, taking in the massive crater of smoking slag which had once been an alley. In the center of that crater, he saw Ellia and Gilead, sword in his hand.

"Don't touch her!" He stumbled to his feet, fell, and tried to rise. Ellia didn't see him. She looked up into Gilead's dark, broken eyes, and her own filled with tears.

"Please…" She whispered. Her father looked at her, and his face hardened in an agonized resolve.

"The girl is gone." He said, his voice cracked. "You can't fool me. This is just her shell. No mortal could contain your power and still keep her soul. You killed my daughter, and I will avenge her with the rest of your victims."

He raised his sword and drove it into her chest. As the tip pierced her skin, she exploded into flame. Rowan screamed. His cry of agony echoed in Ellia's ears as the flames engulfed her. When the flames were gone, nothing was left but ashes, which drifted to the ground in a small heap. Gilead watched them, and tears slid down his scarred cheeks.

"The monster is dead." He said heavily. "She will plague this land no more."

Face once again as emotionless as stone, he turned to leave, his sword point dragging a furrow through the dirt behind him.

Rowan stood in his path, his muscles trembling unsteadily. One eye was swollen almost closed, and a nasty bruise was forming on his forehead, blood trickling from it into his eye. In his hand he still clenched his knife.

"You killed her." He whispered, his voice shaking. "You killed Ellia."

"There was no Ellia." Gilead replied coldly. "I killed a monster, which was poisoning your mind. You were her thrall, but I have freed you. Why are you still here?"

Rowan began to tremble more violently, but it was with anger, not weakness.

"I loved her!" He cried, his eyes blazing with raw emotion. "I loved her, and I would have gladly died in her place, but you took her from me!"

He leaped at Gilead, knife drawn, his expression murderous.

Ellia stood on flat stone. All around her, the gray, featureless surface stretched to every horizon. There was light, but there was no sun. Myth crouched a few paces away, her wounds bleeding fire.

"Well." She hissed, spitting sparks. "You've turned out to be almost more trouble than you're worth, girl. Although, I must admit, you have your uses. That last part was a move even I didn't know you were capable of. I wonder how it is that you have my power, and yet can do things that I never could."

Ellia took a shaky breath.

"It's because I'm not you." She said, a bit of fire returning to her voice. "You're only a part of me. My soul is my own, and you can't touch it."

Myth laughed.

"Only a part of you? Child, you're only a part of *me.* I made you what you are. I guided and orchestrated your entire life."

"That's not true." Ellia whispered, feeling doubt creeping in. "Firth made me, and I chose the course of my own life. You were only ever a nightmare."

"Firth?" Myth snorted. "Firth is fake. A silly story. All that Creator of the World stuff is nonsense. *I* created the best creatures on this earth."

"Everything you made is broken." Ellia whispered. "You poison them with your own twisted pride."

"I gave them magic!" Myth snarled.

"Then who gave you magic?" Ellia argued, her voice rising. "That magic was not yours in the first place, and you merely passed on the gift."

"Ha!" Myth laughed. "That's ridiculous. Are you broken, too, then? I made you."

"You did not." Ellia's voice shook.

"Didn't I?" The dragon leaned closer, her hot, smoky breath hissing through her grinning black teeth.

"Was it not I who pushed the Starfall smugglers to steal you from the house of the Baroness? I who gave the oracles dreams about you, so that the Elves would count you as one of their own, instead of having you killed as a mistake and embarrassment? I who whispered to the Queen's pride, causing her to give you an important place at court without asking questions about your abilities?"

Ellia stumbled away, shaking her head. The dragon leaned closer, her smile malicious.

"When you struggled to master your powers, I went to your rival Jasper where he sat in the Library, stewing in his own jealousy and trying to plot some kind of revenge. I was the one who pushed on his mind and told him about the legend of the Mirror of Souls. I was the one who planted the plot in his mind, and told him which cave to trap you in. I was the dragon who fought for you in the cave, so that you conquered the Monster in the Mirror and mastered your powers. I was the one who told Lord Iberus to come fetch you from the city when the Kurdu laid siege to it, putting you in danger. It was always me."

Her hot breath whipped Ellia's hair around. Ellia shook her head.

"No." She stammered, trying to deny it. "That still doesn't make me you. I'm not a monster. I'm not."

Myth looked amused.

"How so?"

Ellia wracked her brain, trying to think of something. She hunched over, hands pressed to her temples. She tried to think of anything that might separate her from what Myth had caused her to become, but all she could say was,

"I'm not. I'm not."

Myth grinned.

"You see? I made you everything you are today."

"Rowan." Ellia gasped. The dragon frowned.

"What?"

Ellia straightened.

"Rowan. I love him. You don't love anyone. You don't even know how to love. But I love him with everything in my heart. So you didn't make me. You only tried to break what was already made." She met the dragon's astonished eyes.

"But you can't."

They faced each other on the gray rock, the wounded dragon and the exhausted Human. Ellia was tired beyond belief, but she was not broken. She met Myth's eyes, and her own held more fire than the Dragon's.

Myth snarled.

"Impudent girl. I was going to let you live, but you are becoming insufferable. I don't need you anymore, to come back to my full power. I may not have made you, but I can kill you. It would be so easy. Like breathing. I need only kill this one small piece of your mind, and you will be gone forever. Then I will rise, and no one will dare stand before my might."

She reared back, and her chest began to glow with inner flame. Ellia frowned.

"Wait a minute. You can't kill me here. This is my mind."

The dragon grinned.

"Does it matter? You are alone here. I will kill you,

and then it will become my mind."

Ellia drew her knife.

"You're wrong." She said. "I'm not alone here."

Then she split. Suddenly, there were six creatures standing on either side of her. Every one of them was vastly different, but they all moved with Ellia to stand facing the dragon. Myth reared back, blinking in utter confusion.

"How is this even possible?" She demanded. Ellia looked around, then shrugged.

"I don't know. It's magic. You can't explain it, and it doesn't ever make sense. All I know is, your power isn't the only power I have. I was given something else, too."

With that, the creatures attacked. The wounded dragon screamed, clawing and biting. She stumbled, then spread her wings. With a tremendous roar, she threw herself free of the creatures. She careened drunkenly through the air, the tear in her wing bleeding. She crash-landed on top of Ellia, one gigantic claw pinning her to the ground. Ellia gasped, her heart pounding desperately as a talon sliced into her, threatening to pierce it.

"Your powers are not enough to stop me." Myth hissed. "Your love is not enough, for what good will it do you when everything you love will soon be dead?"

She opened her mouth. She heaved, and fire splashed in short bursts from the crack in her chest. She heaved again, and some of it came up and hissed between her teeth onto Ellia. Ellia felt it eat through her skin, melting a hole in her torso. She knew she was dying, and she closed her eyes. *I've failed.* She thought, *Oh well.* But then she remembered watching through Myth's eyes as she landed in villages and hamlets, blasting and tearing apart the mortals without a thought. She remembered that one mortal boy who had first wounded Myth with an arrow down her throat, how the dragon had torn him apart. *Am I really just going to lie here and let that happen again?* She wondered. With a gasp, she opened her eyes. The dragon glared into them, full of triumph, even though her life's blood leaked out of her.

"Die, mortal." She laughed.
Ellia shook her head.

"No."

They were both dying. Ellia clung on to her life by a tiny thread. The pain was so great, she felt she was drowning in it. Still, she held on. Her body seemed broken beyond repair. Only her mind still clung to life, but it clung to life with a fierce desperation which Myth could not match. The dragon was growing weaker. As her strength leaked out of her with every heartbeat, Ellia's tiny thread grew thicker.

Slowly, her body knitted itself back together. She pushed herself up, and the dragon's claws bent backwards to let her. Myth stood frozen, gaping.

"This is my mind." Ellia said, and her eyes were full of certainty.

"You can't have it, and you can't return to kill people."

The dragon growled and snapped at her, but she grabbed hold of it's teeth a few inches from her face. They cut her hands, but she focused, and the cuts healed.

"You can't kill me here." She said. "Not unless I allow it. And I will never allow it, no matter how much you hurt me. Because I don't care if I get hurt, as long as it means you can't hurt others."

Myth broke free and bit deep into Ellia's arm. Ellia let her. With her other hand, she stabbed her knife through the dragon's eyes and into it's head.

"*You* can die."

And the dragon did. As she watched, it shriveled and broke from her mind, falling apart into bits of howling darkness that gradually faded. Slowly, the hole in Ellia that Myth had left filled with something else. All the anger she had felt faded into hope. She looked around at the gray plain. A door opened to the outside, and she stepped through it.

Rowan grappled furiously with Gilead. His breath whistled raggedly through his lungs, and the blood in his eye blinded him. The older elf seemed slow and tired, however, and Rowan was only just fast enough to escape his blows. On the ground, the small pile of ashes swirled, then exploded outwards. There was a flash of flame, bright as a sunset. Rowan stopped fighting, staring over Gilead's shoulder as a flaming creature emerged from the ashes. It was a bird, but its wings burned with a thousand tiny tongues of flame, and it's feathers were all the blazing colors of fire.

Gilead took advantage of Rowan's hesitation and swung his sword at his head. However, he was suddenly hit by a sharp blow to his arm. The sword flew from his grasp, clattering to the melted ground.

He whirled, and the Phoenix became Ellia, who slammed into him with all her weight as she dropped from the air. He fell to the ground, and she crouched on top of him, her knife at his throat.

"Don't you *dare* touch him." She growled, her flaming wings slowly fading. His eyes widened.

"Dragon." He choked, and his voice was despairing. He relented under the pressure of her knife, all the fight going out of him.

"You live." He gasped bitterly. "Kill me, then. For I have failed, and have nothing left to live for."

Ellia sat back slowly, and put her knife away.

"The dragon is dead. I killed it." She said. "And

I've had enough of killing things. I would never kill an innocent man, anyways."

She looked at him, with eyes that were no longer golden. Instead, they were a kaleidoscope of colors, fractured like broken glass, and filled with sadness.

"Especially not my father." She murmured.

Gilead stared into her eyes. He saw the truth there. Gradually, the bitterness and twisted hate unraveled in his own. Ellia could see the dragon's poison losing it's hold on his mind. Only the pain remained, and tears began to slip down his face. He reached out, still somewhat unbelieving, and touched her face with his rough, calloused hand. The tears came faster.

"I have been no father to you." He whispered. "I killed you. Or at least tried to."

Ellia felt her own tears start to fall.

"I don't care!" She sobbed, suddenly so overcome with weariness and emotion that she could barely get the words out.

"I don't care if you're horrid, and self-centered, and proud, and heartless, and broken like everyone else. Because you're my father, and no matter how horrible you are, you'll always be better than having no one at all."

Gilead looked at her incredulously.

"How could you possibly be so forgiving?" He asked, disbelieving. Ellia gave him a watery half-smile.

She glanced at Rowan, who winced.

"Well... I've had practice." She said.

Chapter Thirty-Three

In Which the City is Somewhat Trashed

***

"The worst earthquake ever was apparently caused by a young Dalian woman named Sheile. She tried to pry apart two rocks to free a trapped pig, and the ensuing chain reaction reached all the way into Kurdu, where it knocked over a town. Legend suggests that this was the start of the thousand year hostilities between Dalia and Kurdu."
— Glazgo son of Glopzite, (A Better History of Alaria).

***

The silence was lifted from the city, but the rain was still falling, and the elves were still fighting. Ellia crouched behind a demolished grocery stand with Rowan on one side and Gilead on the other, his sword over one shoulder. Together, they examined the scene in the street. The entire area was flooded with Faerie now, all the way from the west gate to the palace. It seemed that they had gathered from all around the city to join in the magical civil war that was now erupting. As well as the fighting in the street, many Faerie were perched on the roofs of houses, raining arrows across at

317

each other. Dalians, trapped in their houses while the ground rumbled and lightning flashed just outside, screamed in terror. Ellia looked swiftly around.

"This needs to stop!" She yelled over the noise. Rowan choked out a laugh.

"You don't say?" Despite how he pretended to dislike his race, he looked crushed at the sight of them killing each other in the street. Over by the gate, the Dalian guards had given up on defending the walls and were instead trying to drive back the invading Elves. Ellia stared, and as she stared she noticed something else. Many of the elves were frowning in confusion as they fought, the pride and anger melting from their eyes.

"We need to get their attention." Ellia decided, turning to her two companions.

"If we can get them to stop fighting and think for a moment, they might come to their senses."

Gilead looked out at the crowded street, his eyes narrowed in thought. Then he gave her a small smile.

"If their attention is what you desire, I will get it for you."

He leaped over the grocery stand and strode boldly out into the open. Gripping his sword in both hands, he beat back the fighters with lightning quick strokes, making his way to the middle of the street. Ellia and Rowan shared a glance, then hurried to follow in the path he had made. Gilead's sword began to glow. He flipped it around, raised it into the air, and then, with a yell of "Stop!", He drove it with all his strength into the ground.

Instantly, glowing cracks radiated outward along the ground. The street split in half, the cobbles coming loose and falling into the crack. Houses tilted toward their neighbors as cracks raced down the alleyways. Trees were uprooted. In the distance, Ellia could see the city wall crack in two places. The gate buckled on it's hinges. Beside her, Rowan let out a soft whistle.

"That," He said, with admiration, "Is Spell-metal at it's finest."

The fighting Faerie all stopped for a moment to regain their footing. As one, they turned to look for the source of the commotion. Seizing the moment, Ellia jumped to the top of an overturned wheelbarrow and spread flaming wings wide.

"Stop it!" She yelled. Her voice carried through the stunned silence like a whip crack.

"What are you fighting for?" Ellia asked. "Lord Iberus is dead. Your council may disagree on something, but that is no reason for you to be killing each other. You accomplish nothing but your own defeat this way."

The elves were silent. Ellia could see the dragon's anger slowly leaking out of them. Nevertheless, even without it, many of them still glared murderously at each other. One soldier turned to Ellia with wounded eyes.

"We were fighting for you." He protested. "We were fighting to protect Myth, that she might lead us into our glorious future."

"Myth is dead." Ellia said it for the second time that day, and she could feel the effect of the words ripple through the crowd like a shock wave. The Faerie looked stricken. Many slumped as if in actual pain. Others protested in shocked tones. The Dalian soldiers stood looking on in confusion, gripping their weapons warily.

"I killed her." Ellia added, knowing it was probably the wrong thing to say.

"So if it is for Myth that you fight, your quarrel is with me. Stop killing each other."

She clenched her fists, expecting a thousand arrows to come whistling her way, and ready for it.

However, nothing happened. The Elves still stood silent. Many of them were frowning, as if trying to remember something. They rubbed their eyes as if waking up, staring around in slow realization. They saw the broken city, the dead and wounded lying around. Many stared at their bloodied swords in dawning horror. Elves who had never cried began to weep at the sight of their dead comrades. Everywhere, people and Elves were crying. Ellia hopped off the wheelbarrow and pulled her tattered hood over her head. Rowan was gazing about in wonder.

"I never thought this was possible." He whispered, awe-struck. "Of course, I hoped… But it was never more than wishful thinking. I never thought my people would be able to heal." Ellia nodded, feeling her words stick in her throat at the sight.

"It's not over yet." She whispered. "Let's go find my friends."

Before they had gone far, Chadwick found them. He came down the street in a fast shuffle, dodging cracks and trees. He was clutching a book, and his face was ashen.

"Ellia!" He gasped. "Whatever you do, don't become a dragon. You *can't* let Myth out. I just found the records of what she did the last time, and it's horrifying…"

He stopped short as Ellia turned her multicolored eyes on him.

"It's all right." She said, giving him a hug. He returned it somewhat uncertainly.

"Oh… Okay." He stammered. Rowan tapped Ellia on the shoulder, and she broke away.

"What?"

He jerked his head in the direction of the palace. Captain Gwylan and his soldiers were advancing warily down the street, dragging Jasper with them. When

Gwylan caught sight of Ellia, he stopped in confusion. His soldiers stared openly at Gilead, unnerved by the sight of the tall, scarred elf with the huge sword. Gilead sheathed his sword and held up his hands.

"He's a… friend." Ellia assured them. Gwylan seemed to take her word for it, and turned to her, his brow creased with worry.

"Ma'am – I mean, Ellia. What's happening? How was the city destroyed so quickly? We were on our way to the dungeons when the roof suddenly collapsed…" His soldiers all had their swords out, and they glanced around with fear at the smoke, rubble, and trees everywhere.

"Is the city already conquered?" Gwylan asked, a slight shakiness to his voice. Ellia shook her head.

"I'm not actually sure." She confessed. "It was the elves who did most of the damage, but I'm not sure if they still want to fight."

Instead of looking reassured, Gwylan looked more worried.

"The Faerie Devils are here?" He asked. Both Rowan and Gilead winced. Gwylan saw the look and instantly regretted his choice of words.

"Sorry." He hastily apologized. "The… Elves, are here? *Inside* the city? We're doomed."

He looked hopeless.

"Not yet." Rowan reassured him.

"My people have finally come to their senses. If you do not attack them first, they should give you no trouble."

A crash reverberated over the city. Instinctively, everyone turned in the direction of the sound.

"But *they* might." Gilead remarked dryly. The group hurried out of the alley in an attempt to see what was happening. There was another crash, and the already broken gates shook on their hinges. Ellia groaned.

"Seriously? I thought we already dealt with those guys."

The gates crashed again. Pieces of the barricade split away and fell down onto the heads of the waiting soldiers. Roy's statues clambered up onto each other and braced themselves against the gate, but they were thrown backward by the next crash. The elves were still gathered in the street, doing nothing as the humans ran around in panic.

"I should probably go help." Ellia sighed, feeling unutterably exhausted.

Gilead stepped into her path, looking annoyed.

"No, daughter. I've had enough of seeing you in danger. These humans will be fine. I understand you feel invested in this city, but this is not your fight, and you're barely standing up. Just get those you care about, and we should leave."

Ellia shook her head, feeling tears spring to her eyes. It was wonderful, this feeling of having a father who cared about her, but she couldn't take his advice. She turned to him, meeting his eyes, willing him to understand.

"It's not just about protecting my friends, father." She explained earnestly. "It's about these people, *any* people, really. It's about preventing them pain. It doesn't matter who they are. What matters is that they're killing each other for no reason. People are going to die. Children are going to lose their parents and grow up like me. If there's any way I can prevent that, I *have* to."

She stared into his eyes, and her father nodded, slowly.

"I felt the same way, once." He said. "They called me a hero, but that's not why I did it. It was always about preventing pain, preventing death. If that is the way you choose, I will walk it with you." He drew his sword. All around them, Gwylan and his men mimicked him. One of them tied Jasper to a post at the side of the road and left him. He began thrashing and yelling things in indignation, but everyone ignored him. Rowan was having a heated argument with a group of elvish council members.

"You have to help us!" He pleaded. "Look how much hurt you have caused these people. Will you do nothing to make it right?"

The gate shook again. Already, there was fighting on the walls as some of the Kurdu climbed over using ropes. The elves watched, and their leaders turned away, expressionless.

"We cannot." One woman addressed Rowan, looking a bit regretful.

"Already, too many of our people have died. We must take the wounded home and tend them. These mortal's lives are not as important to us as those of our own people."

"Please." Rowan's dark eyes were full of pain. He gestured to Ellia, Gilead, and himself.

"Are we not your people? Am I not your brother?"

The woman looked conflicted. Her expression was remarkably similar to Rowan's own.

"I would stand with you, if only because of our blood." She said. "But no one else would stand beside me."

Lady Eaglenda stepped away from the body of her son and came over, surveying the scene. Her eyes were heavy, but they held a hint of tenderness as she looked at Ellia. Then she looked at the elves, retreating down the alleys with their wounded, and her eyes turned hard.

"Just *what* do you think you're doing?" She demanded, her voice sharp as a whip crack.

"Stop. As Firstborn, I command you to stop."

Without Lord Iberus to oppose her, the elves turned to her obediently. Several of the council members looked annoyed. Lady Eaglenda fixed them with a glare.

"*You* may go." She spat. "Take the wounded home and sit there in your cowardice. As for the rest of us, we will not turn tail and run. Are we not still the strongest nation on this continent? What have we to fear from Humans?"

At that moment, the Kurdu burst through the gate. The waiting Dalians threw themselves into a desperate last stand at the gate. Roy's statues and Burke's fireballs fought with them, but they were swiftly being driven back. Still, the elves stood and did nothing, undecided.

"This is not our fight." One man protested, his ancient eyes flickering with doubt. Lady Eaglenda looked as though she would like to smack him. She grabbed Ellia by the shoulder and turned her to face them.

"Look." She snarled. "This Starfall saved us from the poison that was destroying us, causing us to slaughter each other pointlessly. We can all feel that poison clearing, and we all know that it was slowly killing our souls. After all this girl has done, are we going to walk away and leave her to die? One of our own, and a hero, no less?"

The Faerie didn't answer, but Ellia saw many of their eyes fix upon her with a new fire in them. Lady Eaglenda turned to her.

"I will fight for you." She said, loud enough that everyone could hear her over the roar of battle down the street.

"And any elves who still feel honor will fight beside me."

Ellia felt a lump of gratitude form in her throat,

and she swallowed.

"Thank you." She whispered. Then she turned and began a weary, stumbling run up the street.

Chapter Thirty-Four

In Which a Wizard Gallantly Protects His Shrubs

***

"This was not such a good idea."
— King Goldbow the Aged, who decided to start a war with Darkwings, and then was killed by them.

***

In the heat of battle, Kurdian soldiers rarely notice anything beyond their next stroke, block, and the next heartbeat that tells them they are still alive. However, when a glowing chasm suddenly opened up, separating them from their enemies and causing several of their comrades to fall to their deaths, the Kurdu could hardly fail to notice. They fell back, yelling, then braced themselves to leap across and attack the Dalians on the other side. Only, the people on the other side were no longer just Dalian. In fact, most of the Dalians had been shouldered out of the way by an army of Wood Demons, their unnatural eyes glowing with power. In front of them, a terrifying, scarred demon pulled a giant glowing sword out of the earth and twirled it like it weighed nothing.

The Kurdian soldiers backed up, their battle cries dying in their throats. Beside the tall, scarred warrior, a slight girl suddenly flared flaming wings and leaped across the chasm. With her changed eyes, not all of them recognized her; However, none of them could mistake that particular shade of golden light that flickered in the air around her. Every one of them had seen that same light coming from the creature that had destroyed their war machines.

"I thought I told you to scram." She said wearily. The soldiers looked at each other warily. Ellia looked around at them, and suddenly the thought of killing even a single one of them made her feel sick. They were just men.

"Here's the deal." Her eyes scanned the crowd until they settled on a group of people on horses who looked somewhat superior.

"Leave now, return to your land, and no one will die. Fight us, and we will destroy you."

There was a moment of silence. Then a young man pushed his way through to the front. He looked no different from any other soldier, save that he wore a golden chain around his neck, and the soldiers parted for him like water. He had dark blond hair, and little braids in his beard. He removed his helmet and ran his hand through his short hair, then regarded Ellia with pale violet eyes. His gaze moved from her to the army behind her, resting on the unbroken line of beautiful, terrifying elves. He showed no fear, but his brows creased in a troubled frown. He turned back to Ellia.

"You speak for these people?"

Ellia nodded.

"In part."

As if sensing the beginning of a truce, several of the more powerful elves and a few human captains jumped across the gap. Lady Eaglenda and Gilead came to stand next to Ellia. However, no other Kurdu stepped forward. They seemed to trust the one young man to make decisions for all of them. He looked the Faerie up and down, his gaze growing more troubled.

"If we leave, will you swear not to pursue us?" He asked Ellia. She shared a look with Lady Eaglenda, then nodded.

"As long as you go directly back to your land, no harm will come to you from me or the Faerie folk." She confirmed. "I cannot speak for the Dalians, but frankly they are in no shape to pursue anyone."

The young Kurdian let out a snort of reluctant laughter.

"True."

He was silent a moment, then sighed heavily.

"My father would never have accepted defeat." Ellia held her breath, watching the conflict in his eyes. Then a flicker of a smile crossed his face.

"But he is dead, and I am not such a fool." He gave an unhappy laugh.

"We will retreat."

Ellia felt the breath leave her in a relieved sigh. The young king turned and began giving orders to his captains. Gradually, with much confusion and shuffling, the Kurdian army began to gather their wounded and march back out through the broken gate. A few Dalian soldiers tried to start a halfhearted victory cheer, but most of them just stood there, numbly watching ash drift through the air of their broken city. Several groups of elves followed the Kurdu out the gate, but Ellia was not worried about the Kurdu breaking their word. There was honesty and honor in the young king's eyes, and she knew that he would not back-stab them as the Dalian king might.

She swayed on her feet, feeling a sudden strong desire to sit down. Someone took her arm and gently lead her back toward the palace. Ellia leaned against him gratefully.

"How come you never get tired?" She asked. Rowan laughed.

"I do."

"No you don't."

Rowan held up a hand in mock surrender.

"Fine, you've got me. I don't. Ever." He reached into a pocket, then handed her a rock-hard biscuit.

"It's because of these." he told her solemnly. "I raided the pantry before the battle. I must say, your Dalian friends are incredible at making biscuits. Why, you could even build houses out of these things."

Ellia grimaced and threw the biscuit at a tree, where it knocked a dent in the wood.

"I know. It's why they're so hard-headed, because of eating these things. Let's go raid the pantry again and find something better."

They passed Jasper, still tied up in the empty street. He turned his head at the sound of her voice, but she didn't even look at him. Smoke and ash swirled around them. The cracked street was filled with trees, and the houses leaned crazily against each other. Terrified families were beginning to emerge from these, looking around in horror at the rubble of the city.

"This isn't what I expected victory to be like." Ellia remarked after a moment.

"We won, but it doesn't feel that way."

Rowan glanced around.

'No, it doesn't." He agreed. "I haven't lived long enough to see many wars, but I'm pretty sure this is normal. The soldiers celebrate, but the ordinary people just try to keep on living in the rubble. They aren't happy, but at least they're not dead, right?"

"I guess so." Ellia sighed, rather dejectedly. They walked for a few more moments, then she glanced up at him.

"What now?"

He looked at her a little quizzically.

"You're asking *me*?"

"Well, yes." Ellia faltered. "You're not planning on… On leaving now, are you? Leaving me?"

"Of course not." Rowan looked down. If she hadn't known him better, she would almost have thought he blushed.

"It's just that, well, I know you've forgiven me, but I wasn't sure that you would still want me around, now that you don't need me anymore."

He shifted his feet, and nervously flipped something gold through his fingers. Ellia put her hand over his, and he went still.

"I'll always need you." She told him seriously, holding his eyes. "So don't you dare leave."

He smiled, and turned his hand around so that their fingers interlaced.

"I won't."

The gold thing flashed again in his other hand. Ellia felt her curiosity stirring.

"What's that?"

He opened his hand and showed her. In his palm, a tiny golden bird rested. For a moment, Ellia was confused, but then she remembered something. She turned her arm around, took the bird, and held it to the scratched hole in her Starfall cuff. It fit perfectly.

"It broke off when you blocked Lord Iberus's blade and saved that assassin." Rowan reminded her. "I kept it, because it reminded me of you. When you saved that man, who you should have hated, something changed in you. It was like you had suddenly stopped playing the part of a Starfall slave, and had finally broken free. You weren't afraid of us any more. You didn't seem afraid of *anything*, and you were so sure of yourself, that we were the ones who felt afraid." He smiled at her. "You revealed something about yourself then. Something none of us had expected. Instead of letting us kill the assassin, you made the decision to save his life. We Faerie aren't used to forgiving each other. We usually don't, even if the offense is small, so it was shocking, what you did. I think that was the moment that I realized that I loved you. I also realized that I didn't deserve you. I thought it was too late. I was sure that you would hate me forever, and I knew that I deserved it, no matter how much it hurt. But then, I hadn't counted on your amazing capacity for forgiveness. I still find it hard to believe. You're… You're incredible, Ellia."

He stopped talking. Ellia stared at him.

"That," She said slowly, "is probably the most romantic thing anyone has ever said in the history of Allaria."

Rowan tilted his head, and a bit of mischief flashed in his eyes.

"Do I get a kiss then?"

Ellia met his eyes with a grin of her own.

"Yes."

✳ ✳ ✳ ✳ ✳

It was a full week before King Rudbeck returned. He stumbled into the city in the middle of the night, with a mere handful of companions. One of those companions shared the tragic tale with his wife, and by the next day the story was being told all across the city.

It seemed that King Rudbeck had, indeed, been ambushed by Kurdian assassins while he was in the Wildlands. He had been searching for the elves, and the attack was completely unexpected. The fight was very fierce, and they would have all died, if it hadn't been for the sudden intervention of a strange but very powerful wizard. Apparently, this wizard had attacked the assassins with many terrifying magical weapons, driving them off and saving the king. The entire city was abuzz with speculation, wondering who this strange man could have been. Ellia thought she knew. Just to be sure, she tracked down the king's companion and questioned him.

"Yes. A wizard saved us." The man looked tired, leaning on the door frame of his house.

"But the strange thing is that he didn't seem to notice us at all. The assassins were hiding in a field of bushes, see, and he came flying down from the hilltop at them, yelling something about tea, and bushes, and stomping. We could make no sense of it."

The man rubbed his jaw, looking down at Ellia with a frown.

"He did say something, though, that made us think perhaps he was there to help us after all."

Ellia waited.

"Yes?"

The soldier frowned.

"He called the assassins kidnappers. We were out there looking for the Queen's gold Starfall, you see, who had been kidnapped. When the king heard that, he thought that perhaps the old man was saying that the Kurdu were the kidnappers. He tried to talk to the wizard about it, but the old man just ran away. He didn't even stay long enough to let us thank him. So, we didn't find the Starfall, and we came back for reinforcements..."

The man suddenly stopped, trying to see into the shadows of Ellia's hood.

"Say, aren't you the girl who-"

"Thank you for your help." Ellia interrupted him. She tucked her arm with the golden cuff behind her back and hurried away, ignoring the soldier's shouted questions.

Rowan was waiting for her.

"Why are you smiling?"

Ellia couldn't contain the grin on her face.

"No reason. I was just thinking about an old friend

of mine. What do you know about wizards?”

Rowan looked confused. “What does anyone know about wizards? They’re very secretive, and supposedly very powerful. I’ve never met one. Why do you ask?”

Ellia felt her smile grow wider.

“I have.”

Chapter Thirty-Five

The Old Man Gives Sage Advice

"Most humans need a good rock to the head. Not the king. He already has a rock *for* a head."

— The wizard Ham, in response to King Rudbeck's attempt to talk to him.

Several weeks later, a wind swept through Alestromaria. With no one to control the wind anymore, the leaves drifted down, forming a thin silver carpet on the ground. Ellia walked through the wood, trying to be as silent as it's Elvish inhabitants. It was very challenging, but that was good, because it distracted her from her thoughts. During the past few weeks, she had rarely been separated from her father, but today was different. She had woken up in the morning feeling empty. It was the sort of emptiness that made her want to be alone. She walked aimlessly, trying to place the emptiness inside her. She had been happy there, in the Elvish court. The Faerie were recovering, and they welcomed Ellia as a heroine. Her father was still very solitary and depressed at times, but he, too, was recovering. For a time, Ellia had been content to live with her father and Rowan in the wood. But now she was restless. She could not shake the feeling that there was something that she still needed to do, some part of her that was unfulfilled.

She tripped over a root, and cursed. A soft chuckle sounded, over to her left. She whirled and peered into the trees.

"Well." A gravely voice said, "I assume that this somewhat colorful vocabulary signals the arrival of our young, hot-headed hero?"

Ellia caught sight of a face among the shadows, and recognized her old acquaintance, the gray-bearded elf. He was once again leaning against a tree, seemingly asleep. He opened his eyes a slit and regarded her solemnly.

"Your eyes are different." He noted. Ellia smiled.

"I still don't know your name." She realized, coming to sit beside him. He chuckled again, closing his eyes.

"Few do, because few bother to ask. It's Haldren. And you're Ellia, the pride and joy of all Faerie."

Ellia wasn't sure how to respond. He was silent for a moment, his face so relaxed that Ellia thought perhaps he was sleeping. Then he opened his eyes and turned to face her.

"So, tell me, Ellia, what is troubling you?"

Ellia stared at him.

"Why do you think anything is bothering me?" She demanded. Haldren gave her a bland look.

"It's obvious." He stated. "You don't hide your emotions very well. I am also a very perceptive person. So, do you care to talk about it?"

Ellia looked at him for a long moment. For some reason, she felt that this was a person she did not mind telling things to. He seemed trustworthy, and wise. He also reminded her strongly of Chadwick. She sighed.

"It's just that I feel kind of aimless." She admitted.

"The battle's over, the dragon is dead, and now I can live happily ever after, I guess. It's just that I never expected happy ever after to be so… Boring. I feel unfulfilled. There's something I feel I still need to do in Dalia, but I can't think what it might be."

"Ah."

The old man nodded.

"I thought as much. You're restless, aren't you?"

Ellia nodded. She hated to admit it, because she felt that a normal person in her place should feel content. She had her father, and Rowan, so what else could she want? But she wanted something more, despite her happiness and love for them. The old man gave her a knowing smile.

"You need a purpose. A higher calling. I recognize the type. Your kind never rests while there is yet evil in the world."

She frowned.

"What do you mean?"

"It's in your blood." The old Faerie explained. "It was in your father's, and it's in yours. You're a Hero. A Warrior. All Humans have flaws, and Heroes are often also flawed, but in their purest form, your type is motivated by the desire to protect the weak and make right injustice. You generally feel strong empathy toward the powerless. Is there, perhaps, some evil in Dalia which you feel you have not yet righted? Some person or persons in a harsh situation toward whom you feel empathy?"

Ellia nodded, slowly.

"You're right." She realized. "I have all this power, and it doesn't feel right to just stay here and not use it. The Elves don't need me like the people of Dalia do."

She stood up.

"Thank you, Haldren, for your insight." She gave him a genuine, relieved smile, then turned to go.

"If Rowan or Gilead comes looking for me, could you tell them that I'll be back shortly? I have unfinished business with King Rudbeck and his queen."

The palace gates still hung crookedly when Ellia approached them, but the guards in front of them were just as snotty and stuck up as they had always been. They were standing there, stiff as boards, dressed like glittering peacocks, and paying no attention to anyone. It was lucky, she reflected, as the King appeared to have put a price on her head as a runaway Starfall. She stood there indecisively for a moment, her hand absently reaching up to finger the small golden bird hung around her neck. Her cuff was gone, her eyes were a different color, and her hood was pulled over her head, but people around her were still starting to take notice. There was a certain aura of power hovering around her, and a strength in her stance that made her stand out. She took a deep breath and strode up to the guards, pulling off her hood.

"I believe the king desires to see me." She said.

The guard turned on her, his face flashing annoyance. He opened his mouth to speak, but then it hung open in astonishment.

"You!" He snarled, drawing his sword. However, the other, older guard stepped in his way.

"Wait, Bronk." He placed a restraining hand on his companion's arm, then turned to Ellia.

"We're supposed to arrest you." He told her apologetically. "But you saved our city. My wife is alive because of you." His eyes shone with gratitude. "If you walk away right now, We'll pretend we never saw you."

Ellia smiled, touched by his loyalty.

"No, It's all right. You can arrest me." She held out her wrists. "Only please take me directly to the King. I want to see him."

The guard nodded seriously, taking her arm. The other guard looked doubtful, but he said nothing, pulling out rope to tie her wrists with. He tied them as securely as he knew how, his face serious. Then he took her other arm and hauled her through the palace gates. Ellia tried to hide her smile at his sincere belief that he was the one in charge. It was only when they approached the Throne room doors that the guard began to falter, uncertain. Ellia went limp, making herself seem as small and nonthreatening as possible. The younger guard still looked wary.

"She's dangerous." He protested uncertainly. The other guard glared at him.

"Just bring her in." He snapped. They dragged Ellia through the doors, and she raised her head to look around.

The Throne Room was filled with people. It seemed that, now that the danger was passed, the Nobles had returned to court, each with their own complaints about their destroyed city properties. There were guards everywhere, along with servants and spies disguised as servants. Even the queen was present, for once actually sitting in a smaller throne beside her husband. She seemed quite resentful that the King was once again occupying the throne, shooting baleful glances his way. As Ellia entered, every eye turned to her. For a moment, her old fear returned. She stood frozen between the guards, heart pounding. *No.* she thought, pushing away her panic. *I'm not that slave anymore.* She lifted her chin and met the King's eyes with a cool stare.

"Your Majesties." She included the Queen in her glance, dipping her head, but refusing to bow.

"I believe you sent out an invitation for me. It was rather rude, but I decided to accept anyway."

The king's face turned purple with suppressed

disbelief and rage. Every one in the room knew that the king had sent out an arrest warrant for Ellia. Most of them couldn't believe that she was standing there unchained.

"What are you doing here?" The king demanded. He turned to his guards.

"Why isn't she chained in the dungeons?" Some of the guards started forward, but their steps were hesitant. The ones holding Ellia's arms let go and backed away. Ellia stood straight, fixing the king with a blank look.

"Why should I not be here? I saved your city for you. Why would I be chained?"

The guards hung back. King Rudbeck looked from them to Ellia incredulously.

"*You* saved the city?" He gaped, and next to him the queen gave a scornful laugh.

"You could not have saved the city, Starfall." The king growled, less amused.

"You are nothing more than a tool. A tool belonging to my wife. *She* saved the city, as much as I hate to admit it. Just as a hero defeats the monster, though it is the sword in his hands that pierces it's heart. You are a sword in my wife's hands. And then her sword ran away. You are under arrest as a defective weapon. The punishment for a runaway Starfall is death."

The guards stepped forward and cautiously surrounded her. Ellia smiled.

"Your majesty," She addressed the king patiently, "I am no one's sword, and I did not come to turn myself in. I came with a warning."

There was a collective gasp. No one, not even the queen, spoke to the king with such impudence in public. The guards drew their swords, and King Rudbeck jumped to his feet. The queen also jumped up, placing a restraining hand on her husband's arm. He whirled on her. She met his glare, baring her teeth in an attempt at a loving smile.

"One moment, *dear* king. Let us first hear what my servant has to say for herself." She turned to Ellia with a smirk.

"This had better be the right kind of warning, Starfall. Be very careful what you say next, for the words may be your last." She sounded commanding, and, with her voluminous skirts seemed to dwarf her husband. Ellia wasn't sure what sort of a power game the queen was trying to play with her husband, but she refused to comply.

She stepped forward, holding the Queen's eyes.

"I would first like to let you know I am no longer your slave. And I would like to warn the king about the slaves he keeps."

She turned to King Rudbeck, her eyes flashing.

"Selling and buying humans as weapons is despicable." She told him, her voice cold.

"And if you do not free them, I will."

She could feel the magic flickering around her, so strong that it was almost visible. Flames began to lick around the ropes on her wrists. She held the king's eyes as her bonds burned away and fell to the ground. The King stumbled backward, away from her multicolored gaze, his face red with fury.

"Kill her!" He snarled. The Queen just stared at Ellia in stunned surprise. The guards charged, swords drawn. Ellia didn't take her eyes away from the King's.

"I'll only warn you once." She cautioned. "You would do well to listen."

With that, she burst into flame. Burning wings swept the guards backward as the Phoenix sped upward in a column of fire.

Shocked cries filled the air as everyone in the room stumbled backward. The king stared in stunned silence at the smoldering hole in the ceiling. Slowly, he walked forward and looked up through it. The sky above was empty.

"We can't fight that." A guard whispered. "Did you see what she did to the Kurdian army?" Another asked.

"No, we can't fight her." A third guard agreed. The king whirled on him.

"Shut up!" He snarled, but his face was pale. The Queen's inscrutable mask of make-up was cracking. She looked utterly dumbfounded.

"I think… Perhaps we may have underestimated that girl." She said in a tight voice. The king didn't argue.

Afterword

In Which the King's Parenting Tactics are Called Into Question

***

"Although the title of worst rulers of all Time officially goes to King Ferdinand the Bloody and his wife Gertrude, it is generally agreed that King Rudbeck and Queen Pricilla are the worst parents of all time."
— A critique of the present monarchy, by the Philosopher Pollo, who was later beheaded for his disrespect.

***

It was several weeks before anyone noticed the abduction of the Royal twins. Their nurse noticed, but she was so grateful that she said nothing of it. It was not until their birthday that their disappearance was discovered, and by then no one had any idea where they might have gone. They would reappear many years later to claim the throne, but that is another story. They grew up loved and cherished in Alestromaria, and they changed so much for the better that no one who had once known them as screaming children would ever have recognized them.

When they discovered the loss, the Royal

couple's first and last reaction was to blame each other. They had one long, screaming argument in the throne room, and then promptly forgot about it. They paid so little attention to their children that the loss changed very little about their lives. The rest of the court looked on, and were secretly relieved, thinking of the water that would no longer be dumped on their heads during feasts.

On the same night that she confronted the king and abducted his children, Ellia met Chadwick one last time in the garden.

"Will you come with us?" She asked him, her eyes pleading. "Here, you are nothing but a tool. In Alestromaria you would be free. Everyone has powers there. No one would exploit you."

Chadwick looked at her, standing there with an adoring child hanging on each arm, and he smiled sadly.

"I'm sorry Ellia, and I will miss you." He said regretfully. "But I have a place here. Yes, they use me. But my position here is not something I'm ready to give up. I'm at the center of this tangle of politics, master of all the kingdom's spies. This is my web, and this spider is not ready to leave it."

Ellia nodded, discouraged, but not surprised.

"All right. This will be goodbye then."

She shook off Myria and Myrgen's clinging hands long enough to give him a hug.

"I'll miss you too."

"Goodbye Ellia." He held her tightly for a moment, then released her. "And good luck with your task. If anyone can free this kingdom's Starfalls, I believe it is you."

Ellia felt tears sting her eyes.

"I hope I see you again." She sniffed. Then she turned, wrapping an arm around each of the Royal twins.

"Hold on to me." She instructed. Then she became a Griffon and flew over the palace wall. Chadwick watched her go, his eyes filled with sadness. Then he, too, turned and walked away.

✳ ✳ ✳ ✳ ✳

Captain Sheryl waited until the storm had passed before venturing down into the hold to check on his passengers. The hold of the ship was built like a prison. He had to unlock several sets of barred doors to enter, and he locked them behind him. The only things in the hold were four people. There was a woman with silver eyes in the corner, a young man with rust red eyes against the far wall, and two small children clinging to the bars. Water sloshed across the floor.

The captain banged on the bars.

"Everybody still alive?" He demanded. The children's eyes were wide.

"Are we going to drown?" A girl of about ten with white eyes asked nervously. The captain sneered at her.

"I don't think you Demon-eyes *can* drown." He laughed. Across the room, the young man started up angrily. He strained against the chain binding him to the wall, glaring at Sheryl, who chuckled nervously, backing away.

"No, you're not going to drown. Storm's over." He said, turning to go back up the stairs.

"We'll get you to the market soon, then you'll stop being my problem."

He suddenly stopped, turning back to face them. The woman was still huddled in the corner, but the young man looked rebellious. The captain shook a finger at him.

"Don't try anything." He warned. "It's only open

ocean all around. Nowhere to run. Besides, if the garrison boats see so much as a flicker of magic coming from this hold, they'll blow us out of the water, and we'll all die. Trust me, slavery is better than drowning." Sheryl neglected to mention the fact that the garrison boats had in fact been blown off course by the storm, and were nowhere to be seen. The absence made him nervous. The other thing he failed to mention was the fact that they were no longer on open ocean. Instead, they were sailing passed some Dalian Nobleman's summer island, and would soon be turning up into the mouth of a river. He said nothing, only turned and began climbing the stairs.

Suddenly, the boat was rocked by a tremendous blow, throwing Shale into the wall. There was a thump on the deck above, and the sound of running feet. The captain staggered to his feet, face pale. He hurried up the stairs, unlocking the barred doors as fast as he could. In his rush to reach the deck, he neglected to lock them behind him. The boat shook again.

The captain burst onto deck just in time to see a flaming ball of fire rush passed him and explode against the wall.

"What in the name of Firth was that?" He demanded in what he liked to call his Captain's voice – loud, braying, and annoyed.

"That was a fire-stick." Said an unfamiliar voice. "I bought it off a wizard I met in the hills."

Two elves were standing on deck. One was a tall, dark-haired boy with a grim look and a sword in each hand. The other was a girl with brown hair, many scars, and an impossible color of eyes. She was holding a metal stick in her hands. What most alarmed the captain, however, was the utter lack of his crew. Even as he watched, the last two sailors dived over the side in panic, their clothes flaming. He ran to the rail and leaned over. In the sea below, every single member of his crew was bobbing, paddling madly for shore. Captain Shale turned around slowly, clutching the rail behind him. The two elves were watching him silently.

"How did you get here?" He managed weakly, a sinking feeling in his gut. The two Faerie exchanged a look, and the boy smiled.

"The same way we're going to leave." He said. The girl nodded to him, and he disappeared down into the hold.

"Hey! What do you think you're doing?" The captain started after him. The girl stepped in his way. The captain stopped. Then it suddenly occurred to him that he was alone on deck with nothing in his way but a single, slight girl. He grinned.

"I'm captain here." He growled, drawing a knife. "You think you can drive me off my own ship?"

The girl said nothing, just took a step backward. He kept advancing and she kept backing up, until she was just a few steps from the rail. Then she spoke.

"We are going to take your Starfalls now, and set them free." Her eyes were, strangely, sympathetic.

"This time we will spare your life. However, if you ever try to ship or deal in Starfalls again, we will not be so merciful."

The captain laughed. Then he lunged. The girl took one final step backward, launched herself into the air, and flipped backward over the rail. Captain Shale stared. He walked to the edge of the rail and leaned over, scanning the water. The girl was gone. He started to laugh, then his blood ran cold as something huge moved under the boat. The ship lurched suddenly sideways. He was thrown against the side. A shadow fell over him and water rained down, though the sky was clear. Hair rising on the back of his neck, he looked up.

The creature looking down on him was one that

very few sailors had ever seen, and yet all sailors dread seeing. It's scales were the size of shields, it's fins like sails. It's body wrapped around the boat, tipping the entire thing so that the Captain slid toward its huge face. It opened its mouth, full of gleaming, dagger-like teeth, and hissed. The captain curled up into a quaking ball of terror. The monster bent down, closed its teeth on the back of his coat, and lifted him off the deck.

Rowan emerged with the captive Starfalls to see the captain dangling like a broken doll from the serpent's teeth. It swung its head and flung him out into the sea. He could just be seen in the distant waves, struggling toward land.

Ellia landed on deck and walked over to the group of Starfalls. They watched her warily.

"You're free." She told them, smiling. "To stay, or to go. We're commandeering this ship for our cause to save Starfalls. Would you like to join us?"

At first, the group just looked at her, disbelieving. However, slowly, their faces lit up with answering smiles.

The end